Straight Commission

A Novel

By Matthew Cahan

For My Mom and Dad, and dear friend and mentor, Jim Corder.

Table of Contents.

I.

Frank Cusco works on his own. Travel, lots of it. Windshield time, lots of that too. Cheap motels from time to time, and even cheaper meals most of the time. $29.99 a night with free AC and cable. Late check-in and express checkout. There is no manager looking over his shoulder. No coffee area, no water cooler, no mailbox. In fact, there is no office really, except the vehicle he hops in and out of all the time like an interstate cowboy. There is nobody gossiping about the new office secretary, and there is nobody searching the Internet in the cubicle next to him. Working alone affords him the freedom, or, the autonomy to sell. He sells materials to companies making things that make the world go.

Things that make the world move, and things that make the world move fast.

Engine blocks. Valve Bodies. Transfer cases.

He sells himself so his products don't have to do all the work. If they buy him, they are more likely to buy what he is selling. It has worked that way for centuries. Everybody selling something to somebody, that is the way of trade. But times were slow, and in this day and this climate, manufacturing jobs disappeared like virgins on prom night, dashing off to Mexico, and of course, China, leaving a sunken wake of dwindling profitability for the entrepreneurial souls left behind. In other words, the pickin's had gone from slim to none, and slim had gone on and got the hell out of dodge.

But working out there on your own like Frank, working straight commission, it was still possible to make a good living, a damn good one in fact. Carving out a niche for yourself is the key. Finding that place between what is most effective, and what matters the most to the client. Finding that place on your own and operating within that space almost as valve, understanding and synthesizing the intersecting elements of critical energies in such a way as to allow them to perform at their best and, most critically, to use a true salesman's term, comfortable.

Frank was there to make them comfortable, while they made things to make the world move. And move fast. Fast. Fast. Fast.

He checked his voicemail, two small orders already this morning. He deleted the messages quickly, not even smiling at the recognition of new business. They were small fish. There were bigger ones out there to fry. Still though, if the net wasn't out in the water all the time, he'd never catch any.

Frank hustled from one potential account to another, racking up miles on his vehicles and frequent stay points of his motel rewards programs, developing an acute independence.

He was a professional in charge of himself, working straight commission, which, to him, was the only way to work if you were a salesman. Nobody constantly telling him what to do and how to do it, and no ceiling to what he could make. The autonomy was not without its sacrifices though. There was no guaranteed salary. No company benefit package, insurance, retirement, 401K. That was all left up to him, even his expenses. And, moving from place to place every year or two in search of more fertile territory and staying away from home for days, even weeks at a time weren't the most conducive element to maintaining relationships; hence, the breakup with the girl he knew he could, should, and would marry the timing was better. And, when he had enough steaks in the freezer.

Every salesman dreams of the accounts that will by their very size and potential profitability, supplant all others and wipe away like a monster wave at Waimea Bay. The type of accounts that once garnered would come rushing and sweeping in rolling sets to settle all debts and forge future security which until then had not existed. Investments at desirable interest rates, retirement plans, a new home or homes even, trips to places that only were real on a map or the Internet, or the chance to settle down in one place and marry the one who had gotten away. Frank was no different, and most of what drove him day after day, mile after mile to knock on

11

door after door to dial number after number, and endure rejection after rejection was the hope that eventually all of the no's, and all the "we're happy with what we've got" and all the painfully endless waiting in parking lots and plant lobbies, at least one of those babies would come back yes. A bigger yes than anyone had ever seen. One yes that would spawn possibilities in his life otherwise impossible.

Just one big yes baby.

He phoned the company plant and the secretary answered.

"Good morning. This is Rachel. How can I be of help to you?"

"Now, Rach, you know better than to ask me that."

"Oh, hi, Frank, how are you doing today?"

"Well, any better, and it'd probably be a crime." Frank answered.

She giggled, but it was brief. He was calling to check on orders.

"Let's see, Frank, you got one about twenty minutes ago, and another one just before you called. Were your ears burning?"

"No, but maybe I need to try that reverse, inverted psychology thing…"

"The what?"

12

"You know, start thinking about a customer, particularly one's who haven't ordered of late, and somehow that'll trigger them to put in an order. Make any sense?"

"Hey, Frank, you're the go-getter, whatever works."

"I'll be on the cell."

"Be careful out there."

"You bet."

Two little dudes, well shit, they were better than no little dudes at all. He almost forgot about them as he sped on down the road, thinking crisply and decidedly.

One big yes baby.

He was almost there a few times. That was when those floors, and the rugs on top, got jerked out from under him. That was the tantalizingly precarious element of the business that separated the men from the boys. Months, years of work could go up in smoke in seconds, vaporizing your efforts and your income in a flash of uncontrollable circumstances. It could break the spirit. So many promising salesmen simply gave it up. They couldn't take the taxing tide of unsecured income streams. Some guys just didn't have the stomach. Not that keeping a healthy stomach was a bad way to go.

Frank's boss had made it big working straight commission back in the sixties, seventies, and eighties, before cellphones, email Cracker Barrels and Hampton Inns. He was such a good salesman, and businessman in fact, he eventually started his own company and made it entirely sales driven. He told Frank the very first day he started, "son, I don't give a shit what you do with your time, just get the orders and take care of the numbers, because if nobody is out getting the orders, then nobody else will be working." There was more of a hint of pride in his voice. He had the air of a Sergeant Major. A marine, a devoted husband and father, and one man you didn't want to piss off. But to know him and work for him as Frank did, you wanted in the worst way to carry your share of the water and make him proud.

The salesman were the ones out on the frontlines for the company. And it was understood that it was not like working in a time clock business, of any sort. The reality was it was a tedious grind, a thankless endeavor, and a mostly unrewarding toil.

The boss had told Frank that if their job was easy…then every asshole in town would be doing it.

The boss had also told him very early of the critical importance to having an ever-deepening cache of contacts within industry, and even semi-related industries. You'd never know when a small, seemingly unimportant piece of information obtained from an obscure and seemingly unrelated source could be invaluable, in a given set of circumstances in the future.

Envisioning the matrices of industry supply chains, at least to Frank, was not an image of unbreakably interlocked, chrome-set ovals' but rather a melee of pissed off cab drivers honking and stomping and screaming at or among each other at a dead stop during downtown rush hour. But the more and the better of these guys he knew, the easier it made getting around town. It was like guerrilla networking. Not that Frank ever confused his job with fighting a war, but he did feel sometimes that there was a need for a certain trench warfare mentality in his job.

Frank rolled along, and he thought about the first time he called on American Toilet Co. He always stayed at the motel near the interstate and drove the fifteen miles rather than spend the night there. It may have flourished at one time, but not now, not for a long while man. It always seemed to be raining, snowing, or enveloped in gray in that small industrial town in eastern Ohio. Only one big employer was left, and they were making crappers, lots and lots of crappers. Most of the town had one family member working there, in one capacity or another, and they were all long-standing union members. He'd park across the street, in the lot of an abandoned VFW Hall, trash scattered about, and parking pylons askew, the asphalt

15

gnarled and cracked. The plant literally took up two city blocks, with the main office building towering along the avenue. Its tinted windows set imperviously on each level, imposing, daunting, and cold. Frank would stand alone in the lobby and dial his contact's extension and get the voicemail ninety-five% of the time, and then knock on the door until someone happened to come by. The other five he was too busy, sorry just covered up right now. When someone did stop and pop open heavy glass door a crack, he'd politely ask them to give his card to his contact, immediately say thank you, and then be on his way. Frank didn't want to come off pushy, rather appreciative…knowing that it accomplished nothing if he forced the issue at that moment. And it took an entire morning to get there, do his thing, and get back out of town and on down the road. All that "just the leave a business card." The consistency was the point. Showing up, letting them know he was there, and staying in front of the customer. Long haul man, not the short sell.

Frank thought about the gray and depressing scene in that town, and the continual unsuccessful attempts to contact his contact and he didn't even blink. He knocked on this door for three years before he got his foot in.

Three years man, and after an additional six months of painstaking testing and evaluations, he had finally gotten a full commitment from management to change his product. They had signed off on the quality control requirements; purchasing was on-board in lieu of the significant cost-savings they were realizing with the switch. Even the chemists were excited because of the environmental benefits. The initial orders had been placed. Everything looked rosy.

And that's when it went right down the crapper.

It began on the back shift. The operators were refusing to work with the product after they were informed a plant-wide change had been made, by management. Their reasons ranged from incompatibility with the current process to the smell was noxious and causing headaches. Frank knew something was rotten in Denmark. The trials, the research, the lab work, and the performance to this point had proved undeniable. There wasn't a snowball's chance in hell they wouldn't have made the switch if there were any chance the product could cause any type of physical problems with their workers, or if it would be problematic in their applications. This was a big fluffy feather in the caps of a lot of people. Attaboy, all around.

But to the operators, that didn't mean shit.

Frank left several messages with a contact of his that worked on the shop floor. He was to meet with the leadman on first shift. A guy with whom he'd spent the bulk of the evaluation period working. A guy who was critical to both

Frank and the management that insofar as evaluating the material, and eventually determining whether it would be of value to American Toilet Co. And a guy who, having worked for American Toilet Co., for twelve years from an operator to lead man to shift coordinator that knew the score, he was fully aware of the benefits associated with a potential change.

Thom. Pronounced, Thom.

Come on, dude, call back, Frank thought. Rolling into town his mind was working, inherently examining the roller coaster ride of a straight commission salesman. In high cotton one day to picking shit with the chickens the next.

Just like that.

Motherfucker, Frank thought.

The material had tested very well, but later on it had run into some problems when handled by the operators on the line, on third shift. Frank thought it was a little strange that every test he had witnessed in the company of several chemists, engineering managers, and production supervisors had gone considerably well. They were not plant-wide tests, but each one was representative of the potential large-scale processes in which his product would be implemented. Weeks had gone by, and the communication lines Frank had spent the better part of the past three years developing were evaporating. He couldn't get any decent information out of the engineers, the supervisors, or the chemists. He needed to get them from someone on the floor.

Thom was a guy he met when he'd first started calling on American Toilet Co. He had worked his way up from third shift operator to lead man to process engineer. Being a union-shop, Frank dreaded calling on them because they were notorious for being highly, highly resistant to change, of any kind. And, as an outside supplier, he wasn't allowed to even turn a wrench on the floor, lest he run the risk of getting tossed out on his ass. That was part of the deal.

Thom was a baseball fan, and so was his boy. Frank had put in a call to a friend in Pittsburg and landed a couple box seats to opening day of the new stadium. Thom told Frank he had taken his kid out of school for hit and borrowed his mother's Oldsmobile to drive up to PNC ballpark.

He checked into the Hampton Inn and took his *USA Today* with him to the room. The sports page was the only thing worth reading in that paper, he thought. There was always decent coffee in the lobby, and clean bathrooms. Smart traveling salesmen would stop off at the nice motels when they had to drop a bomb, as it sure as hell beat the gas station where you needed a key chained to a wooden club to get inside. Frank was no different. His voicemail indicator blinked on the cell phone. He thought about his boss and how he had marveled at the increased efficiency the invention cell phones provided.

How'd we ever get along without these bad boys?

It was easy to get acclimated when getting in touch with people was the lifeblood of your livelihood.

Frank, yea, it's Thom here…meet me out at the Hungry Hogg off 57. It's about two miles south of the motel on the right-hand side. Can't miss it. 5:30. The robotic lady-like voicemail voice indicated the end of the message and Frank hit the #7 button to delete.

The place was painted red, and Frank noticed two long tin vents poking out the opposite sides of the rear of the building with words either missing or hanging crooked-like teeth lost in a playground fight. There was a large satellite dish in the back of the parking lot, enclosed with a chain link fence. The gate on the fence had a "Beware of Dog" sign by the handle, and as Frank walked past sure enough there was rottweiler asleep by the power box on the base of the satellite. Frank guessed the owner was concerned that someone was going to pull up to the satellite, break into the fence, and yank that thing out of the ground, essential wiring intact, and somehow to that motherfucker on downed the road. He thought about asking Thom about that when he showed up, but you never knew, the owner could be his uncle or something, so he decided against it.

Thom turned up a few minutes later. He wore a faded company hat, and his hands were black from the soot and grime he had been working with all day. They shook hands in the doorway of the place and walked inside. To Frank, it looked like a lodge inside a coalmine. Everything was a blinding dark, with the smell of grease, smoke, sauce, pork and beef wafting about. After his eyes adjusted, Frank could make out the other side of the room a solitary cash register and the cooks behind a counter busily working in the white clothes with read stains on their aprons from their chests to their bellies. They found and sat in a booth against the wall on the side of the room. Frank figured some of the guys in there may have wandered in during the Depression and never left. A waitress named Dottie took their orders for two cokes and disappeared leaving a pair of gravy-stained menus. Frank downed half his coke instantly. They talked briefly about the recent death of Dale Sr., the great NASCAR legend who'd died in a wreck at Daytona the previous Sunday. Thom went on for a minute about it, noting that it wasn't Sterling's fault they were just racing. Hell, man, shit happens, especially at 190 miles an hour.

That is fast, Frank thought, real fast.

Racing was big around here, and although he'd never been a fan before taking this job, he quickly learned the value in developing a working knowledge of it.

They ordered two beef platters, and they came back in a matter of minutes on plastic plates that looked like they were from a junior-high cafeteria, small mounds of soft dark smoky flavor. Mac and cheese on the side and two small plastic bowls of coleslaw came neatly alongside like scoop of whipped cream on a big sundae. Frank saw Thom take his hat from his head and cross his hands quietly and pray before diving into his meal. Frank likewise bowed his head and gave thanks, finished, and reached from the pepper while two truckers opened the door to leave and squinted at the equally blinding gray light outside. He was careful not to eat too quickly and kept pace with Thom. The waitress suddenly appeared from the roomful of shadow holding a full pitcher of coke. Only her arm seemed visible as she expertly poured each glass to their limit and then disappeared back into the dark. She returned quickly to check on their meals and leaned down to ask Frank if it was one check or two. He nodded for one, pointing to himself and then swiftly handed her a twenty.

"It's all yours, hun."

"Well, thank you, sweetie, you all have a good one now."

"We will, you too." She smiled like a grandmother would, and Frank smiled back. Thom barely looked up at her, still mashing his meal, leaking bar-b-cue sauce down either sides of his mouth.

After they finished, they walked outside and across the whitish and jagged gravel toward Thom's pickup. He leaned on the side of the tailgate and lit a cigarette. Two large smokers were parked on two-wheeled trailers with "for sale" signage on the front. Custom Hog Roasting. 444-3232.

Frank was fully aware they hadn't talked any shop and was just about to bring it up. Sometimes it was better to hang back, wait for the moment to present itself, and pursue the particular topic. And sometimes, it was the other way around.

Thom was looking at the ground and then shifted his eyes to the parking lot.

"The union ain't gonna 'low management to change any current suppliers, no matter how good the product is; it's not a matter how much money it saves, no matter what, man. They the ones who have to use the stuff; they the ones who have to make the parts, man. Hey, man, Frank...it ain't nothing 'gainst you, or your product, or your company...people just don't like change. And, man, they also don't like it when management comes in and forces a change down their throats. Change, man...people just don't like to change, I guess." He wasn't quite stumbling over his words, but he wasn't cogently conveying them either. His voice had a preemptive rush about it, sounding like he was trying to let Frank down as easily as possible, but without appearing to compromise his allegiance to the union.

His hands had a motion of sagging resignation, while he stuck them forward while they were still in his pockets.

Frank felt a chilly swath of reality whirl around him as he stared at the gravel for a moment and then at Thom. The cold wash of anger and frustration spill over him from his eyelids to his ears; all that he could hear and see pissed him off to no end.

One more free meal, huh, Thom? That it? Couldn't have returned one of the many calls instead of dragging me into that cancer factory? Of course, these were questions in his mind, not on his lips. The union had made their decision. Whether it was legitimate or not, a fucking act of Congress would get them to do otherwise. Frank knew it and he suddenly felt like smoking a cigarette. He stared back at the gravel and let the urge pass. He knew with an onrushing certainty that the recent collapse of communication, the sudden deference to voicemails, and unreturned phone calls were only a cover for what had really been going down behind the shop floor doors.

24

The union was telling management to go and get fucked, with Frank and his product unwittingly acting as the go-between.

He may just as well have been a rock, bottle, or brick somebody picked up in an alley during a nasty scrape to hurl at the enemy.

Thom just kind of looked at him blankly, not seeming to understand. He didn't seem to grasp the situation from Frank's standpoint, and that may have been what pissed him off the most. Frank's anger was brief, and he had trained himself to turn it into a focused, if not objective, awareness. But boy, some, if not most, of the guys he seemed to deal with acted as though guys like him just cruised around playing golf and cocktails and dinners at the Olive Garden. They didn't work for a living. In fact, they had the easiest gig around. Frank wished they had to spend their days and nights on the road making a living with a box of business cards, a calendar, and an atlas. Knock on a door over and over again until you can barely remember the last time someone gave you five minutes of their time. They'd see that if nobody was out there actually getting the orders, then nobody else in the company would even have a fucking job. They'd fucking realize then.

Did this guy think he drove all the way out to this shitbox to buy him some fucking bar-b-cue?

25

The moments were longer than moments, but not by much. Frank knew that the longer he dwelled on the conversation, despite the kick in the gut that it was, the worse it would feel. And, he would, absolutely no way in the only world that he only did, and ever would know allow himself to appear unprofessional to anyone in the industry. Absolutely motherfucking not, but then when out in the alley, that was, then and now, and would always be a different story, and with that he swallowed with a little difficulty and looked at his silent contact, standing in the early gray evening colored in red and black flannel.

Thom didn't know what to say beyond what he had. Frank knew that too. He shook his hand and thanked him for being up front with him, even though it was after they had eaten.

"Say uh, Frank…you uh…think you might be able to get them tickets again next year?" Thom asked.

Frank almost laughed and thought putting Thom's dentist into a higher tax bracket but thought better of it.

"Don't know, Thom, never can tell."

On the way back to the Hampton Inn, Frank checked his voicemail, and the latest order had come in just before the plant closed. How many was that today? He did the math in his head. They were little dudes, but they still counted.

26

Unfortunately, the big daddy had just told him to go on back to the hotel and eat a shit sandy. It had basically told him that he wasn't getting another crack no matter what, and it didn't matter one bit of difference whether he'd spent the better part of the past three years busting his ass to bring a great product that would help the company on every level it could.

Life sucks, man, so go get a fucking helmut.

The next morning, he woke up to the sound of the sports channel blaring on the television.

Dah Na Na. Dah Na Na.

It wasn't a second before his mind acquired an acute awareness to his surroundings, and then almost by default, he remembered the events at the Hungry Hogg and getting the bad news.

Losing the big daddy.

As he regained his bearings, he walked to the coffee maker and fought the urge to get angry. It was too early, and too late for that. So, he turned on the water in the shower, hopped in, shaved, and proceeded to get dressed quickly and assuredly.

Another day, another dollar.

He turned onto the on-ramp and headed south, leaving the town and the previous day behind him.

The sky was so steeled gray that there was a blinding effect, almost like the sheer brilliance of sunlight that forces one to squint and hold their fingers on a downward diagonal rail to their forehead as a sort of shield. The cold blanket of Midwestern cloud cover. It was getting on into winter. Stripes of white paint padded the asphalt every few feet, droning a dotted line which dissected the road like a border or a railroad symbol on some old map.

Keeping his eyes to the foreground, the world moved steadily toward him in a continuous and breezy panoramic drive-in, and the engine inside his chest murmured steadily too. The half hemisphere of silver and gray and shrouded clouds made the brown earth even more brown, while the beheaded and flattened stalks were still and made no sound at all. Neither did the billboards.

In this early morning, the only sound in or outside Frank's head was of rubber rolling over crushed and melted rocks turned into interstate. There was no radio signal to be had out here, and that was all well and good because this was the time of day that needed silence. A full day, especially at the beginning, is a lot to contemplate. The number 32 exit was only twenty-five minutes away, the meeting only thirty, leaving five minutes to park and saddle up. Frank continued to breathe slowly and deeply, swirling in his head the possible avenues of dialogue that may present themselves once he entered the plant through the rear exit door next to loading bay #3. There were good and bad aspects to making a call in the morning. It was a visit that hadn't been planned until yesterday, for the simple reason that there were certain intangible elements to a surprise visit, that didn't necessarily associate themselves with one that was scheduled. People can sometimes emit a greater, or maybe a more receptive, amount of energy when posed with an unexpected change of routine.

He checked his voice mail and another small order came in early from Utah. Well, Frank thought, I'll be dipped. He'd called on that company some three years ago and had given up to a large extent on account of their seemingly slow response. But what the hell, man, he thought, another one to add to the pile. That was always good news.

Generally speaking, when it was early in the morning, and late in the week, it was the best time for Frank to not only get into see Syd but also get the time he needed to ask the questions he'd carefully constructed. And Syd, being a man who was difficult to pin down, would probably not be apt to volunteer any information unless the time was right.

Frank flicked his blinker up and gently slid his car over to the right with just two fingers, barely noticing a bus of college cheerleaders waving behind shoe-polished windows as they sped on past, with sparkling faces and bustling pom-poms.

The Shell station was the only outpost at the end of the ramp, and two eighteen wheelers were still parked on the shoulder, brown exhaust puffing from silver tubes like a couple of big and sleepy old men still snoring the morning away.

Frank squinted up at the cab as he slowed to the stop sign, watching a man in a red-hooded sweatshirt squirt out and down to the ground like a hot dog from a bun. He quickly righted himself and shot Frank a frazzled and freaky glance. He squatted and scurried underneath the trail after grimacing at the smell of the cab. Frank didn't think much of it, but he briefly imagined living in his vehicle day and night like most truck drivers did and grimaced himself. Shit, the days could be bad enough.

He quickly eyed the green digital display on his dash. Nine minutes. Can't be late. Nothing debilitates a business relationship faster and more assuredly than lateness, even if this was a surprise, it was a matter of policy.

Syd was not in his office, and nobody was in the break room either. Frank set his satchel down beneath a bench outside his office, put on his safety glasses, and tucked his tie inside his shirt. Safety first. He waved to some workers he knew, and nodded to others, making eye contact all the way. In

30

the offices on the one side of the plant, they're all types, and any number of meetings that could be going on, with Syd being involved in any of them. The problem was, with this, a recently set visit, he just might catch Syd in the middle of a clusterfuck.

The presses were being cleaned with highly pressurized dry ice machines, blowing foggy and frozen vapors onto their surfaces removing particles, grit, excess aluminum, zinc, or magnesium. The operators were more than likely taking coffee and/or having a smoke, and Frank moved behind two press-lines to see if he could find someone to help him locate Syd.

Just as he took a couple steps, he ran into Raymond, the first shift second line lead man.

"Holy dog shit, Frank what in the sam hell is goin' on?" He hollered, happy to see him.

The patch on his shirt was ridden with soot and graphite, leaving only the A visible.

"Just seein' how you're doin', young man." He responded, smiling. Raymond was pushing sixty-five, easy.

"Well, man, can't complain, 'course if I did wouldn't do no good."

"I hear ya, you seen Syd?" Frank asked.

"Sure, come on."

Raymond motioned for him to follow and turned back between the press line. Blasts of steam shot in short gasps as

31

the presses opened, the smell of hot and volcanic aluminum leaking into their nostrils.

His face and neck were streaked with dark trails, and one operator leaned his arm backward into a glowing reservoir, dipping a ladle into a bright orange pool of liquid fire, scooping a portion, and turned to pour it down the sleeve into the press. Raymond paused at the control panel and studied the digital display. Enormous bursts were being launched from the exhaust ports, and Frank watched the shiny steel cylinder slowly inch forward, gently nudging the slug of molten aluminum into the cavity. As it filled the recessed areas of the press, it rose to be flushed with the surface, the opposite side of the press closed on it like a coffin lid, squeezing it with thousand pounds of pressure. It ran for a full cycle, and Frank watched as the walls of the press disengaged. Steam wove and zigzagged up and out of the press, revealing a dull and oddly shaped form of metal. There were miniscule numbers embroidered on its surface, and the quick and buzzing arm of a robot lurched forward, stopped momentarily, spun like a drunk pony, and reached in with two large cleaving claws to remove the part from the cavity.

The robot dropped the part into a basket, and an operator with large gloves reaching to his elbows picked it up for inspection. And the process began again. Frank realized he'd been staring and turned to see Raymond light up a cigarette in the midst of all the heat, steam, and pressure. He looked at Frank and slightly grinned.

"Hope you weren't planning on going out to dinner in those clothes, man."

Frank smiled and shook his head. Raymond motioned with his hand for him to follow. When they found Syd, he was immersed in what appeared to be a man-made clusterfuck.

Three process engineers were standing behind him at his desk, all arms folded, all eyebrows crinkled, and all heads nodding and shaking without a hint of understanding. Two younger guys who had the look of interns stood back away from the desk, not wanting any part of the action. Syd's supervisor leaned over the desk from the side, pointing with a Phillips screwdriver and raiding his voice with each sentence.

What the fuck, Syd? What the fuck? He kept asking.

Getting louder and louder with each fuck.

He held his gloves in his hands and his hands were on his hips, glaring downward at Syd. Frank noted Syd's upper lip folding up, and most definitely holding back a strong desire to tell his supervisor to settle the fuck down, turn down the volume, back up the ego, and put it in park. Instead, he took a brief pause in the gaining questions to break in and issue several directives to the engineers as they started nodding in unison. The supervisor barely looked at Frank as he jerked open the office door and left in a huff. Syd hadn't made eye contact with Frank, but had he they both would've smiled or even laughed if the current situation been so harried. Then the engineers filed out and split up into different directions on the shop floor. The noise burst in the office while the door was open and then silenced when it shut.

Syd exhaled and swung his chair around to squint closely into the computer monitor. He clicked and double clicked sharply.

"Sorry, Frank, not a good day today." Syd said.

Frank glanced outside onto the shop floor and watched Syd's supervisor wave and point the Phillips screwdriver over the heads of the two interns and in the general direction of the broken press like a history professor hungry for tenure.

"Not at all, Syd. Figured you might be covered up. I'm sorry to have caught you at a bad time, just wanted to stop in and see how you all were doing." Frank answered setting his briefcase in a corner out of the way.

"Appreciate that. Things are rough all over right now. As you can see." He answered, motioning around the office in reference to the preceding chaos.

"Sure, looks like everyone is on edge."

"Yeah. But that press being down is a drop in the bucket." Syd said, a serious glint setting over his face.

Frank made sure the door was closed securely and pulled a chair up opposite Syd.

"Word is you all are up for sale…thought I'd ask you up front." Frank queried respectfully.

"You sure do have your ear to the ground. Their positioning us that's for sure. There are officially, just rumors. But I think they've got a buyer on the line. We haven't been making for a good while now. Costs are way up, competition from Mexico and China is killing us, and at the end of the day, we just can't keep making our parts and selling them for a profit. They never did get out and try to find something else to do. And it's caught up with us." Syd's face said it all. He'd been there damn near twenty years.

He'd have to uproot his wife and kids and go wherever he could find a new job. As soon as that thought crossed his mind, Frank looked up at him.

"I'm going to be calling on a customer later this month; we've been working with them a long time. Great guy. I can put a word in." He said, without hesitation.

Syd looked at him with something close to disbelief in his face.

"Hell, Frank, you'd do that?" Syd asked.

"Damn right I would." Frank responded. Syd pushed slightly back in his chair and mentioned that he had family outside Nashville. Then they got back to business. Frank asked how he was fixed for lube.

Outside the office, the sound of horn blared on and off as a forklift backed up carrying a skid with four fifty-five-gallon drums bound in shrunken plastic like four fat and dismembered cows; its yellow siren circled alerting those near of its presence.

They shook hands and Frank pointed to the back of his card, where his cell was written in large black numbers.

"Just holler when you can."

"Thanks again, Frank. I'll talk to you soon." They spoke over the cacophonic squeezes and gasps of the presses, and as Frank headed out, Syd was immediately swarmed by operators needing help and engineers needing guidance.

Frank maneuvered his way back through the press lines and toward the smoking section. The last row ran a separate compound than the others in the plant, and only had one operator per shift, versus the seven, nine, or eleven on the others. Frank knew all three and stopped to give the middle-aged man named Jamke a stainless-steel lock-knife with a small chain with his company logo on the face. The bones in his back were poking outward through the back of his shirt, and he nodded his thanks to Frank through toothless jaws. As Frank inched outside, the gray was even brighter and more immense. Several people were clinging closely to each other and the tiny space heaters at the corners of the smoking patio. Frank stopped near them, handing out a company pen to each of them, rattling off a quick joke about the weather, and declined a cigarette.

Frank bent sharply in his knees, raised a fist to his mouth as though he were hoisting a trumpet, and announced that he was freezing his white ass off and needed to get out of the cold. They waved and thanked him, and as he unlocked his car door, he looked up briefly to see still outside and standing in a small circle, extending their hands to display their shiny blue presents, barely shivering and looking downward at them talking.

It was 7:16. He pulled out of the parking lot and stopped at a truck-stop near the on-ramp to the interstate. He called the boss.

He had a certain boom in his voice. Authoritative. Motivating. Self-assured.

Not a man to fuck with.

"Frank, how are you doing this morning?" He asked.

"Not bad, just trying to stay ahead of the rent, man." Frank answered.

37

"I know the feeling, fast son of a bitch, ain't he? What's going on?"

"I was in to see our friend Syd this morning." Frank said peering by habit into, within, and behind his mirrors.

"Oh yeah, how's he doing?" The boss asked.

"Well, not so good. They are for sale all-right; he thinks they've already got a buyer on the line. Probably going to close the plant by the end of the year. The parent company is in real trouble, hemorrhaging money in some of their other plants so it will probably make more sense to shut the doors, lay everyone off, and clean up the books a little before they try to sell.

"Yeah. That's what happens when you can't adapt." The boss stated evenly.

His voice was deliberate, and his words were, like always, right on the money.

"How are they fixed for product?"

"Probably another three to four month's supply will last them to the end." Frank said.

"It was nice while it lasted huh?" The boss asked in a way that revealed a shared understanding.

"Yeah." Frank said, letting out a breath that said it all.

"Frank, I know it stings, but you got to remember, the great thing about what we do is that we can pick right up and move on down the road. Most people can't."

"I know, but…shit, boss, you just wish one of these accounts would give back the same thing you put into them, you know…stay solvent at least as long as it took to get in the door."

"Listen, Frank. The big ones come and go, and every guy like us is always out there chasing them and fighting tooth and nail over them. But just because they're big doesn't mean they're not as vulnerable as a little dude. Sometimes a few tiny holes in the right places can sink even the biggest of them. And another thing, the big ones *know* that they are, believe me. So, the dynamic within them can be a lot more volatile, even unreliable. That's part of the deal. But the guys that make it in this business are the ones that are out there…out there day in and day out humping it up and down the interstates, state highways, county roads, and side streets bagging the little dudes…the little fish that over the course of a year, or tow, or five or ten, can add up to a damn good living. And they're great too, because you generally don't have to put the time and energy into them that you would on the big bastards. Then if you lose one or two, it won't kill ya. You just get back up the next day and get a couple back."

Frank was sitting in the lot of the truck-stop, impervious to rumbling trucks clumsily turning into elongated parking spots.

39

"You know what, Boss? I think I knocked off six or seven in the past couple days."

"See, what I mean, kid, now stop wasting time in the Flying J lot talking to me and go out and get some orders."

II.

He could hear the blades of the chopper cutting through shallow night sky. His belly clung to the dirt, needles from the cacti piercing his rotted jeans. Darting around the scrub brush were high-powered beams of light from border patrol trucks, driven by heavily armed men on the hunt. Rafael turned back and saw the eyes of his younger cousins pasted wide like two possums. He motioned with his fingers to stay still. They had practiced hand signals. They had been eating as little as possible, moving low under cover of darkness close to the ground, working their way north for almost a month, and now they were within sight of the river. Just another hundred or so yards. It was said that the last hundred was the longest and the hardest. They could hear the dogs now. The chopper had banked to the west, and the elliptical glow of the spotlight scanned the terrain. Rafael reached for the cross around his neck, holding it between his skinned fingers, saying a Hail Mary in silence. He had said so many prayers without even hearing his own voice, that he almost wondered if he'd had one anymore. The memory of leaving his parents, his wife, and his two daughters and trying to get north, hiding in the desert, eating snakes and rabbits, and rationing water like a camel, came to him while he lay in waiting. He hoped he'd have enough strength to make the swim. He hoped his cousins

41

would stay still. The barking they'd heard dwindled, seemingly headed west. It might be that the larger group from whom they separated the previous day was discovered. They were traveling with children, women, and older men. Rafael knew that their chances were better in smaller numbers; there would be smaller targets and could move a lot faster. He had considered staying with the group, which numbered over twenty because his cousins were less afraid, they stopped talking about the possibility of being caught, and they played with the children.

Rafael inched away from the cacti, lifted a finger below the moonlight to his cousins, and he could barely hear them move in behind him, dragging seared logs and reeds. They'd kept the materials for the raft in their bags tied to their legs. He peaked forward toward the rising grade amid the jagged branches of mesquite trees twisted like dried cracks in a river bottom that were stolid against a backdrop of held breath and coyote calls. His heart pumped endorphin-rich blood, running counter to the calmness he was determined to maintain. He prayed again. They crawled like commandoes through the dirt, tearing the worn fibers of their clothes against rocks and twigs and sand. An hour must have passed, as they closed in on the international border. For the first time in their lives, they would be traveling abroad. Albeit without passports, green cards, or boarding passes. They were risking life and limb to find work. Simple as that. Their families had struggled for two generations, raising corn and failing to sell it for any profit. His two little girls cried often when they were hungry. They wore homemade clothes owing to his mother's and grandmother's ability to sew. He wanted his daughters to go to school. He wanted to buy his father a television. He wanted to have a cupboard full of food every single day and every night of the week. His friend Cesar sent money every two weeks. He'd gone north two years before, and no one heard from him for two months. His mother cried every night, his own trying to console her, comfort her, reassure her that he was okay. That he was probably so busy working in a nice restaurant or a factory that he just didn't have time yet to send word. They prayed, kneeling below the turquoise coated statue of Our Lady of Guadalupe surrounded by candles on the dirt floor of their two-room clay house, aglow with candles and worry. Rafael worried for his friend too. He wished he had gone with him. He felt both helpless and regretful. He wished he could have been with his friend, maybe able to help, knowing they would watch out for each other. He also longed to work alongside him, whether it be on a farm, picking strawberries or in a kitchen loading and unloading a dishwasher, earning wages, and currency of much greater quantity and value than anything available to him back home.

It was a long time before they heard anything from Cesar. But when they did, it came in the golden form of a Western Union envelop. Enclosed was a picture of him standing outside a rusted chain-link fence which encircled a large metal building with a square sign that red RDP Rubber Co., Ligonier, Indiana. There were also 340 US dollars. It was as though Rafael had sailed from Spain the way an explorer had and landed in the new world and become an instant celebrity in his village. They celebrated long into the night. He was alive and not dead from heat exhaustion or drowning or shot by a gringo border agent. Not only was he alive but also he had made it to a place called Indiana. The father at the village church helped him find it on a map. It was all the way at the top of the United States, near Michigan and the great lakes, almost to Canada. He was working in a rubber parts factory. There were lots of others there too. They even had a tienda on the main street.

The money came every two weeks like clockwork.

This made Rafael wish that he'd left with Cesar even more.

When they crested the ridge, Jose slithered up right beside him. They looked down on the water moving southeast, languidly. It was far but not too far across. The moon, the great big spotlight in the sky, was slipping behind gusts of clouds. Thank Jesus for the clouds. They looked at each other, sharing fearful mud-ridden grins.

Easing down the ridge, they could hear the water. Rafael spun his index fingers quickly, and pointed toward the bags, indicating it was time to assemble the raft. He looked in the direction of the border patrol trucks, the chopper, the dogs, and the spotlights. He knew that he'd have to scurry to another ridge to take one last look.

III.

Lots of times we get shot at. That's why we like to stay close to the tree lines. Kind of keep their shape as hidden as they can. Some old rancher with a double barrel shotgun or smart-ass kid with a rusty 22 or a CO2 pellet gun with nothing else to do some afternoon might get lucky. Blow out one my wings and sink my ass to the dirt like a stone and then I'd be waiting on a few from my tribe to circle on down and get the rest of me. That'd be some irony for you.

People don't give us much respect. It perhaps is, or because of our nature, I guess. We pick at the dying. And eat the dead. That's not something people see as a convivial way to make a living.

Does anyone ever smile when you point one of us out while driving through the country? Nope. Most people snarl or sneer or swerve their car at us if one of us happens to be too close to the road. Saw my brother get blasted into a thousand specks one day when we found a doe half on and half off the shoulder. Its eyes were frozen white. Its intestines were spilled out onto the concrete and the flies were there ahead of us. I always warned him not to get too close to the road. He didn't listen much though. Thought he knew better. He went right up to that doe and hopped around to get a good angle at his head and right when he bent down that silver chrome bumper of that

46

old Bronco smacked him into nothing. Didn't even see it coming. He was at least three feet from the right lane. That son of a bitch meant to grease him.

Someday I just might find that Bronco twisted around a tree somewhere off the side of a two lane with the driver hunched dead over the steering wheel and take his tongue out first. Then his eyes. Get what I can before the ambulance shows.

Most people just don't know that someone or something has to do what we do.

Nobody stops the truck with a wave and invites the garbage man inside for a coffee and biscuits, but everyone needs their shit taken out once a week.

At the minimum.

Makes you wonder what would happen to all the bacteria that can spread disease if we didn't come around to get it?

Nobody ever gives us credit for that.

IV.

Taylor sat at the table, with a napkin beneath his cocktail. His legs crossed under the table, keeping them still, his stomach accepting the alcohol as a settling agent. There were almost as many strippers as there were customers. It was early on a Wednesday night. No bachelor parties, no college kids, just solitary men sparsely seated around the club, alone and watching. He didn't feel like he thought they might, but sometimes he did. Tonight wasn't one of those times. He knew that his favorite stripper was working tonight. Jasmine. She was Hispanic, smooth skinned, and had a voice that purred in Spanish. She also spoke English, and that was equally as catlike. She sometimes tied a rose in her hair and winked at Taylor while he watched. Her eyes looked only at him, daring his to look back. Her hips moved slowly and subtly suggesting the things that could make a man lose his ability to reason. And they only moved for him. Or so he thought. Or so he knew. As far as he could, his state of mind in a place like that.

He sipped on his bourbon and coke, and felt the cool air swirl around the place, the mini spotlights rotating sharply in elliptical patterns on the stages, over the tables and onto the shirts and faces of the customers, and then back to the strippers. The supposition in the air was enough to make his

48

legs shake. All of it in the open, and in the dark. Sex for sale. Or the appearance and prelude to sex for sale, an illusion disguised as an inviting opportunity. They dangled it in front of his face as soon as he walked in the door. He smelled it in the cheap perfume. He saw it in the convincing and seductive looks from their eyes. They wanted him. He could have them. It was real. Of course, it cost money, but what did that matter? Didn't everything?

It appealed to certain people. It being the seeming closeness to sexual intimacy. Maybe to those who couldn't get it, or get it on any other way, or those who didn't have the nerve, skill, talent, or inclination to…find it on their own. Maybe to others they were just diversions, driven toward shady images of lust, or out of boredom. Some others looked at is as just a good time, a night out with the boys, or girls. Maybe some were in fact girls finding a way to test the water or attempts to turn on their boys. For others, they could just be exactly what they looked like, sick lonely perverts relegated to an isolated, imaginative relationship with women who sold their skin and their movements for money. Taylor was different though. Taylor wanted a relationship. Taylor wanted to find a diamond in the rough.

A sweet-sounding waitress came by his table. She leaned down in front of Taylor, slightly blocking his view of Jasmine. She smelled like Chanel. Not the cheap stuff most of the strippers used but that he didn't necessarily mind. Her outfit was dark, tight, and somehow both more, and less revealing than what the strippers were wearing offstage. Her shapely legs were clad in fishnet stockings. She smiled in a sweet way; her eyes were wide and young.

"Having another one?"

"Sure, why not? Taylor said.

"Don't have to work tomorrow?"

"Oh yeah, but I've got a driver and a tolerance." He smiled as she cleaned his ashtray and he saw the definition in her arm, slight but strong.

"That's cool. I wish I had a driver, or a car."

"How do you get to work?"

"Bus. I'm finishing school and can't afford my own." She shrugged, still smiling. Making honest small talk. She was awfully cute. But his thoughts drifted back to Jasmine, as she finished her set on the main stage. He turned toward her and felt a stir in his gut.

"I'll be right back with your drink." She replaced the ashtray and moved away in the dark toward the bar. Taylor sat up in his chair and righted himself. The ultraviolet lights in the club brought out splotches of detergent in his jeans, the same pair he'd owned for four years, and still hadn't figured out how to wash properly. Jasmine collected bills of cash from the stage floor on her hands and knees, not looking at anyone. She even moved like a cat Taylor thought, shuffling his hand to his back pocket. He pulled out his wallet and held it between his thighs, knowing he had over three hundred in twenties in there. Easily enough for plenty of private dances. His heart pumped a bit faster. The waitress came back with his drink and set it down gently on top of a napkin. She smiled again and she noticed his hand shaking just slightly as he reached for it. She was off just as quickly. Jasmine sauntered off the stage and was met by another stripper, waiting with one leg on the steps, trying to appear elegant. She was a fake blond, with fake breasts that bulged through a white satin nightgown. Jasmine took her hand and helped her up the steps and descended into the company of several men waiting for her attention.

Taylor was disappointed; he'd been beaten to the punch. Where had they come from? They weren't shy about approaching her. He was certain she'd seen him. He had hoped she'd come right over, seeking him like he was seeking her, so that they could escape to the private confines of the VIP Lounge, where he'd buy her a drink and talk to her about things she would think were funny while she rubbed his head and slid closer to him on the intimate fabric of a ripped couch he didn't even notice. Then they'd get into the first private dance. She'd slowly take off her lingerie, and he'd stop her, ask her to keep it on, just to leave a little to the imagination. She'd abide and tease him with her eyes and her hips, suggesting again, and then again, and then rubbing his legs with her knees, spreading them so she could lean closer and slide up onto him pressing her head, breasts, and stomach against his raging...shit! She'd gone off with two of them, without even looking at him, holding her gown in one hand and her cash in the other, straight toward the curtains underneath the purple sign that read, VIP Lounge. Shaking her ass automatically outside her silver G string.

She stopped and spoke with a big, bald man in a tuxedo shirt and tie outside the curtains. He leaned over and said something to her; she nodded and turned to the two guys. They both wore shirts with wrinkles up their backs. Sleeves rolled up and their ties loose from their necks. One was taller than the other and he said something to her. She nodded to him and said something back to the bald man. He nodded and looked back toward the main stage, sniffing his nostrils and clasping his eyes under his belly. Trying to look imposing and succeeding. Jasmine placed her hand on the arm of the taller customer and whispered into his ear. He smiled. When she finished, she turned and walked toward the back of the room, where a door opened revealing a brief and bright light. Two strippers emerged in full dress, and Jasmine entered after they headed toward the main room.

Taylor watched and sipped his bourbon.

Was she ditching them? Did the big bald man in the tuxedo give them the shaft because there were two of them? Maybe she was going to change into something else and come back over here and sit down. Tell him she had to make an excuse to get away from them, imagine the two wanting her by herself.

The waitress came back. She held her tray over one shoulder, her other hand on her hip, looking down at Taylor with a turn in her upper lip. Her eyes soft and gentle.

"Another bourbon, sir?"

"Yeah, and tell that grease ball not to drown the bourbon this time." He immediately felt bad for speaking that way toward her, and a little scared that she might actually repeat what'd said. The bartender was a grease ball, gold chains, pinky rings and all, but he was also built like a brick shithouse. He could probably bench press 400 pounds. Or four strippers. And he could probably drop kick Taylor across the parking lot like a nerf football. She looked back at the bar and then leaned toward Taylor.

"You okay? You sure you want another bourbon? Or, how about some water?" She asked. She was nice on the ears and eyes. Her voice sounded like a college student, a young kid with a straightforward and easy demeanor, just being nice to a nice customer.

"Yeah, that'll work, but I'll take that bourbon too. And you don't have to tell the bartender what I said." In a beveled effort to salvage some humor, wishing he could pull what he thought was an overstated and unsolicited thought back from his lips into his mouth and brain. He turned to look at her, and the music seemed distant, so did the dust catch in the swirling arcs of the stage lights.

She laughed a little, sensing his unsureness.

"Don't worry...they water down all the wells in this place." Half rolling her eyes in the direction of the bar. She leaned a little closer, and her hair smelled better than a bed of roses. "That's...where all the profit is." She didn't quite whisper, and she didn't quite flirt, but she tossed her hair around her shoulders as she turned.

Several songs passed. The strip bar soundtrack. ACDC, Whitesnake, Aerosmith, and Cheap Trick. Songs that were on every classic rock station in every town in America. Perpetually supported by teenagers first picking up on rock and roll and those who were once teenagers when the songs first hit

54

the airwaves. And, of course by the DJ's in the strip clubs. The bourbon was doing its thing on Taylor, and the ashtray engulfed cigarette after cigarette. He didn't see Jasmine. The two guys in shirts and ties were gone too. He wondered if they'd gone back in the VIP room when he hadn't been looking. There were other naked women on the other stages. Or almost naked. He didn't like to approach the stage, with a one-dollar bill in his hand, standing in the lights among all the other customers like a hypnotized dog, begging and thankful for a quick brush against their breasts, the briefest and most exposed of moments of supposed satisfaction for all of a dollar. But he did anyway. This one was stunning. She couldn't have been more than twenty-one. Perfect, tight body. Blond hair. Moves. She wasn't getting too much attention as the crowd had thinned out a bit. He still had his twenties, and his lust. What the hell? He knocked his knee into a chair at the next table as he moved toward the stage, and righted himself, hoping no one was watching but not altogether caring. The music rang louder and louder. *Here I go again on my own, going down the only road I've ever known.* He made to one side of the octagonal stage black sheen littered with currency. Some wrinkled and others folded. Ten, twelve bucks at the most. He looked at the dancer, she was rolling on her back, kicking one leg over the other, her hair falling backward on the stage, her lower back slightly raised up revealing hips that Taylor wanted to hold as they curved like a woman's hips should. She did not beeline for him, rather finished her dance move elegantly, and raised herself to her knees, covering her breasts momentarily by crossing her arms, her hair falling now over her face as she smiled flirtatiously at Frank, shooting her blue eyes at him, winking without closing an eyelid. She slowly dropped to her hands and made her way to him, hands and knees hips and eyes. He felt his legs shaking. His stomach bubbling. Heart pounding.

She got close enough to taste and rose from her knees placing her arms around his neck. The perfume may have been cheap, but it smelled like a thousand roses right then. Her body was even more perfect up close. Sliding back down with her hands on his sides and hips and, then gently gliding on her back, running a hand from her lips to her nipple to the crease in her G string while seeing into Taylor's eyes. Pushing on her heels and bending her knees just a bit displaying the desires of any sane, straight man.

Then it was done. The song ended and Taylor was entranced. She bounded to her feet and kissed him on the cheek. The DJ clamored for applause.

"Let's hear it for Simone on the main stage...gentleman let's puts those hands together out there...these ladies are working really hard tonight so let's give them a hand."

Squatting, she stuck a thumb in her G-string and gave Frank an expecting look.

"You want to do some privates?" He asked as he placed the five-dollar bill against her skin. The elastic snapped back and took possession. Well earned.

"Sure. What's your name, cutie?"

"Taylor. What's yours?"

"Simone. Where are you sitting?"

"Right over there, I've got to use the restroom."

"Okay, I'll meet you in five, cowboy." She kissed him again on the cheek and spun to collect the dough on the stage. Taylor felt a wisp on relief, and excitement. He walked to the restroom, past the bar and the grease ball behind it. There was a sports page above the urinal. An old man with a tuxedo shirt and tie sat by the sink. There were bowls of jolly ranchers, breath mints, and single cigarettes. As Taylor went to wash his hands, the man squirted a milky white shot of soap into his cupped hands. He waited for Taylor to wash and rinse and then handed him a paper towel. Taylor would've felt a little strange if this were the first time a man in the men's room had helped him wash and dry his hands, but this wasn't. The man looked

57

all of eighty, and Taylor felt a twinge of pity for him. A man that age shouldn't be handing out towels in the men's room of a strip joint. There was just something tough to digest about it. He dropped a five spot in his tip jar and noticed that it was full of fives and tens and some twenties.

Taylor had a solid buzz on now. The place was even less crowded, at least in the main room. There were strippers in full dress seated at the bar, eyeing him as he walked past to his table. The bartender glanced his way while cleaning glasses and puffing out his chest. It was a shifty darkness surrounding him. Lights dancing like strippers, and music swaying like ice cubes in a tumbler. He found his table, a full cocktail, and a smiling stripper in a lace nightgown and pencil-thin pink panties.

She was smoking a Marlboro light, and stirring a drink with the other hand.

"Are you having fun tonight?" She asked.

"Hoping to in a little bit…" He said as he sat, raising his eyebrows quickly and glancing at her, trying not to spill over in excitement. She was so hot she was smoking. He reached for the remainder of his last bourbon and coke, downed it, and fished out a cigarette. She giggled and slid a lighter over.

"What's your name again, sweetie?" She was looking at him with a certain focus. The kind of focus that Taylor was hoping for, someone interested and someone stunning. He looked back after he lit his smoke and answered.

"Tell me yours again." He said while already knowing, he was just trying to play it cool, any way he could.

"Ah…you don't remember my name…that's a first." She tried to sound offended, half kidding and half serious. All of it a tease, all of it playing along in the make-believe middle ground that Taylor and all the customers that blew their money and their wads in places like this night after night found themselves trapped in. Playing a role that every guy who walked in expected them to, ever eluding sexual fantasies for sale. They dangled the translucent desire like bullfighters, and the closer the customers got, the more it cost them, and the harder they tried to get a date or to get them to meet them at some bar or somewhere after work. And there were those who were somehow caught up on the idea that they could rescue them as though they were innocent stray puppies who just wandered into a strip joint and naively began to take off their clothes and swing around upside down on a pole and who, really… in fact, wanted some sucker to take them away from all of it.

"Wait, I remember, it's Simone." The song had ended, and it was time to get some privacy.

"That's right, sugar, you ready for some fun?" She leaned closer to him, rubbing his knee with hers and her breasts against each other, licking her lips.

"Oh, yeah, let's go."

She slid upward from her chair, sipped the final finger of her drink, set it down, and took Taylor's hand. He could barely feel his feet as he followed her. If he could rationally seal out the crowd, the scene, and the situation, he'd have felt like the luckiest guy on the planet walking away with a girl that fine. He could almost do it too, after enough bourbon and too many lonely nights, he could just about fuse the what if to the what right now. Almost.

The VIP Lounge light blazed a solid white over the bald head of the bouncer in the doorway. Simone didn't do much as motion toward him, and flung the curtain to one side, gripping Taylor's hand a bit harder as they entered.

There was an array of cubby hole-like booths stationed around the room. Almost like escape pods in a spaceship. He continued to follow her as she weaved through them, some back to back with men's legs stretched out or bent at a ninety-degree angle, women astride them or crawling around or

60

arching their asses into their crotches. He noticed but didn't look too long.

There was one in the corner, completely out of view of the others, except one directly across. Jasmine sat with one of the men from before, still in her skimpy outfit, apparently engaged in an interesting conversation. Again, he didn't look for long, as Simone took both his hands and firmly and full of intention, guided him to his seat. Taylor sat and looked up at her like a high school boy, engrossed.

The next song began, and it was a funky, hip hop tune. The walls of the pod drowned out everything, making Taylor feel even more secretly ensconced in the place he was after all night long. Dark, intimate, no one in sight. Just him and the stunning vixen he'd pulled of the main stage a few minutes before.

She began to glide to the music, closer than breath, letting her knees rub his and her hands mover over her breasts, smoothly untying her see-through top. Taylor reached for her hips and she pushed them away at first with a smile, and spun quickly, dropping her ass into his crotch and his breath popped like a balloon. He reached down and tried to adjust and cursed himself for wearing jeans. She leaned back lower, and her hair was in his face, grinding away. Somehow his vision was more focused, noticing the smallest intricacy of the woven strands in her panties which purposely exposed, and concealed her incomparable ass. His hands found their way to the top that was tied in tiny knot. She was pumping now, and he reached again for her hips, and again as soon as he applied the slightest pressure she retreated, standing up and spinning again to face him. She smiled as she looked at the bulge in his jeans, and swiveled herself into an array of voluptuous movements, showing the slightest biting of her lip.

Selling it all like it was a brand new fucking Cadillac.

The sound of the bass subsided, and the DJ's voice reappeared in the invisible world outside the pod. Distant, but there, as he slumped in his seat. He righted his package and sat up.

"You want another one, sweetie?" Simone asked, leaning close and this time sounding a little less sweet and a lot more direct.

"Yes, I do."

"Okay, that one's twenty-five, and each song after that is too." Did she say too, or two?

"Okay." She smiled again and turned to look behind her. Jasmine was sipping her drink and gave a little wave. Taylor couldn't see Simone's face, but what he couldn't see was another smile. Then the music started. He sat back into his escape pod and fixed his package again.

She continued her efforts. And he rewarded her. Saying yes to more and no to nothing. She elevated her seduction and her feverish and pulsating routine with each song. Grinding and riding, tabulating and charging. He whispered and she moaned. He wished and she granted. He was hers. She owned him for her time. And he owed her for hers. The cost didn't mean a thing. The moment did, at least to him. He thought he wanted a diamond in the rough. But now he just wanted more of this. It was a substitute. But a very convincing one. Just without the love, or the loving for that matter.

And now, he was like the rest. They came, they drank, watched, wanted, drank, and in most cases, they lost themselves in what they what wanted to lose themselves in. That's why these places did so well. That's where all the profit was, in the hope. Like the lottery. That's what all these strippers were, fucking scratch (and in some cases…sniff) off lottery tickets. The potent realness of that thought was gone as soon as Simone leaned into his ear again.

"You wanna have some real fun, sugar…"

"What kind of crazy question is that…?" The demonstrative nature of his reaching for his wallet was more than enough of a yes for her. And she smiled, again, but *this* time with excitement. She hugged him like an excited teenager, kissed him on the cheek. She giggled and looked again at

Jasmine, who was alone now, rocking a lime green heel loosely from her foot under sexily crossed legs, watching with eyes that could have smelled of any number of things. The guy with the wrinkled shirt and loosened tie had gone.

Taylor was hammered.

A different waitress came up to the pod. Before she could ask for anything, without even looking at him, as though the stripper on his lap was his date, asked if they wanted anything. And before he could respond, Simone told her she wanted a glass of the best champagne in the house. Dom. And Taylor saw what he ordinarily would have identified as a condescending and callous tone…only at this point he merely registered, and didn't judge, a way to place an order. And the waitress took it without a hint of insult and looked to him.

"Would you like anything, sir?"

"Yes. Yes. Yes." He raised his arms, motioning toward all three women in his field of vision. The all laughed, sharing a giggle at the man. He was funny, they couldn't deny that.

"This guy needs a Budweiser, a pack of Marlboro lights, whatever she's drinking, whatever she's drinking, and…whatever you're drinking, baby…and put it on this bad boy." He leaned forward and pulled his wallet from his back pocket. The AMEX card shone greenly in the neon and dusty light, with the A-M-E-X letters illuminating in bigness through the plastic as though they were fingerprints under a forensic crime lab light.

"Okay, sir, I can do the drinks on this card, but if you want to put the dances on it, you have to get some funny money." Taylor had, and he kept his eyebrows raised.

"What's funny about my money, girl?" The strippers kept giggling, sipping, and looking at each other, intermittently glancing at Taylor and the waitress.

"Well, you have to give me your credit card, I'll go run it at the bar, and they will give you cash, or funny money…that you can pay the dancers, like it's cash." Hmm. Frank would've thought, if he was thinking. So why do they have to do that?

"And, they charge you 20 percent on the dollar for however much you want to spend, it's a better deal than going to the ATM, they'll charge you 25 percent. Basically, you tell me how much you want me to run on your card, and whatever that is, minus the twenty points, I'll bring back to you in funny money, and you can use like cash, for…these lovely ladies." Taylor glanced over to the other pod, and on cue…Simone and Jasmine were sitting close, rubbing each other with their hands intertwined smiling and sending a vibe to him that to ignore would make him crazy for the rest of his natural born life.

"Run it. 500." He said, not looking at the waitress.

"Okay, and you know that you'll only get 400 in funny money?"

"Yeah, sure, go ahead."

"And the drinks, how did you want to take care of those?"

"Can I pay with funny money?"

"Yes sir, yes you can."

"Make it 750."

"Okay." And she was gone. And Frank opened his arms again. Knowing that there was something about his credit card being run and drinks on the way that he was the motherfucker in charge.

The strippers settled back in on either side, chatting it up and carrying on. The buzz was whirring now. Taylor was jamming with the party he'd found for himself. They got out of their pod, and walked over to his, their hips had an illuminating streak and their eyes were the circuit bridges to the idea in his head when he took the cab to the place earlier that night and the skipping his heart had done making eye contact that night with Jasmine, the shaking in his legs the burning in his throat and the bulging in his…wallet, it was all on now. All of it happening in between their eyes and his. This was the way he would've drawn it up, and it felt like he would've guessed. But guessing didn't feel as good as right now.

"You're ready for us, baby?" She giggled as she asked.

He didn't answer.

The songs went on and on. Then they ended.

The strippers had moved back to their pod to gather their purses and their clothes. When they returned, they found Taylor still slumping, but pushing upward slowly from the pod. His shirt was ruffled, and one side drooped over his belt. He glanced at them and reached in his pockets. There was a wad of gobbled cash, and funny money. He'd paid the waitress between one of the last songs. The strippers were the last to get paid. He felt sure he had plenty. What did he get in funny money, 750, 1000? The girls came up to him.

They were chewing gum quickly. And looked different. The lights that were hidden had come on. It no longer looked to Taylor like a high-dollar upscale private party room, but a dirty and rotten room with skuzzy cubicles and torn carpet littered with stains and butts. The strippers looked ten years older, pale where they'd been tan, tired and worn out where they were sultry and young. Their eyes blinked with something between anxiousness and detachment. Taylor was still awash in the last seven songs, or was it nine? He didn't know and was glad he'd no stain in his lap. Although there was a close call.

"What's the damage, girls?"

"Uh, it's 900, for both of us." Nine what?

"You mean 450, for each of ya?" Taylor asked. Unsure but far from sure. Jasmine was chewing gum more quickly than Simone and glancing around even quicker. She jumped in too.

"Yeah." Simone didn't contradict her. She just chewed, and blinked.

"Wait a sec…that's like thirty-six songs, we didn't do thirty-six songs." Taylor slurred his words and didn't know if he believed them either. They were back there long enough. Shit.

"What's the problem here?" The bald man with a goatee, and the big arms asked, leaning in his tie was looser than before.

"There's no problem, we're just settling up here." Taylor said, instinct trying to intervene in any potential problem. They guy shot his eyes at him and looked back at the girls.

"You need to pay us, sir." Jasmine said, arms folding.

"I'll pay you what I owe, not double."

"You owe us 900 each, doubles are double."

"What do you mean?" He asked, trying not to see double.

"We told you, if you get us both, you pay us for it."

"That's the deal man, you get two, they cost twice. Double your pleasure, double your taste amigo, now you need

68

to pay the ladies and be on your way, we're closing." The guy had shifted himself squarely at Taylor, and sounded like a used car salesman, but looked like a bailiff.

"That's not what they said, man, are you kidding me?"

"Listen, pal, do you want me to call the manager, and the police?" Taylor instantly knew enough that he was up against it now. He envisioned trying to fight with a manager, this goon, two strippers who had just turned on a dime, and maybe in front of a cop who probably was paid by the owner of the place, that he was getting it up the ass in the VIP room, all with a buzz that could wash an aircraft carrier and knew that there was a good chance he'd end up in an alley with no wallet or a jail cell with no shoes.

"Here's what I got…I think I'll have to get some more." The strippers swiped the wad from his hand like it was heroin. Simone licked her thumb and flipped the small orange packets, stapled at the top. The thin paper flapped against a cardboard bottom. Simone came up with 640. Frank was surprised. He looked at the bald guy.

"Where do I get more?" He acted resigned but felt a stinging and burning. He was pissed to the core, but it was a nugget in the deep resides of his gut. Distant and quiet but definite too.

The bald guy made like he was escorting him, motioning out the door and almost grabbing his arm. He didn't and Taylor walked out and toward the bar. A guy in a sleek Hugo Boss looking suit sat in a barstool, stirring a highball with jewelry on his fingers. Gold bands and diamonds. He afforded Taylor a brief look and felt his hair sharply and looked back at the television as the sports channel ran scores on the bottom of the screen and web gems on the upper part. He said something to say to the bartender, who just nodded, and moved over to Taylor.

"What's up, partner?" He was fat.

"I need some more funny money?" Taylor handed him his American Express card. This one was going to hurt. But not as bad as the alternative he reasoned.

"How much?" He picked up the card and looked at it in the light.

"Uh, 900 I guess." That should be safe.

"You got some ID?"

"Here." The bartender held it up into his face, looking down and up like he was behind the counter at a liquor store and Taylor was a high school kid.

"All right, that's you, Henry." It's Taylor dickhead. He swiped the card and waited for a receipt, bobbing his head with the techno beat coming from the bar stereo. The loudmouth on the microphone from earlier had sat next to the guy at the bar.

The credit card machine buzzed with acceptance, and Taylor felt both relieved and angered. He signed the slip and the bartender stacked several orange packets on the bar.

"Be careful, partner...5's is in play." he winked and smirked, then laughed like a high school bully as he walked back toward the guy in the suit and the disc jockey. Taylor felt himself getting pissed, wanting to tell the guy to fuck himself and that he'd knock his teeth into the back of his throat if he said anything back. But instead, he sucked the anger back down and looked at his new currency. There were 5's in play. Each packet had a 5 instead of a 1 on it. There were fewer in each stack, and he had to lick both hands to separate them. He turned and found the bouncer talking with Simone and Jasmine. They took the money faster than before and kissed him dismissively on either cheek.

"Come back, sweetie...it was fun." And they were off, and the bouncer began escorting Taylor to the exit. He was sobering up with shame and anger now. Flushed with the sinking awareness from the roller coaster of emotions that had been both excited and dulled in the recent hours, he ambled to the door unsatisfied, used, and near two thousand dollars poorer.

71

"Hope you have fun spanking off your sorry knob tonight…" It was the voice of the bartender, and he sounded like someone does when they are trying to show off. The guy in the suit was laughing, like the guys Taylor had seen in the mob movies, jeering and callous. Taylor heard others too, and the bald guy right behind him was one of them. He turned and the scowl was automatic.

"Hey, you turn around and keep going, pal…" The guy had his arm on Taylor. He noticed Jasmine and Simone laughing at him too, while they leaned into a lighted window, apparently exchanging stacks of funny money…for real money. He didn't see them laugh too long at him though because the next thing he knew he was in the parking lot, but they were the last thing he saw.

And there he was, alone in bad part of town, his clothes reeking of cheap perfume and wrinkled as though they just came out of the dryer and staring up at the neon sign overheard. G's Gentleman's Club in pink electricity.

Wednesday Night. Double Dip.

The cab he hired was one of the few cars in the lot. Thank God. Taylor walked over to it and knocked on the window. The cabbie was dozing. He rocked awake and squinted out the window. He recognized him and fumbled for the lock. He flipped on his light and Taylor got in.   "Back home, sir?"

"Yeah, you remember the address?"

"Got it right here." He held up a piece of crinkled paper, Taylor leaned forward and saw something that resembled his address and grumbled an affirmation. He fell back in the seat and felt exhausted, dirty, and like a chump.

"So how was it in there tonight, sir?" They seemed to hit every red light, and the cabbie had a question for him at each one, looking back in the rearview with a crooked smile and furry eyebrows. Taylor thought about it, and he wasn't sure how to answer. The real reason he was there was that he was somewhat lonely, having been dumped from his previous three girlfriends, he was obviously horny, he had an inclination for the booze, and he had fallen for the trap. It was easy, and he was both vulnerable and lazy. And he had a little cash in his bank account. And for that kind of single guy down on his confidence but up on his sex drive, a strip joint was a safe bet as to where he might end up sooner, rather than later. That in and of itself was to some degree shameful. It was dirty. And it was expensive, even if you didn't get ripped off. But to get laughed at on top of that. That was downright wrong, even if he was the sucker who bit hook, line and sinker and went so far in his mind to believe that he was in charge, from the moment he

73

slipped a 5 in a G-string to the moment the last song of his private dances ended. Then they took his money, laughed at him, and showed him to the parking lot.

"Fine. It was fine." He felt like he was eating stale crackers while he spoke. Bland and lifeless, and even a little salty.

"Sure, sir, fine, it looks like you got stampeded by a herd of twenty-year old tail…fine my ass…" He was smiling.

"Naw, naw, you know how they are…they rub all over you and mess up your hair."

"Yeah sure, your clothes look like they turned you inside out, and with all due respect, you ain't got much hair too mess up sir…" He chuckled at him too. Everybody is a fucking comedian now, huh? He was taking it from all sides, and he still didn't know how to feel. He wasn't beyond accepting responsibility for his actions. He knew going in that he was taking a cheap, well not really cheap, short cut. He knew that he was no match for the bouncer, the bartender, or the guy in the mob suit and he wasn't cut out for a bare-knuckle ass kicking in a strip club parking lot. There was no way that he was that kind of guy. But that didn't make him a chump, did it? He wasn't a chump earlier in the day, before he decided to go to the strip club. He wasn't a chump at work, he ran that place. He thought and thought. The lights changed and the cabbie smirked in his mirror, asking him about the evening, about the girls, about their tits, and about their asses. He heard but he didn't listen. He knew that the thoughts in his head needed a conclusion. Or at least a point at which he could decide what he felt like. There was a bottom and a top to this whole deal. He had been to both in the span of the past few hours, and now here he was…having been shitfaced, dry humped, his balls ballooned in blue, ripped off, humiliated, and now getting carted home by a perverted cabbie with a few wrinkled funny dollars in his pocket. He had to feel something. If anything, he knew he had to know how he felt, and what, if anything, he was going to do about it.

The cab pulled into his neighborhood, and then into the driveway of his townhouse.

"20.25, sir?" That's not even a full dance, from one stripper, Taylor thought. A ride home is not even as much as one in the club. He saw in his head the strippers exchanging their money and heard them laughing, and it boiled him.

"Sir?"

"Oh yeah, right. Hold on a second." He reached in his pocket and pulled out a handful of orange money, laced with green money. There were two fives, and eleven ones, of green. And, there were at least fifty in orange. Taylor wadded it up and handed it all to the cabbie.

75

"It's all yours."

"Sir, uh, what is all this?"

"It's your tip. Thanks for the lift."

"This isn't real money sir, this is…this is monopoly money or something…what do you want me to do with this?" He wasn't belligerent, but more confused.

"Those are two dances and Gentleman's my man. It's all I have; they took me for my last dollar."

"Sir, uh, I uh…"

"Yes, you can, and the next fare, I'll double it." He shut the door and tapped the roof. The cabbie was holding the green and orange bills in the light above the steering wheel, looking confused but not objecting. Taylor looked at him and then he turned for his door. The cabbie honked a few times and drove off. Apparently, it was cool with him.

As he got to the door, he realized he was walking bowlegged, and his thighs were chapped. When he went to the bathroom, he saw that his dick had been rubbed raw, it was bright pink and to touch it burned as though he had the clap all over. His head was pounding and as he flipped his keys, wallet, and cell phone on his nightstand and there was no cash, save one folded orange funny dollar, and no change. He had probably dropped close to two thousand bucks, and this was how it felt.

He was sore. And more than a little pissed.

V.

The smoke in the place was fermenting. The television above was almost concealed. There were color images small and camouflaged behind it, but even still the news made it through the haze. It could have been the altruistic power of television, or the smoke- and gaze-laden eyes of anyone who had sat long enough on a bar stool staring at a TV screen that made it still so irrepressibly visible, and in this case, Frank was on both sides of the bar, and the smoke. Fried chicken grizzled in the kitchen, and the customers sat at tables with barely a foot between them. Green table clothes and silverware that was faded from years of being washed with cheap detergent and city water. Frank was at the bar, nobody on either side of him, drinking double jack and cokes and smoking cigarettes. He'd been at the plant across the street since 4:45 a.m., working with the guys on first, second, and third. His hands had nicks on them, and his clothes were streaked dark. Now it was after 7:00 p.m. There was a news correspondent on the TV speaking from the White House lawn. Evidently, he had some breaking news.

The news was, to Frank, more than remarkable.

The human genome project had been completed. The publicly funded organizations and the private sector had held a press conference, jointly announcing the conclusion of a process that had accelerated at a near incredible pace in recent

78

years and months. The President presided, scientists and chiefs of staff, secretaries, and cabinet members all surrounded him and applauded the announcement.

The public and the private organizations had been racing to be the first to finish, and, or the first to publish their results. Frank had followed the research on-line, checking back every few weeks to see how much further along they were. 30 percent. 55 percent. 78 percent. Then, finally 95 percent. The 95 percent represented a working draft of the entire genetic makeup of a human being. And, there was just something simply astonishing about that. Both in terms of scientific achievement, and potential. Now, there was a marker at which the human species could step back and assess themselves, on a deeper and more profound level than ever before. A molecular level. Laying out the map of the human body, at its most basic and comprehensive level, on the surface beget astounding implications.

"Can I have some water please." He asked, belching quietly. His pants were ruined with mica and his head stirred with the smells of steam, grit, and sweat. He'd been working in the casting plant for several hours on each of the past three shifts. They were in dire need of help. The money they were spending on raw materials was ghastly. It was one of the few times that someone had contacted him to find out about testing his product. Frank came to this town a few years back, calling on them and never getting far. But it had paid off to come by every month or two, drop of his card, and put in the voicemails. Reminding them that he was out there and ready to help whenever he could. Sure, they had other irons in the fire and probably a relationship with his competitor, but that didn't mean he couldn't try. That didn't mean he wasn't going to do his job. And, those negative's, maybe and hopefully, could and would come back maybe, after a few years. And that was all he could ask for. A chance.

His contact in the plant had told him over lunch one day that this bar, and the liquor store down the way, did an amazing amount of business between 6:30 and 7:00 a.m., on the weekdays. The third shifters, leaving work headed straight over as it was their time to blow off some steam. The thought made him cringe. Actually, and literally wanting, and going to get some beers or booze at that time of day? But then again, he'd never worked third shift on a production line, as more than an outside salesman, for months or years at a time.

A fucking 7:00 a.m. happy hour. Damn did that make him shake his head.

His stomach gurgled, as his throat burned. The heartburn was back. It made him wince, rising like a lava bubble in his belly and into his esophagus as though it was a fire in a mineshaft.

Fuck this stuff hurts. He had been out on the road for over two weeks. Sometimes if he got too far from home, it wasn't worth making the trip back because he'd have to turn around the next week and do it again. If he stayed out, he could make more calls, maybe get to know his contacts a little better if not a lot and get a better feel for the local environments. Or, find a good place to get a drink after work, a local place that might be known for great pizza, or in this case fried chicken. The downside to being out that long was exactly that. And it was hopefully going to be worthwhile, but you had to maintain your focus the entire time so that it was, but at the risk of getting lost. That was the thing about the isolation, and the freedom of his job...the autonomy was beautiful, but it had its burdens. You could get lost out there on your own...not just in some small town in Ohio or the back hills of Tennessee or a river valley of Kentucky, but in your own mind. Working alone meant being alone, that was the deal.

Lonely and alone are two different things, but that didn't mean they couldn't coexist.

The talking heads on the news station began discussing the meanings of the announcement and staking out their opinions. The future could be bright. It could also be risky.

Possible cures for long destructive diseases, cornered and solved at the source rather than chronic and horrible treatments were raised by advocates. And the detractors saw the slippery slopes associated with cloning, dangerous clinical trials with previous gene therapy. Cross-firing at each other with their salvos of knowledge and speculation, adding more and less to the facts.

More, and seemingly always, less.

The concept of medicine, directed at the source of the problem, to Frank, seemed to make quite remarkable sense. Why wouldn't it be possible? When you really thought about it…why couldn't it be?

He was neither a scientist nor a scholar, not even a successful schoolboy when he was in school, but he did know what he knew, and he learned it by doing it. And to him, that was the most effective method of learning. No one could tell you the difference if they hadn't done it themselves.

It was also inspiring and lined with hope. There had to be a way to beat the things that were beating us. Cancer, AIDS, MS, Alzheimer's, Diabetes to name a few. And even here in the United States, with the money and the resources and the doctors, people still couldn't win. What about majority of the world population, where medicine…well, where it was a whole different ballgame?

If the human genome project, and the ideas behind it, could isolate the molecular makeup of the human species and lay the groundwork for a methodology, systems, or innovations to bring cures to things otherwise incurable and in the process open a path to understanding ourselves on the most fundament level, couldn't that bring the human species closer together in ways thought unimaginable? Could a scientific discovery based on years and years of research and irrefutable evidence, eventually, maybe raise a level of global consciousness where people realized that they weren't all that different...maybe even transcending the ageless conflicts that hinged upon religion. The alcohol swirled among his thoughts, and Frank found that delving in and out of them was a continuous process. Driving along state highways or back roads, sitting in the driver's seat in an idling car or the hotel or the bar or wherever he was...the seemingly unlimited space on which his thoughts could go, was as vast as it was inescapable. The isolation was something that grew with its own momentum.

The longer he was alone, the more he was.

When could they make that discovery work? How long before a headline became a difference? That's when it would be news Frank thought. Sometimes it angered him how misinformed, and or conveniently angled, the presentations of the news was...as he spent a great deal of time reading and watching it. In the morning on CNN or the BBC America and the *USA Today* in the bathroom, and at countless lunch stops reading the *Wall Street Journal*, *Reuters*, *FT*, the *Christian Science Monitor*, or *The New York Times* or whatever local paper he could get his hands on that day and then NPR and then to the good ones on XM radio in the car during the day and then the local, national news at night. It was a thirst Frank constantly had to quench. If you got time to listen, you better had.

It was a way to stay connected.

He finished his drink and paid his tab, and then walked out into the dark and toward the neon red outline encapsulating the familiar cursively written words, Hampton Inn.

The shower was long and needed. After he dried off and almost emptied the complimentary lotion bottle over his skin, he pulled on some clean clothes and plugged in his laptop. Most hotels were equipped with wireless Internet access these days, and he entered the hotel's security code and was online. He clicked the tiny icon in the lower corner of his screen and his *Outlook Express* opened wide. It was almost 9:00 p.m. local time, and he had received close to twenty emails. Some were updates from the *Washington Post*, *The Financial Times*, and the *Christian Science Monitor*. The news that was widely reported was largely parallel, but the op-eds usually offered different insights. A couple were irritating advertisements for shopping discounts, credit card applications, and others were silly mpeg files from friends who were probably fucking around in their office during the workday finding, reading, and sending off things they found funny. There were also two from potential clients, indicating that a current trial was progressing well, and one that promised they would evaluate his product when the time allowed, but not anytime soon. He sighed when he finished scanning the emboldened messages as none were from the lady, he wished would drop him a line, but rarely if ever did. Good news and bad news were better than no news at all. And the cognizant fact that even at 9:00 p.m. in a motel room, after a long and exhausting day, there was still business to be done. Keeping up with this over-the-email medium was another element of a salesman job that was unimaginably more efficient than the old days. Frank used his cell phone more than a teenage girl and knocked on more doors than a Jehovah's Witness, leaving countless voicemails, and it worked in some cases. But there were some potential customers who didn't have the aptitude for personal meetings or phone conversations but were more comfortable with the quite distance and comfort communicating via email provided. You didn't have to talk to salesman after salesman, you didn't have to leave your office to talk to one in the lobby or a conference room, but you could give and get all the necessary information you needed in an email. Frank was hip to that. Life was an unending, and undeniable two-way street. It was both understanding that and making others understand it that was essential to traveling on it safely and successfully to your destination. And it was all a part of being connected.

He shook his head and rubbed his eyes…the light from the computer screen illuminated in the dark room was giving him a headache.

Looking at the clock, he made his way to the bed, grabbing the last of the complimentary lotion on the way.

In the morning, he made coffee in the bathroom, carefully avoiding the sink so as not to electrocute himself unnecessarily. As he tied his Jerry Garcia tie, he flipped on the television the leading story on CNN was the death of four Marines in Baghdad after an Improvised Explosive Device had blown up their Humvee on a city street. The enemy combatants were using a method of fighting that was both effective, and frightening. Terrorism. Since 9/11, terrorism had become a constant concept that touched every American. It was no longer something that happened only on the other side of the world, to people who were already living under its horrific shadow. It worked both in the combat zone, and in civilian settings. And on 9/11, it had been used on a massive scale on American soil, in the biggest and most thriving American city, to American people and foreign nationals, using American airplanes with American passengers, and it had happened as the terrorists had taken advantage of the most American cultural principles…trust. The openness with which Americans had traveled, worked, and lived was used as a catalyst in combat. No one was safe. And now, Americans were made starkly aware of what had in fact been going on in the rest of the world. It was pure evil, and it would have to be dealt with.

Frank grimaced as he watched the news that morning. His travels were mostly limited to the roads, but he used airplanes too. And it would be a lie to say that he didn't think differently every time he boarded one after 9/11. Who didn't? He thought about that…the fact that in the middle of the Midwest…almost as far away from the parts of the world where suffering, war, famine, disease we're rampant, he was more aware of that fact. At one time, he didn't think about things that way. Sheer distance and the lack of connectivity were conducive to a greater unawareness. But that time was gone. And it wasn't really, a long time ago he thought, making it even more poignant. Change happened fast, real fast, almost so fast you could almost not notice it until things were already different.

And vastly so.

He couldn't help but wonder if and how they could be connected. All the way there, he left the radio silent, in an uncomfortably disquieted effort, to work out his thoughts. Three things continued to swirl with consistent fervor…medicine, communication, and a clear illustration of good and bad.

He also couldn't help but wonder about the miles his thoughts had traveled in his own head while he sat in that pilfered bar, and even on the drive back to the hotel, up the steps and while he slid the plastic card in the slot above the door handle, while the booze swam backstroke in his head waiting the one light to turn green.

He was on the road to another town in another state that morning, hustling toward a lead he'd gotten over the phone from his boss, who'd gotten it from a contact in Japan, and relayed to him with an email. The Japanese were thriving in the United States, with plants sprouting up from Alabama to Kentucky, and Frank was doing his due diligence, finding and following the leads.

VI.

Colin Lien was the youngest salesman at the competition, and the most persistent. He never took no for an answer...that was his tagline. No doesn't mean no, it just means not right now. Sooner or later, the no could be twisted into a yes with the right persuasion. Everybody could be persuaded. He learned that on the car lot back in his early twenties. Those guys had balls. They would turn a beat-up Nissan Maxima with a worn-out short block, duct-taped hoses and 100,000 miles on it for a profit with the right kind of silver-tongued polish. If they came on the lot, looked around for a while, they wanted to buy. Just ease on over and make them feel good. That was all there was too it. And, if they put up a front, or a pretense that they were just looking, you just had to help them see that they found what they were looking for...maybe let them try on your sunglasses if it was a real sunny day, and then never ask for them back. Get them in the office and offer them a soda and casually start showing them the paperwork, just to see what the numbers would be of course. Make them believe you were their friend...that you were looking at for what they believed to be in their best interest...that what you were selling was indeed exactly what they not only wanted but needed to buy.

Who gave a fuck if it might break down in a week? What the fuck? As long as the check cleared.

This latest gig, in the chemical business, was the shit though. Set your own prices...no limit to what you could pull in...freedom, no one sweating you on how you got the orders...yeah this was, definitely his bag.

He was making twice what he made at his last job, selling pharmaceuticals.

That was a good thing because his account at Structure stressed out, so was the one at Kenneth Cole. The shirts were bad ass though.

Colin was on a torrid pace of late. He'd gotten three orders that week. Two of which were commitments for the rest of the year, and the other he wrestled from his competitor after weeks of expensive dinners and lavish, albeit under the table gifts. Golf clubs, brand new Pings. The pit passes for the NASCAR race. A 350-dollar spa day for his contact's wife. Shit, the bastard had better switch over to his product. He was probably getting laid more now than he did before they were married.

His phone rang and he dropped his cigarette out the window and rolled it up.

"Colin speaking."

"Is this my motherfucking money, man?"

"You know it. How are you doing boss?"

"Good, you headed home?"

"Yeah, got a stop to make but after that I should be knee deep in tail by the end of the night."

"Young bastard, wait till you get married and have kids...all I can say is you better enjoy it while you can."

"Marriage is for...the marrying kind." He almost said suckers but changed his mind when he remembered he was talking to his boss.

"Yeah, listen...good job this week, we've been trying to get that business for a long time, but never have been able to." Colin smirked as he liked the props...almost as much as the money. He liked to be recognized, to be the man who can seal the deal and bring home the bacon.

"I just hope they remember who their friends are...they were pretty loyal to those guys."

"Well, what'd I tell you what...grease the skids and the landing is a lot easier. They always cave if you squeeze them hard enough or rub them the right way. Everyone wants a good rub. Salesman 101 Colin, remember?"

"Yes, I do." As much as he liked the praise, he had no patience for the belaboring of lessons learned. He liked to take everything and run, wasting as little time as possible on the shit that didn't matter to him. Thumbing the steering wheel, he wondered how long the call was going to take.

"Now, before you go blowing your commission check on hookers and booze, you need to check with them to get a guarantee of credit, they may be paying late, at least that's the word on the street." Colin gazed squarely ahead of him, his whirling confidence decelerating a bit.

"They have bad credit?"

"I didn't say that, but their customers have had trouble and things have a way of trickling down. The contracts with the unions have hamstrung the Big Three, and they hammer their suppliers like bastard stepchildren. So, we could have some problems, and I don't want to make and ship as much material as they use and then get stuck holding the bag. So, you need to stay after them and make sure we have an understanding up front that our terms are Net 15...not 30, or 60. If I don't get paid..."

"Right, I understand. I'm going back to see him in a couple weeks so I will address it with him then."

"Okay Colin...stay out of trouble and I'll talk to you next week."

"Yes sir. Good-bye." Fuck, he thought. Fucking late payers. That fucker...I hope he...

He jammed his fist around his cigarette pack and bit one by the filter and yanked it out. He snapped his silver zippo open and then shut, inhaling fiercely. He got agitated quickly, and his anxious demeanor gained an almost sinister momentum when his mood swung from near euphoric to wary. He sneered at a trucker who changed lanes well in front of him, and he pressed the gas pedal to the floor.

As he passed, he gave the trucker the finger. He didn't slow to look over at him, just sped on by.

Colin had had several sales jobs. He was in pharmaceuticals for about six months, office furniture before that, and used cars before that after he dropped out of college. This job though, this was much more than his speed. No one on his case all day, no limit to what he could take home, and no corporate policy that frowned on greasing potential customers to go with them. That was what he found worked more than anything…every day of the week and twice on Sunday. Everybody had their price, and everybody liked treats. You just had to find a way to make them feel not necessarily good, but okay, with receiving them. It was like that in all businesses he reasoned. Everybody was in bed with somebody, that was how things got done.

He opened his cellphone and scrolled down. Felicity. Faith. Felicia. He stopped at Felicia.

93

"Hello?"

"Felicia…how are you doing darlin?"

"Fine. Who is this?"

"Colin."

"Oh, Colin." She was busy from the sound of her voice. He heard glasses clinking and voices carrying on.

"Yeah, how are you?" she asked, remembering that this was the cute one from the other night.

"Oh. I'm good, just so busy. School and my other job have been kicking my ass."

"That's rough, where else do you work?" A truck hurtled by him in the slow lane, its suspension rattling. Red, diamond placards indicating Flammable Liquid were stapled loosely to back of the truck. She said something but he couldn't hear, and almost yelled at the trucker but returned to their conversation.

"I'm sorry, guy almost ran me off the road…I, uh, was thinking that I wanted to see if you were working tonight, thought I'd slide over for a drink, or two."

"That would be totally cool." She had a cute, bubbly ring to her voice. She hung up before he could say anything. They had had a good conversation the other night. The bar she worked in was kind of a dive, and Colin usually ended up in one like that at the end of the night after starting off at the more, swanky places. The upscale restaurants which had bar seating were his bread and butter, a good place for happy hour, a cocktail or two and then on to the club, or wherever the wind might happen to blow that night. If he couldn't round up any willing members of the opposite sex to hang with and eventually, hook up with...he kept on trying. And, when the lights went out at the first, second, or third place...he would most of the time stumble into the one where they were still on, albeit dimly.

He remembered drinking himself into a stupor the previous weekend when he met a girl, some girl. It must have been the Zegna shirt and new haircut and the deep wad of twenties he unfurled as he bought his highballs that set him apart from the rest of the stiffs in the joint. Music thumping. It was mostly a hipster crowd, spiked and colored hair, tattoos and piercing. It was a constant thought that he relied on subtly as he got dressed to go out, and as he checked himself out briefly in the mirrors behind the various bars and in the bathrooms, and ultimately when he was prodding himself along on will alone after a long night of partying toward the seemingly kind and interested bartender who saw something different in him that the usual parade of beer swilling, cologne ridden, and not-so-sweet talking jackasses that came to her bar night after night.

The guys back on the car lot used to take him drinking after work. He could swill with the best of them. Wine, liquor, beer. Whatever.

Come by if you want to. That was, well something. If nothing else, if he absolutely had to…he could swing by at the end of the night…after all she did say it was cool.

VII.

"Hey." Taylor's voice was as dreary as it was metallic.

"What's goin' on, buddy?" The accent was deep, Indiana south.

"Not too much, trying to do a little work and nursing a hangover." Taylor's head hurt like a son of a gun, the drinks may have been watered down, but putting them down two at a time still did the trick.

"Is that right? You put one on last night, huh, cowboy?"

"Oh yeah…went right through me too."

"Like shittin' through a screen door."

"Please Everett…I can't go reliving it."

"Well, bud, if it didn't kill ya, it'll make ya stronger, that's what they say down in the Goter."

"Yeah…hey, man, you still know that guy over in India that does that copying…or scanning software?"

"Oh, you mean Haybeeb. Yeah man…I just got off the horn wit 'ol Haybeeb this morning." Why?"

"I got an idea I want to talk over with you, are you working late, or going to the gym?"

"No, I went to the gym every single damn day this week…tonight is my night off."

"Cool. Can I swing by the ranch after work?"

"Why, sure 'ol buddy…come on over."

97

"Good deal. See you then."

"Alright...bah."

Taylor hung up the phone and looked down at his desk. There were post-it notes, reminding him of people to call and databases to update, a coffee mug that still had steam growing north and a crumpled, orange rectangular strip of paper that resembled a kind of currency.

The office was semi-busy, but he had come in a little early before most of his employees and closed the door to his office. He probably reeked to high heaven despite having brushed his teeth four times. It was not an easy task to hide the specter of a whiskey bender and a stripper sandwich from the night before lurking in heavy and dark bags underneath his eyes and on his breath. He was no rookie. And he refused to let a bad night get in the way of work, or at least getting to work.

His company had cut out a little niche in the software market. Their produce was a streamlined database service that supplied restaurant vendors with real-time inventory access and analysis of all current and potential restaurants in their reachable markets. This allowed them to better compile, assess, and use their information so that they could stock only appropriate amounts of items, and ship to customers just in time. Thus, reducing lead time, making more effective their use of floor space, etc.

When the dot-com boom bubble ascended, he had left his job to start his company, and slowly added employees as his own workload grew exponentially until he couldn't keep up. Work was his life. Twenty hours a day, seven days a week. Originally, he had planned on building the business model, establishing a client base, and luring some investors and selling at the height of the IPO frenzy and cash out with a small fortune. The problem was, he invested so much of himself into the idea and the company, that when the chances came around to sell, he never felt right about it. So, he didn't. He was one of the few guys who stayed the course, kept working hard and never went under, or public. Now, after almost ten years in the game he had gotten to a point where he had nine employees who were fulltime, worked hard, and were loyal. His product was profitable, and his work was rewarding. But the reward had a cost. At least to his mind.

All those hours and all that focus left him devoid of a love life. The job begat a shrewdness dealing with people across a desk, or in a conference room, but not on the dating circuit. He put his money into real estate, mutual funds, t-bonds, and drew a decent, but not hefty salary. He studied the market. Followed the trends. Swam behind the big fish when necessary and took chances on the up and comers when his instincts told him too. He was able to reinvest his earnings into the company.

His employees all did well too. And Taylor went to great lengths to compensate them, just a bit more than what was commensurate with their efforts, and value to the company. Hard work and loyalty should always go rewarded, that was something he believed in and it was not unnoticed by his employees.

Especially Sheila, his secretary.

When her husband ran off with some college football cheerleader, he cut her all the slack she needed. He lent her his second car as long as she needed it, paid her gas card, picked her kids up from school when she was in a pinch, and even slid her an extra hundo a month off the books so she wasn't totally strapped. She was in her late thirties, raised in a rough neighborhood, always on time, and loyal as the day was long. She was also his biggest fan. Beyond making enough to put her kids through college and someday sailing from island to island in the Caribbean with a schooner captain that loved nothing more than sunsets, blue water and showing her a great time, she wanted her boss to find a girl who deserved him.

There was a knock on the office door. Taylor looked up from his desk, feeling the weight with every movement.

"Yeah?"

"Taylor...I've got a couple invoices I need you to look at?"

"Okay, come on in." Sheila came through the door and crinkled her nose. Her suit was ironed to perfection and she had a slight fidgeting thing she did with her hands when she had papers or folders in them. Long nails thumping on the edges softly but loudly too.

"Rough night?" She asked as she laid the folder down on his desk.

"Are these current?"

"Yes, they are...I said, rough night?" Taylor looked up at and would've smiled, but his answer was around his eyes.

"You could say that. What else is going on?"

"Not too much, we've got a conference call scheduled at 2:00 p.m. with the delivery company from Franklin, and the new franchise group. Did you go to that awful strip club again last night?"

"Two o'clock, okay...I'll take a look at these and go over them with Ted after lunch, we'll do the conference call in here." Sheila's questions were sometimes automatically avoided, but he was still pissed about getting ripped off, and that he couldn't avoid.

"You did. I can…smell it on you." She said, not in a demeaning way, but more than faintly disappointed. Taylor was not looking at her, but his computer screen, pretending to peruse email or a database or something but just reading the headlines on espn.com over and over.

"Do you have the numbers sorted out for that call?" He asked, knowing she did but hoping she didn't, so she'd leave and drop the issue.

"Yes, Taylor…they are in the folder. I don't…I just don't understand why you go to places like that. I mean…I know why men do, I don't really see the rationale, but I know men and women dancing around in G-strings, and doing whatever it is they do in the VIP room at the back kind of explains itself, but why…I mean, that's not you…you should be out with a nice, I don't know…"

"Sheila." Taylor was still looking at his computer, the pounding sensation in his head was like the drums in Jumanji.

"I mean, there are women out there, nice ones…smart ones, sweet ones who would just die to go out with a guy like you."

"Okay, that's about all the positive reinforcement I can take right now…can you run down the street and get me a smoothie?"

"Taylor, I'm just saying, you deserve better, and I just hate to see you all..."

"All what, Sheila?"

"You know, like you got taken advantage of, by a bunch of skanks who take their clothes off for money. I can't fathom that you'd ever take one of those girl's home to your parents..." Her soft and caring, yet unmitigated and relentless opinions were driving into Taylor's skull like threaded screws into drywall. And the thing was, he knew she was coming from the right place, with the right reasons. He knew better and knowing better was the hard part when you did something stupid.

She was one of those women who, if you didn't know any of her background, not that it mattered, you would swear lived a life of complete, domestic, feminine idealism. From her devotion to her children to her professional demeanor to her hair, clothes, makeup all were above reproach. Women could really pull that off Taylor thought. It wasn't that she didn't mean what she was saying, or that she wasn't those things...it was just that women seemed to Taylor to be so damn good at putting on a surface shade of normalcy and elegance that conveyed an air of complete propriety and good faith. A layer which could disguise the fact that they, and really everyone had personal issues or circumstances at home or in relationships of some kind or another that could be, dark, worrisome, and perhaps scary and in that case, certainly to be avoided if you were an interested man, so far from their present reality that, again, most of the time you forgot that they were or could be there.

That was, of course, before you found yourself neck deep in them.

"Sheila, if you were my mother, I'd be under my desk right now, but given the fact that you are my secretary, and my friend…I'm going to respectfully ask you to stop analyzing my social activities, and please, go get me a smoothie because if you don't, my head is going to explode. Seriously."

She looked at him evenly, still with a caring and familial face, arms crossed, and nails tapping lightly. She finally exhaled with a hint of resignation.

"Bananas, peaches, and apple juice?" Taylor let out a relieving breath.

"Yes, thank you…and would you have them put in a shot of that energy booster stuff?"

"Sure. And here, take a couple of these." She tossed him a bottle of Ibuprofen.

"Thank you, Sheila." He called to her as she walked out, giving him a smile that a woman gives a man she cares for when she knows he's been a bad boy and she is helping him out in the way only she can.

"You're welcome. Oh, by the way, the Dean of the Business School at the University called again. I left his information on your desk. Be back in a bit." She closed the door behind her.

Taylor rubbed his temples, dropped his hands to the edge of his desk, and pushed his chair backward, spinning toward the small ice box in the corner. He opened it and took out an icepack and bent forward pressing it against his forehead. The cold flooded his head and for a moment there was a little relief. He popped two Ibuprofens and dropped his head back on the top of his chair.

Thinking hurt in his current state, but he couldn't help it. The sounds of jeering laughter and the weight of handing over hundreds of dollars to those strippers would not go away. They bent him over alright. Took his ass for as much as they could. He replayed what he could remember, the knowing glances between them and the symmetrical gyrations of their asses on his crotch made at first a little horny, but after that more than a little shamed. They took his ass like a tourist in Havana.

He picked up the post-it. The college was interested in having him be a guest lecturer. It was good idea, he just hadn't given it much thought because of his schedule. He figured he'd call the guy back and listen. But, for now he just wanted to get through the fucking day.

After work, he stopped by the liquor store, picked up a pack of smokes and a twelve pack of Lowenbrau. Everett loved his Lowenbrau.

He pulled up to his house and parked out front. Everett's truck was in the driveway with reflecting stickers on the cab window. Megadeth. Judas Priest. Ozzy.

"Aww, now that's real nice Taylor." Everett said when he saw Taylor carrying the beer.

"Figured you might want a few on your night off. I see you're still waiting on the patio furniture." He had a nice, big front porch but the only things on it were a dead plant, a set of worn wood chimes, several empty beer cans, and an IU flag limply stuck to a windowsill.

"Yea…I do need to get sumthin' out her' to set on…maybe one ah them chase lounges…I could set out here in my speedo and sip on my cocktails while all them desperate hottie housewives are out power-walking! He-he-he!" One thing Taylor loved about Everett was his sense of humor, and the fact that he made himself laugh all the damn time. What a skill.

The house was always clean, and he had antique furniture that came from his folks and theirs too. There were IU basketball posters on the walls, a signed picture with him and Bobby Knight, another signed picture from the '87 championship team, several knockout swimsuit models, and then there was just about every scary poster from every scary heavy metal band that ever laced 'em up. He had a quite a collection of concert t-shirts as well. The one he was wearing was from an Iron Maiden show in '84 with the sleeves cut off revealing tattoos that were just as scary.

That was another thing Taylor loved about ol' Everett, his unique authenticity.

The sumbitch could still make a mullet work.

They cracked a couple of Lowenbrau's and Taylor shivered after he swallowed.

"Atta boy." Everett relaxed into his recliner and raised his bottle.

"Oh, yeah, that was like drinking cat litter."

"Well, yeah, shit, Taylor, I'm surprised you even opened one of them, usually you go into lockdown after a doozy. What's going on?"

"I got hosed last night."

"Well, no shit, buddy, I could tell this morning when you..."

"No, man, I mean I got ripped off." Everett's eyes widened, and he sat straight up.

"Say what bud…somebody break in your place, your car?"

"No, no not like that."

"Somebody hack into your accounting system?"

"No, at the strip bar." Everett was relieved, he was expecting worse.

"Oh, what? One ah them little tramps tack on an extra lappie?"

"Try 30." Everett was drinking, then gagged on his Lowenbrau and spit it back up on his Iron Maiden shirt. He ran to the kitchen and grabbed a paper towel, and meticulously wiped it off. When he returned, he had a stunned look on his face. He also looked like he was going to laugh.

"Say, what now bud?"

"You heard me man, they took my ass for over two grands."

"You're fuckin' with me, ain't you?"

"Wish I were."

Taylor proceeded to retell what he could remember from the evening, including what the girls looked like and how good their tits were, as these were important, if not critical details to Everett. His memory was accurate too. Always had been, even when he was drinking. When he was finished, Everett had put back another Lowenbrau, and clearly understood the issue.

"So? Them sumbitches got you by the short ones and then backed you into a corner and got into your wallet. That bout the long and short of it?"

"Pretty much. I mean, I did go for the double dip action, but they never, and I mean never told me it was going to cost double. That's where they put the screws to me, when the place was closing, and they had the manager, the bouncer, the strippers, and the cop standing around me like a lynch mob. In my state I wasn't about to pitch a fit, you know what I'm sayin?"

"Yeah. That was smart move on your end, cowboy, no telling what might've happened had you tried to take them head on. Because them sum unseemly bastards. I'm sorry as hell you got it in the backside like that, but something tells me you ain't just gonna let it go." Everett spoke plainly.

"Well, that idea I was telling you about..."

"Hmm?" Taylor pulled out of his pocket the crumbled orange funny dollar and handed it to Everett.

"Oh, you didn't spend all your tittie bucks! Hell, you could go back and get another quick looksee at a girl on the main stage buddy!"

"That's not, entirely what I had in mind."

"Well, care to enlighten me, bud?"

"You said you still talk to…to…what's his name, the guy from India?"

"Haybeeb. Sure do, 'fact he probably on the clock right now, over in New Delhi. But what the hell do you want from him?"

"He's the cat who can copy, scan, recreate with that software?"

"He's the one, but what does…" It was dawning on Everett.

"I want him to find a way that would allow us to copy, make, and print a shitload of these funny dollars. And, in such a way that they could pass at any strip bar we wanted them to." Taylor was all business now. As he spoke out loud his plan, he realized that until then he hadn't really visualized it in his head completely. On the wall above the television, Taylor saw another poster completely unlike the others. It had the funny faces of several famous comedy actors in space costumes.

"Conterfeit tittie-bar dollars?" Everett uttered, with a wistful and awestruck tone.

"No, my friend." As Taylor glanced at the poster above the TV, he grinned.

"Space-bucks."

110

"Taylor, ol' buddy, I ever tell you 'at you 'bout slicker den a stray cat coverin' up a turd on an icy pond?"

VIII.

"So, I hear you all have been running some tests with our competition?" Colin asked the engineer. His name was Walter.

"Yep. They come in with a product 'posed to be cheaper. Keep our tools clean longer too."

"Well, how much you run of it?" Colin asked.

"Been on for about a week now."

"All three shifts?"

"Yep. All three."

"Been runnin' that good huh?"

"Sure has." Walter twirled a toothpick between his thumb and forefinger, nodded as slowly as he spoke, and eyed Colin. Slick little bastard. Seen his kind for thirty years.

"Is there something wrong with the T-5757, I haven't been made aware of any problems?"

"Wouldn't say we've had problems, but we're always looking for ways to get better, and save money." Colin sharpened his eyes like an alley cat might.

"I sure do wish you'd a let me know you were testing somebody else's product, that way we could've come in with something we believe would provide you with the benefits you just described."

Walter's body language gave away his feelings. He recoiled, crossed his arms, and shifted his weight a bit.

"It ain't my job to tell my supplier to get me something better. It's yours." He was not sounding like a pissed-off uncle giving his nephew another chance to redeem himself at the family auto-shop, but more like a matter-of-fact man of the working world who'd not easily change his mind.

"Walter, you've been doing business with us a long time, and I'd hate to think you wouldn't give a chance to keep your business." Colin tried to swoon, as was his habit. Walter was having none of it.

"You're missing the point. You've had every chance in the world the whole time you've had our business. Now all of a sudden, you've got some competition in here, some tough competition I might add, and you're ready to give us a better product at a better price. See, what I'm sayin' to you is, why the hell ain't you tried to save us money before? So, now you're telling me, basically, that you've been screwin' us all this time." Walter minced no words. In his world, there was no Santa Claus, and there sure as shit wasn't no Easter Bunny. But Colin's tongue kept on moving, effectively disregarding the dialogue.

"If we can come up with something that will prove out as good, if not better than the stuff you're running right

113

now…will you, rather will we still have a chance to stay on as your supplier."

"You already behind in the game now, but we're looking to find the best product at the best price, and I ain't gonna keep runnin' tests till I'm blue in the face if that means I'm just savin' a couple bucks here or a couple a pennies there. I got more pressin' issues to contend with. So, right now the window is open, but it won't be for long. This boy from your competition…believe his name is Frank Cusco…has really worked his ass off getting in here and his product is worth its weight in gold, so far. You gonna have to come up with something as good or better, and fast, or their stuff is gonna have to crap out for us to stick with you. You hear what I'm sayin?" Walter was a busy man, and as he spoke, he seemed to be annoyed with the time he was spending on this subject. Colin sensed it too, and when he heard the words…crap out…he became alert like the alley cat he was and poised himself to leap from the pavement to the lid of a dumpster to scrounge for some dinner once he caught the scent.

"Understood. I'll get to it right away Walter, in fact, would it be okay if I took a look at the presses where you are having the most trouble so I can get a bird-eye on the application parameters. That way I'll have the most current and critical information to work with when I contact our chemists."

114

Walter accepted this offer and had the smallest hint of resignation in his voice. He reached for his phone and paged Morris, his first shift lead man.

Morris appeared at the office door window less than a minute later. He wore a dusty dirt track racing team hat, and a scraggly goatee.

"Walter, can I call you tomorrow with what we come up with?"

"Yeah." He barely acknowledged Colin as he left his office, spinning in his black vinyl chair toward a file cabinet in the corner. After he'd left with Morris, he glanced upward through the empty door window. Sumbitch, he thought.

Colin reached into his bag and pulled out his safety glasses. He put them on and walked between the yellow painted lines.

"How you been, Morris?"

"Alright, I reckon."

"How's the family?" Morris glanced with an awkwardly confused, but brief look.

"Sister's good, got another one on the way." He answered.

"I meant…uh, you got kids, don't you?"

"None I know of." He laughed roughly, but the awkwardness was still there.

115

"Shit, I could've sworn you had a couple." Colin was sure, but apparently not right.

"No, you probably got me mixed up with some other customer." He motioned for Colin to follow him, as he banked a turn toward a pair of massive machines. They were enormous mechanical monsters. Grunting and squealing and squeezing all kinds of things that Colin could gloss over in conversation, but truly did not understand, or care to know. He figured he'd let it go. Forgetting a misstep was one of his better talents.

"So, how's this new stuff running?"

"Running good. Real good." That was all he said. Shit, Colin thought.

"Walter says you had it on now for a week or so?"

"Yeah, we started small, just a few gallons, and then it showed some promise, so we increased the test range. Little by little, that way we don't go too far ahead of ourselves and wind up eating a bunch of scrapped parts."

"Sure, sure." It was loud all around them, and Colin had to lean in closer to hear, and be heard. He neglected to put in his ear plugs. Fuck the company policy, they didn't do any good anyway.

They watched the press open, wheezing and smoking. The ejector pins raised upward and the metallic shape, oozing gaseous vapor inched toward the open cavity. The robot that

116

whipped forward to grab the part was a full second late, as the part slipped out of the press and fell heavily onto the floor, clanking loudly above the mess of volume.

Holy shit, Colin thought.

"This has been happnin' bout every twenty, twenty-five cycles or so. Parts just drop out like…the craziest damn thing…makes me wonder…if they made the right adjustments, would we really need this robot, or any of em?" He smiled, but not at Colin. Colin wasn't smiling either, but he was looking around. Apparently, there wasn't any food in the dumpster.

"Hey, Morris, listen, uh, where's the head?"

"Back the way we came, take a left and you'll see it at the end of the row."

"Thanks, I'll be right back, I've got a couple more questions for you if that's cool."

"Yeah, I got something I need to check on, meet you back at Walter's office."

"Cool." he reached for Morris' hand and tried grab it like a bouncer and give him a half hug, but Morris didn't turn toward him, and uncrossed his arms for just a second and shook Colin's sharply.

"Perfect." He smirked briefly and made his way out.

He walked toward the head and nodded to the hourly workers he passed. They all cast their eyes on him as he did. But he kept moving. Quick and agile.

He found the restroom but didn't go. Instead, he kept moving past, toward the back of the plant, near the loading docks. He kept going until he saw the painted words, storage, above a chain-linked cage in the rear. The supply room was guarded by a fat man by the name of Wallace. Colin, as sure as though he'd been born for it, interrupted Wallace from his issue of Guns and Ammo. His name was on the patch above his left shirt pocket.

"Say, my man, you got a second?" Wallace barely glanced up, his greasy hair was meticulously combed, and his shoulders were square and looked as though they could haul a thousand pounds of sheetrock up Mt. Everest.

"What can I do for you?"

"You keep the lube supply back here?" He more than glanced up now and lowered his magazine.

"So, what if we do?"

"I need to…check on it."

"And I need a blowjob in the Bahamas, pal." He said dismissively, looking back down.

"Yeah, yeah, don't we all? But who do *I* have to *fuck* to get into this cage?" Colin asked with a sneering indignation.

118

"Go fuck yourself, pal. And you still ain't getting in here." Wallace laughed, which was a merging of a snort and a breath and went back to his story about the "unconstitutional" efforts by some liberal organizations to outlaw the possession of AK-47s.

Colin looked sideways quickly and reached into his bag. He pulled out a hat with the Chem-Friends logo on the front, and a wad of cash, then slid the money underneath the hat through the slot in the cage door, nudging the edge of the magazine.

Wallace lifted the hat slowly, and the bushy eyebrows which covered the cavernous wrinkles in the skin of his forehead lifted like peacock feathers. It was a frozen moment. And there seemed like there was a yellowish glow around the money. In that moment, he was opened and closed, with adrenaline, anger, envy, lust, jealousy, regret, and almost every Sunday School house lesson he ever learned or forgotten; he had chosen his own choice.

Right from wrong. Good from bad. All that shit. And just as fast the poignant image of a silver Rolex squashed all the other thoughts like a piano falling out of a ten-story building onto the dutiful pavement below.

Wasn't nobody looking out number except number one he thought. And with that he got up from his chair, looking

119

around like a nickel-bag dealer and pulled the ring of keys from his hip-pocket.

"You got one minute."

"More than I need." Colin uttered.

He maneuvered to the rear of the supply room, scanning drums and totes like he was a robber in a bank vault, looking for the most valuable bearer bonds amid stacks of ones, fives, or hundreds.

When he saw the blue, 8 ½ × 11-inch paper, taped to a 55-gal. drum labeled "trial lube" with his competitor's company name on it, he sneered again.

The drum was sealed shut. Both bungs had never been touched since the day they were sealed.

Colin set his bag on the top and pulled out a pair of channel locks with blue grips on the handle and a small container of viscous fluid. He opened the channel locks and dug into the grooves and forcefully pushed counterclockwise. At first it didn't budge, and he said fuck loudly, but silently in his head. Fuck, motherfucker fuck, fuck, come you, motherfucker, fuck and fuck.

Then it moved, maybe a quarter of an inch. But that was all he needed. He spun the bung opener quickly and opened the drum. He poured his fluid from the little container into the drum like he was a surgeon in the ER, methodically

120

but with the utmost sense of urgency. He turned the bung wrench the other way, closed the drum, smiled and patted the side like a daddy putting to bed his baby.

He looked at his watch as he exited the cage. Wallace looked up nervously, but not suddenly from his magazine and didn't nod.

Colin didn't nod or look at Wallace on his way out.

"Thanks. See you next time."

"Yep. See you next time." Wallace said.

No, you won't see me again, but thanks for the love, motherfucker.

The rest of the afternoon he had chills running up and down his arms and legs, the hair stood up on the back of his neck. The breeze through the driver-side window had an extra coolness. He felt like he did when he was a kid, tiptoeing up the stairs and creeping down the hall into the bedroom to swipe a twenty out of his stepdad's wallet. He had really pulled a fast one this time though. It would be several days before they pulled the contaminated material online, and the thought of the presses locking up like jail cells made him smile like a bandito might. Fuck them before they fuck you. That's how it was in the big leagues.

He pulled off the interstate to take a leak at a rest area. The eighteen wheelers had the south side for parking, and the cars had the north. He veered to the right and as he glided toward an empty space, he saw a coach bus offloading a group of elderly passengers. Colin saw a long row of them filing into the main building were the restrooms were located. About the same time, he realized he had to piss badly. He slammed the car door shut and slipped on the curb, nearly busting his ass, but recovered and moved to a trot along the sidewalk and up the gradual ramp to the door, passing the myriad of elderly folks with walkers and floral shirts that reminded him of his grandmother. Several men wore dark colored hats with USS Navy insignias. As he ran past and pulled the door opposite, one that was being held for a lady in a wheelchair, he felt a rap on his shoulder.

"Hey there, young man…you ought to be a little more courteous." Another elderly lady who was pushing lady in the wheelchair now had a cane in her hand.

"Whatever, lady." Colin sneered and brushed passed the wheelchair and then inside the building.
He didn't look back, but he heard a several more voices rumbling their disgust. He didn't care though, what the fuck were they gonna do?

Inside the men's room, there were more old folks, and he felt like he was going to burst. As one man exited a stall, he snuck in front of another who was obviously waiting to use it but had turned briefly to look at the doorway.

Colin drained and exhaled.

The old man who was waiting realized that he had been skipped in line.

"Hey, you must've seen me standing here." He said as he rapped on the door.

"Too fast for you, old man, I'll be out in a minute so hold your fucking horses." Colin shot back out of the side of his mouth.

"Why, you little son of a bitch." The man's voice was withered and had a sound that was somewhere between a rumble and a tremble.

Colin zipped his fly and pushed the door open, glaring at the man. The man's eyes were full mostly of disbelief, and a little anger.

"Careful, old-timer, I might just yank out your hearing aid and flush it down the fucking toilet." He said as he washed his hands and fixed his hair in the mirror.

Several old men were looking back at him in the mirror with disdain, and surprise. They were as stunned by his actions as they were by the man who had been waiting for the stall and was literally standing up to the young man in his fancy clothes right there in the rest area bathroom.

123

"If I was fifty years younger, I'd flush your *head* down that toilet, you little…" Colin was pulling brown paper towels from the dispenser and smiling a bit.

"Well, I got news for you, you ain't fifty years younger and even if you were, I'd kick your ass." The other men in the bathroom grumbled together with more shock in their throats, all collectively wishing they were in fact fifty years younger so they could teach this little prick some manners. It was unfathomable to them a human being could be that insolent, and disrespectful. And somewhere, way back in the deep recesses of his mind and soul, it was equally as unbelievable to Colin that he had acted the way he did and said the things he had, just so he could take a piss. Then the fraction that notion disappeared was replaced by the selfish, ignorant, and contemptible self-interest swell that had dominated his personality longer than he could remember. Somewhere along the trail any chance that he would allow himself to care for anything or anyone not directly involved in his own satisfaction had gone by the boards. He smiled again, because he liked it that way.

He slid out the door and into the main foyer of the building. He saw the vending machines and the help desk and the ladies' restroom on the other side. He thought about getting a coke, but before he could move over the machine, he spotted the lady with the cane, standing with seven other ladies, all of whom had looks in their eyes that could sear the skin right of his face. He didn't look at them long and headed for the door.

"You better hope we don't run into you again, you little bastard." She said, and she meant every word. Colin just laughed. The old bag had balls. Then he almost strutted out the door toward his car.

It was another hour to the house. As he sped back toward the city, he smoked and listened to the pulsating beats his rave/club compilation. He was into that scene for years. Late night body bumping sweat slinging techno dance parties with glow sticks and ecstasy. It gave him goosebumps to think about right then, as he pictured the bartender with the tight ass looking up from the bar as he walked in and gently biting her upper lip.

When he arrived home, he opened a bottle of tequila, and slammed down a shot. He showered, and after drying off, he checked himself out in the bathroom mirror. He flexed his triceps and turned to admire the ridges in his shoulders. His abs weren't what they used to be, but he didn't have a gut like most of the guys his age. It was a quick and slippery slide from a once chiseled twenty-five-year-old to a lazy and soft thirty-year-old if you weren't careful. He snipped the curling black hairs from his nostrils, and plucked a couple from between his eyebrows, rolled on some speed stick, and patted on some after shave. Then he sprayed on the Dolce & Gabbana. Liquid gold.

Then he took another look. Damn, it was good to be good looking he thought. He got dressed and felt like the winning power ball ticket going out the door.

When he got to the bar, he had a rush of anticipation whirling inside his stomach. It was on the second floor of building in the warehouse district. A bouncer stood under a light outside.

Colin guessed he went 300, easy. He wore a long black leather jacket and a look on his face that said bad mofo. There was no line, so Colin decided to try and strike up a conversation.

"How are you doing, man?" Sounding cool and tough.

"It's alright. You got an ID?"

"Sure do, but I don't look twenty-one, man…" Trying to joke.

"Don't matter how old you look." He answered, gruffly.

"I hear you, pretty slow right now, huh?"

"Mmm hmm." Colin's ID disappeared into the bouncer's hand. And he waved him in, his mammoth hands reassuming an interlocked position below his stomach, not paying Colin any more mind.

"Thanks, man. "He felt a small pelt of dissatisfaction at not being able to endear himself to the bouncer, feeling as confident as he did. It never hurt to make friends with the big man who worked the door. But he quickly blew it off as he climbed the stairs two at a time.

The walls were painted a deep rustic red, with crazy ass zombie art hanging about. He pushed through purple velvet drapes in the doorway and immediately set his eyes on her.

Felicia was sauntering around the other end of the room, picking up stray bottles and bobbing her head to the house music. The place was about half full, and as he made his way toward the bar, he heard his name. He was walking around a pillar, with a miniature Greek statute inset about waist high. The voice didn't register at first and having lived most of his life in the area, it could've been anyone. But it wasn't crowded enough for him to get away with ignoring whoever wanted his attention, so he pulled on the pillar with one hand, turning back to see who it was.

"Colin Lien, ain't this some shit…I don't believe it." A guy about Colin's age emerged from a corner, where a small group of people were sitting on leopard spotted couches around a curved coffee table that seemed to be only a foot off the ground with lava lamp-like fixtures casting a bluish hue in the background. He had a three-day stubble, slickly moussed dark

127

hair and a swab of gum in his mouth, gnawing down on it like a bobcat. It took a moment, but Colin recognized him.

"No fucking way. Ollie, when did you get out?" They shook hands and hugged like old war buddies.

"Man, what's it been four, five years?" Colin asked, sizing him up.

"Actually, well, yeah, man, you're probably right, whenever it was, you left the lot." Ollie shrugged.

"I guess so, shit, what the hell you been up to?" Colin was genuinely happy to see someone from the past, and didn't want to chew him out, turn their back or throw a lamp at him.

"Well, you know me, man, little ah this little ah that." He smiled furtively and kind of motioned with his head to the corner. Colin titled his and saw what appeared to be a couple of shapely Latino girls sipping on their cocktails. Ollie was a bit shorter than Colin and wore a white v-neck designer shirt under a black jacket. Probably Armani from the look of it. Possibly Zegna. He also had one nice piece of hardware wrapped around his wrist.

"Mmm-hmm. Nice. What are you doing for work?"

"I, uh, well, shit, man, come on over and join us, let me buy you a drink or two." He said as he lightly grasped Colin's shoulder, gesturing toward his two friends.

"Yeah, man, sure." He figured, since it was still early and she hadn't seen him yet which was good because he didn't want to overplay his hand, and he hadn't seen Ollie in a long time that he ought to go have a couple with him and hear what he was up to. It didn't hurt that he was apparently outnumbered.

"This is Colin Lien, an old friend of mine. Colin, this is Sorroco, and Maria." They both raised their hands to meet his, and they shook. Both were offering demure looks. They went back to their cocktails without saying anything. A waitress came by and whispered into Ollie's ear, glancing at Colin. He nodded and asked Colin what he was having.

"I'd like a Dewar's and water."

"Dewar's, fuck that shit man...bring us a couple Glen Livet, angel."

"No problem, Ollie." The waitress answered, smiling at Frank.

"Dewar's? Are you kidding me...that stuff is like drinking gasoline." Colin sat in a chair that looked like something in a futuristic sci-fi movie made in England. Ollie sat on one side of the couch, facing Colin.

"Glen-Livet, shit, my boss is the only guy I know that can afford to drink that stuff." Ollie smiled and patted his Colin on the knee a couple times. He offered him one of the shots that were on the table.

The clinked glasses and put them back. It stung for a second but felt better the next.

He lit a cigarette and offered on to Ollie.

"Got my own. So, didn't you start selling pharmaceuticals after you left, is that right?"

"Just for a while, but it wasn't my thing. Too many people on your ass, too many rules on what you can and can't do. "

"Then what?"

"Actually…got into working straight commission…manufacturer's rep."

"No shit?"

"No shit."

"Man, I remember the kids who were loaded to the gills back in high school, their Dads were mostly 'manufacturer's reps'." He had a bounce to his grin, and to the look of interest it purveyed.

"Well, I ain't complaining. But, I ain't exactly rolling in diamonds and furs like you, apparently." Colin responded, glass in hand and high dollar scotch on his lips.

"Well, I did alright on the lot back when the SUVs were moving hot and heavy. But after that Bridgestone/Firestone tire blowout, it went soft and I wasn't about to sit around with a bunch of middle-aged jackasses smoking Kool's and talking about how good ah athletes they were in high school." Ollie leaned forward and back, swatting Colin's knee again with the back of his hand.

"I hear that." Colin said.

"Yep. So, you on the road a lot or what?"

"Fair amount. Less than my boss thinks I am. I need to have my time and my space, you know…at least enough to get my thing on." He was starting to feel the tingling gibe of his buzz going. It was good too. He went on to share several highlights of his career. Ollie listened intently, and continually nodded in an approving way. Then he somewhat subtly changed the subject.

"You still partying?" Ollie asked. Colin responded with a look. One eyebrow up and curled along the wrinkle of skin above his eye and the other eyebrow down, as if to say…shiiiiit.

"Come on then, fool." Ollie said. And then stood up.

"Where are we going?" Colin asked. But his words were lost in the thumping of the booming beats aloft in the bar. But before he knew it, he was following his friend between strobe lights cocktail tables and mingling hipsters toward the red neon light reading restroom.

When he walked out the music was penetrating, but his level of awareness seemed to skyrocket to a level of acuity that he associated with twenty–twenty vision and insatiable hearing. Kind of like a super-hero who can see around corners and hear things in other rooms and almost knows what's going to happen moments before it does. And as he licked his numbing lips and sniffed his stinging nostril, he walked through the place with his old friend Ollie from the used car lot and the all-night rave parties they used to hit together, dressed to the nines, and scoping the surroundings like he was rock star at an after-party. That's when she did a little double take from behind the bar. She was washing pint glasses in a soapy sink with her hair pulled back in a ponytail and as she shook the suds from them, she looked twice at the tall dark and sexy guy casting a pulsing look in her direction room the other side of the bar. She didn't flinch, but it was all she could do not too.

Did he just wink or was it me, she thought? The lighting was glowing, and the moment was gone before he or she could be sure, but inside somewhere, where her heart got excited, she knew that he was checking her out, and there was something familiar about him. He was walking with Ollie, and he wasn't friendly with just anyone, that was for sure. She went back to the calls for gin and tonics, vodka cranberries and jack and cokes after she dried her hands, lifting her eyes subtly to check him out one more time from the back.

He could feel her look and being looked at like that made his stomach swirl and his ego bulge. But he was determined to play it cool, and to make sure he didn't look back at her, he slapped Ollie on the back and cracked a joke. It wasn't easy, but he managed to pull it off. Ollie was hopped up and laughed, even though it must have been hard to hear him.

"And what have you two boys been up to?" Maria asked, or it could have been the other one.

"Just catching up, love." Ollie smiled at her and leaned down and kissed her neck and taking her hand in his clasping it tight. The inquisitive but still sexy look on her face turned quickly to excitement as her eyes suddenly lighting up like fireworks.

"Go on, baby, we'll be right here." He said. And she reached for her friend's hand as they stood and straightened the material of their dresses, one of them taking the other in her hand and swaying their hips with a sudden lift to their gait.

"So, what's the story with those ladies?" Colin asked after they sat and lit into two fresh slugs of scotch.

"They're hot, aren't they. Cuban. And both of them moved here from Miami. Maria's cousin is a friend of mine, actually we do a little bit of business together, and her friend Sorocco moved here kind of, like a traveling companion."

"What kind of business you into, man?"

"Buy and sell cars still, a little real estate, rental properties you know…couple other things. Try to stay diversified." Ollie puffed on a cigarette, one arm outstretched over the back of the couch, sniffling and rubbing his nose with the inside of his thumb, his eyes not darting, but alertly scanning. Colin didn't press him past that. And he thought about getting a drink at the bar. But the two girls from Miami returned from the bathroom with eyes aglow and instantly blunted that notion.

They were smoking hot too, playfully flipping their hair and sitting on either side of Ollie.

One lit a cigarette and ran a finger across her collarbone with a very thin gold necklace gleaming as she did so. That one was Maria, had to be.

"So how long have you known each other?" She asked.

"We go back a few years. Used to work together." He answered.

"Ollie was the best of the crew though; he could close anyone anywhere anytime." Colin wasn't above giving his buddy some props, particularly in front of these two girls. But he tried like hell not to stare at the way her dark and slender legs shifted over one another. Sorocco looked on and Colin glanced at her, zeroing in momentarily on the hardened nipples emerging through a silk dress. He leaned forward and started to ask them about themselves. Music they were into. Favorite cities they'd been to or hoped to visit. Shows they recorded on TIVO. He kept on with the Scotch too, as Ollie was still buying.

Silver tongued devil. That's what he was thinking to himself.

The girls wanted to dance. Almost on cue. They got up from the couches and reached for Ollie's hand.

"No, not me." He said.

"Oh. Come on...come and dance with us, Ollie..." They purred, nearly pleading.

"Maybe later...I want to chill for a bit." He didn't want to get up, for whatever reason. Colin hadn't danced or even thought about dancing in...he couldn't remember when, but in this moment, Ollie looked over at Frank and suggested they take him for a spin.

"Would you like to come dance with us, Frank?" they asked.

"Love too." he downed the last of his Glen Livet and winked at Ollie. Don't have to ask me twice he thought.

"Be careful, man…they're a couple of pros." Ollie quipped, leaning back and glancing down at his cellphone.

They set their purses down on the table and reached for his hands. Each stuck out like light sabers. He followed them through the growing crowd of hipsters and billowing smoke toward the dance floor aware of the tingling sensation in his fingers as they met with the soft sexy skin of theirs.

They instantly pulled themselves onto either side of him, rocking and rubbing and running their hands over his stomach and lower back. Momentarily gliding backward and then forward with each other. Slipping away from him they danced together, conspicuously too.

It was right up close to feeling as though he'd won the fucking lottery.

IX.

For a second, he was self-conscious, worrying that
everyone might be staring at them, as though they were making
a scene. But when he did pull his eyes away from the girls, he
noticed no one looking. The smoke from the machine and the
cigarettes bubbled into a shroud under which they were hidden.
He felt daring enough to pull Maria closer, so her legs sipped
apart and clung to one of his pelvis swerving and pressing he
squeezed one voluptuous cheek and kissed her tongue first. She
moaned and pulled him closer with a feminine ferocity that
made his blood pressure spike. She then quickly retreated with
a deeper and more determined swipe in her eyes while keeping
her hands on his sides and applied just the right amount of
mmm-hmm so that she turned him and he found himself face to
face with her friend, whose smile was the last thing he saw
before her mouth bit into his. Whirling in his head he
desperately tried to remember to savor the moments, very
aware of his disbelief this was really happening. It was as
though he entered a dream compounded in his favorite erotic
movie.

One that was exclusively written for him.

When they moved away from the dance floor, the girls
were about to head back to the restroom, and Colin toward the

137

bar, he knew he was pitching a tent and reached into his pants to make the proper adjustment.

Maria playfully ran her hand along his chin.

"I hope you're going to come with us later."

"Makes two of us." He said.

"Or three." She giggled and went hand and hand through the crowd with Sorocco as their dresses swayed alongside their hips.

He looked back toward the corner and saw Ollie hunched over with his cellphone glued to his ear, and a guy in a silver suit standing on the other side of the table, rattling one leg nervously, with a gold bracelet dangling from his wrist, pinkie rings shining from, well both pinkies.

Two pinkie rings.

Colin decided against heading that way for the moment and made a move for the bar.

Felicia saw him coming but didn't make it obvious. She was certain he was the one there the night she and Astrid came in for her first time. And, something in her remanded her so that she was a little miffed by the sight of the two Latino-looking girls. She'd worked there for long enough to know how to see through the smoke.

Colin looked at her. She was hot. He tried to get her attention by just leaning on the bar. At this point, he felt he could do now wrong and felt for sure she'd pick up his scent. But when two guys whose attitudes screamed 30,000 dollars a year millionaire slid into an empty space next to him and went jabbering on about what the prime was going to do with the new head of the Fed got their order in for two dirty martinis, he got a little ticked.

"Seventeen buck's, boys." Felicia said, looking directly at them.

They looked at each other and stuck their hands into their pockets, aggregating what they dug out. The line of people began to back up along the railing of the bar. Felicia glanced each way, skipping over meeting eyes with Colin.

"Here you go…thanks." The first one said, handing here exactly eighteen.

"You aren't going to tip the lady?" Colin chimed. The first guy looked up at him, the other tried to ignore the comment.

"What'd you say?" He asked with a small amount of attitude.

"I think you heard me." Colin said evenly. Locking the guy down with his eyes, his confidence still at a record high. The guy tried to stare back but froze up and pulled out his wallet from his back pocket.

139

"I was going to, man…no big deal man just, take it easy." He said, trying to act cool about it. Colin resisted to urge call the guy a punk ass bitch or something to that effect and watched as he laid a five on the bar. They promptly walked away, martini glasses in hand as he turned to see Felicia looking at him with a touch of thanks in her expression.

"That wasn't totally necessary…they would've, what can I get for you?" She asked, knowing she was going to get caught in the weeds if she didn't keep moving.

"Bottle of Bud…actually, make it four."

"Double and double-fisting, are you?" She asked.

"No, my turn to buy the round, that's all." He said.

"Mmm hmm. Here you go. Twelve bucks." He handed her twenty.

"Keep the change." He said.

"Thank you." She said quickly and made to attend to other customers, but before she got away, Colin had a question for her.

"You busy later?"

"Uh, what do you mean?" She was caught a bit off-guard, and despite the building bank of customers, she didn't peel herself away from the look he was giving her.

"Just thought we could maybe catch up at some point, talk, have a drink, whatever works…"

140

"Yeah, I guess so…come back up to the bar when it's not so busy. Okay?"

"Sounds good."

"Sure." She spun the other way and pointed at a kid in a red Mohawk with a nose ring and a cutoff leather vest hoisting a fistful of cash. Colin could barely get a swallow of cold beer down his throat before his dance partners gleefully pulled him by the arms away from the bar.

"Wait, just wait a second. I got some beers back there." He said, but to no avail. They were on a mission apparently.

Ollie was sitting on the couch sweat beading on his forehead, checking text messages on his phone. He was into something. Exactly what it was he could probably guess but chose to remain withdrawn. Wasn't his business. He was just there for the hot ass and party favors.

"We like your friend." Maria said.

"He is a good dancer." Sorocco added.

Colin relished the compliment.

"I was just trying…" The music cranked back up and he didn't get to finish his sentence.

"Are you all ready to get down?" Ollie asked.

"What's the plan?" Colin wondered.

"I'm supposed to meet up with a couple people at a club a few blocks from here, then back to my place, if you want to come with?"

"Come with us, Colin...please." Maria said. Colin looked at the girls, wanting the story to continue, regardless of where it might lead.

"Hell yeah, man, let's get it on." Ollie motioned for the door and they gathered up their things and left as a pack.

From the far side of the bar, having kept her eyes out and her hopes up, Felicia noticed the three bottles standing un-drank in the spot where Colin had ordered them. And she walked that way to put them in the cooler in the event he came back for them, but then saw him walking just for a second under the light above the exit, his back to her.

X.

Frank was supposed to have moved into the apartment three weeks ago. He had planned on having the cable, electric, water, and on by the end of the week. He'd even found the local grocery, the jiffy lube, the liquor store, blockbuster, and pizza place right after signing the lease. But before he could do all of this, he had to get there first.

Only a month before, late on an April night in urban Cincinnati, a young unarmed man sprinted through an alley, separated from his friends, trying to shake the cops on his ass amid shattered forty ouncers and dangling trash from overfilled dumpsters. He almost made it over the fence too. But they got him. Shot him. Dead. He was Black. The cop was White.

The next two days were hot down around City Hall. The building itself seemed stressed to its limits. People poured into protest. Enraged people. Tired of the hell the city had been turned into. The poverty. The crime. Junkies cringing in stained wife-beaters at every street corner, harassing any passer-by. The Over the Rhine area had once been a flourishing spot to shop, eat, drink, and visit with friends. Now it was a just another covey of liquor stores, and all but abandoned row houses, soaking in the humid sun between jagged cracks in the pavement and wretched smells of sewage gurgling from curbside drains.

A rock. A bottle. Maybe a brick. Somebody started throwing something. Somebody got hit. A window broke. A ten-foot-by-six-foot-plate glass window of a storefront might have shattered with a harrowing, unmistakable sound, the beginning…that an incensed mob had been anticipating, and the down sliding unstoppable current may have followed.

However, it happened. It happened.

Anyone driving through the area could expect a pelting from sidewalk standers…hurling anything at their disposal. Business owners were suddenly, instantly transformed into targets. Their stores goldmines for maniacal prospectors, intent on theft and destruction. Someone shot a policeman in the chest. Gunfire pierced the springtime evening from all directions. The alley. The main drag. Rooftops. A woman, pregnant, was taken from her surrounded car by thugs and beaten. An out-of-state delivery man making a stop in the area had his head smashed open with pipes and bottles.

Smoke enveloped the Kroger building. The mayor considered calling in the National Guard.

Frank had finished a workout at the gym downtown. He could hear the sounds, of violence from around the corner as he popped his trunk and dropped his bag inside. Looking back up the side-street, he saw men in t-shirts, some holding various kinds of objects, backing off in a staggered group, yelling

144

things. The view Frank had was between two buildings, at least ten stories high. The perpendicular street was a bevy of confusion. Following the group of rioters were several white-shirted mounted police, dark colored ties strewn downward on their chests. Some tried to hold helmuts in place with one hand and the reins in the other as their horses clopped along precariously through the street.

Frank didn't think long. He just got in his Cadillac and fired it up. As soon as he put in drive, several men rushed to his window.

Motherfucker…you better gimme yo cah! Frank noticed dark streaks down the inside of one man's arm while he draped it over his window onto the roof.

His hair ragged.

Then he dropped it off the roof with a drastic scowl on his face and reached in his pants.

As soon as Frank saw that his arm came back off the roof and the one gold tooth the man had flashed as if to communicate something, he didn't stick around to talk.

He heard a couple of bullets fire and ducked his head down toward the stick. He steered with memory. They faded in the rearview and he wondered if it was real. Then turned. He saw a Saks Fifth Avenue marquee blasted by gunfire, the F and the A barely clinging to cable that kept it up on the exterior brick wall on the department store across the large parking lot, and then turned again. It was always sketchy downtown, but this was something different. Something was going on that was not going on when he had gone into the gym that morning.

He turned again and slammed on the brakes. A truck was stalled in front of him, cars parked on either side making a pass impossible. Frank didn't want to stop moving; the reality was that someone had just shot at him percolating his senses like high-sky air during freefall. All that his instincts told him was to keep moving, handle the situation, and remove yourself from danger. Exit the scene that is uncontrollable. Get out and get safe. Then he leaned carefully out of his window to see around the truck. A group of ten, maybe fifteen, men were spread across the street, making their way toward the truck, and him behind it. They were not police. They were crazy, wild fucked-up motherfuckers intent on hurting, stealing, or maiming, whatever they could get their hands on. Behind him was a lady in a minivan skidded up after taking the same turn he had. She hadn't been as quick to apply brakes as he did and slammed into his rear sending him jolting into the steering wheel. He heard an almost cheering sound erupt from in front of the truck, as though the quarterback of the opposing team had just been knocked over by his own player, awaiting a thirsty onrushing crowd of lineman to hammer his ass into the

146

dirt. Frank felt blood run from his nose, trickling down his lips and onto the powder blue shirt he'd just bought from the Gap. He looked in the rearview and saw the mixed fear and confusion in the face of a mother who had a baby in her backseat. He saw the look of someone who knew they were suddenly in the wrong place at the wrong time, but no earthly idea what to do in or about it.

His eyes went lucidly wide. Knuckles wrenched like swift knives slicing through a dark kitchen.

Frank felt nothing but a calm and silent awareness and knew what to do.

Whatever that was.

He clicked the seatbelt and popped out of the car and ran back to her window.

She rolled it down with a stammering fear.

"'I'm sorry, I'm so sorry, are you…I, I." She managed to say. Frank could tell she was close to frantic. A fender bender wasn't that big of deal on any other day. But she'd seen the same madness that he had, just around the previous corner, she was just trying to get out of there with her little one.

"It's ok, ma'am, is your baby ok?" She looked back, touched the baby with her hand, and nodded. She snuffled.

"Yes, she's ok. Thank God for these seats. What is happening, someone just tried to break into my car, they…they…had a gun." She was almost in shock.

"I know, we need to get you out of here. Lock your doors, and when I come back here, you just follow me. OK?"

"But what about…"

"Just do what I'm telling you. Lock your doors." He saw her nod again for a moment and ran back to his car. Sweat was running down his legs and through his shirt too. He dug into his briefcase that his boss had given him the week before he'd first gone out on the road and pulled a long and heavy silver crescent wrench from the side pocket and ran to the cab of the truck stalled in front of him.

The group of men looked like something out of a nightmare. An angry mob of nightmare men for real meaning to swallow their intended victim.

Hatred glared from deeply white eye sockets.

Reason was gone. Long gone.

The truck cab was empty, the engine still running. Somebody had either left it to be stolen or had been taken by force.

He stared down the group; his hands wanted to shake but they didn't. Just sweat.

They kept coming at him, and he did something that felt completely unreal, unnatural like rain without clouds. He cocked his elbow back and raised his other hand.

"Back the fuck off." He heard himself say. But they kept coming, within thirty feet. The man out front had a long metal pipe in his hands. He swung it wildly over his head and pointed it at Frank. They part staggered and part sauntered over the street as though the asphalt was shifting beneath them like walkable lava. There were red marks on his clothes, more than likely blood. And he damn sure wanted more.

"Fuck you, muthafucka…you one…" Said a ripped young man probably younger than him, biceps like pythons and abs like large pebbles in close order, one gold teeth gleaming in the unreal daylight.

He hummed that crescent wrench as hard as he could. And it dangled over and over a few times, and by some miracle, it caught the leader in the forehead.

When it did, his eyes strung wide and one knee buckled.

Then his pistol discharged.

The man next to the leader sent a freakish howl up into air between the buildings.

His foot exploded.

149

Tattered white pieces of shoe sprayed up in the air like popcorn and then landed in the street and lay in front of him. Blood spurted upward and he went down. He tried to grab at his foot and some change spilled out of his pocket.

Frank just stared at all of them for a second.

"Get the fuck out of here...NOW!!!" They moved back down the street, eyeballing him as though he carried an amulet that rendered them forceless. And they did, scattering like dove when a hunter emerges from a hidden spot after taking one down. The second in command was splayed on his back and hollered in pain. They just left him there. After several solid moments, they were gone. Frank sneered his upper lip and walked backward toward the minivan. The lady was frozen.

"Ma'am...ma'am!" She took her hand back from her mouth and reluctantly turned toward him.

"I need you to follow me, my car is right in front of you...we're going to take a right at the stop sign and then head straight to the onramp for the interstate...OK?"

"Can you drive?" He asked.

"Uh...I...yes. The man there...will he be OK?" She still bordered on being in shock.

"All you need to do is follow me; get on the highway and get home, you and your baby...can you do that?" He

150

looked at her unflinching. She nodded again, checking her little one, who was still happy as a clam in the car-seat.

"OK, just stay right on me." He got back in his car and steered around the abandoned truck and the man bleeding, alone in the street. Wanting to grab his foot with a bullet hole in it, but the pain created a distance like a canyon. He just wretched and howled. He swiped for Frank's tire as he passed as though he could puncture it with his fingernail.

When they were out of town, by about fifteen miles, the lady pulled past Frank slowly and whispered thank you through the window. He saw the baby in the backseat, its head leaned over, gazing toward him. He pulled off the interstate to fill up, thinking that it'd wouldn't have been long if they'd have kept coming.

But one thing he knew as sure as he was born was that no matter what them sumbitches were not going to get that woman, or her baby. That was for damn sure.

XI.

Frank had developed the market in and through Ohio, from the rust belt to the river. The boss had charged him with that opportunity. There were still a lot of calls to make there, despite the decline in the automotive industry, and manufacturing on the entire domestic scale. Depending on how quickly the market was developed, it would be necessary to hire someone who planned on living there for a long time and cultivating a necessary area over the long haul. It took Frank roughly a year to do so. Before that he was all over the place, from Texas to California. Even Utah.

But, for him, and for now it was onto Indiana, the heart of the heartland. The Big Three were still major employers throughout the region, and their suppliers were also there, and Frank was the low man on the totem pole, rather he was the youngest, the only one who was still single, without kids, and thus the best suited to move from unchartered territory to unchartered territory with the sole intent to grow the business from nothing to something by establishing the relationships where the company needed a presence. The company was small, just starting out when he joined up.

He was still out on the road trying to nail down an account when his old lease expired, up near Findlay. His cellphone had gone bad, due to a recent coffee spilling incident

152

in and around the console, and it was only a sudden flash of memory that lit off in his head to call the movers in Cincinnati, let them know the key was behind the light fixture next to the mailbox, and to go ahead and pack everything, which wasn't much, and he'd meet them at the new apartment outside of Indy. Only he couldn't get back in time. And when he did, the movers had left everything in the garage.

The week had gone on and on and on...one step forward and two steps back kind of deal. They kept showing improvement, and then something in production flamed out halting the progress. Frank decided that the best option was to stick around and help troubleshoot, kind of babysit the whole deal until things worked themselves out, the changeover would effectively take place and he could take off. But it was rarely if ever that easy. And instead of heading all the way back to Cincinnati, he just stayed through the previous two weekends. Finally, things did work themselves out with production, and the new product began to run across the board with high marks.

So, Frank hit the trail.

And now driving was like hiking. Up a big hill. After working that long and that far from his home, which was now not even in the same place it had been when he started the trip, his mind felt heavy. It was the personal stress as much as anything. Cringing at the notion that he was going to be waking up, in a new apartment in a new town, he felt like a cigarette. He felt like his skin was going to be pulled away from his bones in a vacuum if he didn't. He felt like the snowfall outside his car was pelting his face in rapid succession hot and cold at the same time. He had an immediate headache, a piercing one. He was starving for two cheeseburgers from McDonald's, a massively large coke, and the biggest supersize order of French fries on the planet. He felt like smoking a whole pack of cigarettes. He felt tired, and like sleeping. His stomach turned on its own axis like a gymnast tiptoeing along a balance beam with nausea on one side and fluttering shakiness on the other. He blinked, but his eyes did not gain any more focus. He felt very distant from himself. He felt like it wasn't right to have to deal with a life change right here and right now in the way he was having to. He felt alone.

He must've driven past the turn off…because the signs for cities were not the ones he saw in previous exodus from town. Where in the hell was the atlas? Shit, where in the hell was he? Somewhere near Upper Sandusky, but wasn't that south of Sandusky, up there on the bay? The towns he did past had names like Defiance, Washington Court House, Bucyrus. A red hue wallowed on the western horizon. It was slipping to the southern part of the world. Frank breathed in heavily. How could one week turn into three so quickly? The words that

154

made up the silent gliding sentences inside inched closer to cursory. Son of a...where the hell am I, he thought. It was starting to snow thicker, flying in the faces of his headlights like frenzied moths.

Flipping on the overhead light on the driver side, he dug with his right hand in between the passenger seat and the console, clutching with two fingers at the sunken atlas pages. He got a hold of it and was open to Ohio. He had done it a million times, that is getting lost and figuring out real fast how to get back on the right track, but right now that didn't mean a thing. It just as quickly slipped down to his feet and he felt the pages flap over his dress shoes between the pedals. Fucking thing. God did he want a smoke. One wouldn't hurt. How long had it been? Six months. Just one for the road, it wouldn't lead to anything.

The darkness and the swirling snow alight in every window hinted of outer space. And he started to swerve. The sensation lasted only a second or two, but long enough for him to feel helpless. Luckily, the asphalt opened itself up enough and the tread from his tires bit into it, righting the car and allowing Frank to re-establish control.

It happened quickly enough so that he didn't have time to be scared. He didn't think about being scared. He just kind of noticed the floating sensation, momentarily indifferent to its

155

effect as though it were another of the recent irritants flowering his life.

Fucking snow on a Friday night. He was probably a hundred or so miles from his new home. It was even hard to picture, the apartment he'd rented was one amid several hundred in a complex off a four-lane highway. The folder was in the glove box, the lease and the new address, and the payments and the information that he'd merely glanced over. The fact was he was in such a hurry to get out of Cincinnati, Ohio that he rented the first place he found just outside of Indianapolis that seemed clean, safe, and convenient.

He'd have to follow the two-lane highways through the four way stops until he hit I-70. Then head west. He hoped he'd remember the way once he hit town and ran across some landmarks. Ohio was proving to be a tough place from which to relocate. It was all he could to not to pull over at the gas station for a pack of cigarettes. Anything Ohio made his head pound, his temples clashing like symbols from one of those stuffed toy monkeys. Looking around and man, it was so damn bleak, fucking drab and dark and barren. Sweet Jesus, he thought, if depression was a state, it'd be fucking Ohio. It should be a relief to be getting out of there, but he was trading it for Indiana.

Maybe the miles were getting to him, could be that the hours and hours behind the wheel were wearing him out. Then again wanting a cigarette so bad he would trade an eyeball for one had to be adding a degree of tension. He wanted to gnaw his gums out. He couldn't tell if he was having a cold flash or breaking out into a cold sweat. It had been a long week in a long month, and he'd been so good about staying off the smokes. The idea of quitting, of never having one again felt like a criminal sentence. Like he would always be missing out on something, like having eggs but no bacon. Or sex with no orgasm.

Fuck it. He pulled off at the gas station immediately before his turnoff to I-70. I've been so good, he thought. This fucking place damn near sent me to the funny house to wrestle with the locks on my jacket in the rubber room. He got out of the car and the cool air felt great. It was like being paroled. Fresh air and open space. He stood up and grimaced. Reaching for the pump, he felt a wrenching sensation.

His back was screaming at him. The pain shot like a bolt of lightning from his sacrum up his spine and into his scapula. His neck seized and he felt for a moment that he might be paralyzed. The pain was so intense, his vision went blurry. Reaching for the hood of his car to balance himself, he slipped in the slush and his feet flew up in the air and his back hit the

157

ground first. Fluorescent lights blared downward from the overhang above the gas pumps, and the melted snow seeped through his jacket, shirt, and pants. He was lucky he didn't knock his head on the ground. The sudden pain went away as quickly as it'd come. Embarrassment was the next thing he felt. Within a few seconds though, he was able to harness the endorphins flushing his system enough to pull himself up. There was a couple that were obviously just in from the farm to fill up for the week, who didn't even look his way, and another guy who wore a Reds baseball hat and a camouflage vest. He stared angrily at the pump, watching the numbers roll onward and upward, smoking a cigarette, despite the warnings. No one seemed to notice, or care. Couldn't give a fuck about a guy slipping and maybe hurting himself.

There was a brief sense of shock that filled him, but it subsided as he brushed the wetness from his clothes the best he could. Cold stains soldered his knit pants in darker tones.

He walked with his back hunched over toward the store. Rows of potato chips and beef jerky greeted him. Thin cylindrical bulbs hung in pairs on the ceiling, a couple flickering, fighting for life. Inside them lots of bugs had no more fight in them. He looked back toward the coolers and turned toward the stacks of cigarettes on special.

Then he caved and bought a pack.

And it was a relief.

The woman behind the counter looked at him briefly but didn't show any pity. Frank went to the restroom and took a leak that seemed to last an hour. He washed his hands and pulled a paper towel from a scratched dispenser and wrapped it around the door handle as he opened it up. His back loosened up a bit, and his head felt somewhat clear, but the onrushing of tension he'd felt while digging for the map and dealing with the newness of relocating at the end of a long stretch on the road subsided but didn't disappear. Stress. It had been building up over time, physical, mental, emotional even.

Frank looked at his reflection in the driver's side window. His hair was stressed and receding quicker than he had hoped. His head-veins were bulging, jagged, and angry. He noticed puffy circles under his eyes, and his tie hanging loose and oft center. Pulling on the driver's side door, he slid inside, turned on the ignition and pulled out onto the two-way heading toward Indiana.

He popped the pack of cigarettes into his other palm three solid times, peeled the cellophane with his teeth, and flicked one out and felt the intoxicating singe of anticipation and remorse on his lower lip. Son of a bitch he thought. Just like riding a bike.

Inhaling the first drag showered his lungs with a stinging joy, painful, and relaxing. He dropped the window an inch and held it close to keep the smell to a minimum without losing the light.

Fucking snow on Friday night. New apartment in a new town. Don't know a single solitary soul. New territory, starting over…again. No one did say it was going to easy but fucking a man. Time was moving so much faster now as he got older, still a year shy of thirty, it was more and more evident that the older he got, the faster time went. It'd be Thanksgiving in a few weeks. And November was a short month. Both on the calendar and in terms of ship days. That is the number of days in the month where his orders could get out the door. And the company billed the customer the day the product was shipped. Then you got to Christmas, and end of the year shutdowns. Customers typically closed their doors for two weeks or so for maintenance, inventory, and vacation. Taking on inventory then was not something they liked to do, particularly because they wanted to keep the books as clean as possible at the end of the year, thus orders were down.

Ordinarily, they didn't want to see their current suppliers, not unless they were bearing gifts or taking them out to lunch. After all, it was Christmas time. Certainly not all customers were like that Frank reminded himself. It was just easy to be cynical. Even more snow descended in drifts now, luminous against the backdrop of green roadside signs and reflective stakes, the wipers swooshed away what landed on the windshield.

He continued to smoke and drive and think, trying to keep the stress from bouncing around his cranium like a racquetball.

When he reached the outskirts of Indy, he turned north on 465, toward Noblesville. He exited on 37 heading northeast and looked long and hard to the east for a large apartment complex. A Dairy Queen was just going in at the stoplight. A vet clinic, a BP station, and a car dealership were going in too. Frank remembered the Dairy Queen from the day he signed the lease because he noticed the two large empty blizzard cups on the desk of the leasing agent, and the fact that she had mentioned that her husband liked DQ because the restrooms were clean. When he thought to ask why that was of importance, she indicated that in when he needed to go number two…and they absolutely had to stop…DQ was a great option in that he could do what he had to do, and she could, have a blizzard. It was another mile or so when the sign for the apartment complex caught his eye. He turned right and weaved his way through a labyrinth of residences that numbingly resembled themselves. He popped the glove box and pulled out

161

the folder. The apartment number was on the top right corner of the first page, and he found the number which was between the range of 2005-2280, as the cream-colored sign indicated.

As he pulled into the parking space, which added seventy-five dollars to his monthly rent, he saw a stack of boxes against the door of his garage.

Cock-sucking moving company. Fucking cookie cutter apartment. Why in the hell did he pick that place? Couldn't looked around a little more. Maybe one of those lofts downtown. Oh yeah, he remembered, downtown Indianapolis. What difference did it really make in a town where he didn't even know a soul? He was moving to make money. He needed to get away from anything closely resembling a distraction. Living out in the country, literally would be a great way to focus. Read. Workout. Work. Get ahead. It was the first place off the highway that looked decent. It even had a golf course nearby.

When he'd moved all the boxes inside, he was relieved to find the water was turned on. After taking a hot shower, he wrapped himself in a blanket and coughed. He didn't want to beat himself up for having smoked on the drive. It was just such a long day.

Before he fell into a deep sleep, he felt the shooting pain in his back. It crawled right up his spine like a pissed off radioactive tick.

Fucking bastard shit fuck whore cunt slut fucker mother-fuck! The words ran through his mind. It hurt too much to yell them. Then, just like that, the pain was gone, like a demon after an exorcism.

He gazed like a Cro-Magnon det-hawing from an ice wall. The empty cream-colored walls looked back at him, and after a good while, he exhaled.

The floor was probably not going to help his back, but it didn't keep him from falling into a deep sleep.

He saw billboards advertising XXX Adult book stores. Casinos. Motels. Abortion Counseling. Anti-Abortion. Cigarettes. The dangers of cigarettes. Rest stops. Gas prices. The Ten Commandments.
One read Hell is Real. Another read Jesus died for our sins, what have you done for Him lately?

Foot-High Pies. Amish Furniture. Tom Raper Rv's. Welcome to Kentucky. You are now leaving the state of Illinois. Lookout Mountain 55 miles. Vote Democrat, nobody else does. Re-Elect Harry Harrison for sheriff. They were plotted firmly among the vast sown acreage of corn, soy, and wheat. The rays of sunlight spewed effervescence over them.

Showers of beautiful radiance swelled through each stalk and plant and vine. He found himself driving from the passenger side. Looking in the rearview about seeing the road in front of him. He stuck his head through the sunroof and could swear it was gently snowing, and still sunny. His hair flung upward and backward awash in the wind and when he lowered, and he checked it out in the mirror, and it somehow never looked better. The CD player reached docilely to his ears it was…who was it singing? Of course, he knew it was just a dream and one thing he knew that sometimes in a dream it was difficult to know exactly what you knew. That is to say that in dreams, things could sometimes feel infinitely possible, and at the same time basic motor movements were rendered frozen.

It was Albert. Word was when he hit the stage at the Fillmore west back in the late sixties, with Janis and Jimi on the bill he came out first and blew the bolts off the place. Anyone ever heard of somebody upstaging Jimi Hendrix?

It took time to get his mind around the isolation. And it took even more time to get his mind inside the reality that no one was watching, no one knew where he was at any given time or what he was doing. Inside and out, it was just him. Headed in one direction or the other. Empty fields of agriculture swallowing his vision in every direction. A lot of the time was only billboards, road, and corn.

The clouds clustered and collided with each other, dipping down toward the treetops and swirling well above the highway like a party of salsa dancers.

Every day was evening and morning and afternoon. Frank got hungry. Drunk. Full. Sober. Hungry again.

He lit and smoked the best cigarette of his life. He sucked in the air almost like a chaser. Suddenly, a large cup of coffee appeared in his cup holder. It was perfect with three shots of espresso. Not too hot. Not too bold. He hadn't had a sip, but he knew it was great. Then he saw a paper back on the dashboard. Before he opened the lid, he knew it held two pulled pork sandwiches from a local bar-b-cue place out of Nashville. Complete with the spicy mayo, pickles, and tomato-based sauce. Bar-b-cue chips. Something stung his fingers. It was the gritty-flavored additives on the chips clinging to his hands and sneaking into the tiny cracks in his skin. Then they were clean but still dry. He opened the console to find some hand cream. A gift from his mother. One bottle of the stuff could last an entire winter if he conserved. It smoothed out the dry skin like diving into a pool. He was in a Cadillac. STS. V8 NorthStar. Cut right under the wind. To accelerate all he had to do was tilt a toe. Just a hair. He imagined in this dream breaking the sound barrier without the boom. Quietly doing something extraordinary and beyond his limits without making a noise out there all by his lonesome. In his experience, the folks who really had it going on and did things they were proud of where their efforts exceeded their expectations or the expectations others placed on them, didn't advertise it. It was so beautiful to be here. Out here on the road with an atlas, card, calendar, and a purpose. Nobody really knew what he did for a living. If he told them they didn't understand, most of them. There was no point in talking sometimes. There was much more said in silence.

He flipped the turn signal on and eased over to the fast lane and passed a peloton. They edged into the background and disappeared, then a truck emerged, rumbling forward as though it had gobbled them up and used them for fuel.

He looked again and it was gone.

Frank blinked once.

Then it was next to him, and the driver was snorting something off the dash. He looked like some hillbilly without a month of showers. Then he was black. Then it was one of the Bee Gees. Then he was back to a hillbilly, or a cable guy. He held even with Frank, and though he tried to accelerate up a hill the truck stayed flush. The cord from his CB radio was strewn downward. He angrily swore into it while glaring over at Frank.

Instantly, two more trucks appeared, the cable guy swerving in front of Frank, the rest boxing him in like a convoy. The clouds drew together like a quilt, just like so many days of encapsulating and ominous grayness in the Midwest out on the road. Shrinking the lanes, they moved in unison. Frank didn't budge. He checked his mirrors. One truck in each. He checked his windows. One of each there too. They were trying to squeeze his balls in vice for some reason. His ball didn't feel like being squeezed. They felt like they needed more room.

The front truck was volatile. It was jumbling and bouncing. The bolt on the rear door jiggled and looked like it'd break any second. The placards read combustible. Black and white lettering. Could've been a bomb in there. Maybe a dirty one. The brake lights went red as beets. Smoke whistled from the pavement and the rubber squeezed. Frank didn't blink. But he eased the wheel intently to the right and the serrated edges in the shoulder sent a vibration from the tires to the suspension to the floorboards and the pedals up into the soles of his shoes up his legs and out through his fingertips. Gripping the wheel firmly, he still didn't blink. The right-side wheels passed over and the vibration stopped, but he could feel pebbles bouncing up from the shoulder into the undercarriage into the chassis like a popcorn machine. Then he dropped his toes to the floor. The

NorthStar engine cranked up and he heard the demonstrative pulse of the motor kicking in. All eight cylinders going to work like rocketing the Cadillac past the lead trucker in an instant. He saw smoke shoot from its exhaust ports like a bully getting his pants pulled down at the junior high dance. All three receded like apparitions in the rearview.

The road opened like a freeway in Houston. Eight lanes. Then it thinned to four. Then two.

Frank rolled beneath an overpass. Toll ahead. Fifty cents cars and trucks. He braked easily and passed into the cash only lane. Somehow there were two quarters in his fingers and slowing to a gentle pace he flicked the coins out the window and the red light changed to green.

Roadwork signs emerged within a mile or so, warning that speeding could result in ten thousand-dollar fines and fourteen years in jail. Frank never failed to heed those warnings.

When he was on the road, every single day he marveled at the people that worked on the road crews. Day or night. Especially at night though. He made a point to slow way below the stipulated speeds. He also made point to wave at the workers standing by with the signs, and it was also without fail that behind large gloved hands and hooded faces, the workers waved back. They made it a point too.

168

"Frank, I need you to start calling on the heavy extrusion industry. Ducting too. I need you to fly out to Ogden, out near Salt Lake, there's some guys to call on out near Reno too, and Phoenix. Get on it quick."

"I'm on it, boss."

He woke up and snow had fallen, vast sheets spread over the flat fields surrounding his apartment complex. Texas sunshine was a long way from here. The company needed him in the Midwest, building the markets where they had little to know presence. Even though he grew up in St. Louis, working based in Austin was never going to work. The boss was good about letting him try though. No automotive manufacturing to speak of, only oil drilling parts. Mud-pump motor pistons. Urethane pipes. Off-shore drilling too, high density riser buoyancy modules. Those fuckers were huge. Thirty-five feet long, ten feet wide. Hand laid up with fiberglass. They mopped on the lubricant and damn near half of it went on the floor. They were buying close to a million a year. Twenty-two percent of that would have kept food in the fridge for a good while. And probably him in Texas. If that one had come through like he had hoped he probably could've worked from there. Commuted to the Midwest once or twice a month. He got into the shower, without a curtain.

As he scrubbed, he looked out the small window the snow was everywhere. He dropped the soap and banged his head on the handle picking it up. The shower head coughed, and the pipes rumbled behind the walls. The water stopped, leaving a healthy layer on his skin.

Motherfucker.

XII.

Its wings were mangled and frayed. Stretched out like an old nun's fingers while the breeze moved through them. When he stretched out as far as he could his wingspan went a good five feet. Almost as tall as the farmer he'd feasted on as a young bird. The one who was working a row of beets and corn in his garden during the summer and suddenly dropped to his knees making sounds of pain. Grabbing the overalls in the middle of his chest like they were burning him alive, he fell on his side and everything went silent. No one else was there. Nothing for miles. Just sitting on the roof of his house, he watched the farmer leave his body behind. All of it in seconds. When he knew that he should approach the farmer, he noticed gray strands of hair wafting in the light breeze, a gold ring on one finger and blood inching out of his hip where he'd fallen on his farming tool just before he died. That was a long time ago though. And if he'd been told then that he would never have a taste of a farmer again, he wouldn't have believed it.

He was a tracking a deer that had been clipped by a car and died wheezing on the shoulder of the highway in a seeping clump, its guts swollen and yellow as they hung from its side. The flies were whizzing around as they were the first on the scene. A bluff receded as he pitched to the right and angled back again. He would do this over and over surveying the spot

171

where the prey had fallen, and the surrounding area to locate anything that might make a play for him. Often the animal was only wounded and bleeding and trying to survive with every bit of its breath and its will, so he'd just maintain a steady alternating pattern of revolving circles to keep it in sight. Eventually, the blood and breath always ran out though. One time he watched a male deer crawl for two days and nights with its hind legs crushed and blood leaking a trail through a clearing in a recently plowed cornfield and some of the others had seen the deer too and crowded the little space of sky.

There was going to be more than enough to go around.

The damned deer seemed to always take unnecessary risks. They would try to cross busy highways where the ground was not dirt and grass, so their traction was bad and then they'd get scared and freeze up and let a car or a truck plow the living shit out of them. Spraying them into shards sometimes so much so that it wasn't any good because a more intact body would make for a better meal. It also let him and the others like him do what they were put on the earth and in the sky to do. Clear out the diseases and bacteria that can spread when a dead animal is left alone.

He tilted back a gain and his long talons touched down in the gully by the deer. Its eyes had the lost stare of death in them. It did not make him feel one way or the other.

He needed things to die.

To survive. Always had, always would.

Traffic was not so busy now. He hopped up on the pavement and hobbled over to the center of the deer. The intestines were still fleshy and ripe. The stomach, kidneys, all of it was going to be ripe. He picked at it sharply and pulled a string of tendons from the shoulder to make a little space to get in behind them. Not wasting any time as he bent back his beak and chugged down as much as he could because he knew the others like him were out there, and it wouldn't take them long to come around.

He spun his head when he heard a piercing cry from behind. Silver light bristled off the secondary wings of a hawk. Before he could correct his vision, it had disappeared into the tree line. He saw the slightest movement of branches and then another brief scream. But it wasn't the voice of the hawk.

A car spat gravel at him, and he hobbled back awkwardly with a mouthful of heart lining trying not to choke on it. He plopped back into the tall weeds in order to get some distance from himself and the road.

He swallowed on the blobby bloody flesh in his mouth and tried to readjust his bearings. The hawk had gone in fast and he was surprised to hear him call. If he was diving on quarry, he didn't want the quarry to know he was on it. Maybe he was the kind that wanted to announce its presence, so there would be no questions as to his intentions?

They hunted the living. That was a different skill set.

The hawk was looking at his rabbit and at the buzzard, the deer, and the blood and the desolate farmland.

They spent several moments looking at each other, not quite enemies, most certainly not friends.

XIII.

Felicia was light on her feet. She was excited when she
woke, there wasn't the usual boring lecture in her
entrepreneurial business class on the syllabus today. There was
someone from the real-world speaking. A proven businessman.
Someone who had the literal and incomparable asset of having
done it for real, in the real world, and wasn't the run of the mill
professor who waxed philosophically, albeit harmlessly on the
dynamics of the world of business, all the while doing it from
the confines of a college campus. The class itself was fine, she
was sure to get an A. But grades weren't all she was after.
Since she was a little girl, working after school with her father
at the small grocery store that he owned, she knew that she'd
go into business for herself. Standing on the small loading dock
on the back of the building, she'd hold a clipboard and monitor
the deliveries, keeping track with a pencil and pad, backed up
with a razor-sharp memory. She would go to bed at night and
dream of running a transcontinental conglomerate, or a fashion
magazine, or manufacturing plant. Innovations and business
ideas came to her while she sat on the bus to school, when she
mucked the stalls at the barn out back, or when she sliced
onions, lettuce, rutabagas, mushrooms, or tomatoes before
dinner. She couldn't help it. And she loved the process
involved. At ten, she finished and reread Adam Smith's *Wealth*

of Nations. When she was twelve, she read with a flashlight beneath her covers the Tom Peters books, in one week.

She ate, drank, and slept it.

When other girls were trying out for the cheerleading squad, Felicia was tracking pretend stock investments. She and her Dad would research companies together and make imaginary purchases of stocks. In the morning, she'd fill the buckets with water, even pull out a dead rat or two, replenish the hay, turn out the ponies, and hand feed them carrots. Then rush down the dirt driveway to beat the paper man. He'd usually fly out the window one local after another, but at the O'Kane place, he'd slow down. She was such a darling little thing. What girl was sprinting down to the street at five in the morning to receive by hand the *Wall Street Journal*? She didn't want the paper to get wet is what she had told him, but the truth was, she couldn't wait to get the paper in her hands to see how her stocks were doing. God bless her. Cute as a button. Probably end up running for the Congress or something someday.

It wasn't as though she couldn't have been a cheerleader, she was a natural knockout. Long dark hair, hazel eyes, beautiful features. Boys often called the house, but by and large they wouldn't call back after she'd go on and on about her admiration for Warren Buffet. He father was so

176

proud of her. It was a considerable blessing in his eyes that her academic drive and insatiable appetite for reading and learning about business, went such a long way to fend off the typical popular jocks. Subtly, or maybe not so subtly, he hinted to her that the boys who were intelligent, considerate, and respectful were with whom it was worthwhile to spend time. They had something to offer. Hot shot jocks, rich boys in suits, or slick-talking punks with lines of bullshit a mile wide were a dime a dozen, and not worth a second of her time was one of his not-so-subtle hints.

She couldn't accept the scholarship she earned in high school to the University of Texas at Austin because her father had taken ill. Renal cancer. Exercised every day of his life. Didn't drink, didn't smoke.

Just got dealt a bad hand. He held on for almost four years.

After he passed, she began to isolate herself. It was a task to do the laundry or make breakfast. Menial, everyday chores she used to do with one hand tied behind her back were suddenly a heap of immovable barriers. The newspapers would pile up in the driveway, and instead of taking them inside to devour like she always had, she would blankly pick them up and drop into the trash bin if she remembered to wheel it to the curb on trash day. There was a little bit of money left in a trust her father had setup when she was born. Some of it had to be applied to his medical bills. The other to some minor debts. The rest would last for a couple months, but after that she knew that something would have to change. But she didn't want to. She didn't feel like she could do anything. Even as the moments stretched into days, weeks, and months, the cloud of depression was amassing thicker layers in her mind. It was a completely new place for her, one that was difficult to understand, much less exit. It had happened upon her without her knowledge or consent. Coercing her into a state of inertia, frozen like a creature in the Land of Narnia.

She was aware that she was not herself, that her mind didn't default to the negative spiral that had enveloped her every thought, but she felt helpless to stop it. It wasn't natural for her to start a book only to feel immediately unable to continue and drop onto the floor in resignation, yet there she was lying on the couch in her pajamas with at least seven face down in the carpet. Her skin was pallid, and wrinkles took on new life about her eyes.

When it became clear that the money situation would soon become dire, her energy level perked up some. The innate motivation within her took a stand against her cycle of motionlessness. It was relieving to her in that she knew that something had stopped the downward momentum. And it was her inherent desire to succeed. There was no way that anything could take that away from her completely. Not even the loss of her father. It was a large part of who she was, and who she felt destined to be. And it had been dealt a heavy blow. But not destroyed. She remembered taking a long hot shower, washing her face and hair with fancy products her aunt had given her after the funeral. She exfoliated, moisturized, conditioned, rinsed. It was a start. She moved onto the laundry. Then the house. She pulled the blinds, dusted them, and the light that rushed in made he inhale deeply, and gave her a bit more energy. She wasn't emotionally, or mentally out of the woods yet, but she had to start somewhere.

After a light dinner, she sat in front of her computer. She logged into her bank account and ran through her finances. It was then she knew that she'd have to emerge from her shell. If nothing else, the bills had to be paid.

She needed a job.

It started when her only friend in town, Astrid, encouraged her to meet her for a drink after several months of solitary mourning. They had gone to middle school, junior high, and then high school together. Astrid was the wild one. While Felicia spent her nights studying, doing homework, getting ahead on her required reading, Astrid would be on the phone gossiping up a storm about other girls or the new hot boy in Spanish class. She went out with the Seniors when she was a sophomore and snuck out of the house more than once to meet her latest boyfriend. She came to Felicia when she lost her virginity to the backup quarterback on their mediocre football team. A square-jawed and pimple-faced senior named Reed who drove a "super-nice" car and whose parents lived in the rich part of town. She cried all night in Felicia's room with makeup oozing from her eyes and down her cheeks, literally revealing the childish face she'd so intently masked to appear older than her fifteen years. Reed told her he wanted her to be his girlfriend for a few weeks. On a Saturday night after a football game, he took her out to Sonic for a Slushy, popped her cherry in the backseat of his leather trim Lexus, buttoned his pants, and drove her home in a flash. Before she could even put on her seatbelt, they were half a block from her parent's house, the engine idling, she overcome with a frozen feeling. He said he didn't want to drop her off at her house because it was quicker to take a left and meet up with his friends. He also said that he'd thought about what he'd said about wanting to have a girlfriend and that he was senior, and he didn't want to be tied down. She meekly sniffled an okay, and he winked at her as he spun off, leaving her holding her jean jacket on the curb, changed for good.

When they graduated high school, Astrid went on to State, joined a sorority, and discovered clubs and drugs. Felicia stayed home, nursing her dying father, and discovered pain and loss.

Astrid's parents had divorced while she was away at school. Her mother moved to Santa Fe with a sculptor she met in an AA meeting. Her father came out of the closet and moved to Buffalo with his assistant. They hadn't gone through the divorce process in its entirety and agreed that Astrid could stay in the house until it was settled, and the property divided and sold. Felicia had wondered why Astrid never seemed to have a curfew, or why her parents never seemed to show up for softball games, or school plays. In fact, she barely knew them only to have occasional dinners where conversation was minimal, and the television was left on in the dining room, the audio up to a point where Felicia had to nearly holler to Astrid to pass the pepper, or pitcher of cranberry juice. Astrid wouldn't look, only nudge the shaker or the juice silently, embarrassed and sadly silent. Felicia always felt as though the strangely loud volume of the television and the shortened and stilted dialogue were a way of ignoring their own lives, their own present, numbing themselves to it like someone having their wisdom teeth removed. It made Felicia so thankful for her father. That he wasn't biding his time until she was gone. It wasn't lost on her that this dysfunctional situation at home was probably the main reason Astrid caught the worst of high school stigmas, a slut.

After barely graduating, Astrid moved home. That summer she visited Felicia at the store, sitting in a red-topped stool behind the counter, and ringing up customers and keeping track of the register. She'd go out back and smoke a bowl when it wasn't busy, then turn on the tiny television above the cigarette rack, watching soaps and game shows, courtroom TV.

It was so nice for Felicia, to have her friend, a friend around. They didn't talk much about the future, both of them not knowing what it held or what they were going to do in it. At that time, when all their lives they were brought up to think the world would be beginning to open to reveal limitless possibilities, they both hinged themselves to an anchor of unknown fear.

It was ironic, and unfair. Those were hard feelings to shake.

In late fall, Felicia's father succumbed.

Astrid was there for the worst of it, trying to help her friend any way she could. She and Felicia would take walks to the park down the road from where they grew up, arm in arm sometimes. The weather turned. The leaves colored orange and red and then fell. They massed on the park ground, in scant

182

layers, listlessly lifting their edges when a breeze was strong enough.

Astrid would stop and light her bowl, or a cigarette, staring off at the pond.

Felicia would often cry.

Her aunt had taken over running the store. And she'd check in once a week at the most, in a daze and despondent. Her aunt would hug her, rub her shoulders, and cry with her. One day, she told her she'd gotten an offer on the property, it wasn't a king's ransom, but it would help with the bills, and she didn't need to be working in there anymore anyway.

Her father wouldn't have wanted that. She told her squarely and deliberately, that life does go on, and it's up to us not to miss it.

Felicia agreed, and the sale went through. That night she called Astrid.

"Hey, sweetie."

"Hi. How are you?" Coughing up a hit, Astrid raised up on the couch.

"Well, I'm…okay. Are you still looking for a roommate?" Felicia asked.

"Yeah, yeah…do you want to move in?"

"I think so, I mean, I need to move out of here. My aunt sold the store. The house is way too sad for me, I can barely

183

move when I'm here…" She felt a little stronger but still like crying.

"I know, sweetie, I'd love it if you moved in. We'd have a blast." Astrid was high and excited.

"Yeah? You think I can hang with you?"

"Baby girl, you have no idea." Astrid said. Felicia smiled.

"We need to celebrate, are you dressed?"

"No, not really."

"Give me twenty minutes to get ready, I'll be over to get you, we're going out, girl." Astrid hopped up off the couch and tossed the phone in the lazy boy, cantering to the shower without a goodbye.

Felicia smiled again into the phone, and with a sudden spurt of girlish, curious excitement walked to the mirror in the hallway and quickly rushed to the bathroom to wash her face.

The vodka tasted rough, despite the cranberry and orange juice, but it had a way of lessening the latent pain that had taken up residence in her psyche, and the constant sadness that had pervaded every thought.

She and Astrid laughed, talked about things she hadn't talked about in such a long time. They played a game they used to in junior high school, picking out people, and racing to see who could come up with the celebrity they most resembled.

184

They found a Gwyneth Paltrow, a Jude Law, and another guy who was short, bearded, and silly and was standing by the jukebox bobbing his head frantically to Jimi Hendrix tune. He was a Jack black. They talked about the girls in high school who were nice to their face, and bitches behind their backs. About who had the cutest eyes, Mr. Givens, from Shop class, or Mr. Traveler from history. He played football at Nebraska. And he married his high school sweetheart. It was amazing the stuff they remembered, and how it was all so distant, yet so clearly recalled. It was also funny how none of the past seemed to carry the weight it used to. How things had turned comical, if not silly.

They were having a time, just the two of them sitting at the bar.

Her friend nudged her, whispering that there was a cute guy at the end of the bar totally checking her out. Being noticed felt good too. Without realizing it, she ordered another sex on the beach. And bummed one of Astrid's cigarettes. The smoke stung her throat, and she placed it into the ashtray. The rush of nicotine swelled, and she felt her buzz zooming. She noticed the guy at the bar looking at her and her heart jumped just for a second. Then she quickly turned to her friend and they giggled. The two of them continued to enjoy themselves, but Felicia sensed that another drink might send her to a place

185

of which she didn't have a full grasp, so she decided to switch to water. Alternately sipping her cocktail, taking small tugs on the cigarette. She wondered if it made her look cool, because it kind of felt that way, but she couldn't be sure.

Could that guy be checking me out she thought?

Astrid knew the bartender. He had thick chest, wore a black t-shirt, and in the right light resembled a young movie actor.

"How are you doing, ladies?" He asked. They were giggling, picturing him in movie scenes, as well as in costume.

"We're good, Turner. My friend was just telling me she thinks you're cute." Astrid said, bracing for Felicia's response. Felicia's face went rosy, her jaw sank like a stone, and she feigned an angry look at her friend.

"Well, actually, I told her you kind of look like an actor, that...I always...admired." She thought it was a decent save. Turner grinned.

"May I ask which one?" He had a kind of feminine tone to his voice Felicia noticed.

"Um...Harry...Ford." She shrugged slowly and sipped her drink through the straw.

"Damn it...I was hoping for a JT." He answered.

Felicia looked confused.

"I didn't know he was an actor." She said. Astrid smiled at Turner.

"He isn't...but he's hot." As he said that he broke into an impromptu dance move behind the bar.

"Oh...my God." Felicia looked at Astrid.

"Yep. Very gay." She said, lighting a cigarette.

"I had no idea, except...well his voice kind of does give it away." Felicia said, going back to her water.

"Real nice though. Hey, I meant to ask you, what are you going to do for a job?"

Felicia exhaled, brought back to reality for a second.

"Well, I hadn't thought about it until recently...you know I have experience working in a small grocery store, but really that's about it. I want to go to school, you know it's like I missed out on the whole college thing. I kind of blocked it off in my mind when my dad got sick...I just...I know I eventually want to run my own business, but I really want to go to school first."

"So? You want to work or go to school?" Astrid asked.

"I guess, I have to figure how to do both. I don't want to work for four or five years to save the money, then go to school, and be in my thirties before I actually get out in the real world you know?"

"You're probably the only girl I know who could pull that off." Astrid said, without a single doubt in her mind.

"Thank you, sweetie. What kind of job do you think would pay the bills and put me through school?" As she finished her question, she looked back at Turner smiling to several customers as they closed their tab. She watched him humbly but efficiently accept a tip in the form of a fifty-dollar bill and move on to the next group waving cash in their hands thirsty for booze.

"You could be a stripper; they do that all the time." Astrid was half-joking, half-serious.

"No way, the sickos in those places...ugh. Besides, have you seen my tan lately, or my dance moves? I would probably break my leg, or the pole." They both laughed.

They kept on for a little while longer, Felicia began to yawn, but she kept an interested eye on Turner, as he methodically poured drinks, chatted up customers, told jokes, and ostensibly filled several tip jars with ones, fives, tens, and twenties. Astrid left for the bathroom and came back with glossy eyes and a peculiar smell.

"Hey, sweetie, it is getting late. Think we better ask for our check?" Felicia asked.

"Hmm? Oh, no, baby girl…let's hang out awhile." She murmured, glancing over where the cute guy was standing, now with some friends apparently.

"I don't know, I've got a lot of packing to do, remember?" She posited.

"Oh yeah, I forgot." Astrid said.

Astrid frowned for a moment, wanting to wait and see if the guy at the end of the bar would offer to buy them a drink, or come over and start talking to them, maybe he had a cute friend. But she acquiesced, and they zipped up their purses, buttoned their coats, and made for the door.

Felicia couldn't help smiling on the inside as she walked past the end of the bar, the cute guy watching her the whole way.

It was enough that he was looking.

The television was still on in the living room as she walked in, noticing the stench of bong water and cigarettes. Fast food wrappers, pizza boxes, beer cans, and ash littered the coffee table and she sighed. Her roommate was slunk under a throw blanket, one pale arm dangling outward over the edge of the couch. It was at least the fourth morning in a row. She picked up the trash quietly, turned off the television, and cleaned the glass surface with warm water and paper towels. Her roommate stirred and groaned.

189

"I'm going to put some coffee on, sweetie. You want some?"

"Hmm mmm." Her roommate muttered.

XIV.

The hall seated close to three hundred. Elevated to the rear. There were a cast of well-dressed college kids seated behind laptops. They had the look of eagerness beyond their years, a function of having possession of a keen intelligence without perhaps the necessary compliment of experience. College kids had a knack for knowing everything, Taylor thought. He remembered being one. It was only after he got out into the real world, he realized how complex, complicated and difficult everything was. It was easy to believe like as a college kid might or does that the world can be conquered.

Or changed for the betterment of all humankind.

Damn near if not every generation said it.

The world is ripe and ready for us to change it.

Then again Taylor thought, why shouldn't they? To a certain extent, it was the belief as much as anything that did in fact inspire change.

He felt good about being there in front of these students. Not overconfident, but confident, nonetheless. It wasn't the first time he spoke to a large audience. He'd given plenty of presentations, power points to potential customers, and pitches to venture capitalists. He'd sold his products by virtue of having brought people in, confidently walked them through the value-added characteristics of his service, illuminating his vision of what it could do for their company, and walking out of the room with the business.

It was a lot more nerve-wracking in those days, when his livelihood was on the line. But he did feel a little nervous for some reason. There were some cute girls out there.

Taylor introduced himself. He went briefly into his work history, and the background of the company he had built, and continued to run. When Taylor had returned the Dean's call, he was immediately put through. The Dean was a polished salesman. He lauded the success of Taylor's company. Taylor addressed the audience.

"The current state of the manufacturing sector in the United States is a telling representation of the potential issues brought on by a globalized marketplace. If we take the automotive industry as an example, we can clearly see the problems facing once well-established, profitable companies such as General Motors and Ford; DaimlerChrysler is avidly trying to find a buyer of its Chrysler unit, Goodyear has been staring at bankruptcy for one reason they never capitalized on the golden opportunity they had to grow their market share during the disastrous situation with Firestone SUV rollovers. Instead of pursuing an aggressive marketing strategy, lowering prices and seizing on the safety concerns of most SUV owners looking for replacements for their Firestone tires, they sat back and raised their prices figuring that customers would come to them because they had to, and they could make even more margin.

"Companies such as RVW Corp., a onetime behemoth tier 1 supplier in the automotive industry, got caught up in the idea that they needed to buy all kinds of smaller companies, paying too much for them, with the notion that they would become a one-stop-shop for their customers. Well, when you pay too much for companies that make have plenty of pre-existing issues...such as, pending asbestos litigation, or are simply in businesses that are inherently altogether different from the business that you, as the acquirer, have been successful in, you put yourself from the get-go at a serious disadvantage. Where are they now? Chapter 11. Probably looking at Chapter 7. Insiders say that it's doubtful they'll ever make it out. Other similar outfits have all gone into bankruptcy. These are, or shall I say were, corporations that have been staples, if not pillars of job security and manufacturers of widely desired products for the American consumer. But, one principle in a market economy that stands the test of time...adjust or die. Simple as that. What happened to them is not unlike other companies that have gone obsolete for a variety of reasons. These are the ones that are fresh in our minds and tied to the memories and psyche of the American economy, and the American worker, and the American consumer.

"I remember when it was becoming clear that the Chinese were going to begin opening the doors to capitalist-type business ventures, and the first American companies began closing their doors and moving operations over there to take advantage of the massive savings in labor costs. Everyone from managers to hourly employees broke into a collective cold sweat. And as well they should. If a company could pay a worker, for example two dollars a day versus fifteen dollars an hour, plus benefits to in theory do the same job, of course they would at the very least investigate the opportunity, if not jump right on it. The problem with the American automakers in this case was, to put it bluntly, laziness. They didn't want to adjust to the changing dynamics within the marketplace. As a growing culture of financial managers took more control of these companies, they became more focused on profit, rather than product. Increasing margins, rather than enhancing value. These financial managers, and the mentality with which they functioned, centered around a principle of driving down costs. It was symptomatic of the greater issue.

"Concentrating on growing short-term margins, rather than the fundamental principles upon which the company had originally been founded and flourished. Manufacturing

194

products that bring a qualitative value to their customer's lives. Ladies and gentlemen, entitlement, does not exist in the business world. There is no empirical law that mandates what works today, won't be challenged to work tomorrow. Or what is profitable today will be profitable tomorrow. There is however, to my mind, an empirical law that says, if you can't stay competitive, you won't survive. That sounds simple, of course. But in can agree in this business, to call reality, and within it as it sustains itself, it most certainly is not. And, if you don't believe me, with a cautionary and justifiable sense of apprehension, then, as the market as it currently, and amidst its currency, exists, will always refer you to do, and that is to go and ask the fucking shareholders.

"Now, more specifically, what led to the downfall of these companies? There are several prevailing factors, as anyone who may have read in the news in the past few years will note. First, exorbitant health-care costs. Second, exceedingly large pension commitments. Third, ill-conceived, and poorly designed products that have not proven competitive in the current marketplace. It was recently reported that for every GM owes health care and pension/retirement payments for two retired employees, for every one that is currently working. We're talking massive, albatross like overhead. Couple that with competitors such as Toyota, Nissan, Honda,

195

and KIA. Companies that are making more desirable cars with reduced depreciation, enhanced features such as hybrid technology that deals with the ever-rising prices of gasoline that do not have the overhead. That don't have a union presence in their plants. That have less debt and more cash. Companies that are putting plants in the United States, hiring US workers, and selling to US customers.

"Now to management. One of the strategies that the corporate entities such as GM, Dana, and Collins & Aikman used and relied heavily on was leverage purchasing. I call it that for lack of a better term, and it's a pretty basic description of how the purchasing departments went about squeezing their suppliers year after year to grow or maintain their margins.

"This strategy in my view, was and always will be a path to failure. Its very essence is flawed, because it inherently shifts the onus to become more profitable on someone else. Now this is not to say that a company shouldn't always be looking to lower costs, but it is the way(s) in which they go about it, and the ways in which they work with their suppliers that are critical. Simply demanding that every year the supplier must lower their cost by say 4 to 6 percent, a common practice in the automotive business, from the Big Three on down to the tier 4 suppliers. They would issue "award letters" to suppliers at the beginning of every year, congratulating them on becoming, or remaining valued suppliers to them. Then require that they reduce their costs, provide a letter indicating how within a matter of weeks, or risk losing the business altogether. This is just an example, but typical of these corporate purchasing strategies. They would also press their smaller suppliers to accept sixty-, or ninety-day payment terms. The idea was, that they could leverage themselves to a point with their suppliers that they could not risk losing the business because they were who they were. Ford, Chrysler, GM, etc. The problem was, and is, if you allow your company to be beholden to a customer, and bend over for lack of a better term for whatever demand they put on you, sooner or later, you're not a supplier, you're a hostage. And your destiny is tied to them, which is exactly the place you never want to find yourself in in a global, completive market.

"When you look at the number of small businesses in the United States, and how many people they employ, the type of philosophy they have to have in order to survive, you really can get a better understanding of the overall equation. By that I mean, if you look at the smaller, quicker, lean, precision-oriented companies out there prospering versus the gigantic sloth-like corporations that are failing, you can really see the type of mentality it takes to survive in today's global marketplace."

Felicia was seated in the third row. She wore a new skirt, a red alpaca sweater, and her narrow-rimmed glasses. She listened intently, took copious notes in her computer. She had read *The Reckoning* by David Halberstam again recently. In one of the preeminent books on the automotive industry in the twentieth century. It had chronicled the US automotive industry and the rise of the Japanese. Toyota and Chrysler. There were symptomatic points in the each that paralleled today's issues, as the guest speaker had highlighted. It was an interesting talk. The man knew his stuff. His background was also interesting, as it was in computer technology. A far cry from manufacturing. The seamless nature by which he related his thoughts on the current situation in the US manufacturing sector was poignant because he was able to understand, dissect, and apply the common threads that existed in his business. That kind of ability was something she identified with. Going back to her childhood when she would pour over the *Wall Street Journal* reading articles on the steel industry, or the oil and gas industry, and in turn integrating simple axioms such as supply and demand to her father's store. What items grew legs and jumped off the shelves versus the ones that collected dust and so forth. As he went on, she lifted her head up from her notebook for second or two more than she normally would have. There was something familiar about him.

She couldn't put her finger on it for bit. Not trying to look for too long, she returned to pecking away at her keyboard.

Taylor was in his element, business jargon rolling off the tongue like dealing cards out of a blackjack shoe. Trying not to speak with his hands too much, he nodded his head for emphasis. The recall of countless business plans and presentations came to him like breath, and his confident rose with each eloquent sentence. He forgot about the bevy of attractive coeds with their eyes in his direction for most of the talk. Then he noticed a brunette with fierce attentiveness and stunning legs in the third row. He couldn't help it his eyes though. She was more interested in what he was saying, at least it appeared that way. She whipped away at her laptop like a pro, glancing up for a second but continually returning to her notes.

Then he looked once more.

Her eyes were curious, and serious. They were angelic, and intelligent. She slid her glasses off her face and tilted her head for a moment, her mouth turning up on one side in a knowing smile.

His heart stopped, and he heard himself stumble. Uh. Uh. Uh. If there were crickets in the lecture hall, they could've been a symphony.

XV.

She caught herself looking at him, realizing that while he looked back at her, he was losing his way up there. He was very cute. Not just because he was in fact an attractive man. But he was looking at her, right at her in that great big room that had been transfixed on his every word and she knew something the rest of them didn't. It was just between the two of them. And, in spite of the circumstances, seeing a man caught like a kid stealing a brownie from the kitchen counter was so endearing she could barely stand it.

"I'm sorry you all, I just uh...totally lost my train of thought for a second, what was I saying?" Taylor asked.

"You were touching on what, as applied to small business, it takes survive in today's global marketplace." Felicia chimed. She felt so natural sounding off like that. And it also made her heart leap a bit. Maybe more than a bit.

"Yes, thank you...Ms.?"

"O'Kane. Felicia O'Kane."

Taylor concluded his seminar, thanked everyone for having him, wished them luck, and deliberately glanced at Felicia when he added that he'd be happy to stick around and answer any questions.

XVI.

Frank was in the press line office, early on a Thursday. Ireland, Indiana. His customer, Ireland Transmissions and Plastic Products had been there since the early fifties. He taken over the account from the boss, who had earned the business after calling on them for eight years.

It was crowded with first shift lead men, a couple maintenance engineers, the mill room supervisor, and their foreman, the great Lucas McIlroy. He'd been their twenty years. A decorated Ireland policeman of twenty years, and the US Army prior to that. Old school. Say what he meant and did what he said. A man of respect. And nobody, whether a paycheck-to-paycheck operator, a hustling salesman, or somebody in upper management wondered who was in charge when he was on the plant floor. A man with whom it took quite some time to earn his respect, but once you did, he was on your side until the end. Frank had been working with him for almost ten years. And would drop everything if Lucas called and needed something, anything. He rarely did. But it was a no matter what relationship as far as Frank was concerned. It was the rare situation that transcended business. Frank respected him and busted his ass for him, and the company. They'd stuck with him for years, and that kind of loyalty was few and far between.

He told Frank a story one time about when he was
growing up on the farm. His daddy had fallen off the tractor
while out in the field and broke his leg, yelling for him from
the tall corn. When he found him, he was grunting and
moaning and cussing, and bleeding like a sieve. He told him to
go on and get the truck from the barn, and the cloth stretcher in
the back. He had only driven one time and that was on the
fourth of July when his daddy had gotten into some shine and
let him take the pickup out in a small spot in the field that he
hadn't tilled. When he got back, his daddy was in a pool of
blood, his leg twisted all up underneath him and biting into a
clump of wood wrapped in his bandana. His heart was beating
like it'd been struck by lightning he said, and until this day he
didn't know how he got his daddy into the bed because he
weighed two-hundred pounds at night and at the time he only
weighed one hundred pounds soaking wet. Must have been the
adrenaline. His daddy yelled at him to take him to Doc
Dustenhoffers place on the near side of town. He ran every
light, even though there was only two back then, but cut off
anyone and ever grandma and whoever else was in the way.
When he got there, he heard his daddy ramblin' something
awful, using swear words he never heard nobody say. He
rushed inside passed the nurses and old people in the waiting

room screaming lord God bloody murder for Doc
Dustenhoffer, to come outside because his daddy was hurt bad.

The Doc still had his stethoscope is his ears and his
white jacket on when his face when whiter. Blood was dripping
through the holes in the bed, through the undercarriage and
onto the street. He said "Lucas, boy, I want you to help me
with this stretcher here; we gonna take your daddy inside."
They had to operate right away cause of all the blood loss, and
Doc Dustenhoffer had me hold daddy down while he operated,
blood squirting up on the ceiling, on his headlight, on him, me.
Daddy was going on about the war and how he come all the
way back from France only to fall off a fucking tractor. He
said, "I marched through the Ardenne forest in the unending
snow with trees shattering like bottles, taking shrapnel for
breakfast lunch and dinner, and a fucking tractor, you believe
that shit, Doc?"

"AAAAAAAAAAAAAAAAAAAAAAAAAHHHHHHH
HHHHHHH!!! Motherfucker!!!!!!! Motherfuck…those
fucking French cocksuckers I ever tell you; I hate em more
than the Krauts cause they're trading sides all the time…at
least AAAAAAAAAAAAAAAAHHHHHHHHHHHH!!!! At
least you knew dem sumbitches was trying to kill you."

That's when the Doc put him completely under. Think
it was morphine. He shot him up with a needle six inches long.

The Doc looked at Lucas and told him to listen and listen real good. He said, "Lucas, I want you to…" I kept looking at my Dad, with a bloody stump of tangled flesh and bone abandoned like a kid with a kid at a Nebraska emergency room for a leg, and his eyes glazed over like he was watching angels on the ceiling, drooling all over himself…and the Doc pulled me away. "Lucas" he said, "I want you to go on across Main to the weld shop. You tell Earl…you know Earl, don't you, boy?" "Yes sir," Lucas said "he and my daddy are friends." "Good boy, you tell Earl I need a six-foot tall man leg, and you tell him I need it now or your daddy won't ever…you just tell I need it for your daddy quick fast and in a hurry. Go boy, run." Lucas ran over there and he thought that he was too scared to cry, cause if you're a little kid it's hard to cry and run full out, you gotta stop somewhere and hide behind a tree or something. But Earl saw me comin' and he pulled off his mask and the sparks from his torch died off and he came over to me asking what the matter was.

Lucas told him what Doc had told, and Earl run clear across his shop and lit up that torch, cut a rod the length of a walking cane 'bout a quarter inch wide, and rushed right past Lucas out the bay door to the street and onto the hospital. Lucas just ran after him.

When he got back, the Doc said, "Lucas, I did call your mama and she's on the way over from the school. I want you to wait out here in this room for her. Nurse Lydia will tend to you. Your daddy gonna be alright." He just as quick went back in that room.

What Lucas found out was they used that rod to hold all the pieces of bone together and sowed it up in him, keeping his leg from having to be cut off. He was laid up for a good while, drank a lot of shine. And anytime it rained, he swore like hell about how he hated the French.

"Jesus." Frank said at the time.

"He he. Yep, they did things a little different back in those days." Lucas said, never taking his eyes off of Frank's, and smiled.

"Daddy never did speak no German after he come back from the war."

"Not even in Ireland?" Lucas looked at him from above his glasses.

"Don't get cute with me, son."

"No, sir." Frank said.

This particular day, everyone was in the office when Frank showed. And when he opened the door, he felt a cool breeze as it was the only air-conditioned spot in the plant. The room kind of lit up too.

"Hey there, old boy!" "Where the hell you been, stranger?" "Well, look at this good-looking son of a buck, shit I better make sure my old lady doesn't know you're here." "It's good to see you again, Frank, you doing alright?" It was as warm as a weekend with old friends when he walked in, shaking hands, and grinning ear to ear. Toward the rear of the office, Lucas was squinting at his computer screen, hunting and pecking, trying to block out all the chatter so he could get his work done.

"What do you say, dude?" He smiled when he stood and shook Frank's hand. If you weren't ready for it, he'd crack damn near all your knuckles too, Frank thought.

"Good to see you, Lucas, how you been?"

"Ah hell, Frank, the house, car, boat, wife, girlfriend...they're all ninety days late." Still smiling. His posture that of a load bearing wall. There was limited space in the office, but the others respectfully made a hole so they could come together for a second.

"Hey, Frank, I tell you that that guy from your competition was in here other day?"

"No, Lonnie, you didn't. You all go out on a date." Bursts of laughter spilled out from the other guys. It was not a crowd in which you'd want to be squeamish, or without a sense of humor. Lonnie playfully sneered at them.

207

"Shit, he come in here with shirts, nice ones too…had collars on them, company logos. He gave us some golf balls too. You bring us hats, pens, anything?"

"Yeah, in fact, I did." Frank replied.

"Well, where are they?" Lonnie asked, pushing the issue a little.

"At the bottom of every drum, keep looking they're down there." More laughter. Frank got a high five from the lead man. Lonnie threw his head back and went back out onto the floor. As he walked out Lori-Ann brushed past him, with a serious look on her face. She had been there probably twenty years, and her daughter eleven. Her hair was tied back in a bun, white socks neatly pulled up low on her shins, and wearing a red St. Louis Cardinals t-shirt. She was the Quality/Inspection Supervisor, and in her arms, she carried a cardboard box full of rubber gaskets. They were marked with yellow dashes indicating defects.

"Howdy do there, Frank? You married yet?" She asked, resting the box on the desk and folding her arms.

"No, ma'am, I'm still a free man."

"Well, don't you go waiting forever." She smiled a kind of motherly smile, and patted Frank on the arm. Everyone was standing around, waiting for the inevitable lashing about the bad parts.

"Lucas, we need to figure what in the hell is going on with the 4049s, and the 2348s. Look at these. Look." Lucas was seated at his desk, and he reluctantly put on his glasses, squinting like a jeweler at a cache of suspect diamonds. Lori-Ann stood over him, one hand on her hip, glancing at the other guys with a look that said, 'any of you all got something' to say.'

And not one of them did. They just looked around like they were invisible.

"I'm goin' to check on the 3994s. They said they're havin' trouble with them too." She turned and left, and they watched her pass through the big panel glass window above Lucas' desk and looked out onto the floor. A few seconds went by and the guys, except Lucas, leaned forward silently, peering around the corner watching to see if she was gone. Just then Lori-Ann stuck her head quickly back around the end of the window, and everyone slid back to their earlier stances. It was a funny scene. Lucas was still looking at the parts, turning them over and holding them into the light, scanning every millimeter for the culprits Lori-Ann was harping on.

"She gone?" He said without looking up.

"Yep." They said, almost in unison.

"Frank, you know her Indian name is three horses, don't you?" Lucas asked.

"Excuse me, her what?" Frank hadn't heard that one before.

"You know how Indians give their kids names? You know how they have babies inside the teepee, well after they're born, they come out the teepee and the first thing they see they name their kids after it."

"Okay." Frank went along.

"Nag, Nag, Nag." The joke went over like all the times it had before. Frank ate it up with a spoon. They broke the mold with Lucas. No two ways about that.

"Alright you all, go on and git. I need to talk to Frank here." With that they all filed out. Toolbelts clanging and readjusting their ball caps.

"How's your boss, Frank?" Lucas asked after shaking Frank's hand again.

"He's doing good, busy as ever, still cracking the whip."

"How's his grandkids?" He asked.

"Doing fine I believe, he's down there in North Carolina 'bout every chance he gets." Frank replied.

"Good. Boy, they'll wear you out. You should see my youngest granddaughter…whew, she's a dandy…ornery for a four-year-old, but cute as she can be."

"I imagine."

"I was just puttin' in a requisition for another month's supply, Frank, you all handle that?" He said. Damn, Frank thought, he never got tired of hearing that sweet music. It was like a load of his back and a needed breath of fresh air all at the same time.

"Absolutely, in fact it should be made and already on the floor, ready to ship by 3:00 p.m. today." He responded immediately.

"That's good. You know those boys like Lonnie were just messing with you bout the freebies…but their rep has been wearing out my phone, and Susan up in purchasing. He keeps hitting her up with a bunch of crap about better pricing and all that. She keeps harassing me about trying his stuff, always on the lookout to cut costs. I told her that there's a lot more to it than price, but they don't know that up there in the office. Sooner or later, I'll have to try it." He didn't have to say it was fair warning.

"I understand, Lucas. Competition is a good thing. All we ever asked for is a shot. If we can't earn the business, outperform, and out-service our competition, then we don't deserve it, or deserve to keep it." Frank said. And he meant every word.

"Aw shit, Frank, you ain't gotta sell me on nothing. You all the best vendor I've got, that I've ever had. They gonna

211

have to bring in some miracle shit or can my old Irish ass
before they get you all out of here." Lucas said. It made Frank
feel proud. He almost wished someone else could hear the
compliment. This unexpected validation, somehow it didn't
feel fully recognizable without a witness.

"Thank you, Lucas. How is that new job running?"

"Well, let's walk out there and take a look." They
walked out into the plant, and Frank felt like he had Secret
Service protection next to Lucas.

He nodded to several operators, ones with whom he'd
worked in the past. He stopped for a moment to shake hands
with Virgil, a wiry man in his early sixties. He had a lawn
mower fixing business on the side and Frank asked after that.
Kept him busy, he said, and asked Frank where all he'd been
lately. He listed a few towns in surrounding counties. Virgil
had a silver star from his service in the Vietnam War, and was
sober for twenty-five years. Frank promised to bring him a
company hat on his next trip and then shook his hand again
caught back up with Lucas.

XVII.

There was a coyote waiting in Del Rio. Behind a construction site. They were putting in a new Hampton Inn and had just finished digging the culverts, serving as suitable spots to hide from the Border Patrol. He was a Mexican, probably fifty from the look of him. Rafael was still tingling with endorphins after making it across. They had not been rounded up. They didn't drown. And they were across. Highway 90 gleaned to the north. Traffic was light this late at night. Their clothes had begun to dry out, for a while as they ran through the thick mesquite fields, hearts blasting and heels hoofing they had seemed to add fifty pounds to their body weight. On top of that, the anxiety and thoughts of the unknown seemed like anchors from which to break free. And now they were. They felt a momentary sense of lightness, a euphoric sensation, as though they'd shed the shackles of their limited futures for a frontier of promise. They'd made the most dangerous part of the journey. And to be free and starting anew was the lightest and brightest feeling they'd ever felt. A roar of an air force jet seared the evening sky above them, then another and another, continually conducting training missions out of Laughlin Air Force Base only a few miles away. Transfixed and still, they sat in a concrete culvert, resting their feet on the side opposite and

213

above a trickling stream and stared at the darting red and white lights from the wings and tails as they hurtled in perpendicular patterns.

"Rafael." Jose asked

"Si?"

"Tu sabes sj el coyote estare aqua?" Julio asked. He was the youngest of Rafael's two cousins, and the most afraid.

"Si, no hay problema. Necesitamos esperar."

"Cuanto tiempo?" Jose asked.

"No se, no precocupado amigo, estamos in Los Estados Amigos ahora." The three of them smiled at each other, incredulous. Rafael twirled the image in his head that had been the motivation all along. On each letter that carried US currency, and stories of life in a land of promise, he stared and memorized the city of origin on the top left corner of the envelop. Ligonier, Indiana. Ligonier. He sometimes would mutter it to himself back in the village or in the field toiling in the heat for money that was worth little to nothing. He said it to himself unconsciously, as though it was a way to convince himself to decide to follow his friend (cousin?) to America and find a job, learn different skills, and make the money he knew he'd never have a chance to make in Michoacan. Ligonier. Lee-Go-Near. There is a job in Lee-Go-Near. There is hope.

One day he said enough and decided. It was straight up the belly of America, almost to the Great Lakes. He had heard that there were jobs in carpet factories in Georgia, and strawberry picking jobs in California. Maybe somewhere he could work in a kitchen. These were other ideas he milled over, but in the end, he stuck with what he knew for sure was real. After all he had seen the letters, and the money that came inside them. Someday, he could send that same kind of letter.

A flashlight flashed twice and the two turned, started and frozen like baby dear. A man in a straw cowboy hat, a checkered red shirt beneath an unbuttoned and torn-up jean jacket, boasting a protruded gut, and lit cigarette in one hand.

"Quien es Rafael?" He asked.

"Como?"

"Quien es Rafael?" Only this time he sounded gruff, closer to hostile. Rafael held his breath and looked up at the man. He had loosely been given instructions not to respond when asked his real name, because he could work for the Border Patrol. It was rumored that they were either using or paying to use coyotes to turn over illegals they were either scheduled to meet, or ones they just happened upon. The tactics had changed as the Immigration Bill had come to the forefront in both the public debate, and in Congress. Enforcing the borders was a driving issue, and the Border Patrol was under pressure to ramp up its numbers. Then again, if Rafael did this, he ran the risk of losing his connection to transportation. And then what would they do? He studied the man as best he could in the seconds they looked up from the culvert.

"Si, me llamo Rafael."

"Bien. Mi nombre es Eduardo. Esperando para treinte minutes. Vengan aqua." The three of them climbed out of the culvert, with their whole lives in their hands, about to entrust them to a man who profited by the trafficking of human beings.

A week earlier the coyote, Eduardo, ambled into a Flying J off I-10 just west of San Antonio. Jacked up trucks and SUV's pumped three-dollar gas in the summer heat. It was over one hundred degrees, at 6:45 in the morning. He chewed on a toothpick and the leather laden skin on his face looked like an etching on a cave wall, his wrinkles deep and aged as though streams of water had formed them over a thousand years. He had spent most of his life on or around the border. He had first tried to cross when he was seven. He lost his two brothers, a sister, his mother, and his father to the river during a flash flood in the middle of the night. They were washed away like reeds, the sound of the currents we're so loud he didn't hear any of them scream. Even if they did. Wandering the northern bank for three days with no food and no water he blankly hoped he'd find one, some, or all of them. One was all indeed. His sister. Her lifeless body half immersed in hot mud one leg being nudged by small lapping lisps on the river's edge. It was while he was trying to dig her out, still in a suspended state of reality that a burly arm grabbed him by the back of his neck and yanked him several feet in the air.

The border patrolman was the biggest man he'd ever seen. Blocking the sun with his wide shoulders, green uniform and gleaming badge. A massive pareda of a man. His sunglasses were menacing, his face red with disdain and his jowls grinding away at a bulge of tobacco. In their frames he caught of glimpse of his own reflection, and he felt separate from himself. In those glasses he saw a tattered and frightened boy, tiny as a mole. He looked back at his sister, dead as she could be and felt a jolt to his jaw. He was back to himself in that moment and that was because a tide of hate rushed through his body like the river had done to his family and his world only the night before. The border patrolman shoved him down in the mud again and again and his only instinct was to fight until he could run. But he couldn't manage successfully on either account. The border man lifted his boot with demonic authority to his stomach, or his head anytime he reached all fours. He heard him say something about how his kind were a sorry breed. He heard him accuse him of trying to rob a dead little girl.

217

Eduardo thought for sure he was going to die.

He heard some rocks scuttle underneath the border man's boots. His head was full of blood. Traumatized beyond authority.

For some reason, the beating stopped. Later in his life he wondered often if it was a dream he was living in that day and night because he couldn't be sure. He couldn't be sure if he survived because out of the swollen concussed left eye, he could swear that maybe he saw a glimmer of a white-stomached red tailed yellow eyed bird swooping in like a heat-sinking missile and gripping with its talons the border man by the outside of his neck and hailing a wild-pitched scream the border man stumbled back and waved his arms at the sky like he was shot up the ass with slow moving cyanide.

The heat swarmed his eyes and ears and the last thing he saw before he woke up in the deportation truck was of his sister, still half in the mud.

It took him nearly twenty attempts before he made it across. By that time, he was twelve. And he could work in nearly any capacity that paid any kind of wage at the time. And he did. From Brownsville to El Paso, ranging up and down the border towns following the dollar.

pavement. It could easily overtake 100 degrees before breakfast.

As they drove back to the Flying J, Eduardo handed Slim the envelop. He opened it and flipped through a stack of bills. He also looked at the paper which detailed the time and place to pick up the mojados.

When he got out of the car, he grunted, slammed the door, and waddled back toward the building.

Later Eduardo drove back toward Del Rio out highway 90. He smoked cigarette after cigarette, gazing out the window at the vast stretches of mesquite. Barren and burnt. All the way to the border.

Eduardo remembered hunting rattlesnakes near dawn in Uvalde county when he was fifteen. One of his friends had howled from behind a myriad of bushes. When he found him, his skin was turning blue and he held his forearm like a vice grip with his other arm. They both knew he was dead, but his friend didn't want to believe it, didn't want it to be true. He just howled and shook his head, squeezing his arm, holding it up near his head as though he could choke off the venom from hijacking his bloodstream and hurtling toward his heart. The twin bite marks were dark and unmistakable. Eduardo stared at his friend, silently. He had learned, subconsciously perhaps, to engage in a mechanical detachment from crisis, or pain. He beat the bushes nearby with the sharpened stick he carried, a sack in his other hand. The rattlesnake lunged out from the dirt in an attempt to take its second victim, but Eduardo was quicker. He bagged it and beat it furiously for several seconds, and then broke its neck. He turned to his friend, who was convulsing near a rock pile, foam bubbling at the edges of his mouth. Eduardo stepped nearer to him and watched the life flutter out of him in slower, fighting gasps, his eyes rolling behind his lids like deep sea divers falling backward from their boat ledge.

He emptied the sack with the dead rattler, curled, and crooked at the feet of his friend.

XVIII.

Frank rode the rails in his new territory of Indiana with a vengeance. The weeks slipped into months, and the seasons were distinct. Hot in the summer, crisp and cool in the fall, barren and frozen in the winter, and fresh and bright in the spring. The land was captive with agriculture. Wheat, soy, corn, a lot of corn. The ploughing, sowing, growing, and reaping took place on either side of every road he traveled, for miles. He racked up ninety thousand miles on this Cadillac in the first year. It was a painstaking process to start from scratch, particularly in a business where the length, and strength of a relationship generally corresponded to conversion and retention. Here, like before in Ohio and Mississippi before that and Texas before that, he was a stranger to those he had to ingratiate himself, an unknown factor up against some competitors who'd been working the state for ten, twenty, hell maybe even thirty years.

Undaunted, and happy to be out of Cincinnati, he knew only to redouble his efforts. He made every call he could, even late on Fridays, when he'd already logged 1,500 plus miles for the week and longed for an ice-cold Budweiser at the local bar and maybe a game of nine-ball, he'd go an extra thirty miles out of his way on a hunch to stop in on a guy he'd been calling on but had not nailed down for a meeting. He knew the faster he got business, and the more of it he got, the sooner he'd be able to make the next move, wherever that was. But after two years in the Midwest, having grown up only six hours west in St. Louis, he knew if he wasn't careful, he'd find himself accelerating toward a long slow death on the stretches of asphalt dissecting the endlessly silent cornfields.

The green John Deere tractors rolled over the land with their unvarying yellow wheel wells. The solitude of a farmer, Frank thought. Not unlike that of a salesman. Just out there, on your own. No one to keep you company except the sights out the windows, the sounds from the radio, or the voices in your head. And those could drive you just about fucking insane.

The time was the thing. You could stare through a windshield for only so long before things started stirring in your head. Any number of things. Voices. Conversations. Memories. It wasn't all that long before you might go over every single thing you wished you could do over, again and again. You'd even plot out exactly how you'd make the exact opposite decision that turned out to be the wrong one. Life was so simple in the rearview. It was figuring the world in front of you that was the tough part.

Frank thought about growing up. Going to Cardinal games. Cheering through the night as a little kid when Bruce Sutter struck our Gorman Thomas swinging to clinch the World Series. Sometimes he'd imitate the great Mike Shannon the long-time voice of the Cardinals sounding off out loud while covering a long stretch. "Here's a swing and a long fly ball in the gap and watch Willie run folks as he's around second, headed for third he's coming around third and there's gonna be a play at the plate and here's the throw and he is…SAFE!!! And the cardinals take the lead 3-2 with a ringing two run double by Ozzie…Whoo-Hoo!!! Alright!!! I'll tell you what Jack…I could sure go for a nice cold frosty Budweiser right about now…he he he."

The Cardinals had the lion share of fans throughout the Midwest. That was always nice about working that territory, because in every small town, there was a devoted group Cardinal faithful, and it was a nice thing to always have with which to identify with among potential customers. It was a unique love affair that they had with the organization. For one reason, back when they original franchises expanded west, the Cardinals were the furthest. And they had a very powerful radio signal from KMOX out of St. Louis. The 50000-Megawatt signal broadcast into the night to homes in every small town from Iowa to Louisiana. Kentucky to Nebraska. On top of that, the minor league teams that fed the Cardinals were located throughout these areas, and the kids that started out there and eventually made it to the Big Leagues were heroes in their hometowns and counties, reinforcing the local love for the Cardinals. With St. Louis being the nearest "big city" to a lot these small towns, families would make summer pilgrimages to a ballgame.

The Cardinals were a storied franchise. Second only to the New York Yankees in Pennants and World Championships. They consistently drew close to, if not the maximum number of fans to home games every year. It was reported that in 1990, when they finished dead last in their division, they managed to bring in 2,900,000 adoring supporters through the turnstiles.

Frank thought about his family. He thought about his friends. He liked to reach out often. That was one of the beauties of the isolation. That and the invention of the cellphone. There was no shortage of opportunity to catch up with people. What else can you do in a car for that long anyway?

Fortunately, he could usually catch one of his friends at any given point in time.

XIX.

Felicia stuck around after several students milled about Taylor, asking a myriad of questions relating to the current job market, what types of skills are most marketable coming out of school to potential employers, what sorts of salaries they should expect to be paid. Taylor answered each one earnestly, if not expeditiously. He had fought the urge to look directly in her direction after humbly nodding during a brief ovation after the seminar, and again as several precocious students hit him up for additional insights. But he kept her figure in the corner of his eye, enough to make his heart skip one or two beats. She remained seated with her shapely legs crossed over one another beneath the writing desk. After the students filed toward the door, he went back to the podium to reassemble his notes and allocated them to the appropriate folders, not wanting to make the first move. As she stood, he caught her legs again out of the corner of his eye, toned and longer than the last day of school, he could feel her approaching the podium, more and more nervous with each step. At the last moment, his self-doubt overrode his excited buzzing in a cruel jolt. Did she remember him from the strip joint? Where he'd drank himself into a blinding mess, covered himself in pole dancers, and gotten ripped off by the scumbags that ran the place.

"Hello, Mr. McCullough?"

"Please, call me Taylor. What's your name?"

"Felicia, I enjoyed your talk today."

"Thank you, it's very exciting to come here, I enjoy doing it."

"Have you been doing it long?"

"Not so much, it wasn't until our company got on the radar of the business school, that they approached me to do it." He explained.

Felicia brushed a dangling lock of hair behind one ear, holding her folders and binders against her side with her other hand, reminding Taylor of the rare, intelligent and beautiful girls he'd watched, but never known back in college that exuded a sexiness that was back then exceedingly intimidating. But what about now? He was perhaps less intimidated by her, but that didn't mean he wasn't instantly nervous, here, talking one on one.

Felicia had waited on purpose. There was something about him that intrigued her, something at connected with her. It might have been a sense of vulnerability. He was definitely not a fast-talking womanizer type, but probably thoughtful, intense behind a slightly nervous veneer. Someone very capable in his professional realm but lacking somehow in confidence. Not because he was incapable, but maybe because

230

he just didn't know how…how to be confident. There was something about him that reminded her of her father. He had never looked at or after another woman after her mother passed. He was too committed to her. She searched for something to say.

"Have you…I mean, you didn't go into your company's particular business model…I was wondering, if you might talk a little bit about that…it's just that I've followed the IT industry with great interest for some time, and it's always so much more educational, and exciting to learn about it first-hand, you know from somebody who is actually in the industry, and has had success, rather than the newspapers, industry journals, the internet or whatnot."

Taylor was flooded with a brimming surge of confidence. He didn't know why but knew if felt amazing. And it was amazing, he thought briefly, that this young girl could send his heart soaring with just the smallest of courtesies, and a question of genuine interest.

"Well, I…I'd love to. I mean…gosh, what would be a good…" He semi-stuttered. Trying to figure out what to do and say. His instincts were moving in the right direction, but they didn't have the traction, or the muscle memory to make it happen with efficiency, like a baby trying to stand but wobbling and tipping over back down on its bottom. Could it really be this hard to ask a girl out?

Apparently so.

"I know a place. It's only a couple of blocks from here." Felicia said. It was endearing to a certain degree to watch a man nervous around a woman, but only to a degree. Taylor remembered the place from several interviews he conducted with potential employees back when he his startup was in its infancy. He hadn't been there in years, but it was a good place, with good coffee, and the pseudo sheik music that one could sort of hijack a sense of coolness while it paced the background of conversation. Stereo Lab. They always seemed to play Stereo Lab, he remembered. It was one of his favorite bands. Good Karma he thought.

Good Karma.

"Great, you want a ride? I have a car outside" He asked.

"Um...no, I don't have car, but it's really not far, we can walk." She answered.

"Okay, after you." He said, hoping he could scrape the rust off quick.

He tried not to stare at the way her bottom swayed as she leaned into the auditorium door and it opened to a vastly more exciting world.

XX.

When Colin woke up, he felt a tight, blocking sensation in his throat. He rubbed his forehead, with one hand, and felt a similar clogged feeling in his nose as he tried to breathe. The two girls from the club were on either side of him, cooed in their covers breathing quietly. His first instinct was to verify they were still asleep, then slink out of the end of the bed, locate his clothes, and put them on quickly and shimmy out the door leaving any promise of a future dinner, movie, or picnic back in the bedroom. But he noticed something out of the corner of one blurry eye, something that sparked an instinct which far exceeded the need to escape the scent of a one-night stand…not only the pile of cash on the nightstand, but at least four fat bags of Peruvian cha cha cha.

It came back to him fast, the night before and running into Ollie, doing a couple bumps in the can, grinding it up with the two Latina ladies in the bed next to him, then onto another club, some more drinks and cha cha cha, and eventually finding himself back at what was presumably Ollie's apartment. Then being led into the bedroom by Sorocco, and her inserting a CD into the player, running her hands down her sides when the beats radiated out of the speakers, then pulled her dress over head in a flash revealing low-cut red panties and a matching bra. The next thing he knew he had her face first in a pillow spanking her because she was undoubtedly a bad girl. He continued to survey the scene and realized with a rising sense of pride that he'd had his first threesome, and pretty much threw down like a kingpin the night before, and it was too fucking awesome of a moment to spoil by the inconsolable paranoia that came with those kinds of thoughts. He could rationalize just about anything. That's what made him good, he thought to himself. And he studied the room as though it was a painting he'd been working on for weeks, content and riveted by his accomplishment.

The room was awash in white silk sheets, tangled around the dark hair of Maria and Sorocco, the High-Def system was blinking repeatedly as a CD was had been muted some time during the night, sunlight raining in like a supernova through a large, ceiling high panel of glass onto the hardwood floors. He did manage to slide out of the bed, but did not go for his clothes, just noticed himself in an array of mirrors, stacked like blocks on opposite walls.

He stopped and looked at himself in the mirror with the sly and cocky smile that he believed he deserved.

\

XIX.

"Well, listen, we need to talk soon."

"Alright, well, I'm getting ready to go into a meeting."

"Frank, this is not something that can wait."

"Well it's going to have to... I'll call you after the meeting." Frank said. Closing the cellphone and sliding it into his pocket. It was a long walk to the plant office. Most of the time, the visitor parking was right out front, but this one was a good 200 yards away. There weren't as many cars in the lot as there were spaces. That wasn't a good sign. The economy had slowed down, that was for sure, and the automotive business was in the shitter. They were making antivibration parts for the Big 3 but were supposedly picking up a good chunk of Mercedes business. That was promising.

He heard his footsteps clop along the parking lot. His briefcase felt heavy and he gripped the handles tight. The wind was crisp. The rope clinging up the metal pole whipped and bowed. Frank hated talking to Simon sometimes.

Who likes talking to their accountant? He wondered. Shit. They always just tell you about how your money is fucked, save more, put some in the IRA, 401K, take some out every month for taxes. All that crap. As an independent contractor, it was on Frank to manage his own financial planning. Unfortunately, that was not his bag. At least, he hadn't made it his. It got put in the pile to be done later every time he thought about it. All that time on his own out there on the road, there were so many chances and so much time to take care of the little things that could make such a big difference down the road but he never stopped and took the time. No excuses. That wasn't it. He just found himself choosing the path where he had the most momentum, the strongest tailwind. Keep hustling. Keep making calls. Steer into the tunnel. When it feels right, accelerate into the turn. Stay in your lane. Eventually it will pay off.

When you're on your own sometimes, it was hard to see everything around you, even though you were staring at it the whole time.

The meeting went well. The purchasing agent was a nice enough guy. Ordinarily he tried to avoid them like the fucking plague. Mainly because they would always hit you on pricing, also because they were just fucking dickheads.

This was a nice change. The guy had worked in production for a good while. He knew the process and didn't have a chip on his shoulder, no perceptible ego he wanted to throw around for the sake of throwing it around. They were interested in a product that would bring a cost-savings, and that was the name of the game anymore. Everything had gone up. Gas. Resins. Compounds. Electricity. Steel. Rubber. Fucking everything. Cutting costs was more important now than ever.

Simon's name was highlighted in the scroll menu. Frank knew he had to call him back. But he really didn't want to. It was one of those intuitive clashes that weighed on him. Knowing you had to do something but not wanting to. When you're out there, man, it is every bit as hard as it can be to force yourself to do things you know you have to do but you don't want to because you're the only one who is there to enforce the rules. And once you shut that voice down, it gets easier to do it again, and again.

Anyway, Frank thought. Simon was a good friend and he trusted him. Especially because he told him things he didn't want to hear. So, he hit send.

"Frank? Hold on a second." He said after one ring.

"Yep." Frank paused for a construction crew as they waved one-way traffic through. Frank waved to a man in a striped reflective vest and orange hardhat. Then he eased past and turned right toward downtown. They were hanging lights and decorations for a parade. Main street was one and a half blocks, they had a clothing store and a bar, three-story buildings with thin windows for eyeballs. The dust could be seen from the street. Several Marines were coming home from Afghanistan that Friday.

Simon clicked back over.

"Frank, you still there?"

"Yeah. What's the story, man?"

"Okay, do you have a minute?" He asked, Frank could hear him click away on his computer.

"Yeah."

"We've got a real problem on our hands. I hope you heeded my instruction about putting some money away every month." Frank grabbed the wheel tighter. Feeling like he did when his mom had busted him trying to sneak back into the house in the summertime after he'd already snuck out.

"You're up to your ass in back taxes. And there isn't much time left in the year."

"What about the extension?" Frank asked.

"That was in April, Frank. We're coming up on August. By October, you're going to have to come up with 30k." Frank thought it would be bad. Knew it would. But that was partly why he drove right past it when it tried to creep into his consciousness, every time. If he kept moving forward and farther away eventually it would be too far in the rearview to catch up. It was so recklessly and stupidly immature that he couldn't believe he'd allowed himself to do it. That was what

238

went right through him more than anything. The IRS would undoubtedly end up getting what was owed to them one way or another, but they could quite frankly blow it up their ass.

That still didn't matter much because he was instantaneously more upset with himself.   Frank continued to work tirelessly in his new territory. He spent nearly every night of the week at a Hampton Inn. Piling up frequent stay points. He was already a Diamond VIP member, but now he was reaching an almost unprecedented level of reward redemptions. He could take a week in Hawaii, including first-class air fare and a five-star Hilton. Same deal at the Waldorf in Manhattan. Europe. Australia. He could have free nights for a month at any of the locations in the United States. But any vacation was a long way off. It was nice to have it in the back of his mind though. It was kind of was like a prize waiting for him in the distance. A reward. It helped.

So, waking at five and filling up his to-go mug with the robust house blend, he went about engaging his craft. Knocking on doors. Door after door after door. He would fire off thirty or forty samples a week for preliminary evaluations. And follow-up accordingly.

Slowly but surely the business came.

His best attributes were not spinning a line of bullshit a mile wide to coerce potential customers into going with his company, sucking up, or passing bribes. His strengths were rooted in perseverance, tenacity, and honesty.

Frank turned to conversations in his head he'd had with the boss. Especially when he found himself pressing asphalt a hundred miles from home on a Friday night frustrated as all hell because a promising lead had turned out to be a wild goose chase or a trial had fizzled out after perhaps looking good from the outset.

"There are no shortcuts, Frank. You…just have to grind it out."

The way it worked, in most cases, was Frank would dig up any and all leads he could, try to establish contact, and if successful, he'd have to present himself, his products, and the capabilities of his company in such a way that it would be worthwhile for the engineer, production manager, or whomever to investigate further. It sounded easy enough from the outset, but Frank soon realized that no matter how good he might sound on the phone or look in person, trialing new products and possibly implementing a change in the production process was a major, major undertaking. Why? For one thing, the products he sold could be otherwise described, in extremely basic terms as industrial Pam. The shit people spray into a pan, so the eggs don't stick all over it. Well, when molding a rubber, foam, plastic, or composite part, or casting a zinc,

240

magnesium, or aluminum part, what you put on the mold to keep the part from sticking was inherently critical. Primarily because if a part stuck, it was scrap. If a rubber grommet exhibited "knit-lines" where the rubber did not flow sufficiently through the cavity due to improper or excess release agent, it was scrap. If an aluminum valve body revealed under infrared examination to have "high porosity" or water molecules encapsulated inside the part, it was scrap. If a urethane console showed "pock-marks" tiny holes on the skin of the foam where the water in the release agent hadn't flashed off quickly enough due to insufficient heat and attacked the foam in its liquid form, it was scrap.

And scrapped parts could sink a manufacturing company faster than bacteria could a cruise ship.

Plus, it was hard enough to find one that worked in the first place, so to stop production to merely try another product that had no guarantee of success, was usually frowned on by engineers, or production personnel who, in their minds, already had enough on their plate. That wasn't to say all of them. It was just more common to find resistance when trying to get in the door than not. In addition, and this ran to the root of the challenge in pushing the products Frank pushed, was that when operators became used to using a specific product, it was very difficult to convince them to change. Part of that was

241

psychological. Some operators had worked a single press for thirty years, with their faces in temperatures in excess of 350 Degrees Fahrenheit, breathing in ghastly vapors, and handling searing hot parts that burned through their gloves. To Frank, they were the key to making a sale. His ideal situation manifested itself when he got a chance to go out on the floor and work directly with the operators. It was more often, than not, would make or break him.

"That's a tough a job as there is. These people are the ones who use our products. They're also the ones who know the application, they know the process and its intricacies, what is critical and what isn't, what to look for and what to anticipate. They'll probably all resist you at first, that's natural. But you have got to be determined and shoot them straight. Let them know that you need their input, that what they say matters, and that you want to help. That is what you have also have to do, is to sell them on, is that you're there to make their jobs easier. And you must show them respect. Of course, you're in there to sell your products, that isn't any secret. The company cuts the checks, but the operators put the juice to the steel, and they will raise holy hell if you come in with something that locks up their mold, if it smells a certain way. You'll learn more in one day, at a press with an operator than

you will a week with some engineer in his cubicle." The boss
had said.

One early summer morning in Ligonier, Indiana, Frank
pulled into a gravel parking lot adjacent to a railroad pass and
large grain silos. His trial began at six, and there was a man
waiting for him in the office.

He was nice enough and had only recently been
promoted from the line to supervisor. His name was Gary. A
young guy, close to Frank's age. He had shaggy blond hair that
pushed out the back of his Dale Jr. hat.

"Hey, man, uh, I'm ah gonna take you back 'ere to the
press line, and you go on ahead and set up and work with
Cesar. He's, uh, a real good operator and will help you run
this...ah trial." He was scratching at his beard, shaggy as well
beneath a longer grown goatee, apparently trying to remember
something else that he had to do.

"That'd be great, Gary, I think we've got something
that could work out well. It's a water base like we talked about
and is probably cheaper than that solvent you all are currently
using." Frank said, restating his main selling point.

"Yeah, uh...that'd be good. They uh...far as I know
they've been using that solvent base from Chem...Chem-
Friends I think for years. Long as I've been here anyway. It'll
probably be a tough sell because I think they in pretty tight

with the plant manager, but like I told you I been…uh…instructed to try new products that could save us money, and if you got a better mousetrap, shit, we'll have a look and hopefully it'll do good. I've got to warn you though, some…uh, these people in 'ere are…uh, resistant to change." Gary cautioned.

"So am I." Frank said and smiled.

He eyed the station over toward the press, and Cesar look up at him briefly, lifting a smoking array of black rubber parts and stacked them on a sheet of thin plastic. Frank shook hands with Gary and walked over to the mold.

Cesar wore a camouflage t-shirt, old blue jeans, and reebok high tops.

"Como estas?" Frank asked.

"Bien, bien. You speak Spanish?" Cesar asked, a little surprised.

"Un pocito solamente." Frank answered, opening his case.

"Oh, si." He said and smiled. It was seldom that a gringo spoke Spanish, particularly in a remote farming town in northeastern Indiana. Frank had noticed as he drove into town through a faint and wispy fog a sense of desolation as he pushed the brakes at the lone remaining red light. The scene was complete with a vacant drive-in theater, a closed down

244

Dairy Queen, and boarded up three-story houses. As he pulled onto the main drag, he eyed the worn-out remnants of shops on either side of the street. He wouldn't have been surprised if a tumbleweed rolled out in front of him. There were faded signs for Maggie's Hair, Ted's Hardware, and a Ruthie's Flowers. The stores were probably out of business for ten years, at least. But nothing had replaced them. No businesses had come in and removed the signs and put up their own. Except for several toward the very end of the street, within a stone's throw of the factory. And, most notably, their signs were not in English. They advertised a variety of Mexican products. Huevos. Musica. Chorizo y Bistec. Televisions. Western Union. It was as though the small town had been abandoned and left to die as the factories all save one had closed their doors, but had been found years later by wondering pilgrims who wasted no time in resuscitating a more than adequate infrastructure to build and work and live.

There were more towns like this one in the upper Midwest. Towns that had once housed several thriving automotive suppliers, providing decent, working class wages that spurred an entire local economy spilling over into family-owned retail shops, gas stations, and small diners. Towns where parents raised their kids, supported high school football,

245

held Church picnics, and worked for the same company their entire adult lives.

Cesar turned back to his press. The molding blocks of aged stainless steel separated with a squeal, the top part raised, sending steam slithering out of its pores and toward the plumbing lines dangling above.

Frank pulled out a one-gallon container that was wrapped in plastic with the lab number marked neatly on the label. The batch and expiration date were coded on the lower right and left sides, respectively. The rule of thumb with a water-base shelf life was six months from the day it was manufactured compared to a solvent-base, which has a shelf life of a year. The problem with going from solvent to water was that a solvent, despite its obvious environmental and health concerns, was that they worked. Solvents were excellent catalysts, they flashed off the mold surface in a matter of seconds, leaving the release film behind. Once sprayed or wiped properly on the mold and given adequate time to cure, it would bond to the surface creating a film and if viewed under a microscope would look like the graph paper in math class. If it was over-applied and not given enough time to "bake-on," it would look like a messy glob of mashed potatoes, leaving little chance of success. It was also invisible to the naked eye, if you were to run your finger across the surface it would appear as though nothing was there. It was counter-intuitive, to both the salesman and the operator, and more than a little disconcerting while waiting for a closed mold to open.

Cesar lifted a long copper wand, with a small tank attached to it. It was caked in black grime. He raised the wand and doused the mold with the current product, sending a flood of fumes into the air. The unmistakable stench of solvent tried to gather around Frank like a phantasm, but he'd enough experience to stand back and place a clean cloth over his nose and mouth and turned his head for good measure. Cesar just turned his nose up a bit, unwittingly basking in the stench and squinted as the solvent baked into the mold surface. His spray wand produced a cone-like mist that covered the top and bottom plates that percolated into the intricate rivets of each cavity. Above the mold was a large metal cylinder, at least seven feet in length and eight inches in diameter, tilted at forty-five-degree angle into the press. A long, black, snakelike trail of uncured rubber fed from a bin behind the press limped into cylinder, to be forced into the press for the curing cycle. The molds were running hot, at least 350 Degrees Fahrenheit, which boded well for Frank's sample, because the water did not flash off the mold nearly as fast or as well as the solvent, and the hotter the mold, the quicker the water would get forced out and allow the release film to cure to the surface and allow for film formation. The uncured rubber had been coated in a calcium stearate solution to keep it from sticking to itself and make it easier to feed into the press. This solution was a mess; it came in a powder form and was diluted with water. It was nasty, but it was cheap. And most companies went with it for that very reason.

Cesar reached for the inching rubber and tugged it to keep it from snagging on the edge of the bin and impeding the feed to the press. Frank continued to set up his tiny spray apparatus. It was a HVLP or high velocity low pressure gun, with a two-quart pot. It had a regulator for both fluid and air, and he set both for 30 psi. Any higher and it could break up the emulsion in his product, and in turn he'd only be spraying water onto the mold surface, making a lockup certain.

"Do you like your spray?" He asked Cesar. Cesar looked at him and shrugged.

"Es, ok. Pero…smell, no bueno." He made a face.

"Si, es un…solvente." Frank answered.

"Si…solvente."

"Solventes, muy malo. Very bad for your health." Frank said, looking at Cesar evenly. He had had his face right in the press, nearly inside of it and had flooded the damn thing. He didn't need that much really, not that the Chem-Friends rep would tell them that. The trick with these types of products was

248

that the less was better. But chemical theory and production processes were two different things. He did not get into taking shots at his competition, which he believed was unprofessional. It was for pretenders, short timers. And a waste of time. He wanted to prove his own products. But it was common sense when someone had their face in a shower of isopropyl alcohol sucking in fumes eight hours a day, that replacing it with water was a good idea.

Cesar nodded, but Frank was unsure if he understood.

"Tengo un producto de agua." He held up the container for Cesar to read, and he momentarily leaned closer, and studied its markings.

"Es agua?" He asked. Flakes of black rubber flash were clung to his face, neck, shirt, and hair.

"No todo, pero casi." Frank answered, instantly unaware of his own limitations in speaking Spanish.

"Oh, si." Cesar nodded again and returned to his work. He slid beside the press, read an antiquated computer readout, and then pushed a large green button.

The press squeezed shut. And Cesar exhaled briefly and shuttled over to a corner to grab a broom, and immediately set about sweeping his area, collecting rubber flash and debris into a small pile.

Frank saw a dustpan and knelt to hold it for Cesar.

249

"Gracias." He said.

"De nada. El proximo cylce…ah the next round, can we clean…limpia the mold?"

"Si, limpia, si si." Cesar nodded emphatically.

"Y entonces, podemos usar mi producto de agua. Ok?" Frank asked.

"Si si. Agua." Frank got the sense that Cesar normally did not crave attention, particularly from a gringo. But having been singled out to work with a gringo on an important project made him feel proud, and willing to help. And making the effort to speak his native language could have made him feel more comfortable with him. Either way, he could tell this operator was going to be solid to work with, and that was exactly where he hoped to be.

Frank brought enough samples to run the entire shift, and it was early. He pinched up his sleeves and opened his notebook to record all the parameters of the application.

He looked up periodically from his notebook, thinking things through and saw Cesar methodically and at a determined pace run his press, stack his parts, and police his area, and he saw at least seven other people probably with similar sounding names doing the same. In fact, the entire group of workers were Hispanic. The only American Frank saw was Gary, and his boss Dick who passed through the front office only briefly,

250

clenching a binder with jagged gray hair and a hurried gait. Frank caught his eye as he walked out onto the floor.

"How are you doing today? My name is Frank Cusco." They shook hands. But the boss averted his eyes.

"I'm real fuckin busy. What are you and Pancho up to here?" He asked, kind of looking down his nose.

"We're going to run a new water-based release agent; we believe it will offer comparable if not better performance to your current solvent base and will be very cost-competitive. Not to mention the health, and environmental benefits."

"Water base, huh? Never seen one yet that's worth a shit. But I reckon you'll tell me this is the one that will get over the hump?" He folded his arms.

"We'll just have to run it and see. Proof is in the pudding." Frank replied.

"Undeterred."

"Yeah, I've been in this business a long time, and I ain't seen anything out-perform what we got. And quite frankly, I wasn't aware of this trial you runnin today…and if I had a rock, I'd hit Gary right in the head with it for bringing you in like this. We got a lot of orders to fill and every cycle were testing something that…I don't have any confidence will work…shit we're that far behind on the parts we need to run. Nothing against your company or nothing."

251

He seemed to be getting more worked up as he went on. He was tall, and skinny. Nervous type of guy. The kind of guy who liked to throw what little weight he had around when he could.

"Running this type of trial won't take long…if it ain't going to work we'll know after the first couple of heats. If it doesn't, we'll pull it off right away, and Cesar…can go right back over it with the solvent base. There will be issues with compatibility. As I'm sure you're aware, with the price of gas as high as it is, any petrochemical derivative follows suit. And it ain't coming down anytime soon. I would imagine you'd be interested in saving money and, also finding a product less volatile for your employees to work with." Frank answered, laying a couple cards on the table. That seemed to ruffle the boss's already-rankled feathers. Cesar had moved away from where they were talking, and the machines produced enough noise so that he couldn't hear them.

You think you're rattlin' my cage, motherfucker? The thought ran across Frank's head quiet like a smart cat up and or down a flight of stairs.

"Look, Taylor is it?"

"No, it's Frank, Frank Cusco."

"Right, Frank. Look, I ain't so much worried about shaving a few dollars per gallon of the cost of my release products. That's small potatoes. What I need is to get parts out quick fast and in a hurry. The solvent base is good, and it's been in here a long time."

He looked around quickly and leaned a bit closer to Frank, turning slightly and spoke lower out of the side of his mouth.

"These sumbitches come up here in droves. I ain't seen nobody choke and die on it yet." Dick said as though he were cracking an inside joke.

Frank felt his upper lip curl just slightly, and he ground his teeth the smallest bit as turned his back on him and walked away.

He turned back to the press and Cesar was motioning that the press had been cleaned and was ready for the trial.

Frank showed him the spray apparatus and handed the gun to Cesar. It was a small act of trust, and respect. It was critical to involve the operator because as they were the ones who literally worked with the products and because sooner or later, they'd have to run it on their own anyway. He reasoned that the closer to the real production setting that he could conduct the trial, the more legitimate data he would be able to gather. This would allow him to back up its performance.

Cesar sprayed a very nice, even coat on the mold, then another. He pressed the button on the side of the press, and it closed. Several minutes passed allowing for the sample to bond to the tool surface. Then it opened. He motioned to Frank asking if he should apply another coat.

"Si, por favor." Frank said. It was always better to put on too much at first than too little. If it started sticking right away, you were screwed. Cesar nodded and applied it. Frank asked him about the smell.

"Es better, the smell." He said. That was a good sign. Frank was worried that having worked with the solvent-base for so long, he might be so accustomed to the smell that anything could smell worse when first exposed to it.

They waited after Cesar loaded the rubber for the first heat. Frank held up both hands, with fingers crossed and Cesar smiled at him. This was where the rubber met the road.

The mold opened and the parts, which usually clung to the bottom, were rising precariously with the top, barely hanging on. Cesar's eyes opened wide with surprise, and he reached in with one gloved hand and pick the parts out with two fingers. Frank wasn't sure whether this was an improvement.

"Es bien o no?" He asked.

"Bien! Bien! Muy facil." Cesar said, placing the parts in a bin on the floor. They peered into the press to check for any buildup, or residue left from the water-base, and saw none. That was another good sign.

"Un otro?" He asked, wanting to know if he should hit the mold again. He seemed to really like the spray gun.

"No, no es necessario." Frank replied. Now the thing was to see how far they could go without "touching up." That was where real value could be added. Not only did it release well, with no sign of buildup, transfer to the parts, but it might outlast the solvent base. That on top of the fact that it would be less expensive, and Frank would have a Nebraska sized silo of selling points for this product.

He might not be out on his ass after all. He gave Cesar a friendly slap on the shoulder and stood with his hands on his hips in front of the row of presses, trying to calculate just how much these guys used in a month's time. It was a good pop as best he could figure. There was no escaping the fact that solvent prices were going through the roof, the plant manager couldn't deny that no matter how much of an asshole he was.

They kept running, and the parts kept on slipping right out of the mold. Cesar knew his business too. He could tell just from the way the rubber barely clung to the top of the mold by a tiny strip of flash after every heat that he didn't need to touch up.

The clock hit 10:15, and everyone instantly put down their tools and gloves and proceeded to the break room, or outside for a smoke.

XX.

She brought a napkin to her lips and laughed after he told her the story about an old friend of his who grew up with all kinds of animals. And how, this one day, Oscar, Red, and Whiskey had gotten out of the yard and treed a cat down the street. He said he loved animals. She liked that. That he couldn't wait to get a dog when he was able to spend more time at home. Something about that made her feel good too. Then he just went on and told her the story about how when his friend's Mom had gotten a call from the neighbor informing her that their dog, donkey, and goat had the neighbor's cat penned up in a tree. His Mom ran down and brought them back, and the next day the same thing happened. She searched the yard high and low to find a hole in the fence or a missing board or some evidence of an escape route but didn't turn up anything. Then the next morning, he and his mom sat quietly on the screened in porch off the master bedroom and watched as their animals began the day by milling around a small pond. Then Oscar started barking and scooting over toward the gate. Red with his stubby beard and tilted horns made quick thumping sounds with his hooves as he ran up close to stand just below the latch. After that Oscar continued to bark but in a little different cadence, and Whiskey loped over to loom over Red. Oscar started digging with his forepaws right below the gate, his tail wagging furiously. Next, Red brought his head down with his horns forward and started ramming the gate, wham wham wham. Whiskey, the tallest of the trio nudged his nose under the latch as it bounced up and down from Red's head butts below. Once Whiskey had the latch secured with his nose, Oscar ran around both and used his right front paw to pull the gate open and they were off. He and his Mom just watched in complete astonishment. Now seriously, how can you get mad at your pets when they show that kind of ingenuity, and teamwork, she asked Taylor. He just looked at her having laughed intermittently and agreed. She asked if they went after the same cat the third time they got out, but it turned out that they went to another house and got into somebody's garden.

He hung on every word about the story she told about a neighbor, who was a friend of her Dad who was flying back from Detroit after a long week pitching the automotive companies on his website ideas. When the man in the aisle seat in his same row had glanced in his direction after getting repeatedly bumped from behind by a heavy-set, rude, and boisterous female passenger. He described how he didn't want to look in that direction, sensing a looming conflict. And how when the lady boarded the plane, she thumped nearly everyone on both sides of the aisle with her two large bags, while snacking on a bag of Doritos, dropping crumbs on herself and everyone else. Just an unpleasant person who you hoped to God did not take the seat next to you. Out of the corner of his eye, he kept noticing the man's seat lurching forward, and the man getting more and more exacerbated. He had his laptop out, probably composing an email and not even able to finish a sentence. The lady was talking on her cellphone too, loud enough for the entire cabin to hear. It wasn't until the plane took off did things quiet down, but then when the captain turned off the fasten seat belt sign, the man undid his tie and pressed the button on the arm to recline his seat. This immediately set the lady off, because her legs were already in a tight squeeze. She fussed for a minute and tried to move around, scuttling the man's seat in rapid succession. He didn't make a move this time though, just sat there with his eyes closed in full recline mode. Finally, she shook the seat with her hand and said, "Excuse me, hey…excuse me! Can we compromise on this?" She hollered, peering through the gap between the seats in front of her. The man didn't move, but opened one eye, and glanced over at her Dad. At this point, Dad couldn't help but look over; it was like he was part of it somehow. The man gave Dad a look as if to say, "watch this," and turned around.

"Girl, you can compromise yourself to the weight loss clinic."

She put her hand over her mouth and said "Oh My God." Then laughed out loud hard.

He told her about his company too, trying not to sound ostentatious. And she was really sharp. Turned out she would be graduating ahead of schedule having taken a heavy course load each semester. She could get a job anywhere, that was certain. Man, she was smoking too. The whole package. Smart, pretty, motivated, good morals. It was interesting to Taylor that she seemed not to know it.

A sliver of worry crept around the back of his mind as the talked as it always had when he was liked a girl. Going back to fucking junior high man. He'd feel it tingle up his back and then down into his stomach. Making steady progress with a girl was like walking from one side of gymnast's balance beam to the other. It was easy enough the first few steps, but then he couldn't help but glance down toward the end and realize how slim the margin of error was, how precarious each step. The end seemed like an impossible distance. Might as well be a mile. He'd try to overcome his doubts. Come one just one foot in front of the other. Nothing too it. He'd take another step or two, but inevitably turn his eyes up and then off to each side, and his arms would waver and the girl would sense his sinking

260

confidence and her interest would proportionately dwindle and his arms would flail and his toes would slip and then it was over. He'd fall on his ass, hoping against hope that when he looked up, she wouldn't be gone. That she wouldn't think he was a wimp. That she'd come over and help him up with a word of encouragement. That maybe she'd forgive the lack of confidence for something endearing. But that was wishful thinking. Every time she'd be gone onto someone who didn't have trouble with his self-esteem. Somebody who knew what to say and how to stay it. One of those lucky guys that could read girls, pick up on their flirtatious nuances. Ask the right questions with the right kind of look in their eyes that made the girls giggle and twirl their hair and reach to their arms for a playful squeeze and say yes, they'd love to go out on a date. Fuckin A if he didn't want to be one of those guys. But he wasn't, not when he was down on his ass like a sorry little pussy.

He'd curse himself to no end not knowing that was the problem in the first place. The worry wasn't as resounding this time. It was there, but not nearly as bad as any other time when he felt literally helpless. Paralyzed by his own ineptitude. Maybe it was just the moment into which he found himself immersed. Chatting away with this girl and being himself, not worrying about what to do next the entire time. Unfortunately, as he knew all too well, they'd eventually they'd have to finish their date, or whatever it was, and he wanted to see her again that was for sure, but should he ask her out? And how could he do it right without making a jackass out of himself.

Taylor left a generous tip on the table and then held the door for her. She smiled with the slightest glance and subtle step as the smell of her hair sent warm chills aflutter inside him, then found each other to pool together at the corners of his mouth lifting it almost involuntarily into a smile all his own.

As they got outside the sunlight dipped in and was soft and bright. On either side of the street there were cars parked with purple fliers stuck beneath their windshield wipers. People were out and about shopping or sitting at café tables reading, some on cell phones, others typing text messages. The wind blew softly through the trees which leaned above, offering spotted blips of shade. It was a beautiful afternoon. The kind of day you could wear jeans or a pair of shorts. Two gold finches flapped and dipped and then landed on a branch behind Felicia. Taylor took a deep breath, noting the serenity. This must be what it's like when all is right with the world. And just when he thought that, he suddenly felt the familiar thumping of his heart. The sinking feeling was back. The end of the beam was a mile away again, and the ground was going to jump up on his ass and she'd be gone like the finches here in a minute.

She bit her upper lip slightly, looking up at him. She could tell something was stirring. She wasn't sure what, but she thought it was kind of cute. She wanted him to ask her out again. He was an attractive man, more than that even. Intelligent. He listened too, that was particularly attractive. But there was a certain vulnerability there too. She didn't think it was weakness, no, he wasn't weak. She could sense that immediately. It was like…he was trying to figure something out but maybe he didn't know what it was. Just a little unsure, not that he should be or had to reason to be. He seemed interested in her too, she was pretty sure. But she had to get going, her shift started at 5:30. Hopefully, he'd get on the stick and make a move because she was starting to feel awkward with him just standing there, the silence growing. Why doesn't he as me out already, Felicia thought. Maybe he doesn't like me that way. But he acted like he did. She could sense that somehow…unless she was totally off base. Either way time was running out, and although they were getting along great, a brief silence could be dowsed with awkwardness in seconds.

Felicia did notice throughout the story she told that he seemed to have a look of longing that made Felicia feel good. More than good.

Taylor tried to suck up the fear, tried to clear from his mind the mental block that seemed to be an impervious boulder

263

guarding a cave entrance, but he couldn't. It wouldn't budge. And as he desperately in his own mind tried to take the next step on the balance beam, he heard himself utter, "It was good to meet you Felicia…uh, good luck in school."

She was kind of startled when he stuck out his hand. She shook it, but sort of frowned. He spurted out his words, and it didn't sound like the same guy at the podium, or inside back in the coffee shop.

But she started questioning herself. She shouldn't have asked him to have coffee anyway. Why would a successful businessman want to date a college student, he probably shouldn't have worn what she did, maybe he didn't like her body. Or her hair. God, why did she let herself think he was into her?

As she turned, she walked down the sidewalk one arm tucked through black loop of her purse glad for the fact that he couldn't see the red in her face.

He fumbled with his keys and dropped them to the pavement. They clanked on the cement and as he picked them up and glanced in her direction. She got smaller step by step, and he bit into the inner wall of his mouth, squeezing his keys in his fist until they left deep and crooked indentations in his skin.

Walking to his car he felt like everyone around was looking at him. Either laughing or keeping quiet because maybe they were embarrassed for him. This school of paranoid thoughts bounced heavily around his head. Then they instantly joined as one mass forming a surge of self-loathing that could peel the paint off three-story house and slammed the driver's side door loud enough for the people at the table nearby to look up for a scattered second.

He looked in the rearview, his face flushed red and wondered if in fact he had a pair.

Taylor sat motionless for a minute and heard his cellphone beeping. Four missed calls.

All from Everett.

XXI.

Walter got a call at 4:15 a.m. He was going to get up in another hour to walk their dog, a brown boxer/Rhodesian-ridgeback mix before taking a shower, but the last hour of sleep was the most important. Getting woke before you had your adequate amount of rest sucked. It made him ornery. Gave him a strange buzzing sensation too. It took him a moment to gather himself, holding his cellphone up to his face to check the number. His wife groaned softly and turned over onto her other side, pulling the covers over her head. He patted her backside and leaned forward, then swung his legs over the side of bed and felt the creaking in his joints.

"Yeah." He said walking into the hall, toward the bathroom.

"Walter, this is Sam, we got a problem out here on the floor." Sam said; he was the third shift supervisor.

"What is it?" Walter asked,

"All the presses are locked up. Froze." Walter wasn't sure he heard him right. He was taking a leak and looked up, spraying all over the seat and the tile floor.

"Shit! Wait…wait a minute. What'd you say?" He asked.

"They all locked up, Walter, we were runnin' that new lube, the one that guy Frank brought in that's been looking real good, 'specially since we put in into the central system and spread it all around the plant. You know?"

"Yeah, so what?" Walter still was half-asleep, hoping this was just a bad dream.

"Well, I don't know if this stuff just went bad on us or what, but we put on a new drum at the beginning of the shift, and by the time it worked its way through the system and into the lines, all of sudden it was like…shit man…like a bomb went off in here. All the presses just stuck like hell. We got maintenance hooking up forklifts with chains and crowbars trying to just get the sumbitches open. It's bad, Walter, really bad." Sam said, sounding despondent.

"Alright, stay put, I'll be in as fast as I can. You call anybody else?" Walter asked.

"No sir, just you. Won't be long for the upper management finds out. The Japanese are coming in later this week too. There's gonna be hell to pay." Sam said.

"You ain't shittin."

He dressed quickly and put his keys in his jacket pocket. The dog was up now, and waiting by the door, anxiously wagging its tail.

"Sorry, buddy, not right now." Walter said as he closed the door behind him, and the dog looked confused, maybe even a little hurt.

XXII.

"You're on fire, kid," Colin's boss said, between mouthfuls of spicy shrimp cocktail. St. Elmo's Steak House was an institution in Indianapolis. The cocktail sauce was legendary, could almost set one's mouth aflame. He was a dapper looking man, in his late fifties.

"You keep racking up orders like this, I'm going to have to bring on some other guys to work the territory." He said. Colin's face went straight and dropped his fork.

"Take it easy, I'm just fucking with you." The last thing a straight commission salesman wanted was for his territory to get sliced up. Take away the real estate and you take away the lifeblood of a salesman. Even if a certain part of a state, for example, was empty as far as potential customers went, it didn't mean that at some point later on a new plant might open up for business. And whoever's territory it was, then they had the rights to call on them. You couldn't hang your hat on previously established relationships or knowledge of the area or anything. If it was yours it was yours, but if it wasn't, then you'd better stay the fuck out.

Poaching was a cardinal sin.

The other part about it was that after working the area for a long enough time and finally converting some customers, of course you didn't want some other asshole coming in a taking the commissions. Every once in a while, some lucky bastard got a nice account dropped in his lap, just by being in the right place at the right time. And if you were not that guy, you had to be pissed off about it. But that was all part of the deal. Sometimes, the ball bounced the other way too.

"I sure hope so, I've busted my balls to steal…I mean earn that business." Colin said. He was dressed to the nines…wearing a Hugo Boss suit that he'd recently bought down the block. Three-hundred-dollar leather shoes. Even his socks ran thirty-five bucks.

"Yeah, I know you did." The boss said, grinning slightly. He was a sneaky little fucker. But he was hitting his numbers for damn sure. Well above in fact. Probably wasn't a thing he wouldn't do for an order. Kind of reminded him of himself back in the day. Boy, did we use to pull some shit…he thought to himself as he dug into is filet mignon.

"It's a good thing our competitor's product turned sour…that'd been your ass if we lost that account. I don't have to tell you what that one brings in every year, or how long we've had it." He said, taking a serious tone, offering an unveiled warning.

"Well, I knew it wasn't going to work once they put in the central system. The chemistry in that product wasn't going to hold up. They could run small production trials with success,

270

but it's a whole different ballgame when they go plant wide."
Colin said, trying to sound wise beyond his years.

"Bullshit, you dodged a fucking bullet. How long had
they been running the competition's product before you found
out? Three months? Four?" The guy didn't fuck around, Colin
thought, best to be careful trying to slip one past him.

"I was just trying to nail down other business and I
can't be in three places at once." He said, still trying to sound
on the level.

"I appreciate that, but never lose sight of what you've
already got." The boss said, easing back a bit, trying to educate
his number 1 earner rather than bust his balls. After all, this
was a kind of bonus lunch. He had a check in the briefcase for
200 big pictures of George. He believed in greasing. It had got
him where he was today. All the other guys who wasted time
dropping off their cards or testing and retesting their products
only to maybe get the business one, two, five years later, fuck
all that shit. Why waste the time when all most of the
customers wanted was a little love, like a golf trip, some
collared shirts, several nice fishing rods? Dinner. Lap dances.
You show me a guy who has some grease in his palm, and I'll
show you a Purchase Order with our name on it. Life was too
short not to cut corners. This kid was natural too. Took to it
like fish to water. That was what the check was for, it wasn't

271

only the customers who needed some love once in a while, if they earned it.

"Yes, sir." He said, wiping his mouth with the napkin.

"Listen, I got something for you. Your bonus." He said.

"Really, no shit. Didn't know…" He thought better about saying anything else.

"Of course, you didn't know, but here. Your commission check should arrive end of the week, so this should make for a pretty good month."

"Thank you. Hopefully next month will be even better." Colin said, thinking it was the right thing to say.

"That's right. But don't get complacent. Easiest thing to do is for you right now is to let of the gas. But I strongly urge you to keep pressing. The world is littered with guys who think they got it made and fizzle out before it ever really gets started." He said, kind of like a coach or a college teacher might. But Colin left college early, and he got thrown off the high school basketball team after yelling back at the coach when he tried to show him how to move his feet during a defensive sliding drill. And when his boss' tone morphed into one of guidance, or advice, he shut it out like a reflex. But still nodded intently to show pseudo respect.

"Now, I've got to catch a plane. The wife and I are headed to Maui. Tell them to put it on my tab." He got up, straightened the pleats in his pants and shook hands with Colin, and with the manager by front door.

Colin sat back down and ran his fingers over the envelop, with the company logo on the upper left-hand corner, his heart ratcheting up its pace. He felt like a kid on Christmas morning.   He raised his head to eye the room and saw people carrying on with their meals and conversations, not paying him any mind. At the corner table, he opened up the envelop and read the written number on the check, followed by a long horizontal streak from the left to the right that he followed as though in entranced in a dream to the other side and read the number again. Holy fucking shit.

It was more money than he'd ever had in his whole life.

His heart was beating like a jackrabbit creeping up behind Mrs. Jackrabbit when the waitress came over and asked if he needed anything else, he said, sure, a shot of Jack.

XXIII.

When Frank pulled into the Mexican restaurant, it was already crowded. He scanned the parking lot for the boss' car, and at the very last spot, he caught a glimpse of the Oldsmobile. It was easily ten years old, but still in great shape. The boss took care of his things. He stood when Frank got to the table. He went six feet three inches, 230 pounds of solid rock. He served in the Marine Corps in the late sixties, going through basic training at Paris Island. After he got out, he sold office supplies, paper, real estate. He also traveled the world, from France to Singapore, to Haiti, making calls. He and his wife moved out to Los Angeles in the mid-seventies. They didn't have a pot to piss in or a window to throw it out of when he first got started. The guys he worked with out in LA were nuttier than fruitcakes too. Some of them sold jewelry out of the backs of their pintos, while all their wives drove Jaguars and Mercedes. They'd go to parties in the hills and he said that you could never really tell who was married to who.

On weekends, he sold the real estate. And one Sunday, he was driving around a nice neighborhood in Pasadena and noticed a young couple standing on a sidewalk in front of a two-story house, probably three bedrooms, two baths. It had a sign in the yard, but there didn't seem to be an agent anywhere.

He drove closer, then turned, and went into the alley behind the house. When he told Frank the story, he mentioned "...now, I'm not going to say I broke and entered...but the fuckin' window was open." So, he parked the car in the alley behind the house, eased over the fence through the yard and on in through the window. He opened the front door and greeted the couple, invited them in, showed them the house, and sold it for the list price. When he called the owner of the real estate company, after getting the number off the sign in front yard...he was more than a little surprised to hear that she had no problem with what he did. Frank loved that story. It was so old school.

"How are you doing, Frank?" He grabbed him by the shoulders and gave him a brief hug.

"Doing alright, how are you, sir?" He answered.

"Just trying to stay ahead of the rent, man. And cut the sir shit, will ya?" He said, smiling.

"Ok. Have you been here long?" Frank asked. It was like he was the coolest uncle and toughest of granddads all in one.

"No, just got in. You should've seen these two kids here with their mother a minute ago. Holy shit, they were all bigger than I am. They must've had seven plates on the table, ten cokes, a basket of bread rolls. They were slamming down

275

the tacos like they were candy, salsa, and guacamole dripping all over their hands and face. And the mom was the worst; she kept yelling at the waiter to come over with more this, more of that. Then…oh shit, then when they got finished, the waiter asked if they wanted some ice cream. I thought, holy shit, you have got to be shitting me. And these kids, each with a taco smashed in their face yelling 'yeah, yeah, we want some ice cream!!!' I thought, Jesus Christ, no wonder there's a fuckin obesity problem in this country." He had a way of talking that couldn't help but take your mind off your worries…whatever they might be. Frank was laughing. It was a nice change.

"Did they end up getting the ice cream?" Frank asked, smiling.

"Yeah, they did, you believe that?"

"So, where are you with Walter? Will he sit down with us again?" The boss asked, changing the subject as only he could.

"We may have caught a break." Frank said, remembering the look on his face when he arrived at the plant, during first shift, the day after Walter had called him about the shutdown. It was ashen, and angry. It said, 'I'm too old for this shit, but not too old to string somebody up by the balls for fucking us like this.' When he signed in at the front desk, the place was eerily quiet. And he felt like he was turning himself

276

to the police station for a crime he didn't commit. He snapped his visitors pass around one belt loop, and they buzzed him in. He caught the glaring eyes of accountants, HR employees, the secretary, even the janitors. Word had traveled exceedingly fast. The company was in it now.

The deepest of shit.

And in their minds the new salesman's shitty product had put them there. When he got out onto the floor, it was like walking into an enemy stronghold, with an entire battalion of troops staring daggers at him. They wouldn't help him when he went to the spray guns to take a sample. He could hear some the comments too. Shitty ass lube you sent in here. Done fucked us good. Don't know why we're fooling with it in the first damn place. Shitty ass lube. It was all Frank could do, not to turn around and say something back. But what? You couldn't just tell somebody on the floor to fuck off. That would only make it worse. If the situation was redeemable at all, it certainly would be long gone if he lost his cool right then. And technically, even though there was not a single shred of evidence to the contrary, it *could've* been the fault of the lube. That was part of the reason he was in there now, facing the music. Standing up for and behind his product like the boss had taught him.

Considering the circumstances, these guys were pissed off and justifiably so. Everyone. He filled up the small container with the same material that was sprayed onto the tools that allegedly caused the problems. The next step would be to take a sample from the fifty-five-gallon drum they were pumping out of. But they were using a dilution tank where they mixed the concentrated material with water to get every inch out of every dollar they spent on the lube. It was a polypropylene tank that was at least five feet by ten feet. Taylor unscrewed the red plastic lid on the top and reached his hand into the tank. And it reeked like a fucking sewer. Frank fought to keep from breathing through his nose, but the stench seemed to seep through anyway. When he felt liquid, he tilted the sample jar to fill it up. The stench from the tank was enough to make him want to puke. He could see black splotches of bacteria caked on the inner walls of the tank. They probably hadn't cleaned it out in years. That was one of the problems with a water-based product in a plant atmosphere. If it were to be exposed to the atmosphere, it was very susceptible to bacteria growth. But that in and of itself wouldn't cause every press to clam up. The integrity of the formulation wouldn't chemically dissipate to such a degree that it would work at all. It had to be something else. But it was necessary to gather as much information as possible to provide to the lab personnel so that they could isolate any and all variables.

After he secured the jar in his briefcase, he asked a man sweeping the floor nearby where the cage was. He looked up through very thick glasses, his hands black with grime and pointed over Frank's shoulder. Frank thanked him and headed that way.

A stocky man with a flannel shirt was holding a steel cylinder in one hand, wiping it out with a shop towel, and blowing on it intermittently.

"Excuse me." Frank said. But the guy kept on wiping and blowing.

"Hello, Excuse me?" Frank inched closer to the fence, raising his voice. The guy had to have heard him he thought.

Do all these guys want to cut my nuts off? He asked himself.

Wallace slowly turned toward Frank, but kept looking at his steel part, eyeing it with care. He moseyed toward Frank without lifting his eyes. To Frank, it felt as though this guy was telling him without saying it that this part was more important than he was.

"Yeah?" Still looking down and then finally up briefly.

"I'm trying to find the lube drums. Do you all keep them back here?" With that Wallace did look up, for more than a moment and scanned Frank's face.

"Who wants to know?" He asked, looking back down at the cylinder, flipping it over in his hands and holding it up into the light. These guys were a salty bunch, that was for damn sure. This guy was maybe one of those on a power trip. Everyone needs to come to the cage for something sometime.

Frank slid a business card through the slot. Wallace leaned over and looked at it. Frank noticed a row of shelves, with boxes of screws, pins, joints piled jaggedly on top of each other. One another shelf rested various casting plates, large wrenches, and tools. Behind them, Frank could see the drums of lube.

Wallace was still looking at the card.

"We were in the process of testing one of our products, and I'm here to get a sample from what you've got on the floor. Can I come in and check it out?" Frank asked.

Wallace went back to looking at his part, only this time he wasn't wiping or blowing. Just held it there and then looked back at Frank.

"Sorry, they told me not to let no one back here till we get up and running." He slid the card back through the slot, and Frank caught a brief glimpse of something on Wallace's wrist.

Something silver. It was a watch band. And from the look of it a new one.

"Who're they?" Frank queried. Wallace in the meantime turned his back on him, setting the cylinder on his work bench at the side of the cage, and walked back around the shelf with the boxes.

"What's that?" Wallace shot back over his shoulder, moving to another task as though the conversation was over.

"I asked you who gave you that directive. I was instructed to take samples from all available outlets. I need to get one out of those drums back there." Frank responded, his patience beginning to wear.

"It won't take a minute." He added.

Wallace ducked his headed behind two boxes, and turned to look at the drums, then back toward the opening in the cage where Frank stood, his heart starting to thump. He grabbed a wrench and drifted backward, peering through the crowded shelves. He then looked sideways, scrambling inside his head for something to say or do to make the guy leave. Fuck, he knew he shouldn't have let that other guy in that time. That was why the plant was down, wasn't it? This guy was coming to see about what had put him over the barrel, or the drum. He hadn't thought about that until now because all the chaos of the shutdown was out on the floor, not back here in the cage.

Everyone was preoccupied with all kinds of shit. Nobody asked him about it. It was like he didn't have no role and no purpose with all the stuff that went on out there. That must've been what he was banking on when he let that smoothly with the fat wad in here. No one was supposed to notice; no one was supposed to come looking for nothing. They always just came ambling up to the cage window looking for a part, or a tool. Clean this. Buff that. "I needed it yesterday, Wallace, so hurry the fuck up." They just came to see him when they needed something. And not one of them ever said thank you. I appreciate you. Fuck, no, they didn't. Been back in that cage damn near thirty years, and no one paid him any respect. He always wanted a Rolex. That wasn't too much to ask for, was it? Damn, that guy keeps saying he needs to get back in the cage. Trying to ignore him. Think he's the only one who needs something back here.

And he doesn't even work here. Fucker won't take a hint. He looks like a cop almost. Coming around here trying to collect evidence like one of those sumbitches in CSI or some shit. The fuck does he need a sample for anyway, not like a little bit can tell you anything. Damn, if my momma didn't tell me never to get in bad with the bad sort. That sooner or later it'd come back to bite you in the ass. Well, shit, how did he know the guy was going to put some damn nuclear glue in that

282

drum and shut the whole motherfucking plant down. Though maybe he was just trying to take some for himself, do whatever he'd do with it. What did they call it…reverse engineering or some fucking bullshit. Fuck me, running, he thought. He also wondered, "I ought to be bow hunting about now, or fishing for crappie not hiding behind the shelves in my own damn cage like some thief in the movies that took place in New York City where the guy ends up trapped in a bathroom stall or something because he's broke and up shit creek without a paddle with all the credit card debt and the landlord fixing to throw him and his wife and kids out on the street so he decides to cross the line and take one itty bitty shortcut thinking nobody would notice, but right then, the world instantly goes upside down and he knows like he does in a bad dream that he is fucked. But no, that money looked too good. And nobody ever just put it out there in my face like at. If he could just go back to that hot second when it just felt like the right play and tell that slick sales guy to go and get fucked a second and third and maybe a fourth time if he didn't leave. Stay honest with the company, be the guy that watched their back. Go and tell Walter about it and maybe he'd tell his boss and they'd put him up for a raise. Yeah, that was what he'd do. Fuck, why don't he just realize I don't want him in here because I got work to do and got a lot of shit to do and ain't got time. Tell him to come back on the back shift and get it from Harold." But Harold barely talked. Lost half his tongue when his daddy passed out drunk on a hunting trip, and Harold was too little to set up the hunting camp and started fooling around with the icicles that clung to the pine branches and one stuck in his mouth. His daddy was so fucked up he thought it was a knife and ripped the thing out with two hands while Harold screamed in terror. And Harold, shit, he was afraid of his own shadow because even his own shadow knew he was a pussy. Hell, he would probably just hide behind the shelf like he was doing and…what would Harold do? He'd probably hike up his britches and hit the fucking trail. But that was Harold, and everybody knew that was what Harold would do. They'd just pass it off that way. Fuck, what would they do to him if they found out he took that money and bought a hot watch and didn't say nothing when all the presses seized up like they did. They might send him to jail for industrial sabotage. They showed a video on it once in the break room. Most people on his shift fell asleep or sharpened their pocketknives or sipped on coffee and munched Doritos from the vending machine. Fuck, they just might call the cops on his ass right then and there.

The wrench slipped out of his hands, and being that he'd turned the screw all the way right a few minutes ago, the top part drove downward into the bridge of his foot. Fucking Fuck. Son of a bitch.

You alright back there? The guy in the power blue shirt called. "Shit-fire, motherfucker, hell no I ain't alright, that thing like to broke my foot." The sweat started shooting out of the pores on his forehead and down into his eyebrows. He pulled a shop towel from his back pocket and held it hard to his face, biting into and the cloth soaked up his saliva, and he could hear inside his head a small squeaking noise as his teeth wiggled fiercely into it.

The fuck was he going to do. He wasn't going to take the heat for this bullshit. Hell no. That other lube guy was the one who did whatever it was he did back there.

His heart was going off now. Could probably hook it up to the space shuttle and launch that motherfucker.

He looked around, and there was only one thing to do.

This time the wrench made a sound that caught Frank's ear sideways as he'd turned to look toward the shop floor to see men yelling over the din of squealing forks and darting sparks from welding tools as they hoisted the top side of a press away from the bottom it'd been sealed to.

Then Frank turned to hear what sounded like a door open quickly and bang hard against the wooden block that was planted against the wall outside. He saw a quick shot of daylight highlighting the cage in the back. And he kept calling for the guy who was acting weird and reclusive wondering what it was that had made him howl in agony and resist letting him just to get a sample from his own drum.

Walter fumbled with the set of keys anchored to his belt in a long loop.

Frank watched curiously. The beginning of a thought germinating. Where had the cage guy gone and why? There was an eerie ambiance at work in the plant. He could sense it in the operators. He could tell that everyone was on edge. It was not lost on him that as Walter found the right key and kicked open the cage door calling out for Wallace that there were plenty of things going on under this roof that had little or nothing to do with him. But what aside from the obvious? That was the question.

Walter yelled for Wallace. A determined and urgent look on his face. He ducked his head around the shelves and stomped to the back of the room and turned quick on his boot heel when he saw the thin sliver of sunlight sneaking in through the door in the back. He dipped his head slightly into toward his chest and push with both hands with a hint of resignation and exhaled loudly.

Frank followed him outside, and Walter kicked a crunched can of Diet coke that clanked a couple times over and over on the concrete.

"Fucking dumbass." He said. Staring off into the distance where a grunting pickup gurgled up the road hightailing it away from the plant like a rabbit trying to elude something way up on the food chain.

After a while, they went back into Walter's office and sat. He rubbed his head and looked up at the ceiling. Frank broke the silence.

"We will begin our diagnostic testing immediately. We will run the full battery and simultaneously send samples to an outside lab with instructions to conduct the same tests. That way we've got an independent screening and will see if our results match up, and what they tell us. We will test the solids levels, PH, density, viscosity, appearance, and odor and run an IR scan. And you have my word, if our product is indeed faulty, then we'll take complete responsibility. If we determine that the integrity of the product is intact, then we'll need to backtrack and isolate every possibility to arrive at the solution."

Walter nodded, and he'd been around long enough to know that it wasn't absolutely certain that the lube was the problem. He'd also seen it for two months without any

287

problems. The reason they were switching to it was that it was an improvement in terms of performance and cost. But it also wasn't the first time he'd seen things go to hell in a hand basket.

XXIV.

Spearing through a wind that belied its own breath, the horizon spun crossways and then tilted vertical so that his wings stretched fully, each feather layered with a deeper grasp of space. There was an opening between blustering tufts of clouds of deep blue that he steered into and slowed, hovering. His neck craned out and down, and his plumage dangled gently in the breeze. The terrain billowed and the fingers of hills joined in saddles created canyons and pathways to lower ground. Water flowed at the deep reaches of these canyons in some places leading to small patches where people had built towns and drove cars and raised cattle. He spied them from many perches. Sometimes daring closely to their fields when the tall pilfered strands of corn had been cut down by slow green machines with yellow rolling wheels leaving lumps of brown dirt and plenty of food. Moles were good. Snakes too. Rabbits usually could make it to the woods and that required a sleeker path of flight. This time he steadied himself in the higher altitude. Only with eyes like his could he see the mammoth machine on the faster moving wheels lurching to one side of the road where the buzzards sometimes gathered to peck away at the bloody red carcasses of deer and dogs and cats even. They tended to hunt in crowds. Sometimes circling for hours waiting for the blood of a bleeding animal to run out and fall to the silent leaves, maybe then one would land nearby and wait. Then his buddies would show. It was in two parts. The front was red and spit smoke. The back was long and metal like a cage and rumbled when it moved. He had followed its path. Earlier when the sun was merely etching the top of itself over the horizon and the air was cooler, he sat with his talons clenched around a telephone line and eyed the human man who also spit smoke from his mouth forcing several other human people into the opening of the back part. They were like the cattle when they were made to crowd into other back parts like this to be taken to places where they were made into food for the human people. He'd seen one of those places too.

The human who spit the smoke pulled down the cover to the opening with his human talons and threw a small burning white stick onto the hard and gray dirt. Then he pulled open a hatchway to the front part and climbed in. The two parts became one long part, and he watched it slowly inch forward and then merge onto the long hard path and increase his speed.

The cattle that he followed had openings on the sides of the back part, and once when resting on a fence post, the truck had gasped to a halt and the brown hairy beasts trapped in the human-made cage glared with dull eyes out at him. He wondered if they knew they were trapped. How could they not? Every living thing must be able to recognize such a horrible

290

fate. To have the freedom to glide through the air and dive through low level clouds and seize on some warm quarry to bring home to mama in the nest with the little ones taken away; no, sir, there could be nothing worse than to lose that. No matter how rough the world was out there. Rather have the chance to take my chances. All you can ask for. You get caught, trapped, hooded, and made to ride in a truck like these humans did to the plenty of others that were not humans and that were loaded onto the other truck would know.

Damn sure he would know.

Then there was the sudden movement the front part made like a rabbit changing course while being chased. Going against the grain. Going crossways across that very same hard and gray dirt toward a long league of green grass that ran between them. But he must not have seen the smaller moving thing behind him with another one of those human persons driving, but he was quick to react and managed to swerve around it, but then his moving thing got out of control, and it spun around like a winged blackbird tumbling down toward the green grass. Something made him inch closer, leaving the telephone wire for a branch in a pine and then to another tree closer behind some flushed limbs for cover.

Some blue jays seemed to scream at the sky, and they could be very nasty.

They were fearless and tenacious too. They weren't
onto him right then, could be plenty of other threats that
garnered their attention.

The big two parted things squealed when the smaller
thing dodged around it and shot past. Then the big thing
bumped and jolted when it dipped into the league of green
grass and turned sharply, but the back part couldn't do what the
front part wanted it to and then the front part and the back part
came apart with the back part crashing over on its side like a
dying elephant. The front part spit out a lot of smoke then, and
as they were joined together in two parts, he thought that the
human in the front would go back and lift the crashed over part
back up. But it didn't. The human jumped out for a second and
pulled something off of his head, and he seemed to look around
in every direction like a scared owl, and then the human person
moved with a lot of quickness back to the front part and
jumped in, slammed the hatchway like he did before only much
harder and wiggled his way out of the league of green grass to
go back onto the hard gray dirt in the other direction. It wasn't
long before he crested a hill and was gone.

He was curious why he left the back part there in the
middle, on its side. And why he left the other humans who
were still in the back part. But those humans did strange things
all the time. They needed moving things to move them. They

292

couldn't fly. And they sometimes liked to point things at you that made loud noises and spit smoke and rocks that could take a wing off in a flash. They were curious things. And it was very curious to him as he watched the moving thing and the human who was driving it inching backward with red colors on the back of his moving thing along the edge of the hard gray dirt toward the spot where the back part of the big thing was tipped over on its side.

Then the human slowly opened his hatchway and got out of the moving thing that wasn't moving anymore. There were no other moving things in either direction on the hard and gray dirt, and he was careful but fast when he ran across toward the back part that looked more like a trap than ever.

XXV.

Felicia stepped out of the shower and bent forward rolling a towel around her head. She looked in the mirror and wished she gone to the tanning bed that afternoon. She wrapped another towel above her breasts and stomach. Her shift started in an hour. It was Friday night and getting close to the end of the month. It would hopefully be a good night for tips.

She pulled on a pair of designer jeans, turning sideways to see how they fit her in the butt. Her legs were as toned as they'd been in high school. And she remembered a crass boy in the class above her telling her how her ass was so fine he could eat breakfast off of it. Maybe lunch and dinner too. It was a disgusting thing to say, but it was a compliment too. She buttoned her jeans and pulled a bra from a shelf in the closet. Her stomach was flat, with tiny knots of muscle showing beneath the skin. Searching through her t-shirts she settled on a black one that read in angel or devil in red letters on the front. It was tight but flattering. That was one part of the job that she couldn't help but like. Tight and sexy were part of the dress code.

After she was dressed and made up, she grabbed her jacket and walked to the kitchen. She filled a teapot, turned on the front burner of the stove, and tore open a small packet of green tea. Astrid was in the living room on the couch, rolling a fatty. She was watching a show about celebrities getting DWIs, going to rehab, and getting busted again within days of being released. Felicia walked behind the couch, looking for her purse which sat on the corner table.

"Oh my Gosh, did she get arrested? Again?" She asked, pausing to look at the television. The screen showed a mugshot of a recent "IT" girl with bloodshot eyes and swollen nostrils staring blankly into the police camera. Next to that they showed her walking out of a high-end shopping mall with glossy bags on each arm and a cellphone in her ear. A crowd of photographers formed a horseshoe around her and as the bulbs flashed, she flipped her hair and proceeded to a waiting Lexus.

"Yes, she was with one of those guys from that boy band, and they were doing lines in the parking lot of McDonalds at 4:30 a.m. And he got charged with public exposure because he was naked." Astrid said, not taking her eyes from the television.

"You'd think they'd get a driver or lock themselves in a hotel or something." Felicia said in mild disbelief.

"I know right." Astrid said, trying several times to get her lighter to spark. Then she held the joint away from her at an angle and lit the end.

"Want some?"

"No, I'm good. Have you seen my purse?" She asked.

"Right over here, hun." She said, pointed to the corner table.

"Thanks." Felicia grabbed it and walked back toward the kitchen as the teapot began to whistle in short spurts. She moved it to the back burner and opened a cabinet and pulled down a mug. She poured the steaming water and then dipped the little pale bag of tea leaves into it. The water turned to light green color, swirling around the string.

"Oh, how was that thing today?" Astrid muttered.

"What thing? Oh, the uh, the lecture." Suddenly feeling embarrassed, Felicia spilled the tea on the counter. Shit. Some of it got on her hand and it burned quick, like a sober reminder. She tore a paper towel from the roll and wiped the counter down, tossing it in the trash.

She thought everything was going perfect at the café. He was smart, funny, good looking, and seemed very interested. She'd given him every opportunity to ask her out, at least she thought she did. It wasn't as though she was an authority on dating or anything, but he wouldn't have had coffee with her and chatted so much if he didn't want too right? Or maybe he found her boring after or during some part of their conversation. Maybe he thought she was a hillbilly after telling him that story about the goat, dog, and donkey. No because he laughed a lot then. But come to think of it he did suddenly get nervous, and strange when they were out on the sidewalk. But maybe that was because she was basically throwing herself at him. She didn't throw herself at him, did she? Well, pretty much by just standing there like an idiot waiting for him to ask her out. And he just said nice to meet you, good luck in school. God, how humiliating.

"You didn't just ask me that did you?" Astrid said, exhuming a cloud of smoke still looking at the television. Felicia wiped up the tea with a paper towel and poured another round of hot water over the same tea bag.

"I know that sounds self-aggrandizing, but..."

"Self what?" Astrid asked, squinting at the television. The IT girl was walking out of the LA county courthouse, without any shopping bags, light bulbs still flashing.

"Stuck up or something. I just, I went on a date today." She said, sounding kind of like a confession.

"You did? A date? With whom?" Astrid turned down the volume, and turned around on the couch, rearranging herself amongst the pillows to get more comfortable. She rested her head on her arm poised to get filled in.

"The guy I told you about, the one who gave the lecture." she said, looking into her tea.

"You did not. Wow, girl. How did that all happen?" Her eyes were open wide with interest.

"I just went up to him after the lecture and we got to talking. He was really smart, a great speaker." Felicia said.

"Is he cute?" Astrid asked.

"Very." Felicia responded with a nod and looked back up at Astrid with a brief look of disappointment.

"Well, what happened?" Astrid wondered.

"We went to a café nearby and had coffee. He was really interesting and was very attentive. Not full of himself, you know? He asked me about my classes, about what I might want to do after I graduate. We told each other stories about…it was going really well or so I thought. I don't know. I think I misread the whole thing." She said.

"Did he ask you out again?" Astrid sounded a bit like a detective.

"No, he just, sort of…it got weird all of a sudden when we were saying our goodbyes."

"Weird how?" Astrid queried, shifting her legs on the couch.

"I didn't want to make another move you know…I thought I was already overstepping my bounds by asking him to have coffee in the first place."

"Wait, you asked him out...that's my girl!" Astrid clapped her hands quickly in front of her face and smiled. That made Felicia smile for a second, then she instantly felt more embarrassed.

"So, how did you leave things?" She asked excitedly, her eyes dilated.

"We walked outside and kind of stood there looking at each other, and it started to feel a little awkward, but I felt sure he was going to ask me out. I mean, it was like...it was going to happen you know?" Felicia said. And in retelling the scenario it still seemed like that was what should've happened, but it didn't.

"Aww, honey...sounds like he just kind of wimped out. Good guys kind of do that sometimes." She sat back down facing the television and reached for the joint in the ashtray.

"Or he just wanted to get the hell out of there." Felicia said.

"No, as hot as you are...he didn't have a wedding ring, or anything did he?" Astrid inquired her voice hollowing as she took a long hit.

"No, he definitely isn't married. That I could tell."

"Maybe he has a girlfriend. You never know with some guys." Astrid surmised as she puffed out a gliding plume.

"No, well maybe, I guess that's a possibility." They were hashing out the evidence like a pair of sleuths. Felicia glanced at her watch.

"Shit, I have to go…so, yeah, I essentially threw myself at him without knowing I was doing it. And he couldn't get out of there fast enough. The worst part is, that being with him, it just felt, natural…you know?" She said, sipping her tea.

"Oh sweetie, I'm sorry. Personally, I think the guy might just have a confidence problem. Either that or he's a dumbass when it comes to women. Some guys just have to get kicked in the balls before they wake up and smell the coffee. And besides, you're not the kind of girl that throws herself at guys. Trust me on that." She turned back to the television.

The IT girl smiled at the cameras and waved sheepishly as she entered a rehab center with her mom at her side.

Felicia slid into her car and pulled out toward the four-way stop and the end of their street. She turned left and headed to the bar. It was a good fifteen minutes to work. And she thought about why things could be so clear one minute and so confusing the next. How could you be sure about anything from one day to the next? She was a healthy, smart, attractive girl but that didn't mean that every guy you liked would like you back did it? Was there something wrong with her? Why didn't she have better luck? That was a stupid question she

300

thought and shook it off as she pulled out onto the interstate. The blinker flashed on and off as she merged onto the highway. The exit to the district was only a few miles or so away and she flipped the radio on. She found a channel playing a hip-hop song that she got into for a moment, then changed it to the alternative station. U2 came on with a poetic song about loss and love and misinterpreted signals and good intentions gone bad or something to that effect. It made her wonder deeper about things. It was natural to want to be wanted, wasn't it? A girl desiring attention wasn't the worst thing in the world. Why didn't he ask her out again? Maybe it was the way Astrid said it was, that he just wimped out. But that didn't make her feel that much better. Would she want to be with a guy who wimped out when it came time to step up? No. She was just like any other girl. She wanted a man to want her. To be in control. To be confident. To tell her things that made her stomach flutter. To touch her in a way that made her get hot down there. She wanted a man to be a man to her. He didn't have to be everything she ever wanted, just what she wanted right then. Maybe a tall one with dark eyes and strong hands. She wanted to be taken. She wanted to do things that would turn him on. Maybe wear slinky lingerie and do a strip tease for him as he sat in chair in a corner suite at a swanky hotel and undid his tie and maybe licked his lips while he watched. Then

301

maybe she'd go down on him with a vengeance. Things that she wouldn't dream of doing unless she was with a man that wanted her too. She wanted to climb on top of a man like that while he was driving his car and make him and make her come like she never had because he would go so deep wide and solid inside her...oh my god, she wanted to be wanted.

A horn blared beside her. She grabbed the wheel hard and veered back into her lane, barely making the turnoff just ahead.

When she got to the club, she pulled around back and parked on the street. There was an entrance at the bottom of some steps. There were cigarette butts and broken glass and a railing that was loosely connected to the cement wall behind it, the screws dandling between the holes and the mortar. A neon light above. Two large green dumpsters were open on the sides, and Felicia walked between them holding her nose. She paused at the bottom of the steps and fixed her makeup in a broken mirror. She took a quick breath to collect her thoughts and went inside.

XXVI.

"Hey man, what you got goin' on, buddy?" Everett hollered into the phone after he saw Taylor's name appear on the caller ID.

"Hey, man, what's up?" Taylor answered. It sounded like he was driving somewhere with all the air whipping around in the background.

"Buddy, we fixin' to get it on tonight!" He yelled back. Taylor pulled the cellphone back from his ear and grimaced. He had reluctantly called Everett back; he'd just been driving around town in a haze, resenting himself each time he stepped on the brake or looked in the rearview mirror. Just a fucking shell of a man. Not even a shell. He wasn't even the skin of a shell of a man in lieu of his most recent failure outside the café with Felicia. God, she was fricking beautiful. He just drove and drove and drove the rest of the day taking lefts and rights and going up and down the streets named after states like Michigan and Illinois downtown replaying the best afternoon he'd spent in a long time with a woman and the smartest one at that, and it kept ending the same way, and every time it, did he just take another left or another right giving himself some more road to find an answer that would let him go home and sleep with himself? He tried to come up with a reason or a rationale or an explanation for not manning up and asking her out on a date or

303

better yet reaching out for her hand and pulling her close and laying a splendid wet kiss on her lips holding her firmly so that she knew he was a strong man who was in control and was letting her know that, but damn, if he wasn't in a time machine so he could back to that sidewalk outside the cafe and do what he should've done, but in fact, he was just riding around downtown in his own car with nothing in it but a lot of gas and when the gas ran out he'd have to fill up again and what would he do then but drive around some more in a spiral that inevitably would not let him escape that same ending. He fucking knew he couldn't go home without the right ending.

"You there, Taylor?" Everett shouted back.

"Yeah, man, I'm here what's going on?" Taylor asked, jerking out of his haze.

"Hey, buddy, I just left the airport. Guess who I got shotgun?" He sounded excited.

"No idea." Taylor answered.

"Give you a hint; he might run a gas station or a Hampton inn in southern Michigan. Ow! Sorry man I'm just fuckin with ya." Everett said to his passenger but into the phone so that Taylor could hear.

"I don't know, man." He really loved Everett, he put the g r e in gregarious and was a good a friend as he had, and he could make Taylor laugh like there was no tomorrow, but

304

right now, he wasn't sharing his exuberance. And with that he sent a bolt through the cellphone.

"Haybeeb! Our friend from New Delhi. He just got in town and guess what he slid through customs like a bag of dope up from Colombia."

"Hay who?" Oh Habib. The guy you work with. What's he doing here?" Taylor asked.

"Hell yeah! He brought one tiny bag which I reckon has his undies in it and another one that's got…wait…one million two hundred thousand space bucks in it, motherfucker!

Oh my. Taylor thought.

XXVII.

"We shut their whole plant down, boss." Frank said.
Grimacing as he did so.

"Who's we? You got a turd in your pocket?" He said,
one eyebrow raised, reaching into his black leather briefcase
and pulling out two folders.

"We got the report back from the labs; we ran internal
diagnostics on the samples you sent in from that drum, and the
retain from that batch number. We also sent it out to two
different independent companies for analysis. And guess what?
The boss queried, while sliding a folder across the colorfully
tiled table, stamped confidential in red ink. Frank opened it up
and studied the comparative analysis charts matching field
sample versus retain sample. There was a drastic difference on
the Infrared Scan. The field sample showed an extremely
higher PH.

"You see those two lines we ran our retain against the
field in three independent labs...and all came back with the
same results. We wouldn't have caught it except the spike in
the PH. That can only be caused by an additive. The
composition of our formulation is nowhere close to that. All of
our retains for earlier batches fall in spec as well. So, this tells
us one thing."

"What's that?" Frank head lifted from the graph. The boss looked at him in total assuredness.

"That's there's something rotten in the woodpile."

"You think someone put something in that drum?" Frank asked.

"I don't think, I'm sure of it. You need to see if you can get back in to see Walter. And show him these test results."

"I don't know boss, I mean...I'll do everything I can but...I'm persona non grata in that place. There saying we cost them over a million dollars in scrap, and downtime, to say nothing of tooling damage." Frank said.

"That's exactly why we need to get back in. They need to understand, in no uncertain terms that our product is not responsible for this. But they also need to understand that somebody stuck it in our back and broke it off, and we're not going to take it lying down." Frank's adrenaline cranked up and met his boss' eyes.

"I'll make it happen." He said.

"Good. Now what are you going to have?" As he opened the menu, he cocked his head to one side and his eyes went wide at the myriad of combinations. You could get damn near one of everything with or without rice and beans if you wanted.

The boss was still perusing.

307

He added matter of factly, "And, Frank, if they give you any shit…tell them they can shove it up their ass or tell them you all can go outside and talk about it, then give me a call."

Frank smiled and loved the fact that the boss was more serious than he was kidding.

Plenty more.

XXVIII.

Colin chopped up four fat lines on the crystal plate on the kitchen island at his apartment. He had sliced through the large rock with a razor blade and spread them out evenly like a sous chef prepping an elegant meal. He got up and walked over slowly to his home theater system and thumbed through a series of DVDs. He found the one he was looking for and opened the case and ejected the tray from the DVD player, blew on it which sent tiny dust particles up into the air, and placed the DVD on the tray and pressed the close button. He had taken a shower after the lunch meeting with his boss, jerked off thinking about a threesome with two movie stars that hadn't actually been in one, but inventing the scene was as much a part of it as anything. Then he got out, dried off, looked in the mirror, and felt like million bucks. More than that. He had recently moved into a loft downtown, pimping it out with designer furniture on his credit card, and loading up on sheik ass clothes from Saks. Right now, he had on a pair of Jhane Barnes jeans, and a white, loose fitting shirt from Zegna. It was good to be making money. In fact, it was fucking awesome. The sixty-inch flat screen came to life with images of stars twisting into the background one after another and he counted them like he had since he was a kid. Every time they added up to twenty-two. And as they cascaded into a ring around mountain top they brightened and then they went dark. The next set of images showed a menu, with repeating trailer music showing his idol. Al Pacino in Carlito's Way. What a bad motherfucker that guy was. This movie had Sean Penn in it too. Could barely recognize him. The opening scene showed Al Pacino's character, Carlito standing up before a judge with a full gallon of gas.

He sipped on some whiskey he had picked up on the way home from St. Elmo's. It was the good shit. Expensive. He swirled it around in his mouth feeling a hot sting in his throat and stared out at the bustling streets of downtown below. The club he planned on hitting tonight was only a block and a half away. He leaned his head against the glass and smiled, his breath fogging up the window in an enlarging circle. Then he walked back to the island in the kitchen, his feet clopping along the prefab hardwood floors.

He looked around the new digs. The four fatties were still there waiting, almost talking to him now. The moment just before everything got started was his favorite. The place was so new he could still smell the cleaning lady.

Looking around the place his mind started concocting scenarios.

Fuck, he couldn't wait to bring the first one back here to watch her get wet as soon as she walked in the door and saw the space, the kitchen, the tall glass pane windows, and the view of downtown. The wine rack beside the subzero refrigerator. The pictures of French street side cafes hanging the brick walls. All the other pictures he'd bought off the walls of the studio nearby. Literally the ones off the walls. Didn't care, just give me the fanciest pictures in here he told the guy. Got the place all sorted out. When she walked in, he could give her quick tour, offer her some wine, maybe a line if she was into that, then maybe play some music and see if she liked to dance and if she did it would definitely be game on so after that part he could finally ease her subtly toward the bedroom and once she saw the four-poster king with two thousand thread count sheets and ten fluffed pillows that'd be the panty dropper.

It was a simple plan, like looking into the future and seeing how everything would go down. And if she was a good one, not some skank he'd call a cab for first thing in the morning, he might make some coffee and eggs for her. Keep her around awhile. In fact, having a girlfriend wouldn't be the worst thing in the world, it could actually be real.

Someone to come home to. Someone to do things couples do with each other.

311

Maybe.

The cell phone rang. He picked it up and read Mom blinking on the screen. He set it down without answering.

He rolled up a hundred-dollar bill and plowed through all four.

XXIX.

Taylor smoked a cigarette patiently and looked at the flat screens. They showed a baseball game between the Yankees and Red Sox. It was amazing how much people cared about their sports teams he thought. It was reported that the Yankee payroll for the year was over 200 million. What a racket. The players nowadays looked like they had air hoses shoved up their asses on a regular basis as big as they were. It had basically turned into wrestling. It was funny too how everyone had their panties in a twist about the steroid thing now when not ten years ago McGwire and Sosa supposedly saved the game by challenging for Roger Maris' single season record and bring fans back in record numbers to watch those two synthetic behemoths smash balls over the walls. It was a shame that you couldn't trust a frickin' baseball game anymore. But if you really wanted to get cynical, which at this point Taylor was verging on, what could you trust completely? The stock market crap game? No. Congress? Fuck no. Strippers? Obviously not. Yourself? Well now, isn't that the best question?

Why in the fuck didn't he just step up and ask her out?

It kept eating at him like a determined termite working his way through the foundation.

313

Every so often he shifted his eyes to one of the girls onstage. They seemed to keep a quick rotation. Maybe three songs and they'd be off to another one, or with one of the many perverted lost souls in there. He wasn't judging them. No. He was one of them. He just wasn't inspired by them like he had been. He slowly sipped on his vodka and soda, remaining careful about his intake. That was part, a big part of his problem the last time. When those conniving hookers took his ass for all that money. His upper lip rose on one side when he thought about it and his nostrils flared. But that wasn't the only thing eating at him. He didn't belong in this place. He belonged out in quaint wine bar with Felicia nibbling on Salmon Cru, cheese and capers and drinking a five-hundred-dollar bottle of Margaux. Talking about things that they both shared an interest in. Business. Animals. Politics maybe. She'd be dressed to the nines he thought. He could tell that she had excellent taste. Unique. Maybe wearing a shawl. She looked like a girl who'd wear one. But no here he was looking at half-naked dancing girls on a quest to give even with them. Fucking A. What a sorry son of a bitch he was. He fought the urge to pound his vodka and soda and order another one to dull the thoughts that ran through his head like rats on a dusty and dimly lit attic floor.

Habib's eyes shot open like he'd just found nirvana when they paid their cover charge and stood shoulder to shoulder scoping out the place. There were several stages, and it was relatively crowded. There was a bunch of boisterous guys surrounding one stage wearing their softball uniforms. At another there was group of well-dressed business types, ties undone and grins all around as they were hard at blowing off some steam. There were the usual solitary stragglers that you almost didn't want to guess what they did, or where they came from.

It was his second trip to the states. Habib had told Everett and Taylor about how he was in love with big breasted blond American women. All of them.

When they sat down at a secluded table toward the back, they ordered their drinks. They toasted Habib and his concerted efforts on the payback project. Everett volunteered to try out the forged dollars first. He said that he didn't want either of them to get caught before they even got started and since he'd been thinking about it non-stop since Taylor came up with the idea, and convinced his boss that he needed to fly Haybeeb over to work on a particular project with him directly, and hadn't had a good lap dance since the night he and his diabetic friend went to the joint outside Loogootee and had to hightail it out of the place because his buddy who usually kept

315

a couple of candy bars with him for the sugar fix had forgotten to do so and when they stopped at the corner store down the road from the tit bar all they had was a frozen ice cream sandwich and after his buddy had gotten a bunch of lap dances from some rather heavy and unattractive stripper and she wanted him to pay up he realized that he didn't have no money so he panicked and reached into his pocket, and it was while she had her head turned looking for the bartender or bouncer when he pulled her G string away from her jungle-bush and stuck that ice cream sandy down there and knocked over a couple of chairs on the way out.

It was because of all these reasons that Everett declared executive privilege and henceforth instructed everyone that he would go and see if could slip one past the goalie.

Neither Taylor nor Haybeeb objected.

So, they just kind of sat there like they were part of a bank robbery team, watching out front while their point man went in back to open the vault.

One song passed, then two. Then a third. Habib started getting his groove on as he began talking in a jagged mix of hip hop and Indian. He told Taylor that he loved the Snoop Doggy Dogg, Dave Chapelle, and he also like the Dixie Chicks but hated George Bush, and that if he could find a way to kick his ass when they were in the building, they'd take him home and make him their own private cowboy. His English was a little tough to decipher at first, but soon enough Taylor got the gist.

After a little while he asked Taylor about what kind of laws they had against counterfeiting in this state of Indiana.

"I'm not sure, Hay...I mean Habib, I mean, what kind of laws do they have against counterfeiting in India?"

"They cut off your hand for it in...ah...how do you say...legitimate business places, but in a naked dancing business place...they probably cut off your dick." Habib said, casting a glance toward Taylor that sort of resembled a mobster.

Jesus.

"Jesus. Seriously?" Taylor asked.

The waitress stopped back with a surprise round of chilled Don Julio Blanco.

"Gentleman, these are from the ladies over there." She was wearing so little, but so much more than the other girls in the place. Setting her tray on the table she handed Haybeeb and Taylor a glass, and grabbed one for herself. She stood back up and turned and pointed.

"See them, they think you guys are cute." She said. Habib was eerily in and not in shock.

"Well, they look cute too, from where I'm at." Taylor responded benignly.

317

"Did they buy you a shot too?" Taylor asked the waitress.

"Mmm hmm." She said as she sat straddling the arm of Everett's empty chair.

"How come?"

"They think I'm cute too, I guess." She leaned forward and toasted Taylor's glass, squeezed his quad, looked over Habib and dropped the shot back in her throat.

"I'll be back to check on you boys." She said, leaving Taylor smelling the shampoo in her hair and to watch the perfect curves where her ass turned into her legs while they made him wish Felicia was there.

He grabbed a cold frosty Bud Light and drained most of it. The chills ran through his skin, but he didn't feel low like he did earlier, and it wasn't entirely the booze boost. It was a different fuel he could feel beneath that. The buzz was good, but there was definitely more as sure as there was no Santa Claus, going on.

And for the time being, that made him feel good.

"So, they really cut off your dick, Haybeeb?"

"Probably only…how do you say…ah…like two-thirds of it. And then make you walk around the town square for days so everyone can see that you only have a nub." He said with a little more salesmanship. Taylor raised one eyebrow right then when he got the shot.

"You're fucking with me."

"Yes. I am fucking with you. Hehehehehehehehehhhhaaaaahhahahahhahha!" Habib let this maniacal laugh out, leaned forward, and grabbed Taylors pack of cigarettes. He lit one up and smoked it like Cheech, hacking up in between laughter. Taylor noticed his face started turning red if that was possible for an Indian guy in a dark corner of a strip joint.

Taylor motioned for the waitress who was headed back in their general direction. Again, Haybeeb's eyes fired up when she caught Taylor's wave. She had hair like Daisy Duke. But not quite the body. However, as far as Habib was concerned, it would do just fine.

"Yes? How can I help you gentleman?" She asked. And before Taylor could ask for another round, Habib stood up.

"Hello, you must be in the Dukes of Hazard. I have seen the movie and the television show. I have the first two seasons on DVD. Is it you please tell me, yes?" He said. Taylor gulped down a swallow and coughed a laugh of his own into his fist.

"Um...uh, excuse me?" She smiled, albeit a little bit stunned.

319

"In New Delhi, we love the Dukes of Hazard, but not the new bullshit movie with that…ah…the boy from the jack-off. We love the old…school." Haybeeb said, raising one eyebrow and shifting his weight just a little bit toward the waitress.

"I…uh, I always liked her. My older brothers loved that show. My friend has the first season too. That Jessica Simpsons got nothing on Barbara Bach." She said. Habib started nodding his head and grinning.

"Um, yes, can we have, ah, two more Budweiser's and one more vodka and soda, darlin?" Taylor interjected, mindful of the potential of bringing too much attention to their particular corner and the fact that Everett had still not come back from the VIP room.

"Sure, I'll be right back." She said, and backtracked from the table, smiling a bit nervously at Habib as she did. Taylor pulled Habib gently by the arm back to his chair, thinking he might try to chill him out a little bit.

"Dude…you have the original Dukes of Hazard on DVD?" That was apparently the wrong question because immediately Habib broke into a…version of Waylon Jennings' famous title song.

"Just some good ol' boys. Never mean no harm." He leaned his head back in the chair and Taylor smiled a real big one.

Man, this cat was a trip.

Right then, old Everett strolled up to the table wearing a grin that seemed to say you ever heard of the cat that ate the canary.

"Well, I'm him." His shirt was untucked all the way around and considerably ruffled up.

He sat down next to Taylor and smiled a new smile when he saw a fresh Budweiser arrive just in time.

"Damn, that's about the best fucking beer I've ever had. Mmm hmm. Whew."

The waitress left and shot a quick look back at Habib who tilted his glass at her, eyes steady in her direction.

As soon as she turned the corner, he turned to look at Taylor, who in turn turned to look at Everett.

"Well?" Both of those looks asked.

"Didn't bat an eye, my brothers. She just smiled at me like she was taking me for a fat wad like any other asshole in here. Now, I suggest you all go enjoy some of those hard-earned dollars."

Habib stood up and made his way to the main stage to entice a stunning blond with insane tits to go back and make some real money with him.

Taylor and Everett watched him, looked over at each other and their glasses made a quiet and beautiful clinking sound.

XXX.

The dirty brown slits of earth between the crops skipped past in the periphery like pages in a book as a reader did flip speedily with a thumb. The road was somewhat open today. But the weather was deceiving. A deep blue sky that grew darker the closer it reached the atmosphere. A tiny sliver of a crescent moon rested, and stars clung to their places scattered but still. He honked three successive times at dog that was wandering absently close to the shoulder in the ditch beside it. Poor little guy must have gotten out of a pasture and through a hole in a fence somewhere. He stuck his head up at the noises and in the rearview it showed its hindquarters and its tail wagged gangly as it bounded away from the roadside into the woods.

A family of silver chrome silos stood stuffed to the gills were huddled off to the starboard. They were segmented in heights, with an angular chute set from the top connected to the others.

The wind glided through the limbs and they glided back. He rolled down the window and lit a cigarette. The air shot a chilly blast through the crack. Tiny dots of ash failed to escape and landed on his black dress pants. He didn't brush them off instantly because they could streak.

He was south of Munfordville, headed north on 65. He'd stopped for coffee at the Hampton Inn in Horse Cave where he read the sports page in the *USA Today*. They were coming down on the baseball players that had used performance enhancing drugs. Supposedly. Now they'd just come out with a report that gave names. Some of the real big ones. But it was essentially heresy. Testimony of some guy that worked in the clubhouse. There was no real way to know if they did it or not. Unless if you believed what your own two eyes told you. Like if a guy's head grew two and a half sizes, at forty years old. The thing about it was that they couldn't prove anything. The drugs were ahead of the tests.

Kentucky had long been Cardinal country. Especially the western part and on up into Louisville. For long time they had their Triple A farm club there, but now it was over in Memphis. West Tennessee loved the Redbirds too.

Frank tossed his cigarette out and rolled the window back up. The last drag got down deep into his stomach and it wretched. He almost gagged, and probably would've puked if he'd had anything in his stomach other than the coffee. Fucking things. Damn it if it wasn't the one thing he couldn't give up. Or one of two.

He'd spent the night in Bowling Green. And made a rare but successful cold call early that morning. A Japanese

324

parent company had just completed construction of an engine plant and was in the process of conducting preliminary trials. Most of the raw materials were already spec'd in from Japan. But they were looking for domestic suppliers. The freight alone would kill them. Frank honed on that aspect, not only the proximity, which made delivery issues a great deal less worrisome. The man he met was local. And Frank was the first American salesman he'd met selling lube. It was fortunate to have caught him early. He offered to bring Frank back in in a couple weeks to meet his Japanese counterpart and bring some samples to start running trials. They wouldn't be up to full production for another couple of months, so the timing couldn't have been better. And Frank knew what they were running, and what he'd bring in that would, or should perform well. Didn't want to jinx himself.

But the day before was even better.

That Tennessee sure was a beautiful place. The people were as nice as they could be. And the bar be cue was something you could bronze. But that was gravy.

Frank had called on a customer that only bought a marginal amount of product. But they had increased their buying recently, not significantly but steadily. It was hard to divide your time and attention the way you might like to. Some people were just like friends, you wanted to call on them more often, but the fact was the numbers were what mandated the time you spent in a certain place. And they respected that down there in Tennessee. What had surprised him was when Gil, the plant manager, production manager, buyer, and the president of the company had taken him to the back where he showed him a drum of a competitor's material. They'd sent it in without a request. Didn't even show up, just a guy on the other end of the phone had called and asked a bunch of rapid questions, some of them abrupt and invasive about their application. Gil was like any businessman, always on the lookout for better and cheaper alternatives and had gone along with this sales call since he'd had a minute before a meeting. And typically, the guy would come down maybe and take a look at what they were doing and maybe bring a small one quart or one-gallon sample with him to run a small test with, but this guy just told him that he knew exactly what'd work for them and that they were the best in the game and if they just put it on line it would do great. Well, before Gil could tell the guy, not that we necessarily would have about the new projects, they were running that didn't have much to do with what they'd been running, and in fact the new orders he'd secured from three big, the three big Japanese automotive manufacturers they were going to have to expand the plant by nearly another 75,000 square feet, bring in twelve new presses and high at least fifty new full-time operators. But since the sales guy hung up before he could tell him all of that, not that he necessarily would have, a couple days later a fifty-five-gallon drum of this stuff showed up with no instructions or nothing.

He just let it set in the back next to some other empty drums back behind the boiler room near the loading dock.

Frank stared at the drum and the label on its side and felt a sneer creep up on his lip. He wiped it off quick though and bent down to study the label. Then stood back up and played it cool.

Gil kind of looked at him, with one eyebrow slightly cocked upward and didn't say anything, just kind of looked at it like was at a piece of an asteroid or a comet or something that had landed right there during the night. Didn't know what to make of it or what to do with it.

"Just figured I show it to you, Frank. But, I ain't gonna test it."

"Why not?" Frank asked.

"Well, for one thing I don't have the time to mess with it really." Gil said. Frank looked right at him as he took a deep draw.

"Didn't care for the man's tone when he called either. Kind of cocky if you ask me."

"That right?"

327

"Cocky fuck. Dime a dozen."

"He a young guy?"

"Maybe couple years younger en' you. Little taller. Maybe played ball as I recollect."

"Hmm." Frank stored this.

Then he explained to Frank the boom on the horizon. Frank leaned on a metal housing adjacent to a large holding tank behind him. Plumbing lines snaked up and around the ceiling above him. A massive 5,000-gallon cylinder three-quarter full of liquid, stood behind him like a bodyguard.

No one was around, just him and Gil, and he had the rare feeling that he'd reached a level in their relationship that was exactly where you wanted to be.

"That's awesome, Gil." He said.

"Yeah...we're trying to temper our enthusiasm. It's a big undertaking for us. But if you don't grow you die. Got to be always be looking for new, different and things. Everybody going green anymore. So, were betting big on the alternative energy thing."

"Sure, as a good long shit you do. We're rockin' in the same boat." Frank said, lighting his own cigarette.

"This new job, these new parts, we're going to need lube too. And you've got the first crack." He said.

Man. This was more than fair.

Gil went on.

"We've worked with you all for a number of years now and you've been one of our best suppliers. Always on time. Never hit us with a price increase. Great service."

"Well, shit, Gil, I wish I could spend more time down your way, but." Frank tended to take compliments sheepishly.

He pulled a cigarette from his shirt pocket and motioned for Frank to follow him over to the door. It opened and a wide-open field of winter wheat glowed green. A bulldozer inched along in the distance and sporadically plopped heaps of dirt into infant pyramids. Beyond them were and a couple men looked through a surveying instrument off to the left, shooting an azimuth.

Frank held out his lighter and Gil nodded when he took it.

"Aw hell, you don't need to worry about that, Frank, I'm the same way. You have to follow the money, or the potential. See that out there. Down to that tree-line?" He pointed with the two fingers holding the cigarette.

"We going to expand all the way out there, add a dock with fourteen bays. Guess it was a good idea to buy all that land when we first broke ground, hell, that was twenty-four years ago. It's fixing to be a ride I'll tell you what. But what the hell man, you only go around this deal once and not one of is getting's out of it alive. So, fuck it, penthouse or shithouse."

Frank laughed, it sounded like something the boss might say.

"The process is unique; we're among the first doing it here in the states. The molds are custom, Europe. Technically, we can make the parts but…"

"But what, Gil?"

"What I'm worried about is labor. It's an involved, and labor-intensive process, and the pool here and in the surrounding counties is thin. We need people that can come in and learn quick and be trainable. Work hard and understand this type of manufacturing process and the demands in a short period of time, so we hit the ground running when we reach capacity so we can really separate ourselves from our competition. We're going to need a manager too. One could handle all the stuff I'm going to have to give up."

"It's funny you mention that, Gil."

"Why is that? You know someone?"

"Matter a fact I do. His shop is closing, and he's got family within an hour of here. Sharp, standup guy. Been in the industry for almost twenty years. The whole skill set. Started out on the floor. Lead man after one year. Team Leader next,

then shift supervisor, eventually production manager. Name's
Syd O'Malley. He's looking too."

"No shit."

"None at all."

"Have him give me a call, will ya? As soon as
possible."

"On your cell or the office number?" Frank asked.

"Cell. Probably the best thing."

"Will do, Gil."

Gil stuck his cigarette in the tiny opening at the top of
the receptacle behind the door on the little square of concrete
and they both walked back inside.

"I've got those parameters for the new projects in the
office, we can head up there and grab em, make a copy for you
so you all can start working on some samples."

"How soon do you need to start running trials? Frank
asked Gil.

"Well, shit, Frank, how soon do you need the order?"
They both laughed. That one never did get old.

"Oh, so wait man, did you want to do something with
this shit?" Gil pointed to the drum.

It hadn't completely escaped his thoughts, something
like that just didn't.

It could be that he should do what had been done to him but in another way. Take it. Study it. Analyze it. Use it. Somehow. Find out where it was being sold in other plants and go at them hard.

Two can play at that game. But as easy as that was it was still cheating. You were either pregnant or you weren't.

Just like the baseball players. They had every excuse in the book. They only had one chance to make it big. The money was impossible to turn down. Almost everyone else was taking the stuff. If you had a chance to make a ton of dough and all you had to do was take a pill or rub some cream on your head or your arms or your ass who wouldn't right? I mean fuck it was a nasty world out there. What was cheating anyway? To one guy, it was sleeping with another man's wife. To another, it was lying to your wife about it. Was it cheating if you didn't get caught? Or if your competition was waiting in the weeds taking shots at your ankles when you walked past. Didn't they deserve some of their own medicine? Some people could do that and live with it. Some people buried secrets so far and so deep that they forgot they had them. Especially when they never got caught. But what then?

You still had to look in the mirror.

"I'd send it back, Gil." Collect.

Gil looked him in the eye. Then smiled the way a proud uncle might.

"Come on, let's go?"

The sun soaked the shine out, and you could catch a bit of the rust beginning to show. The tops of the silos weren't the conical shape, but a half circle like the parachutes that the 101st Airborne used during the Normandy Invasion. Maybe in another life that's what they were.

He hadn't felt this good about himself in a long time, despite the tarred aftertaste of the cigarette.

This morning things were clearer and more resonant to his eye, like the silos and the winter wheat or the barn coming up on his left that must have been a hundred years old with boards chewed out and the joists rotted and the roof tilted in a gradual slide with tree limbs reaching through places that had altogether given out like it was itself biodegradable. Receding slowly into the earth long after it had been retired. A hundred years is a long time if that was how old it was, and now, it seemed to be just easing gracefully toward the ground, like everything and everyone should when their time was running thin.

This part of the world was truly beautiful he thought to himself, but it took the right perspective for him to appreciate that fact, because other times when he was swarmed with loneliness and bitterness it was an ugly and barren and desolate place. Negative thoughts could crawl all into his own mind because he was naturally a social person with a lot of friends, but to make it in this racket he had to do it alone, and that meant, he'd have to be alone, and take a whole lot of rejection.

But, it had to do with the decision he'd made not to do anything with that drum.

It was discipline.

True discipline meant doing right by your own self when no one else was around to see it.

When no one else there to judge your action. No one else there to tell you what it was you were supposed to do. No support system. Just you and your choices.

Frank looked off and saw a green John Deere tractor with solid yellow wheel wells. There was one of them on nearly every acre of every field in this part of the country. It moved as slowly as a barge going up a river against a southbound current. Like it would never get to port. Things looked a certain way in just an instant. As you rushed past in your car or cast a fleeting glance and only had a moment to invest a prediction or a wondering thought about that thing's plight, or its future it inevitably seemed small. Like the tractor or the barge and the driver or the pilot because you were only passing through. Their lives were not even a fraction of importance to yours. So, of course they seemed dim. Frank thought ended and turned back to his own.

He'd passed something akin to a test. Or, a test.

He'd been tempted but didn't take the bait.

Granted, Gil was there, but he was only there green lighting a short cut when nobody else was there to see it. He was opening up a hole in the fence just enough so Frank wouldn't get his shirt sleeve, or his pants pocket snagged if he were to go on and step through to the other side. He'd been there holding open the same way when he we're come back through.

A favor. Just among friends.

But he was just offering, not putting a gun to his head.

Frank thought about going through the wire. No doubt. He thought about cutting the payback check the short way. But something kept him from doing it.

It may have been the miles on the interstates or the state highways or the county roads or the two lane highways or the one ways and all the nights in the sour spring beds with rattling air conditioners and fuzzy televisions or the many times a receptionist turned him away that he both couldn't and wouldn't duck his head and shoulders and slide through that hole in the fence even if just for the slightest of moments when no one would know a thing about it to steal that shit and cut that motherfucker the way he cut him.

But something kept him from doing it.

His boss wouldn't have done it.

Because he would've found a better way.

There was always a better way. You just had to earn it, before and even after you found it.

XXXI.

He was so high he could hunt ducks with a rake if he wanted to.

He walked down Michigan Avenue under the Circle Center mall past the PF Chiang's and Nordstrom's and watched people in Pacer jerseys and jackets cling to each other at the stoplights, waiting for the walk sign to come on so they could get to game against the Heat. The weather had changed for the better, typically it was much colder this time of year. Colin wore a thin black leather jacket with his smokes stashed in the inside pocket. He had something else stashed inside them too. He carried three hundred dollars in a silver money clip, and his driver's license, house key, and cellphone. Keeping a slightly brisk pace, Colin grinned at some women who were walking with their dates going the other way just for the fun of it. He reveled in the fact that they glanced at him when they passed, some even making eye contact for longer than they should. He cocked his head a time or two when their dates caught wind of the passing connection. Just to let them know.

He couldn't help it.

The bar was just at the end of the block.

When he walked in, he stopped for a second and scanned the room like he was the owner.

Then she bumped into him as she was walking back to the bar.

"Sorry oh, I'm sorry, don't I know you?" Felicia asked.

"You know what? I believe you do. Colin." They were close and she loved his cologne. His eyes were a deep color, and a little bit dilated. Okay maybe a lot dilated like one of those rock stars Astrid stared at dreamily when she was either high or sober and he had the same kind of dark rings under them which should've made her some kind of weary but instead seemed alluring and made him even more sexy.

"Felicia." He also had big hands. And he was tall.

She got up around 5 and found a long silk shirt from his closet and slid it on. He was laying on his side with his rippled back edged out from the sheets, his bottom arm tucked under the pillow and one of her feet drooping over the end of the bed. She smiled and made a small sound and then glided over the hardwoods barefoot out of the bedroom and into the kitchen. The fridge was platinum and a cascading light emitted onto her leg as she opened the door. He was, to be sure, a bachelor. She rose up on her toes and looked for some juice. There was one bottle in the back on the top shelf. Behind some big Boddingtons and Guinness. A bottle of Crystal. Some ketchup. Grey Goose. Some Godiva chocolate, and strawberries. She took those down with the juice. What was he doing with

338

chocolate, strawberries and champagne? She asked herself. But didn't answer right then. She silently slid her bottom onto one his bar stools. She picked up the strawberries between her thumb and index finger carefully avoiding spilling any onto the shirt. She sipped at the juice and looked out the window. The city was lit up. She could the see the RCA Dome lit up. The Eli Lilly campus to the east. Red lights lighting up briefly at stop lights and then glowing lower as the lights turned green and the cars they were attached to moving away. Being up high felt good. Seeing it all when it couldn't see you.

The rush of it kind of hit her. She just slept with a guy she didn't know. Hadn't dated. Didn't even know his last name. But the look he shot her every so often from the corner of the bar made her tummy sink and then jump back up and gave her the urge to let out a little scream because you want to smile but you don't want to do that too much because then he would know how bad you wanted to rip off his shirt and wrap your legs around him and ride him until the sun came up. So you just kept that feeling inside and rode an inner roller coaster as you slung drinks and smiled at the other guys at the bar who you knew you wouldn't go home with and watched the tip jar fill up all night long.

And she knew she was going to the moment they bumped into each other when he came in the bar. And she sure did. She did things with him in that huge bed and in the two thousand thread count sheets that she'd never done before. And he knew how to touch her. Just what she had wanted in that moment.

Then she looked over and saw the plate on the counter. She hadn't noticed it before.

She rolled up the hundred-dollar bill and the powder in a clumpy pile right next to it.

She licked a strawberry and tuned out any thoughts of her doting father, her mom, several proud teachers from high school, and the sweet guy that she wanted to go out with but who didn't seem to have the guts to ask her and what Astrid looked like most mornings when she stayed up late and put the bill in her hand and inched over the granite countertop with her nipples hard and cool on the surface and the spot between her thighs getting warm again and that same rising and dropping feeling in her stomach and snorted a sharp burst.

She leaned back and held her finger to her nose, her eyes tingling and her throat burning with the drip. And she instantly felt...

"What are going to with the rest of those strawberries?" Colin asked. Leaning on the bedroom doorway in his boxers.

Wanted.

"You're about to find out." She answered, sliding out of the stool and unbuttoning the silk shirt.

XXXII.

Frank pulled the bolt from the door and swung it back. He had the feeling he should call the police and wait by the side of the highway until they showed up, but something he felt made him go over to the abandoned trailer. He couldn't explain it if he had to. The highway was remarkably empty. No other trucks. Travelers, tourists or vans. Just a wispy and lingering fog and steady slivers of rain.

After he got his bearings from the spin, his heart rate settled back to a nominal state, he instinctively popped the door and stepped out onto the shoulder. He waited for a few moments as though a racing vehicle could rocket through and wipe him out like a bug on the windshield then ran across to the other shoulder and stepped into the high weeds toward the motionless trailer. It was like seeing a UFO land in a desert and instead of running as far away from it and whatever may have had just crash landed into his life he just, breathed in, looked both ways, and went toward it. There were no placards on the outside.

Could be a load of cash in there. Garments headed to New York. Maybe produce. Or explosives. Maybe drums of his product on their way to an expecting customer. But it wasn't any of those things.

He fell back when four sets of eyes met his from a corner between the precarious edges of wooden skids, strewn in a ragged cluster.

He caught himself without falling to the ground and saw the silver white belly of a red-tailed hawk with its wings spread wide with a gliding confidence and then dart with close precision against the impacted gray clouds above and pulled himself back up. It all seemed like a twilight moment, things frozen in plain view and his interaction with the world mattered reverently with each, and every motion. From the moment he steered to avoid the cab as it bent suicidal across the interstate to the first crunch of his urethane shoe sole on the gravel of the shoulder the world seemed incontrovertibly still, with only *his* movement consequential.

When one spent innumerable hour's in thought, like a cowboy building a fence in Wyoming, or a hawk listing amidst midwestern cloud cover, it came to him that way partly as a quotient.

One of them rose and the rest scurried toward the back as though they were prisoners, and he was the guard coming to take them to the courthouse.

He asked if they were okay.

They didn't say anything.

343

Just kept moving to the front of the trailer knocking skids this way and that.

It's okay, he said. But they didn't seem to think so.

Frank was not afraid exactly.

It's okay. He said again. And held out his hands.

They still said nothing. Just huddled closer into the corner behind the pallets trying to squeeze another inch of distance between them and him. Then Frank could make out their complexions, and their clothes. He hoped they weren't carrying weapons. And it hit him.

"No estoy la policia. Yo soy solamente un hombre. Manejando mi coche cuando tengo cambiar lineas rapidamente, porque esto truck, ah…trucko… never mind. Quiero ayudar." He recalled the words from a few courses of Spanish in college as though they were native. Rusty but real.

"No estas la policia?" The one closest to him asked in a quick and quiet voice.

"No. No. Solamente un hombre trabajando." Frank answered. And motioned with his hand toward his jacket pocket.

They eyed him with intense uncertainty. He pulled out a pack of cigarettes. Their eyes opened wide.

"Quieren cigarillos?" Frank asked. Almost a full minute passed.

"Si." The same one answered and eased past his partners in transit and walked slowly toward Frank. He held out a pack with one sticking out further than the rest and the man took it. He couldn't be more than twenty-five. But his face was stained with exhaustion. Frank lit it, and the man closed his eyes as he inhaled.

"Gracias." He sucked it back ferociously, nearly finishing it in two drags.

"Do you speak Ingles?" Frank asked.

"Un pocito solamente." Frank was relieved to an extent. His Spanish was about the same.

"You are afraid of the policia...yes?"

"Si. O el immigracion." He answered. Frank held out the pack again, sensing the man's need.

"Okay. Well. Then you better come with me. Right now. Because someone will call somebody else and they'll be here before long." The man looked at Frank and even in Ingles he understood the gist but did not trust him.

"Donde?" He asked, not wanting to trade a bad situation for one worse.

"Tengo un idea. Mi nombre es Frank." Frank stuck out his hand.

"Mi nombre es Rafael. Mi primos Jose y Jamon..."

345

"Okay. Ahora, vamonos." Cesar motioned to his cousins who were no less nervous than before, but awkwardly and as though they were emerging from a jungle thicket crept from behind the pallet shadows into the inexhaustible gray light outside.

Frank led them across the empty highway. He was amazed that he didn't see one car going either way. How many went by when he was in the trailer? He didn't know. But it was only a matter of time before somebody called it in or a trooper caught an eyeful and picked up the radio.

They got in his car and Frank looked in the rearview before he dropped a heavy foot on the gas.

The Hampton Inn was only a few exits up the highway. The parking lot was empty save a Cobalt and Malibu parked next to the handicapped spots by the entrance in the back. He pulled around to a spot by itself, out of view from the front desk windows.

"Stay down. I'll be right back."

"Si. Senor Frank." Rafael said. Then he repeated the instructions to his friends, and they looked quickly through the windows and slid downward as though making themselves invisible against the leather seats in his silver Cadillac.

His blood was pumping feverishly, but he didn't feel scared. He had the riveting wind inside himself that came from

346

a good source. Despite the obvious legal ramifications, Frank felt okay with himself and this incredibly unknown course of events. Part of it was because he knew in his heart of hearts that there couldn't be anything ultimately wrong with helping some people left for dead on a highway median in the back of a truck. The other part, well…shit, sometimes in life you just must make a choice. Especially when no one is around but you when that time comes.

"Hello, sir. How can we help you today?" A perky lady behind the front desk asked.

"Hi. Have you got any rooms available today?" He asked, noticing the plastic half-cylinder steaming with the heat from a heap of freshly baked chocolate chip cookies on the ledge of the counter.

"We sure do. What were you looking for?"

"I need two, with two queen beds in each. Preferably on the first floor, by the exit, and smoking, if at all possible." Frank responded.

"How many adults and children?"

"Ah…two adults in each, no kids."

"Any groups or conferences?" She asked, tapping her keyboard briskly.

"No. But I've got my Honors card." Frank said and pulled out his Diamond VIP card. She instantly became more attentive when she saw the embroidery on the top.

"Well, thank you for your continued allegiance with us...Mr. Cusco? Did I say that right?" She asked, cautiously but with a smile.

"Sure did." She ran a few more things on her computer and Frank's impressive profile appeared on her screen.

"Wow, you've been with us quite a bit."

"What can I tell you? I'm loyal."

"We sure thank you for that. Okay, we've got you in two rooms, two queen beds for how many nights?"

Good question, he thought.

"Five for now."

"Very good. We can handle that. Should I use the Visa you have here on file?"

"No...actually, can I use Hilton Honors points?"

"Well, of course, you sure can. Looks like you've got plenty."

After he signed for the room, he got back into his car and handed out the little blue envelops with the room numbers on them.

"Estos su cuartos. These are your rooms. Now just follow me."

They had confused and uncertain looks on their faces, but they followed Frank, nonetheless.

He slid one of the keys in the magnetic slot and the door unlocked with a jolt and a buzzing sound followed.

The rooms were across the hall from each other, right on the end. The red light turned green, and Frank turned the handle and motioned for them to follow. All four of them did and their eyes glazed at the cleanliness, the neatly folded white sheets on the beds the large mirror on the wall over a big desk and the size of the television and the small box on the wall that had numbers blinking on it.

It was beyond surreal.

Then one of the guys asked another one a question in Spanish.

XXXIII.

Astrid was trying to squeeze the last bit of butane out of her lighter, but it would only spark as she thumbed it frowning. She loved to wake and bake. She loved to lunch and bake. When she thought about it, there wasn't an hour in the day that she wouldn't go for a hit. Before work, during break, before bed, when she got out of bed to pee in the middle of the night. She considered herself at one time to be what people called a functional pot smoker. Someone who accomplished tasks, or chores, went to work and didn't skip a beat. But now it was like lifting a massive boulder to get up off the couch and carry a basket of dirty clothes to the laundry room or even sometimes to wash her face before bed. Going to work at the restaurant was manageable, for one thing she needed to support her habit and the guys in the kitchen always had the best stuff. But it was getting to the point that she wasn't so much getting high anymore as she was just trying to maintain her buzz. And the little joy of anticipation she used to feel before firing up a bowl had gradually been replaced by an almost robotic dullness. In fact, she barely even noticed that she wasn't doing it for the enjoyment anymore.

She set the lighter down and looked up as she heard someone jingling keys outside the door.

Felicia walked in and said hey very softly, smiling quickly.

Astrid saw something different in Felicia's face. She looked rough. But she also had something close to a sly smile. She still had her natural prettiness, even in the same clothes she had been wearing the night before when she left for work. But her cheeks were a little puffy, so were her eyes.

"Looks like someone stayed out past their curfew." She said, leaning back on the couch and watching Felicia walk into the kitchen, set her purse down on the counter and open the fridge.

"Do we have any juice?" Felicia called from behind the door.

"I think so." Felicia moved several things around and found a vitamin water. She opened it and closed her eyes drinking almost half.

"We need to get some juice. This stuff is just sugar and coloring stuff in the water." She said, walking back into the living room.

"So...where'd you stay last night?" Astrid asked.

Felicia took another drink.

"I went home with a guy I met at the bar." Astrid's eyes launched open.

"You...who?" She shot up like she was spring loaded.

351

"His name is Colin. He has a loft apartment downtown. Really sheik." Felicia reached over and took one of Astrid's cigarettes and pulled a lighter out of her purse. Again, Astrid was surprised. She studied Felicia as she coolly tapped the lighter with her smoke and lit it as though she'd been smoking in French sidewalk cafes since she was a teenager. She watched like a she was seeing a magic trick repeated slowly but not understanding how it worked.

"I thought he was cute. He played it cool but just, you know had it going on. I could see plenty of other girls, cute girls in the bar checking him out. And you know how it can be in the bar some nights, he just stood out from the crowd and got me in his tractor beam or something."

"Did you sleep with him?" Astrid asked, bluntly.

"Oh yeah, like…four times." She said, leaning forward and tapping into the ashtray.

"Wow. Sweetie. I'm…honestly…um."

"Shocked? I know…me too kind of." And she giggled a little. Putting out the cigarette and instantly lighting another.

"Did you…like talk to him this morning?" Astrid asked.

"Actually, we did it a fifth time this morning." She said holding up five fingers and looking at Astrid incredulously.

"When was the last time you were with a guy, like that?" Astrid wondered.

"Too long. Way too long. I mean…he was very experienced… but I think we had a connection, like I wanted him so bad from the first conversation. I felt like he was like…I don't know like a lion or something prowling around without any pretenses or agendas or…hang-ups. I knew right away where things were going to end up. I mean don't get me wrong, he is gorgeous. Ripped Astrid…eight pack. Arms. Butt. Toned everywhere." Astrid was listening intently, and she sensed a fluctuating rhythm in her friend's voice. She was thinking out loud and saying things that didn't sound normal for her. Then again, this was a situation that was quite out of the ordinary anyway.

Felicia went on and described his eyes, voice, his hair, what he did for a living, his apartment. But Astrid got the feeling she was leaving something out.

Felicia squashed out her cigarette and stood up quickly, and sniffled her nose, and rubbed her index finger under it.

"I'm going to take a shower." She said. And got up.

"Okay." Astrid said, and watched her kind of apprehensively. She looked back at the television for a second and turned down the volume on the remote.

Felicia dropped a little bit of coke onto the sink and snorted it sharply before slipping out and leaving her panties and skirt and Colin's silk shirt in a ball by the bathtub and stepping into the shower. Her skin burned quickly pink. She reached for the body wash bottle on the porcelain ledge with her eyes closed and it made a fart-like sound when she squeezed it into the scrub loofah and began to exfoliate. Her heart had a fast-thumping sensation as she couldn't help the images of the night from tickling back and forth in her mind, and her fingers. She was just into the one where he had a strong, surging fist of her hair, and she was looking back at him with her eyes closed when the water ran so cold, she almost screamed.

XXXIV.

Colin went to the gym after Felicia had left. He
coughed a few times while stretching, breathed heavily after
finishing a set of sit-ups. It wasn't as easy as it used to be. The
bicep curls were next, then the pull-ups and the dips. Supersets.
They were a bitch on a morning like this. But he hadn't worked
out in over a week and a half. He didn't want to fall behind.
The ear-pods was jamming. He liked the sensation of sweat
dripping from his eyebrows, getting lost in an absence of
thought and charging ahead like you had your own private
mission. The gym was on the second floor of the building and
had large windows looking out onto the street. It was great
because it was open twenty-four hours a day, seven days a
week. They had all the new kind of equipment. A smoothie-
bar. A steam and sauna in each locker room. And it was loaded
with ass. Almost any time of day there were some young
hotties pumping their toned and tanned legs and swinging their
ponytails on the elliptical machine or a talented cougar
working the exercise ball. Plenty of ass to go around.

Colin strained to do an extra pullup, feeling as though
he weighed three hundred pounds on the last couple inches to
get his chin over the bar. Closing his eyes and struggling, veins
bulging in his neck he tried to kip and swing over but couldn't
quite get there and let go and swung down and almost lost his

footing on the rubber mat. When he opened his eyes, he saw scant flashes of light darting in his periphery. His heart seemed to push the skin over his rib cage forward with each beat. He breathed in deeply and looked at his reflection in the full-length mirrors across from the pull-up apparatus. It was hard to see clearly with the sweat that was leaking into his eyes, so he wiped them with his fingers and took several steps closer.

His eyes were shot full of blood, and his pupils were like gaping black holes. He had puffy rings under the rings under his eyes. Colin instinctively popped his shoulders back and walked to the drinking fountain. Leaning over and closing his eyes again he thumbed the button.

The water ran into his mouth and down his throat.

When he stopped, and stood back up, a woman looked at him like dead in the eyes.

"Hi." Was all he said.

"Hi. You mind if I?" She said pointing to the fountain.

"Sure, I'm sorry." He said moving out of the way but still looking at her.

She was maybe five feet, seven inches, 110 lbs. She had abs and tan skin, tightly cropped hair and brown eyes. Peach colored top, black bottoms. She could've been thirty, but probably closer to cougar territory, in and around thirty-nine was Colin's guess. Only because of the brief look she'd given

356

him, which kind of had a mix of "I know what kind of boy you are and what you were up to last night and you're in trouble with the teacher and also that it wasn't the kind of trouble she'd tell the principal about." And the way she didn't hesitate when she bent over to drink. Not that she stuck her ass up in the air, but more like...discreetly put it out there for a second. Fuck me, Colin thought.

She wiped her mouth with her forearm and her lips curled into a sly smile. But she didn't say anything else, just turned away and moved toward the line of treadmills. Colin got another quick drink and moved himself over to the area where the large inflated balls rested against one another.

Taking one of the bigger balls, he stepped up onto the platform to do both some stretching exercises and sit-ups, and strategically position his line of sight to watch the lady from the drinking fountain start her jog on the treadmill.

His back had been killing him, so he arched over the ball and felt his spine elongate, tweaking near his lower back, and heard the small popping sounds as air released between his them.

The blood flushed his head and he breathed slowly to keep from getting dizzy. He searched the various mirror locations and sized up a geometric trajectory directly in line with a pair of firm buns of the cougar lancing away on the treadmill the way he'd set up a triple bank shot in a game of nine-ball.

His heart throttled forward when he glanced from her butt to another spot on a different mirror and caught her looking at him with that same smile from in front of the drinking fountain. Good God! Was this one way to flirt with a woman? Upside down across the room through a fucking mirror, he thought.

Man, I should go straight to the crap tables.

XXXV.

Felicia stayed in the shower for a long time. Things felt a little strange. Not a little. Maybe more.

She scrubbed hard. Bubbly clumps dripped off her legs and fell to the sink, swirling in mass.

The sobriety of the moment crept up on her like a savage parasite. A few hours ago, it felt wild and cool and exciting to have gone to bed with a sexy stranger and do things that she ordinarily would never think to go near but that was a few hours ago and now that elevated moment was turning into something else. It turned into a sinking envelop of shame. She felt dirty.

Something she wanted to scrub off. She squirted more body wash into the loofah and stared at the tile wall. The water hissed. She wasn't feeling as proud of herself anymore. And she scrubbed harder now, as though she could pull the decisions she made away from her skin if she squeezed pressed and focused hard enough.

When she got out of the shower, she jolted when she reached for a towel. Feeling kind of disturbed with herself.

XXXVI.

Frank felt his cell vibrate in his pocket right as he was going to open the door to the T/A truck-stop. He pulled on the handle and held it open for two ladies that were carrying bags of gummi bears and forty-four-ounce sodas. They said, thank you and he let go of the door. The incoming call was coming from Syd.

"Yes sir, how are you, Syd?"

"Well, I'm making it, Frank. Where you at today?"

"Kentucky."

"Is that right? How's things on the road?" Syd asked.

"If I told you, well you probably wouldn't believe me"

"Ha-ha. That's for sure. I got your message. What's going on?" After Frank left the guys at the Hampton, he'd put in a call to Syd, at the house. Would you give me a ring when you can? Was what he said.

"So, what's happening, Jackson?" Syd asked.

"Believe I got someone you might need to call." Syd paused…for a good few seconds.

"That right?"

"Does the pope wear a funny hat?"

XXXVII.

Astrid went for a walk in the morning. It was early and the fog drifted above the neighborhood streets. She tried to keep her breathing under control, but even though it felt good to be exercising and breathing in the morning air, there were plenty of inert and smoke sweltering nights in her rearview that wouldn't go quietly. She coughed. Then she stopped and her head started to ache. She put her fingers on her temples and rubbed.

The night before after Felicia came home and didn't look or sound like herself, she had spent some serious time thinking about things, and her life. And her friend. At the end of that thinking she started to get scared. And just as soon as she got scared, she had a strange but robust feeling to address what she knew not only from all the television shows she watched to be issues. And she knew that it might be time to make a change. Something about her friend made her look at herself. She waved briefly to a couple walking their yellow lab going the other way on the opposite side of the street. They looked like a nice normal couple. Just out walking the dog together before they started their day. Or that was the start of their day.

She kept walking and coughed a little bit more, and the aching was still there but not as bad as the beginning. After

361

another fifteen minutes, she found herself back at their little house. She stopped and picked up a broom that was resting against the retaining wall alongside the house and swept up the front porch. Then she went in and picked up the wrappers and bottles and pot from the coffee table and threw away the trash and flushed the pot down the toilet, watching it swirl away in green clusters.

She dug through the closet and found the vacuum cleaner. It was covered in dust. She pulled the cord all the way out, plugged it into the outlet behind the couch, and went to town. After that she pulled the blinds and let in the sun that was just steering its way over the horizon and into their neighborhood. The coffee pot was dirty too, so she cleaned that. Then looked for the mop and bucket, and after she found some vinegar underneath the sink, she measured out the right amount and mixed it with some water and then remembered that she should probably sweep up the floor before she mopped it so she went back outside and grabbed the broom. She hadn't had her hair up in a ponytail for a while and she had to look for a ponytail holder because she didn't notice that it kept falling into her eyes during all the activity. Sticking the broom along the baseboards she saw something but didn't pay too much attention. My God, this house was a mess, she thought. She put her hands on her hips and exhaled. But she didn't cough.

It was then that she looked back down at the ground at that thing she had seen a minute before and cocked her head for a moment and then got down on the floor and saw a small business card sticking out from the corner of the fridge. She picked it up and read it.

It was the guy who didn't ask Felicia out. It must have fallen out of her purse when she had rushed out the door on her way to the bar. She never did mention that he'd given her his card.

She spent most of the morning scrubbing and dusting and cleaning and by noon she sat back on the couch and felt the urge to have a bong hit, and a cigarette. The aching in her head which had gone away in the course of the housecleaning, came back with a vengeance.

She started to sweat, and her throat quaked. But she told herself no. No, I do not want either. I just think I do. It's just my mind playing tricks on me.

And with that she didn't. But she did get up and take a shower, and after that she looked at herself in the mirror and promised herself that that was the end of the wallowing, and the dead-end short-term fixes she'd been living on for God knew how long.

Then she put on a clean pair of jeans and a white long-sleeved shirt, made some coffee and got Felicia's laptop out of her room and sat at the coffee table and looked up the website from the business card she'd found in the kitchen. It looked like a very interesting company. And under the contact us heading there was an ad for an office assistant/manager, good wages, benefits, and a chance to move up.

She called the number.

The voice on the other side was sharp, but friendly.

"McCullough Industries, may I help you?" It asked.

"My name is Astrid Shaw, and I'm calling with regards to the office assistant position."

"Yes, well, you're the first to call, we just put that up on the site this morning."

"Oh, okay, then I'll take it the position is still open."

"Yes, it is. When could you be available for an interview?"

"I'm available right now, ma'am." Astrid said.

"Okay, let's see have you worked in an IT business before." Sheila asked. Astrid was reluctant to answer.

"Well, no, I've been waitressing for a few years now after school, but I'm a fast-learner and a hard worker, and…"

"I'm sorry, I don't mean to interrupt you, but I've got another call, can you hold?" Sheila asked and clicked over before Astrid could respond. She was not sure if she sounded too eager or what. She wasn't sure when she had a second to think about it if this would be the right kind of job to apply for and even if she could handle the job which she didn't even know would be like but she stayed on the line and waited anyway. Hanging up out of a small pang of fear was not an option. She told herself to breathe. And she did.

A minute or so later, the phone beeped.

"Hello, are you still there?"

"Yes, ma'am. I'm here."

"Okay. Can you be here at 3:00 p.m. today?"

"Yes, ma'am, I can."

"Well, good, just come on in, park in the garage, and bring your ticket in; we'll validate it for you."

"Okay, great, should I bring anything else?"

"A resume, and a good attitude. Sounds like you already got the latter." Sheila said.

"Thank you, thank you, ma'am. I'll…I'll be there."

"Okay, sweetie, see you at 3."

Astrid hung up the phone, and wished Felicia was there, one to tell her the news and two because if anyone could help her whip up a resume in two hours it was her. But she wasn't. She hadn't come home from work again.

XXXVIII.

Walter walked backed to his office and Frank followed him. He held up his hand and went in alone. Frank turned and stood outside the door, scanning the shop floor. Small teams of guys were working on every press. Some climbed up on top, while one guy strapped a harness on and ran a line to the five-ton hoist above. They were trying to restart the hydraulics and weren't having much luck. Another guy was pounding away at a crankshaft with a twenty-pound mallet, and another guy was holding a torch while laid on his back underneath the press trying to sear some of the bolts free. They were trying just about anything and everything to get the presses open and not one looked promising. The sounds were at an unusual pitch, even for a plant like this. It was like the sound of a herd of wounded buffalo, bellowing as though they'd been instantly paralyzed in the middle of a stampede.

Walter's voice suddenly shot up and he slammed the phone into its small plastic stand, and outside the office Frank stood still. A few minutes went by. People were too preoccupied to take issue with him for the moment, but he knew that wasn't going to last. At some point, somebody would recognize him and pass the word. Then he wasn't exactly sure what would happen.

The door opened behind him and Walter stepped into the doorway. He was a man with a calm demeanor, not one to get riled up easily. But there was a kind of anger in his face right then. The kind that doesn't have an off switch. The kind that takes over when a certain line is crossed.

"You have a cigarette, Frank?" He asked without looking over.

"Didn't know you..."

"Don't make me ask you twice."

"Yes, I do."

"Follow me." Still not looking over at him.

They walked between the yellow lines painted on the floor, and Frank gripped the handle of his briefcase like it was might be the only thing he could hang onto if he were in an airplane that had the fuselage blown out while at thirty thousand feet.

Walter hooked a left and snaked through a corridor where cubicles had been set up. The engineering department. They were people huddled around computer screens in one; another man Walter waved to was leaning back in his chair and holding a phone to his ear nodding and agreeing. Probably not much else he could do. Walter stopped, and the man looked up at him and held the phone down by his chin, raising his eyebrows. Walter didn't say anything, just cocked his head toward Frank and stuck his index finger in the direction down the corridor. The man looked at him for a second, nodded quickly, and leaned forward in his chair. He had on a blue and gray flannel shirt. Big ass boots. And shoulders as wide as the doorway. He hung up the phone and reached into a drawer.

"Come on." Walter said. Frank didn't get to see what the man was reaching for.

The corridor got dark until almost he couldn't see Walter anymore. Then he heard an aluminum handle slam into a door and the dark vanished into gray morning light.

The wind whipped around on the gravel, and nobody was in sight. Frank gripped the handle.

Walter took a couple steps out and wrung his hands out in the wind, cracked them a couple times, and turned around to look at Frank.

"Alright fuck it. Give me that cigarette." He said. Frank reached into his pocket and held out the pack and gave him the lighter.

Right then the door kicked open behind him, and the man from the cubicle stepped through.

"Guess now's a good a time to fall of the wagon." He said, not looking at Frank.

"We done been quit for twelve years. Morris and I made a pact if one of us fell off, we'd both go together. So here we are. You got another one of them, Frank?"

"Sure do."

"Thank you. Morris Carl." Morris did not need Frank's lighter.

"Frank Cusco." He thought about saying something about a blindfold but didn't.

"Yep. Just like riding a bike."

"Just like it." Morris agreed.

"Got off the phone with Marlene minute ago." Walter said to Morris.

"She seen him?"

"Tried to tell me no. But I told her I know about them boys of hers buying up all the Sudafed and propane in Chester County and making that shit up out there in that park, and I'd be fixin' to pay them a visit and the cops were fixin' to be the least of their problems so she ended up comin' out with it."

"Where's he at?" Morris asked.

"That ol' fishin camp his daddy lived in after he come back from the war."

"His daddy would roll over in his grave he knew about his grandbabies." Morris responded.

"God's honest."

"He was one of only a few Marines made it back from them scrapes in the Pacific." Morris said, this time in Frank's general direction.

"Yeah, Wallace never was cut from the same cloth. Lazy. Never thought he'd be this stupid though." Walter said, squeezing in the smoke.

"It's usually only after someone does something like at do you ever know anyway." Morris replied.

"He's the guy from the stock room I guess." Frank asked, carefully.

They didn't say anything, just nodded.

"Well, if you're going to go talk to him. I'd like to come along. My ass is in a sling too." Frank said, unsure as to how that would be received.

Morris and Walter paused, and looked at each other for a long second, and nodded again.

"Reckon it is, Frank. We can go up in the morning you still in town." He said.

"I don't have a motel yet, but I'll plan on it."

"Shit, why don't you go around the building here, get your car and meet me down by the IGA, in the parking lot. I'll call the wife tell her to fix up the spare bedroom."

"Walter, that's very generous but…"

"I ain't askin." Then he smiled quickly both at Morris and Frank, the first time all day.

XXXIX.

Frank waited for an hour or so and watched people go in and out of the IGA. He couldn't help but notice how big most of them were. The moms and the kids. There was a Wendy's in the southeast corner of the lot, and he saw some folks go through the drive thru, park, eat. Then walk into the IGA. What was that saying about not going into the grocery store on an empty stomach?

Walter rumbled up next to him in his big blue diesel truck opposite Frank in the direction police do when they want to talk to each other.

The lift on the truck was so high that Frank had to duck his head out the window to make eye contact with Walter.

"Hope you're hungry, the wife is fixin' up some tenderloin. You ain't no vegan, are you?" He asked.

"No, sir."

"Alright, just follow me down this road here yonder, about five mile to the house."

"Okay."

They drove out over a rolling two-lane and past pastures where most of the work was done for the day. They pulled into a dirt driveway and up a long stretch to a ranch house where most of the lights were on.

Walter pulled off his boots at the front door and Frank awkwardly slid off his dress shoes.

When they walked in, Frank could smell something like heaven.

"Hun? We got company." Walter hollered as he bent down to grab his dog behind the ears. He was a spring-loaded little critter who snuck out of his grip and leaped up on Frank and licked him on the nose in midair.

"Satchel, come on down." Walter said.

"Aw, he's alright, yeah that's a good boy. He got some boxer in him, Walter?"

"Far as we know, he's Pit, Lab, and Boxer. Great hunting dog. My wife found him at the rescue."

The muscles in Satchel's shoulders and hind legs bulged, and he leapt up again at Frank and he squatted down to pet him. He really was a good dog; Frank could tell that right from the get-go, in other words from the beginning.

Mary Ann came out from the kitchen wearing an apron and smiled. She came over and shook Frank's hand.

"It is a pleasure, Mary Ann, thank you for having me to your home."

"Aw, the pleasure's ours, hun, Walter said it wasn't sense in you paying for a motel room when we got the extra bedroom. Please come on in and let me get your coat."

373

"Thank you very much, you have a lovely home."

"Well, aren't you nice. Thank you."

"It sure does smell good in there; can I help you all with anything?" He asked.

"No, it's almost ready…"

"I think the man could use a beer, hun, think I could too."

"Well, why don't you take your guest out to the shop and have you one, it'll be a good fifteen twenty minutes for it's time to eat." Mary Ann said.

They went out the screen door from the kitchen and into the back yard. There was a pathway of large stones set into the ground from doorway to doorway. The yard was fenced in and lit up with portable lights that stuck straight in the ground. To the back corner, Frank saw that they had a large rectangular garden with corn; squash; onions; cucumbers; red, green, and yellow peppers; tomatoes; and zucchini. Each set of vegetables was growing in isolated pods of severed blue plastic fifty-five-gallon drums laid on their sides. Walter mentioned that they worked real good for draining, just drilled a few holes in the bottom with at 3/16-inch bit. In the other side of the yard was a small wooden building, one story. It itself had a small front porch. Two chairs. Walter unlocked the door, opened it, and flipped the switch on the wall inside. There were organized shelves of wood carved figurines all around the walls. He opened a small fridge in the corner and pulled out two Budweiser's.

"Helluva place you got here, man." Frank said.

"Thank you. Yeah, it's what I'd guess you'd call my hobby."

"How long you been at it?"

"Shoot, guess about fifteen years. Learned from her daddy. Man could do just about anything with a knife. Some folks around here will pay a good dollar for birdcages, doghouses, stuff like at. I do it more for a bit of peace of mind, though." Walter tipped back his beer and walked back outside.

He sat down in the chair and motioned for Frank to do the same.

"Say, give me another one of them smokes, will ya?"

"Sure."

"She'll holler at me, but I'm just going to blame it on you." He said as he lit up.

"Well, it's the least I can do." Frank said.

"Look, I was worried about bringing in a new lube, for this very reason. Or something in the same vicinity. It'll be all anyone will say is the cause of the shutdown. Don't matter if that's the truth or not. It's a reason. And people don't care too much about the truth when they find themselves in a pinch.

Now I think you know, and I think I know what really happened. Somehow, someway, somebody got let into the stock room and poisoned your drum. Ain't no other way I can see. Folks in upper management don't know someone like Wallace way me and Morris do. Don't care probably neither. Can't say I blame em. Just way it is. They gonna be looking for a goat, Frank. And that goat gonna be you and might could be me if we can't find the bad guy. I don't know how long we fixin' to be down, but every damn day is costing the company a lot of scratch. And it's going to come out of somebody's ass. Obviously, I don't want it to be me. And, I don't want it to be you, or your company. Not because I like you, and respect you. But because I don't believe your responsible. But don't much matter what I think, you hear what I'm saying." He said, without asking.

"Yes, I do." He said, looking over the short grass as Mary Ann worked her way around the kitchen through the bright windows.

"Good. Let's go on in."

"Walter, thank you for shooting me straight."

"Only way I know how bud, but I'm still going to give you up on the smokes."

XL.

The fog was steady in between the trees, and it inherently sunk down low in the valley, hunting comfort. The way lots of things do.

Dripping dew and fading leaves draped and huddled against each other counting the minutes because fall was whispering in.

He dropped down off a loose branch and stretched out, loping wide winding ahead silently and grabbed onto a solid one.

He looked.

For a good long while he did.

There were beasts tailing this way and that and up against the tide of the river down the valley. They ran hard this time of year. He liked that he could stay awhile and watch them fight like a slew of hornets trying to overcome the run of the water, some leaping out over one another to get up in the front of the line.

All pale and fresh.

They had a hard time seeing what it was that they couldn't see.

Human people used sticks with twine and hurled it out over the water in looping gusts trying to sneak up on them. But that was no way to go about it unless it was the only way.

He let go slightly, and then regripped onto the branch and tweaked himself just a bit to get some more traction.

Then he watched some more.

After a piece of time, they were still fighting the current that spilled over a dead set bull of rocks that had given more speed to the water and he let go of the branch.

His body weight was like an anchor for a second and maybe a half when he stretched out and shed the gravity like it didn't apply to him.

Which it both did and didn't.

He flapped hard and determinedly toward the edge of the tree-line and dodged a swath of branches broken and clumped with pine needles.

Before the one that wanted to flush itself out of the water and into the front of the school knew it was out of the water, its eyes bulged for a moment and then it was dead and being flown away in a world that wasn't a world anymore.

Blood leaked out onto the water below and they instantly moved as a unit darting back down and away under the rush of the tide for safety, but it wouldn't be for too long because they only knew one way that they would eventually have to go.

XLI.

Astrid was kind of nervous. She hadn't been on a job interview in a long time. Not this kind of job if ever. She'd figured an office manager position would be easy enough. But it was still something new. And that kind of stirred her up a little, but not too bad.

She borrowed some of Felicia's clothes. One of her semi-power suits. It felt nicely empowering. It somehow imbued a sense of purpose in her perspective as she did and undid and re-did her makeup in the small vanity that morning. Not pulling on sweatpants and fleece sweaters for a change soberly reminded her that she'd been emptily burning weed for the better part of the past five years.

And putting on something new had a way of making her feel like she was taking a good step forward for herself.

All that was going on, but it wasn't everything.

Sheila came out and instantly made her feel reassured.

"Hello, I'm Sheila Fitzpatrick. Thank you for coming. How are you?" She asked.

"Hi. I'm Astrid Shaw. Very nice to meet you." She said as she stood.

"Astrid, excuse me for saying but that is such a pretty name."

"Oh, thank you. My parents were, well…artists."

"Really. Interesting. Please, follow me. Can I get you anything?" Sheila asked.

"No. Thank you." Astrid said.

They walked through a meticulously designed and organized office area. Astrid was surprised that they were only five people at work in not what she would call cubicles, but open and privately setup offices. They artwork on the walls was colorful and bright. The carpets were new, and very clean. And it smelled good. Not a smell she could put her finger on, but it smelled like an office should, she thought to herself, and reluctantly but intentionally did not smile at one cute young man who she sensed glancing up at her as she followed Sheila into a conference room.

Astrid was less nervous the moment they sat down.

Sheila didn't start to grill her. She just asked her about herself. And some other straightforward questions.

Where did you grow up? What are your interests? Do you have a problem improvising? Astrid didn't have a moment of hesitation either. Surprising herself considerably. And they got to talking. For a good twenty minutes.

About all kinds of things.

At one point, Sheila gently but firmly told her to stop calling her ma'am.

"Sheila, I'm sorry, I just didn't want to sound inappropriate. I hope I can look half as good as you someday."

"That's very nice of you to say." Sheila answered, flattered but not fooled.

But she smiled inwardly sensing that this girl meant it.

"Well, I'm at a place in my life, where I...I need a real challenge, and I think I could be really good here, at this job. I guess it's just a feeling, but I believe that I can if you give me a chance."

"It's not an ordinary office, we move really fast. Being flexible and ahead of the curve is our standard. It's not just answering phones and sending faxes, emails, or flowers. You may find that this position is the fundamental nerve center of what goes on here. In fact, it's where I started ten years ago when Taylor...that's our CEO & President, hired me after I temped for him. It was just a small start-up then, but he had a vision, rather he has vision, passion, and that is something that inspires somebody. Eventually his business model took off, and so did our customer base. But he was very wise not to go public, which he had plenty of opportunities to do. Anyway, what I guess I saying to you is, it's a great place to work if you're willing to be challenged...as you say." Sheila couldn't help but see some of herself in Astrid, potentially.

"It sounds like just the place for me." Astrid fought the urge to bite her lower lip, hoping she did not sound too jumpy. Sheila nodded coolly and looked at her blackberry. After a couple of somewhat tense moments for Astrid she looked up at her.

"Well, good, I'll talk to Taylor either later tonight or tomorrow morning and give you a call."

"Really?" Astrid asked.

"Yes. No promises. But either way I'll be in touch."

"Thank you. Thank you so much."

"Okay, it was great to meet you."

XLII.

Taylor winced.

The pounding was there in his temples like a cop at the off ramp. Sure, as a good and decent shit was intact, and shit-clothed, he knew it would be too even before he dropped backwards on the couch the night before.

The last thing he remembered was everyone yelling, raising glasses before they put down the last of the Don Julio. There was a vague image of Haybeeb getting spanked by two girls while they seamlessly dropped their clothes on the living room floor and started to grind up onto him, while Everett took a couple steps back and just sort of watched in what could only be described as full-on quiet human amusement. Fortunately, the blaring sounds of Mega-Death from Everett's surround sound drifted into mute. And right then it was all he could do to breathe in and bring himself back up and hoist himself up into a sitting position. The red lights on the stereo were still at full tilt, trying to find new tiny rectangles to fill, but there was no sound. The television was on too.

Taylor didn't even bother to swear at himself. It was beyond familiar. Feeling like this. Waking up under a pile of timber. No way to start your day knowing that the day is shot. That another full day is not going to even come close to what it could be because of what he'd done to himself the night before. That hurt worse than the headache. Way worse. Only way to get rid of that feeling is to pour yourself a stiff one as close to quitting time as you could. Just to take the edge somewhere close to off.

But that only led to one more. And after that what would one two or five matter.

He stared at the hardwood for a good while, trying to keep the pounding from expanding.

Then he breathed deep and thought about just what it was he was doing to himself.

And why.

He looked at the maple streaks in the wood for a piece.

Ain't nobody behind the wheel but you. His voice said to him.

"Hey, brother. You want some coffee, Gatorade, sauna?" Everett said, smiling the same smile he was not six hours ago. Only now he was shirtless and hairy and bloated.

"Yeah. But for Christ sakes would you put a shirt on?" Taylor said, each word swung like a wrecking ball in his cranium.

"Ah dude, this is 220 pounds of Hoosier love." Everett said. Walking back toward the cabinet. He opened the door and pulled down a box of filters. Then he reached for the fridge handle. He got out a bag and filled up the coffee pot with water. Pressed the on button and walked back into the bedroom.

He came back out with an Iron Maiden t-shirt, and a pair of jean shorts. He turned off the stereo and plopped down in his recliner.

"You believe that sumbitch? He's a fuckin' wild-man, ain't he?"

"Who?"

"Ol' Haybeeb. Took two of those strippers in the bedroom with him last night. I heard them leave at four thirty or so. They were laughing about how they took all his funny money. I heard them outside my window. I bout had a heart attack after they drove off. Man, those motherfuckers worked dude. They didn't notice the difference." The coffee machine beeped. Everett got up and looked at Taylor for a second, incredulously.

"Not yet anyway." Taylor answered.

"Shit, what are they going to do, man? They were freelancing last night for 'ol Haybeeb far as the tit bar is concerned, if they even know about it. They can't go to the police complaining, now, can they?"

"Ain't the police we need to worry about Everett." Taylor said, as Everett handed him a cup of steaming black relief.

"Well, they can talk to old number 45 they come over here."

"I had a feeling you'd say that."

"Fuck em. Like they fucked you my brother. Only harder. What I say." Everett picked up the remote and put on the sports highlights.

"Sooner or later somebody will catch on. I started thinking about that last night at the club. We need to be careful and not go crazy with this shit." Taylor leaned back, looking at the highlights.

"You worry too much man. I ever tell you that." Everett said. Taylor sensed a caring indignance in his voice.

"Someone has to." Taylor said back. Indignant in his own way.

"That's what the fuck what I mean, man."

"Well, I'm just saying that this isn't the kind of game we need to be playing all over town. That's the smart thing. We got them back pretty good last night, and don't get me wrong man I have no regrets, I just don't want you getting caught up in a jackpot on account of my idea. The people that run these places, if they figure out what happened, which is only prudent to presume that they will…will most definitely come looking for somebody. And we don't want that somebody to be us."

He was leaning up on the end of the couch, looking at Everett with every ounce of self-ownership he could wrestle up from his insides. He had a decent enough handle on his reasons and his rationale, but Everett wasn't having much of it.

If any.

He just looked at the highlights. And didn't say anything back. Some commercials ran. Then more highlights. Everett exhaled big, and he set the coffee down on the table.

"Brother, you are about one of the sharpest cats I know, but when it comes to a couple things, and I only mean a couple now…you couldn't find your ass with both hands."

The logs rolling in Taylor's head suddenly stopped, conjoining their collective weight with undeterred levity.

He felt as though he was locked into a rifle. If he moved just a cunt-hair, the shooter would drop him through the shoulder like a sack of potatoes. So, he stared at the mug on the table, feeling the rigid and impervious impounding strength stacking in order around him and closing in until the only way to stall them was to look up from the table at his friend.

"When it comes to business, philosophy, computers, any of that shit I'll take your word ever day of the week and twice on Sunday, but when it comes to your own self and going

387

after exactly what it is you need to do for yourself, you ain't got no clue. And don't go takin that the wrong way."

He looked Taylor dead in the eye as he leaned forward in the recliner and then took a sip of coffee.

Taylor looked back at him. And it was a good uptown minute before either of them looked away.

"I'm too fucking hungover to take that at all." Taylor finally said, set his coffee on the table, and leaned back on the couch.

"Look, you had the balls to start out on your own, take the risk, and plow your way and carve success when most other people fell flat on their faces. It wasn't nobody else making you succeed, but you. I watched you do it and I respect and admire you for it. Hell, I envy you. Wish I had half the brains you do. But what gets me man, is you can accomplish all of what you did, and still spend the best days of your life half in the bag. And look, I'm the first guy ready to blow off some steam, and I think it's a healthy thing once in a good long while. But rolling solo into the tit bar on a Wednesday for five hours is just a bad formula for the soul. And you got one made of solid God's honest gold, but you're just covering it up when you do that man, taking the easy way when it's really the opposite."

"What do you mean easy?" Taylor asked.

388

"What I mean is it's the easiest thing in the world when you're a successful single guy with a workaholic mindset and no, and yeah motherfucker I mean no, real deep relationship history to go and take the tittie bar bait, or something like that. What you're missing in your life is a good girl, or a bunch of good girls for all I know but instead of getting yourself out there in the mix and dating you figure, you know what, man, I'll just slide over here and skip the long drawn-out shit that you've got it made up to be in your convoluted head and go straight for what you trick yourself into believing is the end all be all. And it's made even more easy because you got some cash. And those bitches can smell that a country mile away. That much we've established, huh?"

"You think it's easy…being a lonely motherfucker?" Taylor snapped. "Do you?" Everett let that sit for a minute. Then he looked down at the coffee mug he rotated slowly in his hands and looked back up at his friend.

"You ain't lonely, man. Everybody, that I know thinks you're the shit. The best kind. Anyone I've met through you I can tell feels the same. The people you work with, Sheila for example, man that woman is a doll. She thinks you hung the moon. Old Haybeeb, man, he told me you would be like the equivalent of royalty in the village he grew up in. Whether he was fucking with me or not I don't know…but." That made Taylor laugh. And Everett.

"Man, I don't what exactly what's holding you back, but whatever it is, I know you can get over it."

They didn't say anything to each other for a thick five minutes. Everett was all but done with his speech. He looked down at his coffee mug and sneered briefly at the coldness of it.

"What I'm saying to you, man…is just get the fuck up out of your own way." He raised one eyebrow, got up, and walked to the bathroom.

For another minute or two, Taylor sat there. Staring at the posters all over the living room wall and stopped of one Gene Simmons. He was looking back at him from behind makeup and long hair. Taylor laughed to himself remembering a conversation he and Everett had about how he was a high school math teacher before he became a big rock star. He didn't believe him then, but he did now. His cell was vibrating and there were already several texts from Sheila.

After it stopped, he picked it up and scrolled.

XLIV.

She wanted to hire a new office administrator. Right away.

He texted her back. Go ahead. He didn't text her that she didn't need to ask him. He truly trusted her judgment more than his own, which was a lot more than he'd ever tell her.

Everett flushed the toilet and washed his hands. He came out of the bathroom and knocked on the spare bedroom door.

"They leave you alive, hotrod?" He hollered. Taylor half-expected to hear muffled cries for help, in Indian.

"I am fucking awake. No need to yell, motherfucker." Habib replied.

"If you need me to call the fire department, I can do that for you." Everett smiled at Taylor and headed back for the coffee.

Habib came out a few minutes later wearing a tank-top, boxer shorts, and draped in a sheet. His eyes were half-open, and his feet barely lifted from the floor as he moved toward the couch. He even had his socks on, pulled up to the calf.

Taylor watched him as though he were a statue that had just come alive before his eyes, in a museum. His hair was standing straight up, and his skin had seemingly lost a bit of color.

"Hey, man, you okay?" He asked.

"Do I look like I am fucking okay, motherfucker?" Habib answered, evenly.

His eyelids opened slightly more after he had some coffee. Everett topped off Taylor's mug and sat back down. Each of them waiting to hear from Habib, with bated breath like he'd just come back from behind enemy lines. He didn't say anything for a while so they turned to the television and caught some more highlights.

It was at least ten minutes before Habib said anything.

"It is not prostitution if you bang strippers two at one time, and pay them in counterfeit money, yes?"

"No." Taylor offered.

"Yes." Everett said.

"Do not fuck with me redneck." He said, while staring only at a space above and to the left of the television. Everett was starting to laugh, a little bit at first and then without an ability to hold it in, and it was utterly shocking to Taylor that, one, Habib had said that to Everett, and, two, that Everett let him get away with it.

"Who gives a fuck? You're out of the country manana." Everett reminded him.

"This is true." And he looked up still looking at that same space only now with a big ass grin.

XLV.

Frank decided to follow Walter.

Walter warned him that the roads might not be too friendly to a Cadillac drive train. But Frank still took his own car. He needed to get down to Ireland later that day, and it wasn't but a fifty-mile drive. If he were to ride with Walter, he'd be adding at least forty-five minutes to his trip. By that time the first shift would be either at lunch or just getting back and that would've been too late to get out on the line and run some of the samples he had in his trunk. They were working on a new product, one that far exceeded existing environmental standards and would be lower cost to the customer.

The woods almost swallowed them as they edged off 37 and passed an entrance to the Hoosier National Forest. There was an abandoned steel mill off way down in a valley. Not a car in the lot. Just a bunch of weeds. Rust etched out along the siding like sap.

The road that Walter turned onto pitched up and went dirt. The trees were like guardians, stoic, skinny, and still. Grayness wafted like a broth behind in front of and around them. Soot brown puddles hollowed on either side where the wheels dropped, and his suspension was tested. Frank started to question his judgment. Maybe it would have been better to ride with Walter. He watched the dually grumble upward and twist over ground rocks and spit mud voraciously backward on his low windshield like brown minnows on the attack. The taillights gleamed and the brake lights stayed off. A gun rack in the cab window. The bed was coated black with Teflon like a hearse for all the dead deer it had ferried. The paint was still as red as the day he drove it off the lot. It was spacious and warm in the cab probably. Clean. Organized. A big silver thermos of hot homemade coffee. Frank was as out of his element as his car. But that wasn't unfamiliar.

It was reassuring.

After what seemed like five miles, Walter reached a camouflaged jacketed arm out his window and pointed to a clearing between some brush. It was barely a road, barely a path. He swung his arm again and Frank took it to mean get out and come up here. So, he did.

The diesel engine was purring. It liked this kind of work.

He tried to sidestep the mud, but it was catching his black dress pants around the cuffs. He got to the cab and Walter stared through the woods.

"Probably ought to pull your car back and park it up on that little ridge back there, the mud should be dry and it's covered in needles and you'll be pointed back down, that way you ain't fixin' to get stuck, we ought to ride up there together from here. His camp ain't but another hundred or so yards up past this hill then down toward the river."

"Right back there?" Frank pointed to a small circular landing he hadn't noticed on the way up, almost like a virginal putting green just fifteen feet or so behind where his car was idling and to the right.

"Yeah, just be easy when you back onto it. The ground could still be wet, and you don't want them tires of yours taking a nap in the mud. Go on, I'll be right here."

Frank ran back to his car and angled the Cadillac easily onto the ridge. He thought he'd get pulled into a quicksand pit at any second, but the needles laid down a lining as though they'd been waiting for him. He gently took his keys out of the ignition, shut the door, and bounded off the ridge and back up toward the truck at this point not giving a shit about the mud splattering up his legs and his jacket because there he knew like he knew his own name that when you were inside reality there really wasn't anything you could do about the shit that flew up or down on you.

The dog was in the passenger seat, and Walter made a coupled quick sound with his teeth and tongue and he hopped onto the console and into the back like a soldier of a lower rank as Frank pulled himself inside. Frank reached back and rubbed his chin. He was good smart dog.

He licked his hand briefly and then set his eyes out the window.

The dually rolled backward for a second then caught some dry dirt and lunged forward. Walter kept it at a slow gurgle when the front-end tilted down and the trees opened and the silted bluffs of a fire from a cabin chimney set loose a glimpse of the camp. They pulled down the thin gap in the foliage with the brush glazing the sides of the truck. Walter put it in park.

"Come on."

The dog leapt on the console and followed Walter out the driver-side door.

Frank got out the other side. Kind of following the dog's lead.

Walter didn't have a leash, and the dog stayed close to him. His ears up and his eyes forward.

Frank was cognizant of his feet sinking in the mud. Making unwanted sounds.

They came around the side of the cabin. One window sown up with grime.

On the front porch, Wallace was sitting. A stack of magazines beside him. Beer cans strewn about the deck and in the mud below. A long glazing descent of brown led to the river and they could hear it gushing with motion. They stopped.

"What kind of beer you drinking Wallace?" Walter asked.

"Kind that gets you shitfaced." Wallace answered. Not looking up at him. The dog wanted to investigate him further, but he knew to heel. So, he did.

"You been up here a stretch."

"Are you working in HR now?" He answered. Wallace glanced over his shoulder to the dog, then at Walter, then at Frank, then back at the dog.

"No, I'm still production." Walter said.

"Didn't think so."

"Why'd you ask?"

"Why's been going around lot lately."

"Bet your sweet cherry pie."

"Bet all of it you got any to."

"On what."

"On what we all end up doing."

"What's that? Dyin. Paying taxes."

"Whatever we decide."

"That right?"

"Ain't necessarily right. Just how it ends up, no matter what you do, there's always a decision come before that."

"See this man here?"

"See two men. And a dog."

398

"He's the man who got the sharp end twisted up in his back while he was trying to help us out."

"Still see the dog."

"He's here to make sure no bullshit pass between us."

"I see. Good huntin dog I reckon. What's that make you?"

"Makes me the man here to ask you to tell the three of us where the poison come from."

"Poison come from ever-where."

"Yeah. But that ain't the question."

"What is?"

"Where?"

"Where indeed."

"Well?"

"See any buzzards on the road up here?"

"Seen some."

"They been feeding good on all them deer. Follow them round the woods after they take a round or get clipped by a vehicle."

"Yep."

"Don't pay much mind to buzzards. No one likes 'em. Prob'ly 'cause they remind us that we all fixin' to end up their dinner. Nobody likes to think of that. But that don't stop em."

"They gotta eat too." Walter said, squatting and rubbing his dog around the ears, trying to ease his alerted mind.

"Yep."

Nobody said anything. Wallace just sat on his wooden chair on his rickety deck looking down at the river like it was going to summon up a solution if he stared long enough.

"Wallace, I ain't got all day so either quit fucking around with me or I set my dog on you."

"Ain't afraid of you or your dog."

"Fear got nothing to do with it."

"The fuck it don't." Walter said and stood back up, taking a step closer.

The dog started shifting its weight, and the hair on its back slid up. Frank was pretty sure a gun was nearby. In fact, he was certain Walter was packing. If he got shot over an account…he thought about that while the river ran. Here up in the woods in the southern part of the middle of the middle of the country, he was chasing down a reason for why his work was not working out. He was hunting an honest answer to his honest efforts. It wasn't what he'd ever pictured. It wasn't the conference room presentation or the wine room in a high fallutin' restaurant where he got the nod, the handshake, or the signature. It wasn't reading a fax or an email in the office. It wasn't a voicemail. The fact was it was here.

He was here. Here he was. Where the, or where this trail had lead him. The small circle in the middle of the ocean where his choices pulled him like a returning space capsule.

He heard the dog's tag clink and rattle. He leaned down on one knee and rubbed behind his ears. Then he reached around his chest and scooted himself in front of the dog.

Frank looked at the old stubborn man in his chair staring down at the water and the dog and Walter. Not one of them was blinking. Or was going to.

A good stiff moment seared on slowing time in a visceral glaze. A pathogenic exercise of dialogic gun fighting.

Then a hawk called out piercing the silence.

He flew down like a red and brown lightning bolt from the woods and revealed himself in the gaping space above the river and between the trees and dropped in as though he were dusting scattered clouds of dowsing agents on a burgeoning fire, but instead, he yanked back on his descent with wings gilded outward and talons flushed and took with him a fish that was swinging its tail wildly above the rushing down swath of water for its last fluid moment.

"Seen me a hawk just like 'at while ago done the same thing."

"Maybe it's the same one."

"Maybe."

401

"Sit long enough and you liable to see any and, just about everything."

"Hope I got long enough to sit." Wallace said.

"Not today you don't."

"That right?"

"You gonna make me do this, aint you?"

Wallace didn't respond, he just kept sitting there. Then he reached for another beer. He cracked it open, took a tug and then lit a cigarette.

"Man come back to the stock room asking about how he can get in. I don't even look at him cuz he was one a them slick haired hot-asses that you see every now and then. Didn't care for his tone either. But he kept on and slid a camouflage hat through the door chute, and it had a bunch a money under it."

"Did he say what he wanted in the cage?" Frank asked, standing even with Walter but on the other side of the dog.

"Naw, just come in and I told him he had a minute to do whatever it was he wanted to do, and then he had to get out. He moved quick too, boy. Man knew what he was doing from what I could tell."

"Did you see him do what it was he was fixin' to do?"

"No, Walter, I swear I just kept my head down and read my mag."

402

"You didn't see nothing?"

"No, I did not see what he did. Man, them drums were tucked out way in the back. Couldn't see around the shelves...shit if I'd a gone back air with him I could probably tell you what he done but I just kept my head down up the front the cage."

"You just kept your head down." Walter said.

"Yes, I did."

"After you took the money." Walter glowered at Wallace, thinking of how much money the company was losing every second one of their presses were down. Frank felt as though he was watching a man peeling back layers of shame and regret, each one dirtier than the one before. Hoping that before all of them were gone he'd come to one that was clean.

Later he'd remember that not once did why and or how in the fuck why did I here ever cross his mind.

It was later after that that he'd gotten word that Walter and Morris had met the sheriff out around the same spot he'd left his Cadillac that day and when they'd walked up together with Walter's dog, they turned the very same corner they'd turned on that very same day and had to rustle off the buzzards with a couple shots from the sheriff's pistol.

Wallace was still oozing from the entry wound under his chin like his last beer that he hadn't quite finished.

XLVI.

While the beeping blurred and the coffee fizzled in the pot downstairs, Taylor awoke and felt distant from himself. Not in the way that a hangover or a strange dwelling consumes someone when they open their eyes to suddenly find themselves unaware of their bearings, and their whereabouts…but distant in the way that he knew where he was, he wasn't hungover, but right then he was aware of an unknown something, a shifted awareness that filtered the green of the carpet through his retinas and the scent of jasmine incense through his nose. A changed, interpretative process active inside all his senses and consciousness. He was aware of it, as he was also aware that today he'd go off and do something he'd never done before, something that would hurtle his life into a reality separate from any he had known. He checked his phone and its time and date. He scratched at his shoulder and flipped the light switch in the bathroom. The shower water steamed up and he squatted in the shower, gripping his knees and stretching the blades in his upper back, letting the water pelt his head and puddle at his feet, blazing a growing redness on his neck. It was almost not painful, almost not awash in heat was his mind and body, as they both were inching toward a place further than he'd known, and he was becoming aware that he'd need every bit of his focus to get there and get back.

His house was silent, except the final beep of the coffee maker. The clock read 8:12. The lady at the drop zone had mentioned that the earlier he get out there, the better off he'd be because the weather could change and he'd need several hours to learn the basics before they went about sending him up in the plane. He already had a quickening heartbeat, and it wasn't even past noon. The thought of jumping from an airplane had always sounded cool. Now the thought of jumping out of one, later that day sounded heavy, loud, all up in his face. It sounded real. But it didn't feel real yet. He moved himself with steps that seemed remote. They seemed not awkward, but remotely manipulated. Somewhere in his head, or in his consciousness, he'd made the decision to do it, and now his body wasn't reacting in step with that decision. There was, maybe not a disconnect, but definite, not a solid fusion between decision and action, they were slow in their beginning as partners. The resulting symbiotic manifestation of the motion between his mind and body was, in fact, forced. He had to make himself do it. And he hadn't even left the house yet.

It was all suddenly, very real, the moment he opened his eyes that morning.

In youth, Taylor thought, there is a chronic tendency to exceed boundaries, cajole and impress peers both known and unknown, test one's own boundaries, or simply cajole and try to impress oneself. Either way, ego is somewhere involved, as well as the unknown itself. Each time he launched a new product or tried to sell his ideas to venture capitalists for seed money, he'd had to size up different reflections of himself in every single panel of glass on every single door. To get in here, you got to see yourself first and know that both you and that guy looking back at you are on the same sheet of music and have got your shit wired tight. Whether that might be looking and looking back at yourself with a smile, a stare, or a smirk they had better be what they were, and they were going to work. You had to both separate and conjoin your professional self and your ego to maximize your acuity, and your effectiveness. And you had to seek out new opportunities with strangers and the possibly stranger, dynamics within certain situations as a habit in order to grow the prospects, increase potential, and eventually capitalize on those opportunities. That was part of his job. That was the job.

But why was it so hard with a girl?

The sun was up and gleaming and he unzipped his cd case and began to flip.

He peeled off the highway onto a two-way and set out deeper between endless farmland. Taylor saw some cows close to the taut wire fencing chewing large chunks of grass like old baseball coaches with swaths of tobacco revolving in their cheeks. Taylor glanced at the directions he'd scribbled on an index card, marking the mileage and keeping his eyes peeled for the turnoff. He lit a cigarette and rolled down the window, slid a CD in, an attempt to find a diversionary soundtrack to his adventure. And that's what it was he told himself, a real adventure. No one knew he'd decided to do this. He hadn't called anyone, told anybody, bragged or confided. He just decided and now he was on his way. And the closer he got, the more his heart skipped and his skin bristled and his head swirled with the near numbing reality; he was doing this of his own choice, and the nervousness all over his body was his mind telling him it didn't want to.

There were housing developments scattering to life on both sides of the road, and there were bulldozers raising and dropping brown piles of earth beyond them, creating driveways and garages and cul-de-sacs. The urban sprawl that had overtaken the plains in cities like Dallas and Houston, were invading the outskirts of Austin. Taylor drove out and away from town and past the apartment complexes under construction as the directions mandated. He had not traveled this far west, to the small town where the drop zone was located until now, and above there was a sky deeply blue, small tufts, trickles, and traces of clouds hanging distant and quiet, somehow giving the vastness of the sky even more enormity.

He called into the office, checked messages. Nothing doing yet today. And the familiarity of his secretary's voice, and the normalcy of their dialogue further imbued a swelling rush of reality. What if this were the last time they'd talk? What if tomorrow they'd be short a boss who had plummeted to the earth under a failed parachute without a warning to anyone? What if they…no more of that thinking, he thought to himself, as he twisted the volume dial on his stereo to loud. He had always used music to motivate himself while running, exercising or before a soccer or basketball game, using the sounds and lyrics and beats to transcend the rising nervous energy into something he could use to elevate both his physical and mental acuity to perform at his very best. It was a reflex as much as it was a ritual. And, frequently it ended up being a distraction, as though the music itself were a vehicle into which he could travel and traverse the workout, the game, or even the opposition remotely. But since his youth and the playing days therein, he was no more a competitive athlete than he was a skydiver. And, perhaps, that had little to do with why he had decided to learn how to jump out of a plane.

The turnoff appeared along the highway, and as he broke from his thoughts his stomach dropped again, as he completed another leg of the directions written in hasty ink. He turned left at the end of the ramp and followed the road 4.4 miles to the next turn and followed it 3.1 miles. At this street, he was to look for a cemetery on the right and make a left. He tried not to think about that landmark, and pulled past state highway 45, onto a farm road which lay below large fields of wheat and corn and cows. The last of the directions indicated driving another mile and taking a last right into the drop zone parking area. He was told he'd see three trailers, several trucks and cars, a plane if it was on the ground and an orange windsock. They were all there, and his stomach stopped. Not dropped, just stopped.

He pulled into the gravel lot and parked. The windsock swayed on a large silver pole, pulling in air and giving the direction of the wind.

East northeast.

A woman in shorts, a t-shirt, and a red bandana over her forehead came walking toward Taylor with a wave. He waved back and walked toward the wooden deck built onto the trailer, which sat perpendicular to another. Thirty yards or so from there another trailer waited, with several guys in their early to mid-twenties sitting on a railing, shirtless and smoking, tanned and carefree from the looks of them.

"You must be Taylor...my name's Ellen Debtfree, don't worry it's not my Christian name."

"It's nice to meet you, pretty nice place you've got out here."

"Oh, well, thank you, the condominiums should be in before next year, but you can't beat wheel estate when you're getting a business off the ground." She smiled and led Taylor past a couple of silent guys in jumpsuits into the trailer. Getting a business off the ground...was it him or were things today either covered in irony or coincidence, or just a little goofy he thought

"There are several others who are supposed to be coming out here today, and we wanted to put you all in a class together, that way we could be as time efficient as possible, but looks like they're bailing out on us. Works better for you though, you can get a little more attention."

"I always enjoy a little more attention."

"Don't we all." Ellen replied as she bustled though the trailer and sat down at a desk. She pulled from a drawer several small packets of paperwork. Releases, insurance, acknowledgements of risk, small matters to take care of before we can get you going on your jump from 11,000 feet she

411

explained, half-rehearsed and half-joking. Taylor was less nervous in her presence, and while talking. He noticed on the walls of the trailer licenses from the states of Maryland, Virginia, Washington, New York, Texas granting Ellen Debtfree authorization to both practice and teach all things skydiving. There were plaques commemorating 1,000 jumps, 5,000, 10,000, and, holy shit, 20,000 jumps. There were pictures of her in multi-colored jumpsuits, sleek blue gills along the legs and shoulders with tinted goggles in varying displays of acrobatic movements amid blue and gray skies and minute topography thousands of feet below. She was smiling in nearly everyone it seemed. It struck Taylor extraordinary, while staring at these pictures that someone could leap from a plane, be pulled to the earth at a speed nearly incomprehensible, and remain so in control, and so calm, and from the look on her face, happy. And now, then and there she was sitting right next to him, this person, asking him to read and sign a waiver releasing her company and drop zone from any liability if he were to be injured, or die in the ensuing skydive. He read and signed, cut a check, and followed her to another room.

It was small, and he sat in a desk that reminded him of seventh grade. There was an instruction manual, and as she left him to read before they began the class, the door opened and a man in his fifties, scrawny and sun tanned, walked in grinning beneath a five-dollar pair of sunglasses.

"Bobby, you look like you've been ridden hard and put up wet!"

"If I was ridden hard, I'd consider myself lucky, Ellen. Is this our student today?"

"Yes, it sure is. Taylor, this is Bobby, Bobby...Taylor." Taylor tried to stand to shake hands and took the desk with him a step or two. He felt the wood dig into his thigh, and he sat again, righted himself and got up.

"Bobby is going to be your jumpmaster today, and he's got over 3,000 jumps under his belt and has been teaching for over ten years. You'll be in good hands. I've got to go and check the fuel on the plane and see about those fools in the packing trailer."

"Sounds good, thank you, Ellen." Taylor sat back down and looked back at the manual.

"So, what's the story, Taylor, girlfriend break up with you, lose your ass in the market, or just get a wild hair?"

"Just...ah, wanted to see what it's all about. See how I might fare."

"Well, it's a helluva a lot of fun, and don't worry, I'm not due to hit the dirt just yet, me and the Lord have got an understanding." Taylor smiled, bullshitting with people was his bag, and it helped steer his mind from the present thoughts that wanted him to not do what he already decided he was going to.

"Is that right?"

"Well, I like to think so. Besides I woke up today and the wife left me, got shit-canned from my job, my grandmother passed away, and didn't leave me nothing, and some gypsy sonofabitch stole my car!"

Taylor smiled, if there was one thing, he knew it was when somebody was fucking with him.

"I'm going in there and talk to my therapist. You go ahead and read up; we'll get together before long." He patted Taylor on the shoulder, grabbed a sports page, and headed into the bathroom.

The pictures were at best basic. They looked to Taylor like a stickman, clinging to a flying coffee table and the stickman falling from the small opening on the side of the plane through the sky like a cartoon character. He heard a flush from the bathroom and Bobby emerged a new man.

"You get through that book okay?"

"I reckon so."

"Well, they'll give a basic rundown of what all goes on, what you have to do, and so on before we go up. A tandem is pretty easy all you got to do is listen to me, hang on, and have fun. Going solo is another thing, were you wanting to do that?"

"Not this first one, I figured it'd be better to go with someone."

"Yeah, it really is the first time, you got no real responsibilities, but you still get the sensation of freefall, and then I'll let you steer once we get under canopy, we'll do some turns and check the world from a whole new point of you, and then you can kind of decide if you want to go solo after that. Most people just like the one-time thing, then they can tell their friends and always got something to remember. I'm going to go check my rig, Ellen should be back in a few, and we'll get on up brother."

"Okay." Taylor answered, feeling more and more the realness that he was not in control, that he was in someone else's ballpark. This was both settling and scary. The collision of doing what his mind and body did not want him to was still there, constant and unyielding.

Ellen returned and brought with her two large, black jumpsuits on hangers. A young guy, younger than Taylor by about five years came in after her. He was already in a green and black jumpsuit, with a pair of goggles in one hand.

"How are you doing man, my name's Collier, I'm going to be up there with you guys today."

"Nice to meet you." Taylor noticed the guy's fleeting eyes and hurried handshake. He was a little pale and smelled like hair gel.

Ellen inserted a videotape.

"Taylor, this is an instructional video all of our tandem students have to watch, it's about fifteen minutes and will give you an idea of the process. After that, I want you to try on these two jumpsuits and whichever is more comfortable without being too baggy, you go ahead and keep that on, they're going up with a load right now, and the next one will be you all.

"See you in a few." Collier said as he bounded out the door with his goggles on his forehead. He flung the door shut, and it bounced back open, allowing a tall prism of light to enter the trailer and shroud Taylor at his little desk. He ran toward the packing trailer and a kid, no more than fifteen, ran up to him with a brown, maybe three-feet wide and long, bag with two shoulder straps. He handed it to Collier, and he slung it over his shoulders, snapping it into place around his waist. The sputtering sound of a single-engine Cessna outside the trailer also rushed inside, whirling dust and blades of grass around and around. Its putting became whirring and got louder and louder like a large, angry metallic bee, and as it grew and grew in pitch and volume Ellen shut the door.

"He's one of our local pro's, he can't stand to miss a load." She said as she pressed play and sat next to Taylor. He saw through the window on the door the plane taxi bumpily back toward the road where he had come into the drop zone.

The video was a closeup of an experienced skydive jumpmaster, walking through the steps of fitting into a jumpsuit, latching a parachute rig around his shoulders while smiling and talking to a student outside an airplane hangar. They proceeded into bigger plane than the one outside, and the jumpmaster continued to smile as they closed the door and took off. It then cut to the jumpers in the cabin, snuggled together with grins and goggles, hands on their knees or kneading together. The door swung open and the earth below looked a million miles away. The student was smiling reluctantly, and the jumpmaster hooked himself to her, from behind. Two exited before them, and then the tandem. The video switched to an upward angle including the plane, and the tandem rolling out and into the expanse. It closed quickly on their faces as they descended, the student agape with sensory overload, her cheeks rippling in the rushing air, and the jumpmaster smiling with calm and deliberate motion. The angles again switched to include the other jumper, swirling around them like a human hawk, his arms and legs arched and extended with total control, weaving and twirling as though he were in a water ballet. And

417

then back to the tandem as the jumpmaster pulled his ripcord, and a thin cable rose from his back. The next shot revealed two cables, hoisting the two together beneath a beautiful montage of red and orange fabric, not falling anymore but gliding above the earth quietly and peacefully. The student only smiled and gasped and then let out an enormous yell of adrenaline ridden ecstasy. Laughing and whooping having the time of her life.

Taylor was feeling better and more excited. It helped to see someone else in his shoes come out with such excitement. He thought less about what he was trying to overcome within himself and was becoming more and more focused on getting up there and having fun himself.

The first jumpsuit Taylor tried on fit like a glove. He looked in the mirror and felt kind of cool.

It was like trying on a tux for the first time. He grabbed a pair of goggles from a hook on the wall and walked outside the trailer. The sun was brilliant, and the clouds had rolled in more than when he'd arrived. They were clumping together in layers like blooming onions, collecting in masses that moved gently and smoothly over the drop zone. The blue of the sky was less prominent, and now seemed more of a spotted backdrop as the shadows of the clouds mirrored their migration on the green grass below. The guys who had been smoking and joking on the packing trailer deck were gone, and only Ellen and the young kid who'd handed Collier his rig were outside, holding their hands to their foreheads and looking up into the wide and open sky. Ellen held a radio in her other hand. Taylor walked over to them and stood looking upward. He heard the intermittent squawking of voices spit from the radio, with a loud humming behind them. Ellen clicked a button with her radio and spit back at them. When there was no chatter Taylor could hear a faint humming overhead.

"Listen for the stall, then they'll be out." Ellen said without looking away from the sky.

"What's a stall?" Taylor asked.

"They have to cut the engine or stall it so they can slow down enough to find their hole and exit." Ellen answered.

"You mean they stall the engine, of the plane, up there?"

"Sure, it's just a single engine, with these clouds they can have a little trouble finding a clearing, or a hole in them to drop through." She made it sound so normal, Taylor started to revisit the craziness in his mind again, all of it seemed so foreign yet he was approaching an intimacy with it at the same time.

"If they can't find a hole, what do they do?"

"Circle back until they do."

419

The faint humming was difficult to hear, and when anyone spoke, Taylor lost the sound. He tried to refocus his ears on its barely familiar pitch and rhythm, but before he could pick it back up, Ellen spoke.

"Stall…hear that? They just cut it, keep your eyes up!" Taylor watched and saw four tiny things, or bodies, begin to appear between a large ringlet of puffy clouds. As he stared up at them, they accelerated and seemed to steadily grow from tiny then small too little and just a little bigger as they hurtled downward. Freefall. Free-mother-fuckin-fall, he thought. The engine of the plane spat to life and regained its sustaining hum, turned away from the area from which it had dropped its passengers, and began to return on a path to the earth.

"They should be pulling in about forty-five seconds, as soon as they hit 2,000 feet." Ellen said as she turned her head away and motioned for Taylor to head over to the packing trailer. The young kid followed and Taylor looked back and saw a popping open of a parachute, like a balloon suddenly and sharply being filled up with air and sealed ever so tightly, as the skydiver cradled beneath it peacefully swayed and swung in the breeze, close enough to the ground that he could make out his feet dangling freely like a child on a swing. He followed the two into the packing trailer and saw a long, silky

420

blue piece of material sprawled on the floor, connected with long skinny strings elongated and flat.

Ellen pulled a container from the wall and held it up with a smile.

"This bad boy is for you Taylor, you go what about, 220?"

"Yeah, give or take."

"Okay, that should be good, it's a big one to hold that weight." She motioned for Taylor to turn around and slid it around his shoulders like a backpack. It was heavier, and more compact than Taylor had thought, but not uncomfortable, in fact, it felt secure, and maybe even empowered. Ellen showed how to hook in around the waist and walked around the back of Taylor to check his container. He felt her adjust the rig, assuredly patted the thing, and came back around the front.

"You got yourself a rig and you're ready to jump, cowboy." She walked back to the door and went outside, and Taylor followed.

Taylor saw the four skydivers flutter down toward the grassy runway. They spiraled in artful angles and closed the distance to the earth like large and colorful feathers. He watched as they pulled down on the toggles, opening each cell of the chutes as they filled with more air, slowing the descent and softening the landing. Each of them stood up their landings, making it look easy and somehow nonchalant. The parachutes collapsed gently to the ground behind them, and Taylor could both sense and see the smiles on their faces as they turned to gather the parachutes by pulling the lines close to their bodies. They slung their chutes over their shoulders and walked toward two kids motoring over on four-wheelers. Hi-fives and avid chatter were being exchanged in a vibrant way as they had just shared an incredible experience, one that was maybe as exhilarating as all the ones before, but not any less memorable. Taylor could almost taste the camaraderie, the joyous synergy of shared endeavor. He longed for it, the unmatched way within certain moments that people could relate to other people.

The humming of the Cessna grew louder, and it zoomed in to land, bouncing gently and kicking up small swirls of dust as the wheels touched the earth. It slowed at a distance and turned almost clumsily over the unpaved dirt back toward the trailers and taxied, wings tilting and the cabin jostling with the pilot becoming visible wearing big shades and a T-shirt. As the plane slowed to a halt, the pilot bounded from the cockpit and walked angrily toward Ellen.

"Fucking thing is out of juice."

"The battery?" Ellen asked, not sounding too surprised.

"Yeah, it's wiped, we're not going up anymore unless someone has some cables, or another battery." He kept his sunglasses on as he spoke, his legs were white and his shorts, shoes, socks, and shirt were jet black. So was his hair.

"Well, keep your shirt on, Ray; we'll get it sorted out."

"I need a Tab." He said with deliberate thirst and headed for a trailer. As he passed, Taylor looked back at him and noticed the back of his shirt. It read in green words fluorescent.

Rehab is for Quitters.

Ellen squinted at the plane as it sat feebly on the grass runway, needing a jump. She pulled at her bandana, looked at the trailer and back at the plane, and then at the parking lot. Taylor's car was the closest.

"Taylor, do you happen to have any cables?" Taylor looked at the plane, and back at his car, and then at Ellen.

"Matter of fact." He unhooked the rig from his wait and shook it from his shoulders and gave it to Ellen. Walking to the car he was thinking only of overcoming a minor obstacle in the way of getting up in that plane and jumping out of it, not about the fact that the plane itself was going to need a jump, presumably from his car and his cables in order to get up there in the first place.

Ellen waved for him to pull his car over near the plane, pointing in the opposite direction, so as to allow the cables to reach from his battery, to the plane's. The pilot took the cables without acknowledging Taylor, and grunted, squeezing the black rubber handles and guiding them toward the battery of the plane.

The kid from the packing trailer approached with a small camera over his shoulder. He looked up at Taylor, scratched at his buzz cut, and looked at the cables linked from a Ford Explorer with 133,000 miles on it, to a plane with probably a lot more on it. It didn't seem to faze him.

"What's with the camera?" Taylor asked him.

"Ellen wants me to take some pictures?"

"Of what?" Before he could answer, the pilot looked back from the engine with his sunglasses on his forehead and near crazed look in his eyes and said,

"Hopefully big fields of dope!!!" Laughing like a bad comedian, he motioned for Taylor to crank up his engine and Taylor turned the keys. The pilot walked to the propeller and gave it a two-handed heave. It took two tries, but the props swung into a violent sounding spin, kicking to life and humming with excitement swallowing any more talk.

Taylor smiled at the kid with the camera, and he smiled back, handing him the camera and motioning to the packing

424

trailer, speaking with his hands telling Taylor that he was going to go and get his rig. Taylor smiled again as the pilot removed the cables from the plane and car's engines, and then absently tossed them into the backseat of his car.

Taylor pulled his car away from the plane and parked where he had earlier. He jogged back to the plane and stopped. He took another look at it and Bobby stood with one leg on the strut, and one arm inside the door. Taylor walked straight and surely, feeling past the worry and well within his purpose.

"Ready to rock and roll?"

"Oh yeah." Taylor climbed inside and found one of the silent guys from earlier, tucked in the back of the rear of the plane where the seats had been removed to make more room for skydivers. He wore a white jumpsuit, his knees pinned up against his chest. He scooted over to one side to make room for Taylor.

As he settled in the back, the smallness of the plane and the humming of the engine, the parachutes on the sky-divers backs and the forward motion up the grassy runway heaped and shrunk reality onto him. Here I go, holy God.

It accelerated and left the ground, rising gradually upward, leaving the people and the trailers to grow distant. His stomach wanted to stay down there, it wished it could return, sinking like a stone in a lake as Taylor swallowed. His palms

425

started to sweat, and his throat began to dry. Bobby was hunched up with his back to Taylor and the other skydiver, talking to the pilot whose earphones were flopped around his neck while one hand stayed on the steering handle and the other waving and pointing at the instrument panel. The clouds smeared about the plane, and the earth became invisible, a milky substance wafted in mysterious depth around the windows.

The rising to altitude was grueling for Taylor, it was slow, methodical, and menacing in its realness. It gave him the undeniable moments to think about everything. To think about the choice, the awareness of his choice and the reality that it was…his decision to be here, right now, so as to be able to do something which ran counter to just about all things rational. Jumping out of a fucking plane.

He thought about any other time he'd ascended from the earth into the sky in a plane, and, became suddenly aware that this was not a commercial flight to Florida, New York, or St. Louis. There was no stewardess, no ginger ale, and sure as shit no pretzels in little silver plastic bags. It all came real. It was sweaty, scary, and real. Twenty or so minutes passed, and they were above the clouds which were distilling into pockets, opening and closing as the plane muttered on an even line. Bobby turned and gave the thumbs up sign and he hoisted the door open, and the cold air of 11,000 feet flushed inside like a bellowing voice. He motioned for Taylor to crawl toward him. He looked back outside and saw more and more clouds.

"Starboard, about ten degrees!" He said loudly to the pilot who listened and nodded. The plane pitched, one wing dropping and the other rising a bit. It turned and a gap between the clouds was directly beneath them, revealing a world of green and brown and dotted life below.

"Okay, Taylor, I'm going to get behind you and hook in!"

"Okay." Taylor moved frozenly, on hands and knees closer to the opening in the side. He felt the bristling cold. Damn it was cold. He felt the loudness, the intense blowing of the air. Bobby inched behind him and reached around, locking himself into the harness on Taylor's chest.

"We're locked in, and I'm going to count to three. When I hit three, all you have to do is roll forward my man, you got it?" They were right on the edge of the plane, with nothing but the whole world, heaven and earth barely an inch away.

"Yeah!" Taylor didn't even hear himself say it, he just stared outside.

"One, two, three!" And on three they rolled.

His stomach now wanted back in the plane, but it neither had a choice nor did the rest of him. He was committed. And somewhere between a sense of relief and plunging excitement, he felt an overwhelming feeling of purity. Totally, regardless of the circumstance, he was embracing his situation. Committed. Fucking free fall. His legs and arms arched awkwardly as he had been instructed. He could feel a man strapped to his back, and the earth rising and rising while the salty taste of clouds rushed over his eyes and mouth. His senses careened into overload, all and everything within his mind rapidly tried to adjust and reach in every direction and toward any dimension available, or imaginable, to obtain, catch, ascertain, that would allow him to gain some, any kind of bearing. There was no basis for the sensations, nothing with which to identify, and certainly no way to anticipate the onrushing boldness into which he'd thrust himself. It was fucking awesome.

Bobby motioned with one arm that they were approaching 5,000 feet. 4,000 feet.

"We pull right at 3,000, okay?"

"Okay" They hit 3,000 feet, and a whistling sound coming from a jettisoned line of fabric was audible behind his ears, and then Taylor felt a sudden, violent lurch under and around his balls. The falling stopped and the harness beneath

428

his legs pulled hard against his skin. His body jolted to what seemed a halt, and the parachute spread wide above them, and he titled his head back to see the most beautiful secure and definite reassurance he'd ever seen.

"Whooooohoooooo! How about that?" Bobby yelled in his ear.

"Unbelievable man, fucking unbelievable!" Taylor yelled back.

"Here, take the toggles." Bobby placed in them Taylor's hands, one at a time.

"Pull the right, we turn right, pull the left, we turn left." He told Taylor.

"Got it." Taylor didn't pull at all at first, he just held on gazing at the beautiful expanse of the world below him, his legs dangling free and his heart pounding. Lakes glistened like gold pools, clumps of trees and pastures of green looked like models on a scale he could hardly believe. The air was warmer, and more still, quiet and serene. The peacefulness was almost as overwhelming as the insanity of freefall, only completely reversed. It was as soothing as the freefall was mind-numbing. A firm breeze sifted about and Taylor pulled on the right toggle, and they glided that way, soaring like a hawk turning in a thermal. He pulled on the left and they shifted that way, he pulled harder and they closed to a downward spin, circling and descending as the trailers became bigger and a four-runner motored toward the center of the field below.

"Okay, I'm going to take the toggles, and as we get really close to the ground I'm going to brake, or stall us out okay, that will give us a softer landing, just keep your feet up and don't let them drift back under mine." Bobby said.

"Gotcha. This is out of sight, man."

"Glad you like it, get ready." Bobby said as the grass became tangible, and he yanked down hard on the toggles. Their descent abruptly slowed, their feet hit the ground and Taylor's weight felled them backward. The chute collapsed softly behind them, and Taylor's heart raced, pumping blood and adrenaline to his extremities and he felt more cogently tied into a moment than he could remember. It had all happened so slowly and quickly, incredibly diverse and extreme sensations smashing over his constitution like powerful and relentless waves against great walls.

They got up and grunted, exhaled and laughed. Bobby unhooked from Taylor, and Taylor shook himself up, gaining his balance and awakening to a sense of newness, washed clean of whatever he was before he'd experienced this almost indescribable moment. He hi-fived Bobby and laughed again.

"Wow that was fun, what a ride huh?" Bobby said as he was rolling the lines in and clumping together the parachute in

430

his arms as the kid on a four-runner pulled up to them. They hopped on and drove back toward the trailer, Taylor was feeling as though he'd undergone a rite of passage, and now he had seen what the others at the drop zone lived for, what the rarified world of the unknown could be like if you committed, abandoned your fears, embraced the danger, and allowed yourself to find a new kind of freedom.

Ellen stood on the packing trailer deck. She smiled at them as the four-runner slowed and stopped.

"How do you feel, skydiver?" She asked.

"I don't know, like I just jumped out of a plane." Taylor answered, as he got off the four-runner he unzipped his jumpsuit, and noticed he sweat clear through his clothes.

"Fun, isn't it?"

"Oh, yeah, I want to go again." He said. They shared a look and short smiles. Bobby walked over to the trailer.

"Go ahead inside with Taylor, grab a soda out of the fridge if you want, he's going to give you a logbook, and show you how to keep a record of your jumps." He followed Bobby and feeling a tingling sensation in his toes and his head. The air-conditioner wheezed and stuck out crookedly from the window.

He showed Taylor the logbook and scribbled down some notes regarding the jump. Exit 11,000 feet. Fifty-five second freefall.

Pulled at 3,000 feet. Hard opening. Good awareness of student before, and during exit. Needs to learn how to relax in freefall. Legs and arms a little wild. Easy landing. Good jump!

"You might ought to do another tandem before you go through solo training. Give you an even better feel for everything." Bobby said to Taylor as they shared a ginger ale in the ac. The nerves were still at work, but the breathing was easier for Taylor. He still was pumping adrenaline like the engine of an eighteen-wheeler.

"Yeah, that's probably a good idea." Taylor responded.

"You get the hang of the freefall, just relaxing and staying focused on what you have to do...you'll get it alright."

"Yeah, that's kind of a crazy concept, staying relaxed while you're falling from the sky." Taylor said, thinking the thought as he spoke it.

"Crazy enough to be the truth, my man...that's the whole key to jumping, just staying cool. Because, eventually you keep jumping and you'll find yourself in a hairy situation, malfunction, getting bumped by another skydiver, who fucking knows, and you'll have to deal with your situation quick fast and in a hurry. And what will save your ass is being able to identify the problem and fix it right away with a cool head. Almost everyone has to cutaway a time or two, and that's probably the most common situation."

432

"What's cutting away?" Taylor asked.

"Your main chute can have a malfunction, get twisted lines or whatever, and you have to cut yourself free and go back into freefall and then pull your reserve. You find out fast how tight your nuts are screwed on when you have to cutaway. Like I said, you jump long enough, you'll have to do it."

That was the first mention, from anyone out there about the potential disasters that seemed to have gone conspicuously undiscussed prior to his jump. It added another level of realness to the already unreal day, carried mainly by the direct and intent tone of Bobby's voice. Taylor guessed he'd had to have cutaway himself, at least once.

"I've got another student here in a half hour or so, Taylor, it was a pleasure, I hope you had a good time and from the look on your face, I'd say you did. Hopefully, you'll be back out here; we always need good people learning this sport." Bobby said, sounding more like a pleased coach than a skydiving teacher.

"I believe I will. Thank you for the learning and the landing Bobby." They shook hands and Bobby headed to the door.

"One more thing and believe me when I tell you this…the most dangerous part of your first skydive is the drive

433

home afterward. So, you might want to wait on the beers until you get home."

"I will, thanks again." Bobby nodded and grinned, heading back out and then back up.

XLVII.

Cesar scraped at his thumb with his fingernail. He got right under the skin and a small patch of red shown through. He sat on a bench outside the office.

The parking lot was mostly empty. No smoke exiting from the vents on the roof of the plant. The railcars that had just last week brought in a load of rubber were silent and immovable behind wafting bare limbs blocking the gray sky like hanging beads in a hippy's doorway. They were no loud squeezing and tearing noises coming from presses and mills cutting and pressing rubber that gave off the indelible steaming smell and sound of production.

Nothing was coming in and nothing was going out.

The supervisor just told him that morning that all hourly workers were being laid off. That management would stay on in a limited role until further notice. All presses would be shutdown. Their customers had gone to Congress to get money to survive so they said and in the meantime their suppliers would just have to twist in the wind.

So that's what Cesar was doing for the moment.

It would not be long before the tiendas in town would have to close because there were no more working people in town to buy things. The problem that was swirling in the air was that towns all over the area, in Ohio, Michigan, Indiana was that no one was immune to the slowdown.

He thought about what to do.

Stay. The money would not last long.

Go home. To work, or for nothing?

There is always a job for someone who wants to work. But where? That was the question whether it was asked in the beginning or the end.

He got up from the bench and pushed his hands into his pockets, thinking about walking back into town.

He heard the familiar rustle of gravel under rubber tires and raised his head into the wind.

Frank jammed his foot on the brake not expecting someone to be walking right out in front of the office.

"Que pasa, Cesar?" He asked after rolling down the window.

"Nada." They shook hands.

"Where is, I mean…donde la gente?"

"No hay trabajo. They tell us…today." He said.

"No trabajo, nada? No mas produccion?" Frank wondered, surprised at the extreme.

"Si. Cesar said, and had a trace of despondence in his expression, but mostly it was one of matter of fact. Nothing could really surprise someone who left his family, crossed a

436

river then a desert and God knew what else found a job learned a set of skills and lived six to a tiny room in another country, Frank thought.

"Can you wait here a minute? I want to talk to you." Frank said. Cesar said okay, and just stood by the car. Frank got out of the car and walked toward the door. He looked at Cesar, who was obviously cold despite his heavy green hooded Eagles jacket.

"Hey man, just hop in here, it's warm, I just want to habla con el supervisor, really fucking quick."

"Si? En el coche?"

"Yeah, si man si. Go ahead. Be right back." Frank heard the door shut and doubted completely that Cesar would steal it. He came back out in a couple minutes and got in the car. Cesar still had his hood up and was somewhat nervously leaning forward where the heat vents blasted hot air.

"Shit man, you getting enough heat? It's colder than a well-diggers ass out there. Sorry, hace frio no?"

"Si, hace muy frio." He smiled shortly and looked at Frank.

"No more work here, no trabajo." Frank said, looking out the window at the railcars, the parking lot, and the building.

"Por los dos? That means both of us si?" Frank asked.

"Si, los dos."

437

"Que hace ahora para trabajo?" Frank asked him?

"No se."

Frank searched his memory for the right vocabulary, thinking how incredulous Cesar might react from his next question. Hoping he could put it correctly in translation.

"Yo encuento sus primos. Desde su pueblo in Mexico."

"Como?" Cesar looked at him like he'd just fallen from the moon.

"Ellos trataran viajar aqui, pero el trucko." Frank made large steering motions with his hands trying to simulate a truck driver losing control of his rig.

"Y entonces, el manejado saliendo porque la policia. Pero yo manejo en la misma carretera de el mismo tiempo, and yo encuentro sus primos, in the back of the trucko. Comprende?"

"No, primos?"

"Rafael, Jose y Jamon."

"Como? Donde estan mis primos?" He pulled back the hoodie and looked at Frank with a look that begged for an explanation.

"They are, sorry…ellos en hotel cerca New Albany, Indiana."

Estan en Indiana?"

"Si. Tengo Rafael's telefono numero. Tu puedes llamarle ahora."

Frank scrolled down on his phone, hit send to Rafael, and handed it to Cesar.

He had to motion a couple times because Cesar was very apprehensive to take the phone. When he did, he held it up to his ear slowly and carefully as though it might explode.

Rafael answered the phone and Cesar's face went from shock to relief to astonishment as Rafael rapidly relayed the recent course of events through the cell phone in exceedingly fast Spanish. So fast that Frank knew that he must have sounded like a total idiot when speaking to Cesar a minute ago. He looked in the rearview mirrors and scanned the area out of habit, and he had to smile to himself at the ridiculous nature of this situation.

From both his and their points of view.

After a couple minutes, Cesar hung up the phone.

Cesar just stared at Frank, in disbelief.

"Tell you what, uh…estoy mucho hambre. Puedo comprarte un taco ye podemas hablar un pocito mas."

Cesar shook his head for a second and blinked his eyes. He was silent for a second.

"Oh, si, very close."

So, they went to the carniceria back in the deserted crippling town and sat in a booth.

XLVIII.

It wasn't much later that day that Taylor was flying back to town in his vehicle. He was blasting one of his favorite songs after another. He smoked a few cigarettes and felt the air blast in from open driver side window. He got off the highway and remembered what the jumpmaster had told him about the ride home. A light clicked red and he braked hard, nearly rear-ending a minivan. So, he let out a long breath, dropped his head back on the headrest, and closed his eyes for a second.

He opened them and turned to look out the driver-side window. The light changed but he kept looking.

His heart dropped like an elevator cut loose from its suspension cable.

Felicia was standing on the corner. Smiling shyly and being pulled close by a tall guy in a dark suit.

The car behind him honked and honked but he didn't move. Just kept looking.

The car behind the car behind him started honking too. The light was green but was going to be yellow soon.

He heard somebody yell out to get moving so he did. He wasn't sure if she saw him. And he wasn't sure if he wanted her to or not.

XLIX.

Frank printed out a google mapped route to the Hampton Inn, New Albany, and the directions to another located just a couple blocks from blade plant. He told them he would meet them at the first one day after tomorrow. He had to make a trip to Ireland first.

Cesar looked again at Frank incredulously. Four of his co-workers had come into the carniceria after he'd phoned. One sat in the booth beside Cesar, and the other three slumped into the booth behind them. Their faces were dark, and they sipped on Mexican sodas. Cesar told them that there were going to go to south, to find new trabajo.
Frank explained the application, and possibly some of the things that they'd be trained on.

"Quien es tu? Realmente?"

"Un comerciante amigo, solamente." Frank responded.

"No, no solamente." Cesar said, studying him.

"Ok, so I meet you in New Albany, day after manana?"

"Si, el dia despues manana?" Cesar shook his hand and they watched the gringo walk out the door and into his silver bullet car.

Frank was out of Ligonier within a couple of minutes. In another thirty, he was on the outskirts of Ft. Wayne. He put the hammer down on the gas and shot in front of a greyhound on I-69 South.

Forty minutes later, he was approaching Gas City, and Fairmont. Birthplace of James Dean.

He bought some roman candles at the gas station and a coffee. Filled up the tank. Gas was running higher and higher. It was over four bucks a gallon the previous August. That about killed him. Seventy-five bucks to fill up. Pretty soon the world had better figure a better way to power our habits he thought.

He called Gil.

"What's the good word, Frank?"

"Man, I'm just pressing asphalt. I get you at a bad time?"

"No sir, what-cha got?"

"Did you hear from Syd?"

"Matter a fact he's here now. Going through the company training deal. Hired in official earlier this week. He's ideal for the slot. Seems like a real stand-up guy. Just like you said."

"That's great. Man, that's great." Frank said, feeling an enormous amount of relief and excitement for his former, and new customer.

"I imagine he might want to holler at you after a while..." Gil said.

"He should have my cell but if not, could you pass it on to him. I had his number from his old employer but I'm sure that's not any good anymore."

"Yeah, I'll give it to him, reckon we're going for a beer after work today."

"Shit, I wish I was there."

"Same here, buddy. What else is cooking?" Gil asked.

"I found nine hourly workers that are skilled, ready, and willing to go to work."

"Is that right? That'll get us started. You wouldn't believe the trouble I'm having just the damn ability to interview potential employees around here." Gil said.

"I worked with one up at a rubber plant northern part of the state. He ran a bunch of different parts." Frank said.

"Compression, transfer?"

"Yeah, both. Worked in the bar well, done a bit of everything, young guy, hard worker. I'm thinking you could train him and his crew up real fast."

"Well good. They Mexican?"

"How'd you guess?"

"Safe to assume." Gil answered.

"I'm sending them your way day after tomorrow. I'm meeting them in New Albany and going to set them up at the Hampton across the way there from your building for a few nights. Can they get into some of those apartments nearby after that?"

"Aw yeah, we'll get them taken care of. They just about giving them leases away. Brand new apartments too. They'll be happier than hell to get some tenants. Wages and hours are going to be steady too. We just got another order fixing to have us busy for a year and a half." Gil said.

"That's great, Gil. Beats the alternative don't it?" Frank said.

"Sure does. Sure does."

"Well, I'll let you run, oh…almost forgot. How are you all fixed for material?"

"Fixin' to write the P.O. soon as we get off the phone, can you all handle double this go around?"

"Absolutely, I'll call the plant right now." Frank said.

"Hey, Frank, thanks for keeping an eye out there. Case nobody ever said so…you worth more than keeping."

"Thank you, man. Talk to you later."

"And later it will be. Stay frosty."

L.

She'd been coming over a couple nights a week here lately.

Come off the road. Have a cocktail. Lean back on the chase. Stare at the lights moving up down east and west on the streets. Flip on the flatscreen. Watch SportsCenter or something.

Reach over. Grab the phone.

Hey baby. I'll be down in a minute.

She had a kid. Eleven. Spent the summers with her father in DC. He was a lobbyist she'd told him one night after a session that about broke his dick in half. At forty, this lady was un-fucking real in the sack. And there was no drama. No nagging. No commitment.

It was great. Fucking. Great.

Apparently, what some people said about cougars was the truth.

And, not but. It wasn't going to go anywhere.

He knew it. She knew it.

She'd be gone in the morning. Just up and let herself out.

He never went to her place.

It was better than great.

Until this afternoon.

He'd met Felicia for a late lunch, and they walked back to his place afterward. The waitress was smoking, and he didn't even look at her when he ordered shrimp cocktail and a filet mignon to share and a bottle of Margaux and he'd gone on and had a couple of grey goose and waters after that and all the while with maybe a cordial break in the dialogue she went on and on about school and work and the gay bartender friend of hers and the other friend of hers...the roommate that she so wanted him to meet and how much of a dear friend she was and how happy she was that she'd put down the pipe started exercising and gotten a new job and how she was always there for her during everything from high school and even after when all her other girlfriends had moved away and especially when her dad died and all that looking at him intermittently oozing excitement he yawned at least twice but had long since learned how to do it and accordingly force the facial muscles to stay impervious. He wondered maybe a second or two if she might have noticed.

Probably less than he did when he thought a customer might have noticed the same stillness on the surface of the dirty wretched cesspool where only plankton survive beneath that being all that was both his plight, and his conscious.

Bottom and of the bottom of the food chain.

447

No matter how smooth the shirts and how spicy the cocktail sauce.

How thick the green wad. No matter how big the steak.

They held hands while they walked. He wondered if anyone saw him. She was smiling a lot and kissing him on the cheek and stuff like that. He was on remote control though. Like it wasn't happening.

The first sign should've been when he smirked at the doorman when the doorman looked up from his paper behind the front desk, said a brief hello, and then did a double take at Felicia. As in, wait a minute man, this isn't the lady I saw you with this morning. The lady from the seventh floor. Colin knew that he shouldn't have given him a knowing smile back.

It wasn't just that Felicia might have seen it.

But it was bad karma to do that shit.

He sat on his stool and looked over the island. Felicia had left a couple of magazines. Ones he'd never think to buy. People. Great Vacations. Cosmopolitan. The Great Vacations was crooked and on top of the others and when he looked at it, he remembered a conversation they'd had about maybe taking a trip to a Caribbean island sometime. He had to admit, it would be a hell of a place to take a girl. And fuck would she have looked good in a suit.

When they got in the door, she dropped her purse on the island with a wild look in her eye and pushed him against the fridge. They kissed for several moments and he was on his heels. Feeling weak. The weaker of the two. He wasn't resisting and he wasn't in charge of the action. That should've been the second sign. Still kissing and moaning quietly they sidestepped a familiar path to the high dollar sheets on his king-size. When they got there he just fell back.

His legs were jelly.

Felicia pulled back the belt while her hair was whipped over to one side and her tongue jetted silently from her lips. He didn't give much thought to his suit jacket wrinkling. She looked up at him as she went down on him and he closed his eyes and put his hand on her head.

He looked at the pictures on his wall. Not even knowing exactly what they were of. Some were blurred in brilliant spectrums. Others were splashed with color. And some were black and white. Skylines in foreign cities. But what cities? Ali and Foreman in Zaire? Who even won that fight? Lauren Bacall? Never even saw her movies.

Then she stopped. Just when it was really starting to feel amazing.

She slowly pulled her mouth off, up, and away from him, as though she were stepping away from a grave.

449

She blinked. Her hair was stringing off to one side and her face flushed red.

"What is it?" He asked.

She stared at the corner of the bed. Stepped forward for and reached as though she were opening a haunted house front door. She lifted the covers by the corner of the bed. And looked straight there. Then pointed with her voice.

"Those aren't mine." And backed up on her feet.

That was all she said.

Cougar thong. And a pair of panties.

Wasn't much he could say to her then. And any attempt was beyond his capacity, within this moment. Nothing in the tank. Not even a stray strand of bullshit he could grab and wing.

Fucking cleaning lady.

Looking back and while he looked at her it wasn't his own regret that he felt, or swayed or weighed him, more than so much as the disappointment for not being more careful.

Bad fucking karma.

And he did feel something as she cried and walked out looking up at him with a couple of spaced, slanted, and stunned stares as she bumped a bar stool going backwards and hurriedly collected her purse from the island before looking back at him

450

one last time with not a hateful, but truthful wide looking pulse.

Saying in undeniable silence that you are a piece of shit.

He wasn't sure what he said back, except that it wasn't an argument.

Then she was gone.

He grabbed his head and walked around the island.

He threw a tumbler against a pane of glass that spit a handful of chards back into open kitchen. A scepter head of impact bashed like a fist. The epicenter of it spread amidst the beveled glass and weaned out and up and down left and right like a baby earthquake wanting to crawl in all directions at once. He called her. Voicemail. Again, and again and again. He mixed himself a drink. Slammed it down. Lined up a couple of fatties. Knocked them back too. Called her. Called her again. Wanting to reach back to the most recent moments of his past and reel it back in and wipe the slate clean with a present brush, but he was a one-way train to the future and the present he'd obscured was gone now if it even was a present once and fuck me if I just knew now what I should've known thirty minutes ago he thought.

He went on that way that night.

Pillaging his demons and the villages where they lived in scanted and unforgiven huts for some unhidden and ethereal treasure and incessantly yet remotely manipulating himself for reasons that were to him, had been, and always would be hidden between the silences of broken glass and dial tones.

LI.

Eduardo smoked.

He waited. Smoked again.

Slim was across the lot, leaning on a low set aluminum rail of a
big rig, talking with the driver who was sitting inside the cab.
Eduardo could see his ballcap with a patch on the front, dark
wide shades, and a ratty beard. Slim looked around and his
armpit hair flared out from his hooped red tan-top sleeves. He
had on dark sunglasses too. Another big rig was parked
adjacent to the rig Slim was standing by. It was idling. It rattled
and shook like an impatient robot child. It was cheaper to keep
it running than to shut her down.

Gas prices had more than doubled. Four dollars at least
for the cheap unleaded. The signs that stood above the lot with
big rotating black numbers were proof of that. In Mexico, the
government controlled the gas. It stayed at or around two bucks
a gallon. That was one thing not fucked up down there. The
American economy once again was beginning to suffer.

He pondered that as he stared across the lot at Slim.

The appetite of Americans was beyond just about
anything. Now the rest of the world was catching up with that
hunger. More people wanted more. China. India. And whatever

they made Americans consumed. The world's biggest customer.

But the jobs that drew so many people from Mexico were drying up. People were not spending like they used to. And it was making some Mexicans decide to go back. He was glad of that in a way.

Something about that stripped away the upper hand that Americans held since they won the war and took half of Mexico. But he was not planning on going back. Being a coyote was like running a funeral home. People always needed help getting from A to B without getting caught.
But since his last group were lost on the highway, his phone was not ringing as often. And business was down.

He had to fix that.
Slim was a pinche fat gringo he thought, as he watched him walk from the rig and on into the store.

Eduardo waited. Fidgeting in the leaky leather seat like a rattlesnake might.

LII.

"Frank, I know you're on your way but, buddy, you ought to be putting a giddy-up in your step because the competition turned up this morning with a couple samples. He's out on the line right now. The press they're fixing to run the trial on is getting' blasted and will be up in bit, so but the pressure is on like I told you the last time you were in to cut costs so we have to look at any way we can to do that." Lucas said, and it was quiet in the press-line office Frank could tell.

"Is that right?" Frank responded.

"Yeah. You got something to run, don't you?"

"I do, a couple pails of two different products. Is there another press we can run on?"

"Fraid not, we'll let ol' boy run for a while and we should know pretty quick how it's going to run, then will stop, dry-ice blast the mold and turn you loose on it." Lucas said.

"Okay, that'll work great."

"Long as you don't mind him being here when you show up…" Lucas said, sounding somewhere between a warning and a truth that needed to be made clear.

"No sir, I don't mind. Not one bit." Frank answered, sounding somewhere not anywhere between adverse or reluctant.

"What time are you thinking?"

"I'm just outside Bedford right now, so if I don't get caught behind some trucks I should be there inside an hour."

"Alright then, go ahead and park out back.

"Will do. Thank you, Lucas."

"You got it, bud."

Frank stabbed the red off button on the cell. He felt a quickening in his chest. A sudden palpitation that conjured a memory of being in sixth grade on the blacktop at the end of recess and agreeing to a time and place to meet a bigger and mean eighth grader to settle something very important at the time.

LIII.

Astrid was taking to the office manager job like a fish to water. She was up at 5:29 a.m. every morning and now she was up to jogging. Two miles at a time.

The phone lines were a little difficult at first, but quickly she figured out how to transfer calls, organize conference calls, put the right ones through to the right people, and put the other ones politely on hold. She'd never used Excel earlier. Now it was old hat. Sheila was also very encouraging. Astrid got to work early and left late. That counted for a lot.

She was starting to understand the business too. A little bit at a time.

Taylor was conspicuously to himself. Rarely had she spoken with him at length. The times he was around he was always friendly and professional. He was precise in the way he moved in and around the office. People responded to him. They worked their asses off when he was or wasn't there. And the people in the office all worked hard, and they cared. That came from the top down. But he did spend a lot of time behind closed doors on the phone and, also out of the office. He had a lot of balls in the air and seemed to be very effective at handling them. But Sheila handled his stuff. She was his lifeline.

"Sheila? When you have a second?"

"Ok, you have that printout I asked for?"

"It's right here."

Sheila picked it up. Her hair was styled. She wore a suit well too. But she didn't try to intimidate. Unless she had too.

Astrid watched her look over the printout thinking to herself something she wasn't too sure about talking about. So, she kept on working on her tasks. Waiting for the right moment.

Sheila moved with authority. She sat in on a conference call and worked the customer on the other side of the line. Stepping in over a salesman that looked unprepared. Astrid could see through the blinds and here through the crack in the door. It didn't last five minutes, but the customer was still their customer when Sheila picked up the receiver and set it back down. The salesman followed her out the conference room door to her office.

It wasn't long after that he left without looking at Astrid, even though he'd asked her out twice before. Sheila came up to her desk a few minutes later.

"Astrid…hi, would you compile these severance, insurance, and unemployment forms in order, send them over to HR for review, and then take a final look at them before bringing them by my office by the end of today?" Sheila asked.

Standing tall in a lavender suit, her face firm with professional taste.

"Yes. Right away."

"Thank you."

She closed her windows. Pressed her toes together and slid her chair a couple feet to the right and pulled down the stack from the upper ledge of her desk.

She went through the documents and cross-referenced them with those pinned up on a board to the desk. Astrid checked them and double checked. Triple checked. Stamped. Shuffled. Patted them down and slid them into a folder. She pushed herself back and stood, holding the folder cupped in her right arm and walked over to the HR department.

When she got back to her desk, she reopened her windows and answered the phone. Taking some calls that were for the salesman that had been let go. Because they weren't easy to respond to, she took their names with polite discretion and their numbers and the time they called and assured them that an account manager would get back to them as soon as possible. When they asked, where was their representative, she told them that he was no longer with the company. Hoping that was the best thing to say.

It was close to 6:00 p.m. when everyone except she and Sheila were still in the office.

Astrid looked around out of a new habit and stood up. She felt like she was tiptoeing over to Sheila's office maybe because of the quiet.

LIV.

Three little ovals. Pale like chalk. Nudging as the days grew on with nodding bulges against the frail shells. Wanting out.

At first, they were just sapling embryo's borne into a tightly woven wired cup. Pale like the shells they broke free from and quickly, then an unnamable blue. Beautiful little beaks whining for nourishment. Demanding air and someday freedom. Sometime ahead their destinies called them like the slithering creatures of the earth would that same day and fear their soaring and stalled hovering and stooping and their terminal descent. Up in the highest reaches of the transformer crevice. Tucked against a metal fixture that ran up down and left and right. Embodiments of what fueled a cache of life different but aligned in a spanning preternatural congruence.

Currents. Resistance.

Long wires stretched from above and around their nest to and from one to another and another and onto others draping down through fields between deforested lands and channeled hilltops feeding hot electric lifelines to the human peoples assembled in their own concentric and communal gravity ridden assemblages from one space to ever-reaching others. But this one was among itself to themselves. When he was gone for long stretches, his little ones cried out wanting their beaks littered.

Come on, Daddy, bring us something because we're itching and hungry and we want to be like you someday.

And he'd be Goddammed if they wouldn't.

Blue little angels for the precious time-being confined to the twig-wrapped balcony home he and their momma had twined up.

They couldn't even stop themselves, yet but they could scream louder than the blue jays did when they saw his daddy in a wooded byre. And they screamed even louder now.

High against a cloudy sky a buzzard looked smaller than it was, and to infant or untrained eyes it could easily be mistaken for their Daddy.

But not when it tilted in from a what was nothing but a black winding spec and slowly but awkwardly dropped in laboring circles and closed the infinite azure space in the sky to the terrifyingly invasive stalking distance suddenly and suspended adjacent to their little home.

The invader steadied itself on the beam. Flapping ugly gusts and peering around in with a monster's head. They hoped it would lose its balance and fall away. But it was agile for a gangly beast. Its grip was generationally experienced. It was bigger than their Daddy. And when it turned and pointed with a

462

loping throat and face cocked like a snake's head it was wide and dark on the beam, and it did not seem possible that such a beast could be inching toward them.

So, they screamed.

LV.

The steam cascaded off the press from the dry-ice blaster. The man's beard leaked out from behind the mask he wore in gray stranded tentacles as he hoisted the spray-head with one arm and two black cylinders on his back. From the frayed edges of his black sleeveless t-shirt, slim-skinned farm-tanned boney arms casted a steady definition with tattoos of blue worn green skeletons, knives, motorcycles, and girls' names faded out over thumping veins that worked their way down his arms like mole tracks in an untended to front yard.

It was an eight-cavity mold, and it was a high-volume part. Which meant that any time that, it was down they were not filling orders. And the time not filling orders was watched indeed.

But if they were going to trial a new lube, they had to clean the press.

It was the only way to get true results.

Lucas watched from the angled spot in the press-line office so that he could keep working on the stack of paperwork weighing down the wooden flat top where he sat. Colin was aware that he was in his line of sight because he had to stand up there next to the press. Those were the rules if he wanted to come in and run a trial. Even though he'd rather sniff around

464

the plant and chat up a cute single mom or sneak outside for a smoke and check his voicemails if he could while they ran his product, he knew he couldn't. This was a real account and he'd been trying to pry it away from the competition for some time and now he finally had a shot. So, he stood by the press and watched.

The aluminum surface gleaned with a steeled shiny cape after the man with the sprayer ratcheted the valve on the bottom center of the two cylinders to the right. Some infinitesimal granular spurts shot out from the antennae like tip due the last escaping bursts of remaining pressure and disappeared in a small space between him and the press as they lost their composition. Colin blinked and stoked out his hand to pat the sprayer man on his shoulder and felt the smallest amount of refraining flesh about a bone as though it was only a blend of tendon and ligament. The sprayer man did not acknowledge the touch save a second stare behind the mask. He carefully lifted the sprayer over the slide on the upright side of the press and turned his back and left Colin there. Walking down the steps and away into the corridors behind the heavy machinery that he could walk safely in the dark. Colin waited for a moment and stepped back to get a sprayer of his own. He undid the screws on all four sides of the lid lifted it out quickly and the throat tubes clanked on the floor. He didn't pay the

sound or potential damage to them any mind and grabbed a
grubby pink liner from his bag and crammed it into the tank,
the cracked walls in the plastic got caught on the rusty blisters
flaring on the inside walls of the reservoir he'd not bothered to
scrub out and cracked in several places. He kept trying to jam it
down in there, but the liner seemed to be fighting like a lobster
free from rubber bands above a boiling pot. Get the fuck in
there, you little motherfucker, he said and no one could hear
him because all the other presses were running full boar but the
operator had stepped up onto the platform in front of the press
and stood with her hefty arms on her heftier hips looking down
at the sharp-dressed salesman kind of from the side of her face.
Finally, he'd forced it far enough down in the tank to be
satisfied that he went for his satchel and pulled out a leather-
man. It took him three tries to find the knife blade, and when
he did, he nicked his middle finger popping it up. He swore
again and blood slowly rose from somewhere down beneath his
skin like a stove burner coming to life. But he didn't stop
himself but picked at the two plastic semi-circles around the
sunken spout and pulled it up like a chicken head. He snapped
the lid off and pried the interior plastic seal off and lifted the
five-gallon pail with two arms and felt a shooting tearing pain
in his upper back between his shoulder blades. It was like
someone had grabbed hold with granite hands of the muscles

behind his scapula and spat fire straight up his spine. But he didn't stop himself then either. Just held the bucket hitched on his hip and the white fluid glugged out in siphoned hoops. Small red rusted giblets floated to the top of the fluid as it filled the tank. It coagulated slowly and Colin stared in disgust from the pain he had in his back that he knew wasn't going to go away anytime soon and the lack of preparation he'd employed in his work at this trial. Fuck it he said to himself. A little rust won't hurt. Aaaaah. Fuck me. Then he stopped pouring off the sample and set it back down wiping sweat off his eyebrows and trying to figure what way he could move that wouldn't hurt his back.

"You gonna stay down there on the floor all day or we fixing to try your juice young man?" Edna asked from the platform.

"Just a second there, I...I just need to uh, cinch this here spray-head up." Colin answered from out of the side of his mouth. He gritted his incisors with each turn of the metal latches between his fingers. Oh, you son of a bitch.

"Well, you better get your ass in the saddle, young man, 'cause this ol' girl needs to make rate." Edna hollered. And she didn't sound like she was kidding.

"Okay, here we go." He used both hands and every bit of his hips to swing the spray can back around and up onto the

467

platform. He almost made it cleanly, but the last edge of the slide stuck out and caught the fluid and air lines and the spray-gun itself squelched against the metal.

He was taking a pained step toward Edna with the spray-pot when it jerked him back.

"Wait there, young man, hold on now." She said and moved straight to where the lines were caught.

"Aw now, you done got yourself twisted up. Hold still now." She inched over to him and his back railed at him with insane wrenching madness. Fuck me, he thought he was going to fall out right there. The spray pot could've weighed five-hundred pounds at that point. His forearms felt as though they were pulling in a 200-pound sailfish in the pacific after a two-hour fight. Fuck me. She got behind him and the only way for her to get to the spray-head that was knuckled behind the slide was to reach around his waist. He could feel her gut, gash along the entirety of his back, and was not cool with that but he didn't have much of a choice.

He felt her head reaching down around under his right arm and he looked down at her and saw sweat and stringy hairs and extended brown moles hanging back against gravity along her check.

"I can't quite reach I need you to squat down here by me some."

"Ah, ah…alright." Colin used his knees and all the muscle that was around them to get down where Edna wanted him.

"Almost got it…hold still." She was seeming to lose her balance, so she reached up and grabbed at Colin's stomach, and he sucked it in when she got hold of it hoping to God this was going to end soon.

"Ok, now give me your arm, young man…I got it." If it was another second he was going to pass out. That was for sure. And he honestly didn't mind that proposition.

But now there he was, standing with Edna on the press-line as she expertly reeled up the spray gun and hose and it hissed a few practice patterns in the open air and adjusted the fluid and air pressure to a fine stream a bumbling fucking moron with a pinched nerve what it felt like in his upper back and a trial to run with a product that may be corrupted already.

But he was still on the platform.

"So, what are we doing?" She was a dizzy blobbing blur across from him there, and he just swallowed and looked at the press.

"Okay, how hot are you running Edna?"

"She turned back to the temperature gauges behind the press.

469

"Upper platen 355, lower 348." She answered, still holding the spray gun gripped in her hand.

"How long are the cycles?" He asked, she starting to come back into focus. His back tensed but not searing like before.

"Five and half minutes."

"Okay, it's up to temp now, right?"

"Yes, sir it is."

"Give it two good coats, then close it up, and run a dummy cycle. Hit it one more time after it opens and then we should be good to go."

She nodded and leaned forward. The pattern was wide and fine. The regulator was set at twenty-five psi on both fluid and air, leaving a controlled amount of pressure behind the product forcing it out in wide prism.

It bubbled up in small circular clumps on the surface of the mold and grizzled and hissed and then evaporated leaving a film only visible under a microscope. Then she hit it again as instructed. When the second coat had been cured off, Edna pressed a protruding red button near the platen gauges and two thin chains dropped the lid of the mold slowly down like a drawbridge to a close and the mold shuttled backward into the press. Edna turned toward a press opposite and grabbed an airline that rested on a hook shoulder high.

The mold opened and the parts clung to the top of the mold. She jabbed the airline behind the edges of the flashing rubber, and they broke free from the surface wagging in the air and were sucked into a chute where they piled up in a plastic tote beneath. The first mold opened, and Edna sprayed it one more time.

"We good to go young man?"

"Yes, ma'am. Go ahead and load."

She dumped from a cardboard crate eight green rings of rubber into the mold and pushed and placed them into each indented cavity behind stained gloved hands.

The first heat finished, and Colin watched not moving his legs. He found a place in his stance where the pain wasn't, so he just stayed right there. It was better to leave Edna to her business because, in fact the product if he could sell it was going to have to work when he wasn't there anyway.

It was a long stretch between the calls and the visits and the card drop-offs and setting the trial date to the actual moment when the product was prepped on the mold and the parts were either going to, or not going to come off the way they needed to. And, well here that moment was.

She got up with the air line and the parts clung to the lid of the press with their stringy flash of excess rubber dangling there like a tortuous secret.

The air blew and so did the parts.

Colin breathed in a hurting huff of relief. Edna nodded toward the mold and blew them down the chute.

She grabbed the spray line and hit the mold again. Then loaded it with another round of rubber.

When everyone went to break, so did Colin. They'd run a least twenty heats, and the parts were coming off well, with no buildup. The release seemed like it was improving with each cycle too. He was worried he was going to freeze within his own muscles standing without moving for so long. It was almost a bigger relief when Edna hung up the spray-line and went to the break room than it was when the first round of parts fell free from the mold. He needed a smoke in the worst way. And when she went left, he went right. Toward the gray light out the back near the loading dock. Easing himself with his satchel in his right hand, grimacing at the knotting in his back his feet slowly nodding over the aged concrete floor amid momentary glances from limping trash grabbers and stiff wristed maintenance men toward the open sky and cold air.

He set his satchel down on the gravel and lit a cigarette. It tasted good and bad too. His head whirled. And he looked at his watch. Thank God, there was fifteen minutes until he had to walk back to the press-line. No one was around. Just a scattered blanch of pickup trucks parked numbly around the lot

472

with faltering Indiana license plates and sputtering googles of smoke steaming up in a fractious and layered and cylindrical ascension to the bigger clouds that were folded in a gray conglomerate concealing any blue.

A truck pulled up. A forklift pulled out a splintering wooden skid with four, full fifty-five-gallon drums shrunk-wrapped on it and dumped it on the bay nearest him.

When the operator gripped the reverse throttle and the forks eased the pallet down on the dock it reared back and pivoted, he smirked uneasily at Colin and swiveled back the other way and whirred back the way he came and reentered the plant from a door up the way. He looked back for a second before he drove through a melee of long plastic strips that hung from the entrance ceiling like benign and wrinkled gate keepers. And he was still there with at least ten minutes left on break.

He looked around out of habit. And then since he didn't see anyone, he went to check out the drums.

It was a bitch getting the bung wrench out of his bag, but he did.

And in the empty wind, he grappled with the bung smiling to himself.

He heard tires grinding gravel back behind where he stood. A sound different than those wrestling inside and out of the plant.

He looked and faintly noticed a Cadillac STS pulling in a spot a good piece from the dock. For a couple seconds, he wondered. Then turned back to drums. Fuck it. Could be anyone.

He heard another sound. Different from any. A howl. Maybe a cry. Something that rifled highly pitched through the blatant sky with relentless abandon.

Something was up there.

So, he looked up.

He stalled against a wash of air and hovered, peering frozen with his primaries etched up and his red-tail rowing down against descent. Stayed there moving in no direction. His nape was a beautiful brown. His steady and rounded wings, outlaying with and between two eyes that could make a marine scout sniper's spotter jealous, and one that wouldn't blink white like his baby's eggs.

Dropping his cere toward home, he tucked in and stooped. Gathering speed like a meteor braking through the last line of atmospheric defense toward the threat hunched, beet bloody redheaded and limping with clutching talons along the metal below.

When seen head-on his eyes were noble.

And huge.

His primaries were elegantly in full. He could hear the cries of the blue ones louder and louder with each closing grapple.

LVI.

The impact sent a hum along the metal in every direction before it drifted into nothing.

The buzzard cackled and furiously rallied its wings in a wild and abnormal wretch as blood sprayed up in the air rising while the two fell interlocked heavier than liquid over and over fitful and his broad gray-black bellyband was searing as his guts and the lined bacterium that went there to sleep once more before dying spat out against the white underwing coverts of his killer.

He saw the world for the first time, with his world upside down clinging to a pained stoking under his skin not given a choice by the spears that punctured his chest. Green meadows and pallid wheat above him and blue sky below flying without flapping and then falling unable to catch an updraft and sift to safety to where it went dark silent and finished.

LVII.

Taylor had not called Everett. He just gave his keys to the valet, buttoned his coat, scanned the neon horizon, and stretched his arms and legs as though he just dropped in from Orion's Belt, while the car went inside.

Then, took a seat and looked.

For a while he sat and didn't say anything except to order a drink. But he only sipped on it. He stirred it with the little plastic red sword at a table against the wall. The girls were like phantoms. Semblances of sex. The music was the same.

The guys from the last time were the same too.

Watching the television at the bar. The big bald fucker with the facial ring of hair. The slickster manager. The uniformed off-duty cop who stood at the entrance chatting with the girl behind the register. Simone and Jasmine. He wondered if any of them would recognize him.

Or the spacebucks.

She looked like the blue way far off behind where any clouds could from the first moment, he saw her.

They did hit it off at the café. For sure man.

Fuck.

They would recognize him. They did have fun before the night was over. Before they took the money. Right.

Yeah right. Before they took the money.

Probably not until they saw him up close. He sipped a little more at his drink when he saw Simone walk right past him. When she grinned his way in her gliding gait she did so as though he was a new or maybe reborn lucky lottery winner walking into the right bar at the right time, he sucked in a large thought. But she did not recognize him. That made it a little more insulting.

Is this where I choose? To go.

Jasmine stepped on stage and she was made up like lighting if a bolt could be sat long enough to apply it makeup.

Is this where? Another breath. And a stare past the strippers into the mirrors that were not opaque.

It is right now.

Am I right now?

Now is now. But here ain't right.

Then what?

That shouldn't stop you.

From what?

Find out.

How?

If you choose to ask, there ain't no need in how.

The waitress came by and said she'd be right back.

Jasmine worked the pole like there was one in her backyard growing up.

"Hey, dude, anybody sitting here?"

"No, man, it's all yours." Taylor answered not hazarding more than a glimpse at him. The guy sat down at the other side of the two-top. Leaned his tangled head back against the wall behind him and closed his shot blood eyes.

"Seen a waitress?" The guy asked. He wore an expensive looking suit, with a white silk shirt and strewn tie. And a puffed left eye.

"She'll be back here in minute." Taylor noticed his eye, and a veiny wrangled bruise down the side of his face.

"Got a light?"

"Yeah." The guy smacked up a cigarette and eyeballed the room. Frank noticed from his periphery that he did not acknowledge a bit of a thank you for lighting his smoke or letting the guy share the table with him.

"Can I get you something, doll?" The waitress asked the guy, setting down a napkin on the table and placing her folded name marker on their table.

"Can you ever. Double Jameson on the rocks and tell the man not to drown Jimmy, ok?" He gave the girl a ten.

"You bet, honey." She said it loud enough for Taylor to hear. And he ordered one more. And she walked off toward the bar.

The guy leaned over at Taylor and asked him if he heard the one about the guy who was beating off in his room one day and his dad walked in and yelled at his son saying to him son didn't I tell you if you keep doing that it'll make you go blind and he looked up at his dad and said hey...dad, I'm over here! And Taylor did in fact laugh but he also kept his eye on Simone who was working the room and had just got up from a guy and gathered her garments free of any second thoughts.

She was back quick with both.

The guy gave her a gentle hand on her hip, and she jumped a bit with a demure look when he reached around to get a handful of her ass.

She smiled and leaned in his ear.

"I like the girl on the pole." The waitress turned around to look quickly with interest of her own. Wanting to know instantly what a man liked. Instinct.

"Oh, Jasmine, yeah, she's sexy."

"But I like you too, baby." Keeping his hand there and she turned back around with a stepped level of interest.

"You are bad." And playfully hit him on the chest. And he gripped her a little tighter and pulled her closer so he could kiss on her neck.

"What happened to your face?" She asked him, tilting back, placing a hand on his chin, and seeing his cuts and bruises for the first time.

"Just a little accident, but you should see the other guy."

"Did you get into a fight or something?"

"Yeah, actually, this guy…he tried to break into my house and…you know what, don't worry about it, why don't you go ask that girl to come over here when she gets done, and tell her to bring a friend for my new one over there." He motioned by cocking his head sideways a little but not looking over at Taylor.

Taylor heard him though. And noticed some had blood had leaked on the cuff of his shirt sleeve outside his jacket. A high dollar shirtsleeve too. But he didn't seem to care. And without getting a clean look other than his profile something was familiar about him. He seemed like he was on something too, had to be.

"Will they let you dance?"

"Well, if they have enough other waitresses…sometimes they do."

"Do they?"

"I'll have to check. Why?" She was resting her black-stockinged knee on the chair between his legs, holding her tray upright under one arm.

The waitress walked around to some tables on the other side of the mainstage.

"Maybe me you and Jasmine there can have some fun. Interested?"

"Maybe."

"Good. Why don't you go get another round for me?"

"What about your friend?"

"Sure, why not, I'll bullshit with this asshole while I wait for your fine ass." He squeezed again and she closed her eyes.

"You're going to get me in trouble I can already tell." She said smiling.

"Hope so. Gone on." He nodded off in the direction behind her and patted her butt one more time, sipped his drink, and stared into her eyes. Shooting fish in a barrel.

"Okay." And off she went.

He reached for another cigarette. Rummaged through his pants again and felt a hunk in one pocket that reminded him he needed to go to the men's room in a minute but didn't find a lighter.

"Hey pal...can I see that lighter again?"

Taylor ignored him.

Colin thought it was because the music.

"Hey buddy!"

Taylor could hear him the whole time, and now the louder pitch irritated him more than a little.

"I heard you the first time." And he turned to look right at the guy.

"I asked you for a light." And he turned to look right at Taylor.

Taylor remembered him now. Staring into this creep and not blinking. Not for all the corn, soy, and wheat in Indiana.

Colin leaned his eyes off first and smirked.

"Sorry man, I just forgot my lighter in the car. Didn't mean to yell. It's just real loud."

"Wasn't until you sat down." That was another offensive move, but Colin didn't want to play any with this stranger, not over a lighter, not after Felicia had seen the cougar thong the other day and walked out on him, not after his boss had cut him loose on the drive back from Ireland because of that shit-storm at the casting plant that would've worked if that greasy fuck from the cage hadn't had gone on and squealed and then blown his head off, and definitely not after

483

he'd already gotten the shit kicked out of him that day…he just wanted to play with the waitress and Jasmine.

"Fuck, if it means that much to you, I'll grab some matches. Shit, it's been a rough day, a rough week man, let me buy you a drink and we'll call it even?"

Taylor looked at him as the guy raised his eyebrows in fictitious friendship.

He pictured Felicia looking up at him on the cross-street.

And that just sent him way past being pissed.

Like he felt when he first started his company. When he couldn't get a job even though he had a great fucking idea, and a better plan. When no one would look twice and remember him.

Like he needed to get his ass up off the sidelines and in the motherfucking game.

"It's alright man, been a long stretch for me too." He said and smiled.

"Cool. Hey, I've got to hit the head. She's supposed to be coming back with a couple drinks, and a couple girls…for us." Colin said, winked, and tried to give the extended finger snap at the conclusion of their handshake but Taylor had already let go.

He took another short pull on his cocktail. He then looked, one a nanosecond from a satellite's engineer would envy, at the bar, and at the stage.

The scumbags the rovers and the tramps.

Standing up, he pulled one twenty out his pocket and left it under his drink.

From the other, he crimped his hand around a brick of space bucks and dropped them on Colin's seat tucked in the back so only he'd find them.

LVIII.

After he got home, he took a long shower.

He lightly peeled open a gas-station packet of Ibuprofens, dropped them back in his mouth, drank two large glasses of water, and crawled in the sheets well before midnight.

"I want to talk to you."

"In a minute."

"No, Taylor. I'm not waiting a minute."

"Sheila, just…just, alright what is it?"

"Did you close all your windows?"

Taylor was still looking at his computer screen from behind his desk and Sheila had closed the door to his office.

Taylor exhaled. He looked up at his secretary, confidant, friend, and lifeline, and clicked on in succession a series of little x's on his screen.

He let go of the mouse and leaned back in his chair, caught eyes with her for a moment and spun back, and opened his little refrigerator and grabbed a bottled water.

"Windows are all closed."

"Have you thought at all about what we talked about a few weeks ago?" She asked, sliding her hand behind her skirt and sitting in one of the smoothed leather seats with oak handles.

486

He opened the water and drank a sip. He spun the lid back on the bottle.

He thought about the day before while he looked at her. Going up in a little plane jumping out of it falling through the sky without a transient grasp of gravity and the getting jacked back into suspension and then steering through the clouds like an unbound accipiter and gliding back into town to stop at the wrong cross-street at the wrong time to see the right girl, he thought about her question.

There wasn't any feigning the topic.

"I have."

"Have you?"

"Yeah."

"And?"

"And, I...love that you are concerned about my personal life, and that..."

"Taylor, honey, I'm concerned about you. And you're too good of a man to go into the wrong rooms."

"I am a grown man, Sheila. And, for better or for worse, I'm going to go into the rooms I choose."

He was not speaking with demonstrative indigence or flailing with deflective denial.

"I know that. But...I think you could do to let go of your...and I mean this in every way that is not to be taken as an

487

affront to your masculinity or your manhood or whatever. But I want…hope you will let go of your, fear. And…honey, if you're truly willing to do that I can help you do that. And I don't mean anything but just what I'm saying. Nothing more than those words and what is behind them." She was gently welling water in her eyes, but still staring right into Taylor's.

He started welling too. Because she was his lifeline.

And she was right.

He got up and hugged her.

When they were done, she exhaled.

"Oh, you've got a meeting today, 1:00 p.m., at the café."

"I do, with who?"

"A new account manager. Her resume is off the charts."

"Okay, we do need someone, don't we?"

"That's for sure."

When he walked out, he stopped at the front desk.

"You know, Astrid, you've been doing a great job here. Hopefully you plan to hang around for a while." He put on his suit coat.

"Thank you, Sir." She beamed.

"Please don't call me that. Taylor is just fine. Oh, and we're going to increase your pay this period. And, we feel like you can start to train with the auditing department. It's really a great place to learn how a business functions, from the inside out. How does that sound?" He wasn't hungover, and the clear cogent contented conversation was coming back to him like a running on an old training course.

"That sounds amazing. Wow, I can't thank you enough."

"Just keep doing what you're doing, we'll talk later in the week." He said, feeling good knowing that it made someone feel the same.

He walked out and smiled back briefly and popped a tic-tac in his mouth.

After he'd gone, she walked over to Sheila's office and was waved in.

"Oh my gosh. Taylor gave me a raise and wants me to start training in the auditing department."

"Well good, sounds like you like the idea."

"Absolutely." The excitement was ballooning inside of her.

"You've earned it, hon." Sheila was proud of her new protégé. She stood and looked out of the windows overviewing the parking lot. It was a beautiful day out there. Sheila watched him go to his car.

Proudly. Hoping.

"Don't you just love playing Cupid?" Sheila asked.

"Maybe as much as you."

LIX.

Slim woke up in a rumbling trailer. Small slits of light up on the top of the aluminum walls. His mouth had a gastric taste in it. His right hand was tucked under his ass. His big fat ass that was tied to a pole behind him with a leather strap that pinched the big ass spare tire that was his stomach. His gut draped over it like a lassoed sea otter, but pale hairy and empty.

The last thing he could remember was walking to the truck.

He turned when he saw Eduardo in the tall rectangular side mirror.

There were others in the trailer. Sitting slumped along the walls. Dark eyes.

He tried to say something. Anything. But he couldn't muster any saliva. A half-filled jug of dirty water was within reach of his left hand. It was bound with a wire that was also tied to the pole behind him.

He poured it into his mouth, and it took almost all of his strength to do it. He could taste dust and some bits of dirt. He swallowed it anyway.

The truck drove on and on. He'd no idea how long it was going to go and how long it had already gone, but he knew why he was on it. Eduardo told him so before he put the white rag over his face.

491

He started to whimper. A shameless act.

He felt the dark eyes of the other men in the trailer, men returning to their home country looking up at him for a moment. No sympathy in them.

"Frank, how are you doing?" The boss asked. Upbeat as always.

"I'm alright, have you got a minute?"

"Sure, what's up?"

"I, I was on my way down to Ireland this morning when Lucas called. He told me that the competition was already in there and getting ready to run a trial."

"Oh really?"

"Yeah, and it was that same prick that put the screws to us."

"Is that right?" There was an instant change in tone.

"Yeah, and as I'm driving into the back lot, I see somebody on one of the loading docks that looks out of place. And..."

"And what, Frank?"

"I got out of the car and just started running. Dead set on this motherfucker and I'll be damned if he wasn't standing with one arm cradled around the drum with a bung-wrench in one hand trying to open it up."

"You got to be shitting me, so what'd you do."

"I, I took him the fuck downtown." Frank was already on his way to New Albany. And half wondered if he was going to have a job when he got there. If not, he was still going to follow through with the promise he'd made. His hand was throbbing where he'd lit up that lowlife sales guy in the side of the face. His heart was slowing just enough to talk, but his hurtling adrenaline was still making a lot of hard and fast left turns.

"Anybody see you?"

"I'm sorry?"

"Did Lucas, or anyone see you when you dropped him?" Frank hadn't expected that question.

"Actually, Lucas pulled me off him. Boss, that man lifted me up like I weighed twenty pounds on a summer day."

"Anyone else?"

"Just the fork driver and Lonnie."

"So, what happened then?"

"I tried to shake loose of Lucas, but that dog would not hunt.

"He had me in a vice grip. I told him that the sumbitch was about to poison one of our drums and if it got into the central system the whole place would shut down. And I told him how it just happened, that I had it on good authority and

493

testimony that this motherfucker had done it and our customer was barely surviving because of that."

"What'd Lucas do?"

"Well, he let me go and moved between me and that prick who was trying to get to his feet and get over to his briefcase. But Lucas saw the bung-wrench laying in the gravel and then went to pick up the briefcase before he could get to it."

"Yeah?"

"And he told the guy to stay right where he was. And opened the briefcase and pulled out a small jar with a smiling face in black ink on the outside. Cute, huh?"

"Real fucking cute. Then what?"

"Lucas asked him what it was and what he was doing with the bung wrench. But the guy didn't answer. He just got to his feet. Looked at his briefcase, at Lucas and then jumped off the dock and took off running. I tried to go but Lucas grabbed my arm."

"That little punk just took off...huh?"

"Yeah, I wanted to go after him boss, but I just felt like Lucas knew what to do right then."

"You're right. And I'm sure he did. What'd he have to say?"

"It was funny, he said…first time I ever seen a salesman run like 'at. Come on, Frank. Let's get you cleaned up." The boss laughed just a bit.

"What you say?" He asked.

"I told him he wasn't any salesman. Nothing but a fuckin' buzzard."

"I've got a call coming in, is the Ireland area code 553?"

"Yeah, Lucas and his boss said they were going to call." Frank said.

"Don't worry about it. Hey, son, I'm proud of you. Be careful, I'll give you a call later."

"Thank you." The boss clicked over, and Frank looked at his pack of cigarettes.

It would've been a perfect time for one. But it was a better time not to have one.

So, he didn't.

He practiced his breathing. Slowly in for several breaths, and slowly out.

Frank stretched his lumbar and looked straight ahead.

The End

About the Author.

Matthew Cahan has worked in the manufacturing industry, focusing on both domestic and international sales since 1999. After graduating from Clayton High School, Phillips Academy at Andover and Texas Christian University Cahan moved to Austin, Texas to become a concert producer and promoter.

The former remains his current profession. He lives in St. Louis, MO., with his badass cat named RayLyn.

This is his first novel.